Born on the
Island

Born on the Island

A NOVEL OF GALVESTON

august, 2011

Linda S. Bingham

NORTEX PRESS ❖ Austin, Texas

This book is dedicated to the memory of the six thousand.
Let it also be a tribute to those who carry on.

FIRST EDITION

Copyright © 2000
By Linda S. Bingham

Manufactured in the United States of America
By Nortex Press
A Division of Sunbelt Media
Austin, Texas

ISBN 1-57168-934-6

Although based on historical events, this is a work of fiction. All characters, with the exception of actual historical personages, are the product of the author's imagination. Any resemblance to actual people, companies, institutions or organizations is unintended. Any errors are the author's own.

Other books by Linda S. Bingham:

The John & Mary Bolt Mysteries

Up In Flames

Flashpoint

Contents

BOOK I

Galveston, 1900–1928

Chapter One

MEG GALLOWAY

My mother was pregnant with me before they set sail from Glasgow. I've always considered it my good fortune that she and my father arrived on Galveston Island in time for me to be born an American citizen. I've never seen that other island, the island where I was conceived, though I had my chance the summer of my seventeenth year, nineteen and hundred, the year of the Great Storm. Mrs. Coolidge wanted to take me with her to help look after Edith.

Although my father had been a school master in the old country, that first year he and Momma were in America he was forced to find work where he could, which happened to be loading cotton on Mr. Herrick Coolidge's docks. When Mr. Coolidge found out that my father was an educated man, he moved him into the counting house of the Coolidge Cotton Company where he stayed for nearly forty years. My mother hired on as cook for Mrs. Coolidge, and it was the beginning of a long association betwixt our two families, the one so humble, the other so high up.

From time to time, Mrs. Coolidge sent for me when an extra hand was needed during spring cleaning, or maybe to sit with Edith, the youngest child. I recall that was the summer Mr. Ned come home from the University of Texas, which made six children to home, 'cause Fern wasn't yet married, although was

3

about to be. There would've been nine kids in the family, but the youngest three, save Edith, had all been lost to the fever, which carried off a number of island children every year.

Edith was ten that summer, a pretty little girl with light brown hair, cottony soft, like a cloud or a mist over her brow, gray eyes like her mother. I liked to sit with Edith 'cause she was good, would amuse herself for hours with her colors and pens, like she lived in her own little world. Her mama often talked to her impatient like and I knew she preferred the ones that spoke up, which made me partial to Edith even more, 'cause she was quiet like me. I still think of her as my little sweetheart, even though she growed up and changed so. And I think that if Mrs. Coolidge hadn't been so hard on Edith she'd be with us still instead of resting in the arms of Jesus.

But there was a streak of granite in Mrs. Coolidge. She'd break a body before she'd stand to see 'em do something she didn't approve of. And it didn't make a bit of difference if that one was her own flesh and blood neither. Mrs. Coolidge was a woman of principle, anybody who knew her would tell you that. She stood for something in this world and she got things done. She was the kind of woman that everybody admired but I don't think many people liked.

Mr. Coolidge declined to build his house on higher ground, up on Broadway where the other fine houses were going up. Said he liked to look out at the water and open up the windows and receive the sea breezes. It were a pretty house, three stories tall, real cypress clapboards painted white, a slate roof. There was a wide balcony across the back of the house off Mr. Coolidge's study on the third floor where he could look out at the Gulf of Mexico and watch the ships come in, which is what I was doing that July day when I was supposed to be dusting the books on Mr. Coolidge's bookshelves.

Mr. Coolidge was a businessman, but he liked books—at least, he had a lot of them, although I noticed that a bunch of them had never been read, for their pages weren't cut, so maybe his books were just another sort of investment. For two hours I climbed up and down a little ladder that was there for the purpose of reaching the higher shelves, took down one volume at a time, dusted it and put it back in its place. I always liked

4

handling nice books, the kind Mr. Coolidge owned, with dark calf bindings and rich creamy paper. My father kept books, a different sort, though he would've liked these better. My dad were the sort that would be happy as a clam locked up in a room like Mr. Coolidge's study and never coming out. He would've started at the top shelf and worked his way down, just as I was doing, reading philosophy and history and novels. Dad never complained that he'd rather be doing something else, but he often commented that keeping books was "awful dry." The alternative would've been humping cotton from Mr. Coolidge's warehouses into the holds of ships that carried it halfway around the world to be made into cloth. That same cotton was shipped back through the Port of Galveston to market in this country and Mr. Coolidge made money all over again.

Of the two, I was more like Mr. Coolidge, who liked the books 'cause they were pretty to look at and nice to the touch, not because of what was in 'em. I know my father must've been sorely disappointed in me that I didn't take after him that way, that all I wanted to do was marry George Winkleman and be a fisherman's wife and raise a family, but he never let on that he wished I'd been different. Not like Mrs. Coolidge was about Edith, and later about Emily. I feel sorry for any kid that comes into the world with a burden of expectations, 'cause even though I ended up never bearing a child, I knowed without having that important womanly experience that expecting something from a child they're not capable of giving never turns out the way you want it to.

Mrs. Coolidge wanted her boys to go into business like their father, her girls to marry boys from well-off families. And, of course, they all had to marry Catholic and bring up their younguns that way. She liked it just fine that one of her boys, Paul, wanted to become a priest.

The summer Mr. Ned come home from the University, he went right into the business with his father. The next oldest, Fern, had made her mother proud getting herself engaged to Joseph O'Malley, a Catholic boy who come from ever bit as good a family as the Coolidges. Fern was a proper lady, even at twenty-two, going off to teas and dedications and what-not with her mother, getting her name in the paper, raising money for good causes. I knowed she was headed for a life very much like the one her mama had, and even though Mrs. Coolidge wasn't big on handing out compliments, she was very pleased with the way her oldest daughter had turned out.

I didn't see Mrs. Coolidge very much, so busy she was with her society work and rarely to home. When I knew she was in I used the backstairs and skulked around in mortal fear of running into her face to face, although I had no reason to be afraid of her, 'cause she'd never said a word to me in my life, but sent word through my mother of what I was to do.

I had made the task of dusting those hundreds of books more lively by working straight across the long row of shelves, rather than go up and down each section, which of course meant I had to move the ladder more often, but that offered variety too. Every time I reached the end, I would look out the window and try to spot George's father's boat, 'cause he was expected in that evening. That's what I was doing when I heard someone come in the room behind me. I knew without looking that it was Mrs. Coolidge and that she had caught me lollygagging. Quick as a flash I jumped down off the ladder and whupped it down to the other end, pretending like I never knowed she was there, scurried up the ladder again and snapped my dustrag busily.

"You silly girl," she said, tsk-tsking her tongue, "you're going about that all wrong."

"Yes, ma'am," I agreed. It was my besetting sin that I hated for anyone to take me for stupid or unlearned, so I tried to explain myself. "I thought I'd add variety to the task, ma'am," I said.

She looked at the window and seemed to figure out what I had been doing. "So you like the water, do you?"

"Yes, ma'am." I turned around to face her on top of my ladder 'cause it seemed rude to keep my back to her when she was talking to me. "My people have always lived near the water, ma'am. But my father says the North Atlantic ain't nothing like the Gulf of Mexico."

"I expect not."

She didn't go away and she didn't say nothing else, so I added: "He calls the Gulf of Mexico a plate of broth, warm and

6

brown. Of course, Scotland didn't have no hurricanes either, ma'am."

"Hurricanes won't hurt you."

"My papa says there was eleven hurricanes last century and that Indianola done give up, ma'am, and everybody moved away and don't live there no more."

"Mr. Coolidge knows about these things, Meg. Do you think he would risk so much money building on the coast if there was any danger? That soup bowl you mentioned protects us—big storms simply wear themselves out before they can reach our fair city. All we can expect from time to time is a strong blow."

"I don't like it when it blows," I said, meek as a kitten and fearful of resisting her.

Mrs. Coolidge didn't look like she was scared of nothing on God's green earth and pitied them that was. She jerked the curtain wider and looked out at the water. She wasn't nearly as tall as I had supposed, probably only about five feet even, but she held herself so straight you'd think she was taller.

I never in my life saw Mrs. Coolidge wear colors but once and that was a sort of peach-colored outfit she wore to Edith's wedding. Even before she was called upon to run Mr. Coolidge's business, she dressed as she did that day, in a black suit with a high-necked cotton blouse I might've ironed. Sometimes she wore a gray suit or an off-white one, but she didn't go in for frills. She had the money to wear fashion, too. Maybe it was 'cause she wasn't pretty that she had never got in the way of fixing herself up, but it wouldn't cross your mind to think about Mrs. Coolidge not being pretty 'cause her expression was that strong and determined.

She would've been forty-three years old that summer she took Edith to Europe, but she seemed old enough to be Edith's grandmama instead of mama. Her hair was still real black, but it had strands of gray in it. She wore it parted in the middle and pulled back and coiled at the nape of her neck. Her eyes were light gray and kind of scornful-like, my mama always said, the kind of eyes that don't gladly suffer fools. Her mouth was tiny and rosebud shaped. Her cheeks had little pouches that hung down, like she had something stored away for later, a chipmunk.

I got nervous, standing on my ladder, wondering why she

7

wouldn't let me get on with my work. Finally she said: "My youngest daughter and I will be visiting your father's homeland next month—we're setting sail for England on Monday."

"Yes, ma'am, I knowed that," I said. How could I help but know it? The whole household was in an uproar getting ready for her trip. My own mother was deserting me and my father to live-in for the whole time Mrs. Coolidge was to be gone. I myself was to come here daily for the next two months to help the housekeeper overhaul the bedrooms. I was glad of the money, which I was saving to set up housekeeping with George, but I was sorry I wouldn't be spending my last summer as a single young lady on the beach with my friends.

Mrs. Coolidge turned away from the window and come to the middle of the room and sort of studied me for a long uncomfortable moment. Was it a test? Was I supposed to turn around and get back to work? Or stand to attention?

"How would you like to go with me?" she said.

If she'd said, how would you like to jump off that ladder and fly around the room, I couldn't have been more stupefied.

"Well don't gape, girl," she said. "Marion has come down with a summer cold and I don't want Edith catching it from her. Your job would be to amuse Edith like you sometimes do here. I wonder if you're a good sailor," she added thoughtfully. I felt like a slave up on the auction block being looked over for defects.

"M-m-m-ma'am," I stammered. "You mean, go on that boat and cross the Atlantic Ocean?"

"That's exactly what I mean!" she rapped out. She was always impatient with people that didn't get it on the first try. I hated to try her patience, but I just didn't know how to say no to someone like her. I swear that until that minute she asked me it seemed like a pleasant enough notion to sail halfway around the world and see my father's native land. But when it was put to me like that, the thought of those miles and miles of deep dark ocean betwixt here and there pressed my heart up against my throat and near strangled me.

"I'll speak to your mother," she said, leaving so fast I wondered if my overactive imagination hadn't dreamed up the whole thing. But it really happened, 'cause I've relived every

8

word she said a hundred times over the years and wondered if it would've changed anything had I gone. I reckon not. I weren't that important. Whether I went with her or not, just about everybody Mrs. Coolidge knew and loved would be dead when she got back from that trip. Nor did I make myself one bit more secure by turning down that long voyage over the water, 'cause when the water gets ready, it comes and finds you, however safe you've tried to make yourself.

I told Mrs. Coolidge I liked the water, but I meant, just to look at. I had a natural- born fear of being in the water and never my whole life learned to swim. It even worried me to engage myself to a fisherman, though George laughed at me for being so silly, said he wasn't going *in* the water, he was going *on* it. I had tried to get him to take the job he'd been offered in a grocery store, but he said his people were born to fishing and he couldn't change.

I don't know what there was about the water I distrusted. People had tried to teach me to swim, but I never could get the hang of relaxing and trusting that the water would hold me up. I just couldn't stand the thought of being miles and miles out to sea with no land in sight and not a thing you could do about it if the sea chose to swallow you up. I thought that if Mrs. Coolidge made me go with her, I'd sure never see my mother again.

My mother never had no more live children after she had me, though she had raised three girls before me that didn't thrive. I was spoiled and petted, spared the hardest chores, and I knew my momma wouldn't make me go with Mrs. Coolidge if I had a mind not to. And so I hid behind Momma's skirts and let her tell Mrs. Coolidge that I always got sick on boats, even the ferry crossing the bay. Mrs. Coolidge ended up taking Lucy Pappas, the seamstress's daughter, to help look after Edith.

I kept an eye on the gigs and wagons lining up along Avenue P in front of the Coolidge house while I turned mattresses and pulled up rugs. Only three people were going on the boat, but it took twenty or thirty to see them off. Edith threw a fit when she heard I wasn't coming and cried so that Mrs. Coolidge sent for me to come as far as the wharf.

I tore off my apron and tied up my hair, presented myself

downstairs in the yard, embarrassed to be seen by all those fine folks in their best clothes. I feared that somehow things 'ud get mixed up and I'd end up going on that trip after all, but nobody gave me the chance to excuse myself, just shoved me onto a wagon seat with Edith and handed me a hatbox to balance on my knees.

I tried to take Edith's mind off where she was going by whispering a story in her ear. She liked to hear the same one over and over—Cinderella, about how the poor little girl had to work so hard for her mean stepsisters and how they made her sit in the ashes, but she was a princess after all, 'cause her little foot was the only one that would fit in the glass slipper.

Edith's momma was in the gig in front of us, along with Ned, Mary and James. Fern and some of the other young people was riding behind in another wagon. Mr. Hampton, Mr. Coolidge's driver, drove the wagon we were in. Ours wasn't the liveliest rig, I'll be bound. Mr. Coolidge never said a word the whole trip, and Paul said his beads, praying for safe passage for his mother and sister, I expect. He should've been praying for those of us left behind, 'cause we were the ones that were going to need it, but of course, we didn't know that at the time. Lucy Pappas, who'd just learned she was going on that trip barely a week before, sat silent and still as a stone, like she didn't know what had hit her yet. I hoped nobody had told her that Mrs. Coolidge asked me first and she was only going 'cause I'd said no. Maybe she'd enjoy herself once they got underway, though it wasn't where I'd want to spend a solid week, cooped up with Mrs. Coolidge on a boat no bigger than the Coolidge house.

Mr. Coolidge sat facing me. I had never had a chance to take a good look at him before, since he was at the office most of the time and I wasn't in his home at night. When he tipped his hat to the household ladies that had come out to see us off, I noticed that his scalp showed pink through the strands of black oiled hair. He wore a handsome waxed handlebar moustache, as if to make up for the thinness on top. He was round and short, stuffed like a sausage into his tight gray suit.

Our caravan rolled proudly up Broadway to the Strand and thence to the wharves, us waving gaily at the people that gaped at us on the sidewalk, like we were in a parade. At the boat, Mrs.

Coolidge told Lucy to take Edith directly to the stateroom and stay with her until she come along. Lucy took the hatbox and Mrs. Coolidge's valise, and I took Edith's hand. The wharf was busy with passengers, their friends that had come to see them off, and dockworkers trying to get the ships loaded. I heard all kinds of foreign tongues being spoke and thought how lucky it was that my father had come from a country that spoke English, which meant he'd been able to advance more quickly to a job where he got to use his head rather than his back to make a living.

The Coolidges had lots of friends, people I recognized from the society news in the *Galveston News-Tribune*. On deck, Mrs. Coolidge had a table laid out with little sandwiches and cakes, and stewards in white gloves served champagne. I would've liked to hide somewhere and watch the swells having their party, but I had to go downstairs with Lucy and Edith. We found Edith's room number, the room she was to share with Lucy. Through a connecting door was Mrs. Coolidge's room. The rooms were about the size of the closets back home, but the walls and ceiling were polished walnut and all the fixtures brass.

"Are you scared?" I whispered to Lucy.

"Terrified!" she said, and looked it.

I felt guilty as could be, so naturally I tried to make her glad she was going. "It's a nice room," I said. "And just think of all the places you'll get to see. And imagine! No chores for two whole months."

Lucy began to look more cheerful and made me promise not to leave her until the party was over upstairs. We could hear a band playing and people shouting and laughing, but we could also feel a slow steady throb down below our feet, which I imagined was the boat warming up its engines. But the party went on for so long that all three of us ended up falling asleep on Edith's bed, probably 'cause we'd had to get up so early that morning. But all of a sudden the boat let out three sharp blasts and we all jumped like Gabriel had blown his horn. Finally it was time to tell poor little Edith that I wasn't going with her.

"But I want *you*," she screamed, throwing her arms around my neck.

"It's all worked out now, honey. You're going away across the ocean to see the sights and Lucy will be right at your side."

"But I like *you*," she insisted.

Lucy looked so miserable I was afraid she was going to cry too. I felt like the meanest person in the world as I took Edith's hand and put it into Lucy's and ran out the door. At the top of the stairs Mr. Coolidge was saying goodbye to his wife. "Have a good voyage, Mother," he said, bussing her on the cheek.

I rushed down the gangway to gain the safety of solid ground and stood there with the others waving goodbye and feeling bad that I wasn't more adventuresome so I could've gone with Edith and been a comfort to her. I knowed things about Edith that nobody else knowed, that she was scared of her momma and that she had a pretend world in her head. She had explained it all to me with these little pictures she drew.

My papa would've give anything he owned for the opportunity I had turned down, free passage to Scotland. But I was American born and bred and didn't feel the same tug as he did for the Old Country. Even Mrs. Coolidge's generous offer weren't enough of a magnet to draw me away from dry land.

I didn't want to bother Mr. Coolidge about a ride back home, nor Ned nor Fern neither, so I caught the streetcar and rode back through town, glad that somehow, in the face of Mrs. Coolidge's determination, I had managed to get my way. I reckon that didn't happen too often.

~~~~~

FAITH KOHL COOLIDGE

July 20, 1900

Lucy lies queasy in her room. Most aggravating when this was what I especially wished to avoid, coddling some sickly female across the Atlantic! I've a good mind to send her straight back the minute we make land, though she may prove useful once we're on solid ground again.

This is my third crossing. Mr. Coolidge, back when he was

not as busy as he is today, went along that first trip. Ned was nine, Fern eight, Mary seven, and James four. I left Paul with Mrs. Chandler, as I expected to take him one day as the eldest of a little group of younger brothers and sisters. But that was not to be. Paul remained the youngest while one after another of the next three failed to survive infancy.

Eventually, I took Paul by himself. Always a serious and thoughtful little chap— perhaps because of the trauma of losing three younger siblings—I knew he would benefit from the trip even without the company of other children. It was during that trip that he decided on a life in the Church. We made a pilgrimage to Rome where his decision was dedicated in a massed audience before the Pope. Then we traveled back across Europe by rail and stopped to look at ancient cathedrals along the way. Paul was not much older than Edith, but Edith will require quite a different sort of tour—I suppose she will view St. Paul's as merely another of Europe's great works of art.

I have some business to take care of on this journey. Mr. Coolidge has an elderly aunt who must be visited before she dies, and he wants me to stop in and see his bankers in London. My own personal goal is to try to overcome a certain prejudice I feel toward my youngest daughter. I despise weakness in myself and must put this behind me! I constantly believe I've succeeded, only to discover it still among my sins. Perhaps the resentment I feel toward Edith has nothing to do with her, but is due merely to her being last in the birth order, a misfortune the poor child can't help.

I grew superstitious after the two little girls died and refused to name the third baby, a boy. Poor little fellow came into the world weeks before he was expected, a pointy face, little stick legs and arms. Mrs. Chandler would've thought me unnatural had I refused to take him to my breast and give him nourishment, but I had a sure and certain feeling that doing so would only draw out his decline and make me more heartsick. Mrs. Chandler had to tease him with my nipple to get him sucking and once he did, I felt how weak was his hold on life. But I was too weak myself to protest and fell into a heavy sleep from whence I awoke to a coldness at my bosom. I pushed aside the blanket to see that he had grown still, as if poisoned by his own mother's milk. I could hardly muster the energy to summon Mrs. Chandler. "Take it away," I told her. "It's dead."

For that's all he was to me at that moment, a bit of cold clay in which life had not taken hold. She let out an exclamation of shock, perhaps at my harshness, and hurried the little bundle out of my sight. I pulled the covers up over my breast and tried to warm myself, but I don't believe the place where he lay his little head during that brief sojourn on earth will ever be warm again.

One tends to think that life cannot possibly go on after some scene of enduring horror, but indeed that is the nature of life, to go on. Only the weak wear their scars visibly. In due time we had Edith, named for one of Mother's sisters. When it appeared that she was a robust child, I sent Mr. Coolidge to sleep in the little bedroom next door and closed that chapter of my life.

August 4

The sea is calm and green today. The choppiness of the last week is finally over. The seamstress's daughter Lucy is feeling peart enough to take Edith to the stern to sketch. Edith is the artist in the family. I shall take her to see the pictures in London's great galleries. I suppose she gets it through my father's side of the family. There was a cousin, I recall, who painted landscapes. I confess that I see little use in it myself, but since she is a girl, mayhap a husband will find it restful to have a wife who paints.

The green hills of Ireland have appeared off our port side. Tomorrow we steam into the Bristol Channel.

August 23

Last evening we called on Mr. Coolidge's Aunt Hilda, up in her eighties, whom I had not met before. We sat together in the little parlor of her London flat and went through the photograph album I had brought along of her American family members, great nephews and nieces. I explained that Mr. Coolidge was busy on a project to expand his warehouse capacity and unable to take a long ocean voyage at this time. I doubt she will be alive by the time he can make the trip again.

Edith had brought along her sketch book and drew an insulting caricature of the old lady, complete with hook nose bending down over toothless gums to touch the famous Coolidge chin. "Oh, Edith!" I chided, but the old lady declared herself delighted with the portrait and said she would keep it forever as a reminder of her irreverent young niece.

Mrs. Wilkes' first husband, Mr. Stanley Coolidge, died some forty years ago, as did the plumber by the name of Wesley Wilkes who replaced him. It is interesting that when a woman turns out to be made of durable stuff she often outlasts the men around her. Mrs. Wilkes asked after my people in Germany and I explained that we had lost touch long ago, that my parents emigrated to America back in '43.

"They were Galveston's first citizens—the City Charter dates to only five years earlier," I told her. I find that most people on the Continent are ignorant of Galveston's history.

"Quite a young city then! And are your parents still living?"

"My mother died quite a long time ago, but my father is only recently deceased. He and my husband were very much involved in building the new deep water port my daughter and I sailed from, one of the reasons I was eager to take the trip. My husband has staked his reputation on that port securing Galveston's position in the world of commerce."

"Was there ever anybody called Galveston?"

"Count Bernardo de Galvez, viceroy of Mexico toward the end of the last century. The old maps refer to the island as 'Isla de San Luis,' or sometimes, 'Snake Point.'"

"Snake Point!?"

"The diamondback rattler. We don't see them much in the city any more—they'd be cut in two by the wheels of wagons and streetcars, but they're still dangerous out on the western end of the island among the dunes. The island had no full-time residents until the coming of white settlers. Savages used to fish there—Karankawas, they were called—but they built nothing permanent. Galveston also boasts a long colorful period when pirates made the island their stronghold."

Mrs. Wilkes shuddered delicately. "I thought my nephew

15

was crazy to up and leave everything and sail off for parts unknown. You ought to come out here, he said, emigrate! No, thank ye. I like me comforts!"

I looked around the crowded little parlor, thinking that my own, by comparison, was spacious, even a little grand. Was it for the comforts of spacious parlors that my ancestors risked their lives crossing the great sea? Then I thought: How aptly the two parlors embody the spirit of our two countries, the one worn out from centuries of use, crowded, stale of idea and depleted of resource, the other boundless of opportunity and expansive of idea and space. Mrs. Wilkes was not willing to pay the price in discomfort and must therefore be satisfied with her poky little parlor.

"What did they intend to do in Texas?" she asked querulously, perhaps sensing my disdain.

"My father had a brother in Central Texas who farmed, but my mother was charmed by the temperate climate of the island and wanted to stay there. She also found it reassuring that a number of Catholic families were already settled there. Even before Father built our house, he helped raise money to build the Ursuline Convent where I and my sisters and brothers were educated. The house, unfortunately, blew away in the '67 hurricane."

Mrs. Wilkes shook her head. "Rattlesnakes and savages, pirates and hurricanes! What an obtuse people you Texans must be!"

I smiled and bore the charge proudly.

Later, I thought about the old lady's remark as I lay in my bed trying to compose myself for sleep. Often before I've sensed the resentment of those who stayed behind, and have felt in my turn the pity and contempt of we who moved on. I thought of my island home, surrounded by the tranquil and bountiful waters of the Gulf, blessed by the benison of warm, sun-filled winters. Yes, there was a price for this munificence—six dead children for my mother, three for me—but neither I nor my father have ever regretted his decision to settle in Galveston.

At home, people still die of fevers and influenza, though fortunately nothing like they did in the last century with yellow fever. Now we know that yellow fever is spread by the salt marsh mosquito and we can protect ourselves. When my mother was a bride, great fever epidemics scoured the island every two or three years, carrying off one in ten lives. Survivors gained immunity and passed it on to their children. During the Civil War it was known that only native soldiers could be safely garrisoned on our island, hence our expression "BOI," or "born on the island."

Three-fourths of the German emigrants died in the epidemic following the 1867 storm, including two of my sisters. People with means generally took to their heels at the first hint of an epidemic, but that summer, the *Galveston Daily News* didn't report the outbreak of disease until the end of July, when already 22 people had died. Shortly, the numbers began to pour in: 596 deaths in August, 482 in September. In all, over a thousand people died that summer, a rate of about 20 per day.

We rejoice in being born on the island, carrying immunity in our blood, but we mean irony in the phrase too. There's an admirable vision in people who see what can be built where there is nothing and have the toughness to overcome every obstacle to achieve their goal; but there is also foolishness in sticking to a course that leads to repeated disaster, like a thick-headed student who won't learn his lessons. Mainlanders accuse us of biblical folly in building our edifices on sand, historical folly in building where the sea has laid waste in the past to our optimism and hubris. It is not easy to answer such criticism. Or rather, it is too easy and not worth saying that nothing can be gained where nothing has been ventured.

It takes a masculine cast of mind to step back and see the larger picture, spread the cost of present human life and suffering over generations to come. Had one's ancestors been content to remain in their comfortable and civilized cities, the world would not have become the broad page on which humans have so large writ their story. My mother, a supremely feminine woman, could not take the long view and therefore she became embittered by the waste and the sacrifice she was called upon to make in the service of my father's dreams. Her entire focus being on her children, she was bereft when she lost six out of the seven, leaving only me. Unlike my heart, hers remained unhardened after those deaths and, only three years younger than I am now, she lay down to take her place among the dead.

17

And so my mother did not live to see me marry the enterprising young Englishman recently arrived on our shores, Herrick Edward Coolidge, who brought family money with him to invest in the cotton storage and compressing business. The bales come to us by rail from all over the South and we put them through our high-density presses, which squeeze the bales into a tighter space so they don't take up as much room in the hold of a ship. I met my husband when he and my father joined forces to make sure the railroads made Galveston, not Houston, their hub. There was the very real danger that if the railroads went north, our lifeblood would be cut off. The railroads have been nervous about Galveston's prospects ever since the '67 hurricane and have talked of digging a channel sixty miles inland to build a port in Houston. Luckily, thirty years of calm weather in the Gulf have put an end to such foolishness.

September 7
    Edith must be dragged out of her room to see the sights. Lucy is not much better—curled up like a caterpillar with the menses. Lord, save me from the everlasting nuisance of females! Tomorrow we tour St. Paul's.

~~~~~

EDITH COOLIDGE PICKERING

I was just a child, but I remember September 8, 1900, as if it were yesterday, not for being the defining moment in Galveston's history, but as the first time I ever saw Mama behave like any other woman, albeit for only a moment.

We had finished our tour of St. Paul's cathedral and were making our way through Piccadilly looking for a place to luncheon. We had left my paid companion Lucy at the hotel that morning, doubled up with the cramps. All of a sudden Mama stopped in mid-stride as if thunderstruck, staring at a newspaper boy hawking his wares.

"Storm of the century!" yelled the youth. "Read all about it! Thousands feared dead!"

Mama stood there stunned, her mouth open a bit. I tugged at her skirt, afraid she was having a fit, not immediately taking in what the boy was yelling. I felt tears crowd into my throat, recognizing that some tragedy had befallen us, something bad enough to stop Mama in her tracks. Then she stepped briskly up and bought a copy of the *London Times*.

HURRICANE HITS GALVESTON, read its banner headline. And under that, THOUSANDS FEARED DEAD.

We were over a week at sea not knowing if our loved ones were among those thousands.

~~~~~

MEG GALLOWAY

The night before the big blow, I caught the streetcar from the Coolidge's house and met George on the boardwalk. We had ice cream, then slipped off to spoon for a bit down on the beach. I remember noticing that the moon was clear, but next morning when I took the streetcar to work, I was surprised to see the two hurricane flags waving on the beach, red squares with black squares in the middle.

Mr. Hampton, who took care of Mr. Coolidge's horses and did handiwork, had been down to talk to the weather station men who told him the authorities had telegraphed during the night to say a storm had crossed over Florida and was somewhere out in the Gulf. A shiver chased up my spine when Mr. Hampton said the waves weren't washing up on the beach like they usually did, little short choppy waves ever six seconds, but were coming in long rolling breakers, which nobody could ever remember seeing on the island before.

All morning we went about our work as usual, me upstairs turning beds, but everybody hanging an ear out into the stairwell to hear the news if anybody come in. People living out on the west end sent word that water was acreeping up over the low-lying spots, which seemed to me like a bad sign, but the only weather we could see from the windows of the Coolidge house was that the wind had begun to freshen a bit. Agnes Miller, the housemaid I was helping, said storms didn't bother her, that all they ever did was blow the shingles off and tear up the trees and shrubbery. We'd just have ourselves a big mess to clean up afterwards. I figured George and his father was taking the boat inland with the other fishermen. I could look out from Mr. Coolidge's study and see a steady stream of boats coming in to safe harbor.

Mr. Hampton kept checking the weather glass. He was worried 'cause he said he'd never seen it drop that low before. Mr. Coolidge sent Mr. Ned home at noon to make sure the girls had come home and to be in charge of hurricane preparations on the home front. Mr. Ned was scared and serious-looking at being in charge of grown men, some of 'em who'd been through hurricanes before he was born. But they followed him right on out the door to get the windows boarded up and tie down things in the yard that might blow against the house. Everybody was worried about Mr. Paul, who'd gone out early that morning to Mass and wasn't home yet, but directly he come in too and said he'd been down on the wharf talking to the fishermen. They said it were blowing up for a bad 'un. By now we could see thin spiraling arms of clouds, like a great pinwheel in the sky, the outer bands of the storm.

We women worked inside, running bathtubs and buckets and urns and anything else we could fill with water to have on hand in case the line that run under Galveston Bay got cut and we had to do without fresh drinking water for awhile. Ever time somebody opened the back door we could see the weather getting worse, the clouds getting denser and darker, the rain falling harder. Finally it was coming down in long solid streams, like fire hoses trained on the house, and the men had to come in and close and bar the back door.

We all screamed at the first big jolt of wind, which the house took like a prize fighter taking a body punch, kind of staggering, then holding. Mr. Coolidge come home about then and stood in the entry hall talking to Mr. Ned and the men. Then he come back to the kitchen and told us not to worry, we were in the safest house on the block. The neighbors must've thought so too, 'cause they kept coming in, in two's and three's, water running off them in sheets. Agnes and I were kept busy passing out towels and mopping water up off the hardwood floors so it wouldn't spot.

The rain come harder, and the sky out the front windows turned black as midnight. Mr. Coolidge made us come out of the kitchen, which was on the south side of the house, which I was glad of, 'cause another minute or two I was about to run upstairs and hide under a bed. Mother and I crowded with the rest of them into the front parlor, good folks and help alike. The lights went out and Mr. Hampton lit a coal oil lamp. More people kept pushing through the front door and we kept getting shoved deeper and deeper into the room, like it was a small room, which it weren't.

The wind was screaming like only a hurricane screams, a high keening sound, a terrible sound. We could only make ourselves heard by yelling right in our neighbor's ear. I had my arms around my momma like I was a little kid again, but there weren't any shame in it. Every face I could see in the pool of yellow light looked anxious as we all thought the same thought—will the house hold? Mary was crying against her papa's shoulder. I wondered if my papa had been let off from the warehouse to go home and make sure our house was all right. I thought about other people I loved and tried to picture where they might be. George might've stayed with the boat, 'cause he'd told me that tying up a boat only gives the wind something to knock it against.

All of a sudden the people around me noticed the same thing I had just noticed, that water was running in my shoe, warm as blood. It didn't take no time at all till it had risen up over our ankles and we knowed it wasn't going to stop. Mr. Coolidge began herding everybody out of the parlor toward the stairs. The ones that had come in last were out in the entry hall and had a head start. Me and Momma were kindly in

21

the middle, and Mr. Coolidge and his children, the ones that should've been first, were last.

Once I turned my back on the light, I never saw it again. It was black as pitch in that entry hall. I had crossed through that way a hundred times before and gone up them stairs, but nothing seemed at all familiar about it that night with so many people pressing and crowding in on me. I had holt of somebody in front of me, but I warn't sure it was my momma any more, and I didn't know who had me from behind. If it wasn't so awful serious, I'd've thought it was funny how all of us were the same there in the dark, scared and blind, servants and gentry alike.

By the time I found the newel post and stepped up on the first step, the water was swirling around my knees. It seemed like somebody had turned on a tap somewhere and the house was just filling up with water. I only made it a step or two, what with all the crush of people against me, when all of a sudden the staircase moved right under me. I knowed I was screaming, but I couldn't hear a thing but the roar of the wind. I slid down to my knees and hung on to that bannister with might and main. The wall to my right come crashing in on me, sending the end of the staircase whooshing out into the middle of the house. I was hurt somehow, but too scared to even figure out where. I knew I had to get to the top of that staircase and on to the second floor, 'cause the house was open to the elements now and water was pouring in. Any minute the whole downstairs was going to wash away.

I fought like a wildcat to get up those stairs, knowing I was pushing past people, but not able to stop myself. I've never doubted that in my right mind I would lay down my life for a fellow creature, but in the midst of fighting to save your own life you don't stop to consider what you're doing, though I've considered it many a time since, thinking that one of those I might've elbowed out of the way was my own dear mother.

I made it to the top, but it didn't do me no good, 'cause the floor wasn't there no more. All I could do was hang on to the big center post that the stairs and all the other floors was connected to. I wropped my arms around that thing in a death grip and felt the stairs wash away out from beneath me. You couldn't even hear the screams of the people that was on those stairs as the sea carried them away.

I've cried a thousand tears that I didn't hang on to Mother's hand so I could've either saved her or we could've died together. My arms were strong from doing chores, not soft and white like Fern's and Mary's. I hung on to that thick white graceful column with the carving round the top, and when it tilted over, that was even better, 'cause then I could drag my poor tired legs up around it and hold on like a monkey on a palm tree. My mouth was open with the terrible straining agony of using every muscle in my body to hang on while the house came down around me. The water against my tongue was pure brine. As the house broke apart, dark shapes moved past me. I was continuously struck and buffeted by falling lumber. I prayed for deliverance, oh, Jesus, oh, Jesus, oh, Jesus.

All through that terrible night I hung on to that sagging pillar. I knew the eye of the storm was off to our west, 'cause there was never no respite, not for hours. The storm finally blew itself out before dawn, and the storm surge drained away and let the waters return to the Gulf.

I could scarce believe my eyes when it got light enough to see, all around me splintered wood, yellow and surprised looking, wrenched from its secret and unpainted places in the heart of the house. And right there in the middle of what had been Mrs. Coolidge's front parlor was a streetcar that the waves had carried down the street and used to batter down Mr. Coolidge's house, leaving hardly two pieces of wood nailed together.

I wasn't hanging on the column no more, just kind of draped over it. I couldn't come down. Out of the corner of my eye I could see a naked human arm sticking up out of the rubbish. I looked away from it and tried to use my voice, but it was all dried up. I reckon I'd been screaming all night. My mouth was terrible dry and I couldn't even cry for that dead body that might've been my poor mother for thinking how bad I wanted a drink of water. My clothes had been ripped right off my body, leaving me just a few tattered rags, but there wasn't nobody left alive in the whole world to see my nakedness, so it didn't matter no more.

Over my head, the sun rose as pretty as you please. Seagulls flew by and looked down at the ruined works of man. The wind was peaceful and sweet against my cheek. I laid my head against that pillar and prayed to die.

~~~~~

FAITH KOHL COOLIDGE

September 20, 1900

    I've never seen such terrible destruction, my island city laid to waste there in the September sunshine. Nothing remained of my home but a blasted shell. There were not even bodies left to bury, for there had been so many, some six thousand, that survivors had to get rid of them quickly, without taking the time to mourn their losses. Most deaths were from drowning. The previous highwater mark on the island had been eight feet, in the 1875 hurricane, but in this storm the water rose to the deadly level of fifteen feet on the low side, the beach side, where our house sat. Ships anchored in the harbor were found twenty miles inland. Thirty blocks of houses and businesses were reduced to rubble and deposited by the waves in a long tangled mass of shattered lumber along the shoreline.

    The convent and church stood. I found Father Kirwin busy arranging shelter for the homeless and feeding the hungry. He took time out to take me into the sanctuary and tell me that not one of my family had been found alive. Several people had reported that our house had been used as a place of refuge, and might have stood had it not been for a loose streetcar washing up and down the street like a lethal battering ram.

    Before I arrived they had loaded seven hundred corpses onto three barges, weighted them with rocks, and committed them to the deep. But within two days bodies began washing up on the beach and they had to be collected all over again and burned. The fires burned into November, some seventy bodies a day. Father Kirwin passed out whisky to the men assigned the gruesome task of feeding the flames. People would go down to the fires on the beach to watch, hoping to identify a loved one and assuage their terrible uncertainty of not knowing whether a loved one was alive or dead. One worker found the corpse of his own daughter and had to be led away, overcome with grief. I did not go to the pyres, but said a prayer for Mr. Coolidge and my children and pitched in to help get the city back on its feet.

On the inland side, as could be expected, there was less damage. The public water system, running deep under the bay from the mainland, was intact. The railroad bridge was damaged, but able to be repaired so that the army of rescuers could come by train to render aid. The *Galveston Daily News* didn't miss an issue, but covered the terrible aftermath of the worst natural disaster to ever strike the United States. Besides the six or seven thousand deaths on the island there were three or four thousand more on the mainland. The catastrophe was of such magnitude that every resource was strained to cope with it, including the ability to compile accurate figures. We shall never know exactly how many people lost their lives, for often entire families were wiped out, leaving no one behind to report the tragedy.

The Coolidge Cotton Company sustained major damage to roofs and wharves, but as I toured the site, I calculated how quickly we could make repairs and be back in business, for it was clear to me that Galveston's fate rested on a quick and convincing come-back from this disaster, else we might as well join Indianola's fate and abandon our island to the sea.

Chapter Two

CHARLES OREN PICKERING

I knew Ned Coolidge to speak to, but he being Catholic and my people being Lutheran, he having money and me getting by with but one good suit, we didn't have much in common. Still, we were both BOI boys up there at the University together and I grieved poor Ned along with my own family that drowned. I myself should've been among their number, but having to support myself in school, my job in the Austin accounting house of Higgins and Higgins ran on through the summer. So, instead of coming home at the end of June, I came home the first week of September and had stopped over in Houston that Saturday night the storm hit.

The storm was still blowing strong sixty miles inland where we were and so we knew it was having a devastating impact on the coast. I hoped and prayed, along with the rest of the city, that Galveston hadn't taken the brunt of the storm direct, and I volunteered to be among the first able-bodied men that rushed to relieve the city on Monday, September 10. What we found was terrible to see. Fully a third of the city was completely destroyed, including the block where I had grown up. Those of us with kin weren't there to pick through the rubble to find our own dead, though, and it was days before I was able to take an inventory of my own losses. There was no sign of my parents, nor two younger sisters. I found the body of Iphigenia, my youngest sister, weighted under a neighbor's heavy cement stoop. I would've liked to buried her, but the soil was too saturated for grave-digging. I said a prayer for her departed soul and turned her over to the body-burning detail.

I knew of Mrs. Coolidge, but only by reputation, you might say. When she called me in for an interview, I could see she was a woman of determination, even if she didn't know anything about her dead husband's business.

"Do you have any objection to working for a woman?" she said. I said not that I know of. And she said, "You've got some practical experience, I take it, in this part-time job you had during your schooling?"

I agreed that I did, but that it didn't run too deep. She said that was all right, because I'd be working under Mr. Galloway who knew the books forwards and backwards. He was the only one in the bookkeeping department that had survived the storm.

It may sound like a strange thing to bind people together, the fact that they're alive, but in the years that followed the Great Storm of 1900, it turned out to be an enduring tie, one that cut across social and financial boundaries. Take my association with Mrs. Coolidge, for example. She was the daughter of one of Galveston's first families, had money long before she teamed up with Mr. Coolidge. In accounts I would read in the newspaper of teas and soirees, charitable events and so on, her name would be prominently listed, Mrs. Herrick Coolidge, right up there with the island's other great family names, the Moodys, the Rosenburgs, the Kempners. I sure never thought I'd one day be working for her, or that I'd see a society lady of her stature with her sleeves rolled up, marching around a decimated warehouse asking questions and giving orders. You'd of thought she was born to command men instead of pour out tea. Not one of them ever sassed her, either, not even when she reached out one morning and plucked a cigarette out of Coleman Vance's mouth and said there'd be no tobacco use on her premises, that it was dangerous and unsightly, not to mention unchristian. Mr. Galloway happened to be there and I heard him say "Tarnation" under his breath. Mr. Galloway's fingers were stained with years of tobacco use, and the walls of his office yellowed from the noxious fumes of ever-burning weed. Instead of giving up his filthy habit, he took to slipping out to an unused dock several times a day. Mrs. Coolidge knew what he was doing, but she never said anything, maybe knowing just how far she could go with the one man who knew everything about her husband's books.

Six weeks after the storm of the century, Mrs. Coolidge shipped her share of the 30,000 bales of cotton that went out of the Port of Galveston that month, setting a new record. After that, no man dared criticize her for being a woman.

People who would've never known one another otherwise were bound together by the simple fact that we were survivors and had lost people that were important to us. Mrs. Coolidge had lost her husband and all her children except the youngest, Edith, who had been in England with her at the time. Mr. Galloway lost his wife, but miraculously learned that his daughter had survived by clinging to the wreckage of Mrs. Coolidge's house, where some forty people had gone seeking safe haven and perished.

Mrs. Coolidge was an example to us all, and we put our grief and our guilt for not being among the dead out of our minds so we could deal with the clean-up. Some of us never got around to properly grieving. It's something I have in common with Mrs. Coolidge.

~~~~~

EDITH COOLIDGE PICKERING

My memories fall into two categories, before the storm and after. Before the storm, I was the youngest of six children. Afterwards, I was an only child. Before the storm, I was pampered and indulged for being the youngest, also for being "different," more dreamy, slower than my generally ambitious and energetic siblings, for taking an interest in books and paintings and music. After the storm, I was expected to put away non-essentials and do my part to help save my father's business and shore up the Coolidge image. Shoring up the image was necessary because my father had been one of the storm prophets that said it could never happen again, that somehow the terrible storms that scoured the island in the nineteenth century were part of what we were putting behind us in this, the glorious new twentieth century. A lot of people believed him and put their money into businesses that were ruined by the 1900 hurricane. My mother took it as a personal challenge to get Galveston back on her feet as quickly as possible and somehow pull victory from the jaws of defeat.

I was only ten years old and not required to participate in the actual re-building of Galveston. My part was to "be good," which meant to keep out of the way while my mama worked nearly night and day to stave off business failure and save our livelihood. Part of being good included not crying over my brothers and sisters all being dead, and my papa. There was no time for grief and there was nothing unusual that summer about losing one's entire family. I found a way to fulfill what was required of me by distracting myself with the recovery of Meg Galloway.

Mr. Galloway had finally found her clinging to life in a mainland hospital. She had been found among the debris of our house, her head cracked open, her leg broken, not to mention being lacerated by flying slate roofing tiles. When I saw her, she was stitched and taped together and in a deep depression over losing her mother, for which she irrationally blamed herself. Mr. Galloway didn't want her to know that her fiance George was also missing and presumed dead, that his father's fishing boat had been found twenty miles up the Trinity River.

I went to see Meg almost daily, since their house was not far from the one we were renting while ours was being rebuilt. "As soon as you get well, you have to come and be my nurse," I told Meg.

Lucy Pappas' mother had been visiting her sister over on Bolivar and had taken refuge in the lighthouse along with about a hundred other people. Mama gave Lucy the job of keeping house and looking after me, but I had learned on our trip that

29

Lucy was lacking in spunk and personality and I planned on getting Mama to replace her with Meg as soon as Meg was able. The worst part of Meg's injuries were to her spirits, for though she had survived the storm, she had lost her will to live. I took it as my personal challenge to turn that situation around.

Everyday I loaded up a little basket with things to cheer her up, a book to read aloud to her, a kitten, tempting sweets, pictures I had drawn. "Oh, Miss Edith," she would moan, "you don't have to bother." I would bathe her face and change her bandages, fluff out her hair to hide the place the doctor had shaved to stitch her up. The doctor had said she would be permanently disfigured by the scars on her face and always walk with a limp, which added to her sense of hopelessness. But little by little, almost against her will, Meg got better. With youthful egoism, I accepted the credit and thought of Meg as one of my creations.

One day, when Meg was still hobbling around in a cast, she said she wanted to see the house, so, with great difficulty, we managed to get her aboard the electric trolley and go downtown, where she got her first look at the wrecked homes and businesses, already giving way to new construction. In fact, a vast new building boom was underway to provide shelter for the more than 8,000 people that had lost their homes.

"Why do they bother?" said Meg. "The sea'll just come again and take it all away."

In the light of day I had enough spirit for both of us, but at night, in the solitude of my little bedroom at the top of the stairs, Meg's pessimism would have its effect on me and I would wake up terrified, convinced that water was rising in the house and afraid to leave my bed to seek comfort or call out to Mama. I began to take a greater interest in the weather, but would hush up when Mama realized what I was afraid of. "Great silly girl," she would scold.

"But what if another hurricane comes?" I finally blurted out, naming my fear. "Meg says they always do."

"We're taking steps," my mother said firmly. "We're human beings, not animals. We needn't be at the mercy of the weather. All we have to do is use our heads, use our resources."

What she was talking about was nothing less than remodeling the island to make it safer for human habitation, or rather, I sometimes thought, safer for investment. After the terrible destruction and death that Galveston had seen, it was easy for city fathers to convince the business interests to subscribe to a large bond issue. They also got the Texas legislature to offer tax relief for a massive three-pronged civil engineering project, a seawall, a grade raising, and an all-weather bridge to the mainland.

The Galveston seawall was one of the technological wonders of its day. Enormous curved blocks of concrete were anchored some fifty feet into the sand. These blocks were designed to take the force of incoming waves and direct the energy upward so that the force spent itself harmlessly in the air. The seawall was fifteen feet wide at the bottom, five feet across the top, seventeen feet high. The surface was paved with great carved blocks of native Texas pink granite to protect the footing from washing out. The essential part of the seawall was finished in four years and more sections immediately planned. Had it not been for that seawall, the nightmare I shared with Meg might've come true fifteen years later in the 1915 hurricane the day my daughter Emily chose to come into the world, a circumstance that kept Meg and me from evacuating with everyone else. But back when the wall was going up, I could have no intimation of what was to come. The wall was merely an interesting place to visit on Sunday afternoon.

A less spectacular but no less marvelous part of the plan was to raise the level of the entire eastern end of the island eighteen feet, three feet higher than the Great Storm had carried the waters. I was twenty-one years old before the project was completed. Long before that, Mama had rebuilt our house on Avenue P and Meg had come to work for us.

When it was time for our section to be raised, Mama hired a contractor to raise the house with several hundred jack screws, inches at a time. The city had been divided into a grid and channels cut through the heart of town to admit dredging barges. A dam was built around quarter-mile-square sections, which the barges flooded with a slurry of water and sand dredged up from the channel and from Offatt's Bay. As the water drained away, the sand stayed behind and raised the level of the block. At the same time, the channel from which the sand was being dredged was improved for shipping.

In all, five hundred blocks of the city were raised that way. Houses and buildings, gas lines, sewers, graves, even St. Patrick's Church was raised, the church that had survived the storm. Sacred Heart Church had been left with only one wall standing. People even tried to save their trees and shrubbery, but nutrients in the sand from deep under the channel were so poor that new topsoil had to be brought in. During the years of raising the city, we got used to getting around on board sidewalks built on stilts ten feet in the air.

The house Mama built to replace the one that washed away was many bedrooms smaller than the original, in recognition of our diminished number. It was still a large house, though, and I wondered about the extra bedrooms, if Mama intended to fill them with additions to our family. I don't know when I first decided that Mama might marry Mr. Pickering, perhaps only because she mentioned his name more often than anybody else's who worked for her. I pictured him as someone like Mr. Galloway, an old man with a beard, tufts of white hair sticking out his nose, which I always exaggerated when I drew him. One night Mr. Pickering was invited to dinner and I was surprised to discover that he wasn't an old man at all, but had been a classmate of my brother Ned's. "I thought you would be old," I said. He laughed, somewhat uncomfortably. His age gave me even more hope that Mama might marry him, and I listened carefully for any detail she might let drop that would indicate intimacy.

In our church there were a good number of weddings between men and women who had been widowed by the storm. I waited impatiently for Mama to announce that she too would be among their number, but Meg counseled caution. "Like as not your mama is too busy with business to get married again," she said.

Finally I asked Mama herself if she was ever going to get married and have more children. She looked at me and said, "That's why I have you. You'll do that for me. Instead of children, I'll have grandchildren."

One thing that was not changed by the storm was that I still attended parochial school at the Ursuline Academy, the Catholic school my grandfather had helped build. I showed an aptitude for fine arts, but was a lazy scholar.

The storm had changed the fortunes of most of my fellow students. Some were orphaned, or like me, stripped of one parent, or were now only children when before they had belonged to large families. Girls who came to Ursuline more recently were excluded from the club of "survivors," were puzzled by our repressed sense of loss and catastrophe, our distrust of balmy skies and clear weather, our conviction that at any moment things could go horribly wrong.

This conviction typically manifested in one of two ways. Some people, like Meg, turned inward and became very religious, minimized life's risks by living quietly, as if to escape the notice of heaven. Others went just the opposite way, recognized the futility of seeking guarantees and seemed to risk more boldly knowing there was nothing to lose. My mother was like that.

Being a physical coward, I practiced a little of both approaches, doing my boldest living under cover of lies and subterfuge. I was a lot more afraid of Mama, herself a force of nature, than I was of God. But ameliorating the effect of her sharp angles and toughness was the softness and tenderheartedness of my nurse Meg Galloway, who never spoke sharply or raised a hand, who would herself cry if I was bad, who always accepted and liked me no matter what I did, and couldn't bring herself to punish me.

I was perhaps thirteen when one of the girls at Ursuline gradually emerged as my best friend, a girl named Amy St. Claire who had lost her mother to the storm. Like me, Amy had been away from the island when the storm hit, and we shared the stunned sense of privilege and awe at being miraculously spared—the nuns said—to do something special in the world. My mother would only allow me to spend the night in Catholic homes, or let Catholic girls spend the night with me. Amy and I would cuddle together in our bed and have long philosophical conversations lasting into the night about what God's plan for us might be. For what great work had we been spared?

We were lonely children. Like most children we knew, we had lost family members to the storm, and we missed them, but it seemed to us that it was the ones still among us that were most absent as they busily went about the work of rebuilding, trying, it seemed, to make something worthwhile of the deaths of our loved ones.

My feelings for Amy were innocent but fervent. I wanted to be with her constantly and was unhappy and moody when that wasn't possible. I wrote her long letters every day, spending more time on these thoughtful epistles than I did my lessons. I didn't know that everyone didn't feel about their friends as I did, not then, not with Amy. My awakening came later with Charlotte.

I quickly outgrew the limited art instruction that was available in my school and convinced my mother—though she thought it was frivolous—that I should have lessons from a real art teacher, a Mr. Chalmers, who was very popular with ladies who painted water colors. Mr. Chalmers did his part to improve my technique and understanding, but his most significant contribution was to give me free access to his art books. I would study the great masterpieces of art and sketch the figures, and it would become clear to me that to escape provincialism I would need to study in New York or Paris. It was a battle with Mama I dreaded, but couldn't imagine losing, for if I lost, how could I go on? Yet how could I convince her to let me leave Galveston when I was all she had?

I also learned from Mr. Chalmers' art reproductions that I had to learn to draw the nude form. I chose Amy to be my model.

Amy was plump and blond, an excellent subject for both line drawings and pastels. At first she didn't feel right posing for my critical consideration, thought she might be guilty of the sin of vanity, but I convinced her that posing for me was actually a religious act, for it was not she who posed for my pen, but a stand-in for the Blessed Virgin, or some other equally unavailable model. And so she would strike a "religious" pose, Mary in prayerful contemplation, eyes closed, hands devoutly clasped, or prostrate before the cross.

I am sorry that none of those early portraits survived. Because of my finicky perfectionism, I was never satisfied with a picture once I had improved and could do better, which meant I was constantly tearing up earlier work to prevent its clumsiness and gaucheness from shaming me. That is why the sketchbook Meg found contained only a handful of compromising studies of my friend Amy and none of our earlier virtuous poses, for by then my nude model had grown quite casual about her nakedness.

We had started out modestly enough, studies of hands and feet, arms and shoulders. Amy would go into my closet and come out with a sheet draped round her and would expose a single area of her body for my abstracted gaze. Her body, pubescent and soft, was not unlike the fleshy Botticellis I studied in Mr. Chalmer's art books.

Although we managed to convince ourselves that what we were doing was virtuous, the secrecy that surrounded the act belied our claim, for we lived in terror of somebody finding us out. Working in bad light, curtains drawn tightly, I would stop often and make fearful inspections of the street below to check for Mama's gig. Meg was no problem—we could always hear her on the stairs because of her gimpy leg, which had never properly healed after being broken in three places.

But it was Meg who cleaned my room, and eventually she was the one who discovered my secret cache of drawings. Meg glanced through the sketchbook and hastily handed it back to me without a word. I knew from her face that this was one of those issues she would have to meditate upon before knowing how to handle.

"Artists have to learn to draw pictures of nudes," I told her. "It's not a sin. There are naked angels in lots of famous pictures!"

Meg left my room in something of a brown study. I almost knew what she was thinking, that this was her fault for encouraging me. Meg herself had often been my subject, fully clothed, of course. I would draw her just as I found her, kerchief tied round her head, pins in her mouth as she stitched lace to a new camisole for me, or sat on a stool in the kitchen mixing up a batch of gingerbread. "Oh, Miss Edith, why are you drawing me right now?" she would say. "Let me fix myself up a little before you do that!" as if I were aiming a camera at her. Meg thought herself ugly, but I didn't see people in terms of ugly or beautiful, only in varying degrees of interesting.

That night, when Meg came in to make sure I was in bed,

she sat down on the edge of the bed and I knew she was ready to deliver her verdict.

"You're not going to tell Mama, are you?" I said.

"What you want to draw pictures like that for?" she said.

"It's art. You don't ask an artist why they draw a certain thing."

"It don't seem right," she said. "Did you make up those pictures or did Miss Amy really take off her clothes?"

I didn't mind lying to Mama, but I always told Meg the truth. "They're drawings from life," I said quietly. "I'm going to be an important artist someday, Meg. You know Mama doesn't take it seriously. If you tell her, she'll make me stop altogether. I'll just die if I have to give up art. Don't tell!"

"I haven't never told on you in your life," she said, shaking her finger at me. "Oh, well, I guess it don't matter since you're both girls. And it's true that them religious pictures are full of naked bodies, but Lord, it just don't seem right somehow."

I nearly always got my way with Meg. She just didn't have the will to scold, and she loved me like the child she never had, though in age we were but seven years apart. In some ways Meg seemed her age, but in others, she was years younger than me. She didn't understand art, didn't understand why I didn't make things pretty when I drew them. Sometimes she would burst into tears when she took a look at some of my portraits of her. "How could you make me so ugly?" she would say. "Why couldn't you let me take that old head scarf off before you started drawing?"

She was particularly hard on her own hair, which was thick and kinky and which I would reproduce in all its mad whorls. She couldn't even brush it, it was so obstinate, but kept it tied up under a kerchief most of the time. Sometimes for church I would fix it for her, piling it on her head and letting little spirals hang down in front of her ears. Sometimes I would draw her like that, make a conscious effort to make her "pretty." She liked those pictures and would carry them to her room, though she only had religious pictures on her walls.

Meg was everything to me, parent and playmate, big sister and sounding board. I treated her like a big doll. She was unique in my world, a grownup who was approachable, who would let me touch her and pet her, fix her hair, play with her hands when they lay idle in her lap. Sometimes I would indulge a mean streak and torment Meg, hide around the corner and jump out and scare her, show up at the dinner table in some outlandish costume, or once, without a stitch. There was no one to see me, because the day help would be gone by then and Mama still at the office, most evenings either taking her evening meal out somewhere or eating off a tray when she got home. Meg was never put out with me, never anything but my most devoted confidante and friend.

"Oh, Miss Edith," she would say. "Aren't you a little imp!"

"Don't call me Miss Edith!" I would tell her.

"Your Mama says I'm to show you proper respect, so don't get on to me about things I can't help."

~~~~~

CHARLES PICKERING

Lots of young fellows in the years following the Great Storm never got around to courting girls and getting married till later. There was just too much to do, and I had thrown in with Mrs. Coolidge, who was committed to doing more than her share to engineer Galveston's recovery. I wasn't very good with girls anyway, so it didn't bother me that there was no time to court and start a family. I lived in Mrs. Beal's boarding house and took my meals there, spent nearly all the daylight hours in the warehouse.

I remember feeling some embarrassment for Mr. Galloway's sake when Mrs. Coolidge promoted me out of bookkeeping to work directly under her, but Mr. Galloway showed no animosity whatsoever and I reflected that he'd probably just as soon not work so close to the lady. I don't flatter myself that she promoted me because of the independence and daring of my ideas. In fact, I suspect Mrs. Coolidge valued me for just the opposite reason: I followed orders and I followed them exactly. That was just my nature, a natural born follower. I never had the temperament for biting the hand that fed me. I liked sure things and wasn't interested in striking out after the unproven. Maybe that's why I never got up the gumption to ask a girl out. Which isn't to say I didn't go out. In fact, I stepped out regularly, four or five evenings a week and twice as often during business hours, for I soon learned that part of my new duties included escorting Mrs. Coolidge to business functions, where, in stupefied amazement, I would watch her get her way with men that had ten times her experience in the world. She didn't do it with coquetry or playing dumb, either; she did it by being the best informed, the most tenacious, the level-headedest, the one armed with the best arguments. I would come away from a meeting where she'd gotten exactly what she wanted and I would think, this lady could run for president.

But Mrs. Coolidge's vision was focused tightly on Galveston, and she paid scant attention to events outside her city except where Galveston's or her own business interests were concerned. One of her areas of concern was helping thwart Galveston's rivals, which after the Storm proliferated. First and foremost was Houston, which two years after the Storm, began dredging a channel for the deep-water port Mr. Coolidge had dreaded and fought. Even closer to home, Texas City began crowing with ambition.

During the Spanish-American War, Galveston had been defended by a regiment called the Immunes, although the regiment never made it to Cuba before that brief war ended. After the war, there was sporadic trouble with Mexico along the border and the Army deemed it prudent to rebuild and make improvements to Ft. Travis over on Bolivar and to Ft. Crockett on the island. Both were newly built before the storm and badly damaged by the hurricane, so the Army co-ordinated its seawall building efforts with Galveston's to make a continual line of defense against the elements. In spite of these improvements, the Army chose Texas City across the bay for its headquarters and sent six thousand men to garrison there. Mrs. Coolidge was an outspoken critic of public monies going to favor a deep-water port right in our own backyard and lobbied Congress not to help this upstart neighbor at our expense.

38

Mrs. Coolidge viewed Texas City, established in the 1890s, as a bastard without parentage. The town boasted no history, but was merely a site cold-bloodedly selected for its physical charms by August B. Wolvin, who had every intention of capitalizing on the advantages of a coastal location without paying the gods of nature as Galveston periodically did. Texas City sat atop a low ridge that afforded protection from high water and came equipped with a natural channel that only needed deepening and widening, which Wolvin was able to persuade Congress to do.

Galveston wharf-owners were outraged. They had worked hard to recover from the Storm and now were being penalized for "congestion and high prices"—which were generally viewed on our side as signs of a successful come-back. But in 1904, Wolvin opened his rival facilities, a harbor, railroads, grain elevator, an oil refinery, and even offered steamship service to Mexico and New York. When it was clear that nothing could prevent Texas City from being there, Mrs. Coolidge accepted it and said, "Well, at least they don't have Opera."

Indeed, the Texas City town site was laid out as if houses and stores were just facilities needed for the port, and nearly everybody who lived there worked in industrial jobs. Galveston gradually accepted the upstart and thought of the town as nothing more than its own industrial arm, a hinterland to send the dirtier jobs to. Mrs. Coolidge never got over a strong prejudice towards Wolvin in particular and his town in general. Privately I thought she was just mad because somebody had come along that embodied her own spirit even more strongly than she did.

Mrs. Coolidge never did care anything at all for the Opera.

~~~~~

EDITH COOLIDGE PICKERING

With the help of Meg Galloway, I was mostly able to live in the same house with Mama and avoid direct confrontation. Meg hated lying for me, but I gave her no choice. Either she was a buffer between me and Mama or I was in trouble. Meg couldn't bear for me and Mama to clash, though I know she thought our skirmishes were only what went on in other homes between strong-willed mothers and their weaker daughters. But I knew our war was more fundamental and serious than that, that what was at stake was my very life and soul.

Gradually I began to understand what Mama had meant when she said, "That's why I have you. You'll do that for me." In her eyes it was quite reasonable to expect me to marry and give her grandchildren, and for almost any girl but me, such a plan might have dovetailed nicely with her own hopes and dreams. For me, that course was impossible. During my late teens, several years after the natural cooling of my intense devotion to Amy St. Claire, I met Charlotte Lattimore and finally learned that my feeling for first one girlfriend then another had not been simply a desire for girlish intimacy. It was passion.

Charlotte Lattimore came to us from New Orleans, a city that in spirit is much like Galveston, both being on the Gulf Coast and under constant threat of inundation. Both cities being old with colorful pasts, cities that make their livings from banking, cotton, and maritime commerce. Cities where graciousness and a buccaneer spirit reside side by side.

I uneasily made the transition from school girl to young woman, which signaled an end of my truce with Mama, who was no longer willing to let me actively study art but wanted me to put it behind as a childish interest. I still held out hope that she would let me go to a serious art school, preferably in New York. I had long outgrown Mr. Chalmers, but was not allowed to seek a new teacher who might help me advance. I felt stuck, thwarted.

Mama was constantly arranging my social life, accepting invitations for me that would put me in contact with eligible young men, encouraging me to follow my dead sister Fern's path to social acceptance. Meg Galloway was deemed to have no style, not a proper companion for a young lady, and was demoted to mere housekeeper and replaced by a Miss Winters who was hired to teach me the social graces I would require to get a husband and to entertain. I despised Miss Winters, a dried up old maid whom I privately derided in Meg's bedroom after hours as never having had any personal experience with attracting gentlemen, a remark which cheered Meg enormously, as she was rather sunk after her peremptory fall from grace. "Don't worry," I told Meg. "I'll get rid of her in six months."

"Don't you get in trouble on my account, honey," Meg replied.

I was as good as my word and several times a day managed to provoke Miss Winters to tears, though she maintained a stiff upper lip in front of Mama and refused to admit defeat of any sort. In the end Miss Winters accused me of sabotaging her efforts and I accused her of being a fraud. Under the terms of a mutual truce, she agreed to suddenly develop a sick sister who needed her in Philadelphia, and Meg was once again installed as my caretaker.

While she lived under our roof, though, Miss Winters managed to spend an astonishing amount of Mama's money on a glamorous wardrobe of gowns for me. She also got me elected to the best social clubs in town, and arranged my debut at the annual Artillery Club Ball in the winter season of 1907. For months afterwards I was duly besieged by young men whom I cynically supposed were as much interested in becoming Mrs. Herrick Coolidge's son-in-law as they were in my fair hand. For Mama had done quite well for herself in the flurry of opportunity that followed the Storm and was only being modest when she claimed that all she had done was to save Papa's fortune. In fact, Mr. Pickering informed me that Mama was one of the island's eleven millionaires.

One of the organizations I joined was The Young Ladies' Poetry Reading Society, which met twice monthly to listen to readings, often by the poet him or herself, followed by the serving of cake and tea. That is where I met Charlotte Lattimore in the fall of 1908. She was two years older than I and not at all wealthy. Rather, Charlotte existed on the edges of genteel poverty and had to support herself as a secretary for the American National Insurance Company, William L. Moody, Jr.'s firm.

I had given little notice to this singular young woman until the night she read Christina Rossetti, whose poems were already richly meaningful to me. Mrs. Isaac Kempner had made her elegant drawing room available to us that evening. Later, I could never drive past the Kempner home without instantly recalling the feelings that swept over me that night as I sat on a floral-print couch with two other ladies and quietly swooned with ardor for the passionate young reader.

It is perhaps common to attribute the fineness of the poet's sensibilities to the one merely reading the poet's words, but there is too that tendency to ally oneself with works of art that best express one's own feelings. So perhaps it was not too callow of me to mystically link Charlotte and the beautiful dead Miss Rossetti.

If I had ever a doubt of my true nature, that was the evening when doubt was forever erased. I knew that I had fallen in love virtually at the first utterance of the fabulous Miss Lattimore, who seemed to me a creation of the small footlights trained on her, or a creature I myself had brought about through the fervidness of my inchoate desires.

Amy St. Claire had attracted me with her difference, her otherness, her soft plump blondness, but Charlotte attracted— if not through similarity—by being what I wanted to be, how I almost saw myself on my best days. Physically, she was slender, breastless and graceful as a young boy. She had hair much like my own, soft and flyaway, light brown in color, which I knew would lighten in the summer sun and darken in winter damp. Her eyes were light gray, with an amazing opaque quality that glassily reflected the light.

> *When I am dead, my dearest,*
> *Sing no sad songs for me;*
> *Plant thou no roses at my head,*
> *Nor shady cypress tree:*
> *Be the green grass above me*
> *With showers and dewdrops wet:*
> *And if thou wilt, remember,*
> *And if thou wilt, forget.*

As she read Miss Rossetti's lines, I had to forcibly restrain myself from leaping to my feet and crying "Bravo!" From the others, the reading received only polite enthusiasm, nothing like the gladness that sprang forth in my heart. I rushed forward to seize Miss Lattimore's hand and introduce myself. Having put her stage presence aside, she reasserted her ordinary self and gravely shook my hand and accepted my flattering remarks deprecatingly.

"Yes," she said, "Rossetti is a favorite of mine. Do you like poetry?"

The truth, of course, was that I was indifferent to words unless they happened to fall from her lips. "Oh, yes!" I cried.

"Do you know the works of her brother as well?"

Realizing that my ignorance could easily disgrace me, I hedged. "Actually, I'm a painter. Have you ever sat for your portrait?"

"I can't imagine why you would say that. I'm not in the least bit beautiful."

I wanted to protest that she was the most beautiful and charming creature I had ever met, but of course I merely offered conventional protest. I asked if I might get in touch with her soon, as I was looking for a model, which she readily agreed to and told me where she worked. Over the three days I forced myself to wait before calling upon her, I existed in an agony of suspense and hope, alternating with the darkest pessimism.

That was the year that Mama, ever the progressive in matters outside her home, embraced the new technology of the combustion engine and purchased a Ford. She even insisted on learning to drive it herself, though she maintained a carriage house and a man to care for the horses and gig for several more years, until the new-fangled machines had proven themselves. Although it was fine for Mama to learn to drive, I was denied such independence for fear that young gentlemen would find such a skill in a prospective wife unflatteringly self-reliant.

I had come to realize that I was Mama's "soft" aspect, her femininity. For herself she claimed the right to drive cars—and men, but for me she had a more traditional role in mind. She had become Papa; I was to take her place. However, in spite of the enormous expense and trouble she had gone to to launch me in society as a public signaling of my readiness for matrimony, I thwarted her by falling in love with Charlotte Lattimore and by coming face to face with my own true nature.

"I'll never be happy calmly submitting to matrimony and allowing my body to become a baby factory to make up to Mama for the eight children she lost," I told Meg.

"What's wrong with marrying some handsome young man and having little ones around the house again?" said Meg.

"Nothing—for any girl but me."

"Why not you, honey?"

"Because . . . because I'm different. Must there be a reason? Can't a body not like a thing without there being a reason?"

"There's always a reason. Nothing happens but what there's a reason."

I didn't feel like arguing, but wanted to return to my day-dreams. A big grin of contentment reasserted itself on my face as I thought of what I had to look forward to tomorrow evening. Only twenty-four hours to go!

"Go away, Meg. I want to dream," I told her.

Meg stood in the doorway frowning. When she was worried, the scar on her forehead turned red. "Don't you want to be happy?" she finally said.

"Maybe I'm not the kind of person who gets to have a long and happy life," I told her earnestly. "Maybe mine will be brief and tragic."

"Oh, don't say that, sweetheart! Think of them that loves you."

"I can't, Meg. I've already given them too much of my time already."

The following evening I had Rallings take me in the gig to Broadway and thence to the Strand, the financial district. Miss Lattimore was to be released from her duties at six P.M. and had agreed to have supper with me at a nearby ladies residential hotel. After delivering us to the hotel, I planned to send Rallings on his way so there would be no spies for Mama lurking about.

I almost didn't recognize Charlotte in her dark and serious office garb among the wave of young working women who poured into the winter street, lit only by the yellow glow of gas streetlights and headlamps of automobiles. The soft brown hair was molded to her head and anchored with a small dark felt hat, the white expressive hands were hidden in crocheted gloves. But the light gray eyes opened wider when she caught sight of me waiting across the street, and she maneuvered through the traffic to reach us. "Miss Lattimore!" I cried.

"Oh, Miss Coolidge, this is such a treat! Usually I've nothing to look forward to but a dreary ride home and a quiet supper in my room."

I felt like exulting, never again, darling! I've come to rescue you from dreariness!

Our rig jostled for space in the crowded street with other horse-drawn conveyances and the ever-growing number of automobiles as the office buildings on the Strand emptied for the evening. After my initial burst of enthusiasm, I found myself tongue-tied with delight. I watched Charlotte's face as the gig carried us in and out of shadows, comparing it to the thousand stored images I had concocted in my mind's eye since that enchanted meeting three nights earlier, which seemed now to belong as clearly to another era as events before the Storm were separated from those that came after.

I saw where romantic imagination had erred. I had made of her a mysterious and tragic creature, when the truth was far different. Away from the crowd of women I now realized had intimidated her, Charlotte was animated and approachable. I almost wished instead she were pale and trembling with dark circles beneath her eyes so that she might find me necessary somehow to her life.

According to plan, I bade Rallings leave us at Mrs. Simpson's Residential Hotel for Ladies on Broadway. Being under instructions from a higher order to wait for me wherever I might go or however long I might be, Rallings forced me to lie. I said that another friend would be joining us soon whose father would pick us up in his car and deliver us home.

"Oh, good! I was hoping to meet some nice young women, the better class, you know, in the Poetry Society," said Charlotte, giving me my first clue as to how I might be helpful to her.

"Indeed? I suppose a newcomer to our city might find it difficult to learn her way around," I said. "I would be glad to introduce you to some people." Personally, I could think of nothing worse than spoiling our friendship with crowds of people, but if it made her happy.

"Oh, how kind you are! You've no idea how I've despaired of improving my social life. Clerks and shopgirls are all right, but they have very little interest in topics of cultural interest. But you're an artist, I recall! Do you do landscapes—or rather, I suppose, since your mother's house is near the water, sea-scapes?" That meant that she had bothered to find out something about me since last we met.

"I'm more of a portraitist. You have lovely eyes. I think they would be very hard to paint, to capture the roundness of the orb, the almost glassy quality of their shine."

Charlotte laughed and placed a little gloved hand over her eyes to hide them momentarily and peeked out between her fingers. "I'm not used to the soul-deep scrutiny of a painter."

"I'm sorry. I do stare."

"You mentioned your need of a model—do you work in a studio?"

"Alas, my mother thinks art frivolous. I'm not allowed the luxury and privacy of a real studio. I work in my front bedroom window where the light is good."

"Your mother is that terribly daunting female, Mrs. Herrick Coolidge, whom they say secretly runs this town. I saw her in the lobby of our building once. Do you have any ambition to follow in her footsteps?"

"None whatever. Nothing could be more boring than the movement of cotton around the world."

"On my level, yes, business is very boring, but on her level. I mean, honestly! Every decision she makes involves big money, people's lives. I've heard she can size up a man in a single glance and either break him or make him her ally."

"I'm rather removed from the world of commerce," I said faintly.

"Oh, but, of course! What am I thinking of! You lost all your brothers and sisters. I suppose it's your job to take their place, to entertain, to bring together the right sort of people in your mother's drawing room."

"How accurately you describe what my mama would have me be and do!"

46

"But your art . . . ?" she offered helpfully.

"I want to paint you, Charlotte Lattimore. Will you allow it?"

"With all my heart!" she said gaily.

~~~~~

FAITH KOHL COOLIDGE

November 3, 1908

It does not escape my notice that in spite of Miss Winter's efforts, Edith continues to wallow in her woozy and self-indulgent fantasy that she is the possessor of some mysterious and luminescent thing called "art." I've looked at her pictures and find them merely sentimental. Wish she'd get over it. Perhaps the best way to deal with this would be to accede to her absurd wish and let her see how far her efforts will carry her, but the young don't realize how little time they have for the essentials. Such a course could easily eat up her twenties when a woman's job is to do her biologic work. If I were an ignorant and indulgent woman I might allow Edith to fritter away her youth and a good deal of my money pursuing this elusive phantom in her head, this God of Art. But then where would she be? Too old to secure a husband and a family. It took me twenty-three years to accumulate what seemed at the time a sufficient bulwark against the vagaries of fortune, but you see it wasn't enough. If Edith postpones motherhood until she's in her thirties, she may not have time. It's a risk I'm unwilling to take. There are not enough of us in this family to take a selfish and narrow view of life. She must do this for me, for her poor dead papa, for Ned and Fern and all the others who didn't get the chance.

Edith, do you hear me? You *will* do your duty by them.

47

Chapter Three

CHARLES OREN PICKERING

I had come to the conclusion that it was time to look about me for a wife before Mrs. Coolidge paid me the extreme compliment and honor of thinking I might be good enough for her daughter. What had started me thinking along those lines was a correspondence into which I had blundered. A lad in the accounts department, Billy Lamme, had gone off to Boston the summer before and met a young lady, a Miss Hazel Brookside, and wanted to court her by mail. Though he had a good hand for figures, his script was near illegible, so he pressed me into service copying out his love letters to this girl in a fair hand.

Like old Cyrano, I began to see ways to improve not only poor Billy's handwriting, but his sentiments as well, because it was clear to me that no young lady as pretty and accomplished as Miss Brookside would swoon with joy over his wooden phrasing. And thus I undertook to sweeten up Billy's letters and that got me thinking about my own bachelorhood and how it might be a good time to end it. I was thirty-one years old, had some money saved up, and had never been with a woman. Some of the young fellers I knew visited the ladies on Postoffice Street, but I'd been brought up to abhor evil in all its guises, and besides, I didn't think Mrs. Coolidge would think much of such behavior if she was to get wind of it.

However, after finishing up one of Billy's love letters, I'd be so agitated, I'd have to get out and go for a walk. Yes, sir, it was time to think about wooing me a lass of my own. I often worked late—it was more or less required of me to keep the same hours as Mrs. Coolidge, who drove herself harder than she drove any of her employees, although some of them might've thought otherwise—so it wasn't unusual to find myself still at the office at ten or eleven o'clock at night. That night, I recall we were working on the Articles of Incorporation for a new company Mrs. Coolidge was setting up, for by then she was branching into other fields. This one was to be an investment house.

Mrs. Coolidge could stand long hours and missed meals better'n anybody I ever knew. She didn't even seem to visit the ladies' cloakroom all that often. Me, at the end of a twelve or fourteen-hour day, I'd be dying to work the kinks out of my legs and get something to eat, look at something besides numbers for awhile. But Mrs. Coolidge seemed to hate to have to give up for the night and go home. I didn't have anybody waiting for me at home, but she had a little girl—a big girl by then—and though I'd never say it to her face, it seemed somewhat unnatural to me that Mrs. Coolidge didn't want to go home and be with Edith.

After we'd closed up our files and made the big oak conference table tidy, she commenced to waxing philosophical, telling me about her plans for the business, things I was to help her watch out for, remember. We ran over our schedule for in the morning, plotted our tactics for the meeting we had with some German bankers. I figured maybe she didn't have anybody to go home to after all. Like as not Edith was already in bed by that hour or else out having a good time with her friends. Maybe Mrs. Coolidge was as solitary as I.

I didn't dare take out my pocket watch and look at it, but I figured it was nigh on to eleven o'clock, dead of winter, the cold creeping up from the warehouse below. I was tired and hungry, wanted to get home to the hot meal Mrs. Beale always laid aside for me, and hit the hay. Or maybe I'd work on a paragraph I'd been cogitating for one of Billy's letters. We had talked over all the things we needed to talk over, Mrs. Coolidge and me, and were the last souls in the office, but I always let her indicate when it was time to leave. That evening she seemed altogether disinclined to go home.

I was so tired my hand was jerking and I put it in my lap and held it down with my other hand. How could she keep on like that? She was glancing over her list one last time to make sure we hadn't missed anything. She was a list-keeper, Mrs. Coolidge. Out in public she liked to impress people by never being seen with a piece of paper in her hand, but always having the facts to ready in her head. It was my job to carry the valise stuffed with paper, to supply her with a number or a name on an instant's notice. I knew why she didn't want a woman secretary to do that for her. She liked to have me there as a living example of a grown man, twice her size, meekly taking orders from her—bound to have a calming effect on other men; whereas if a pair of ladies showed up, some men might think they could take advantage of her.

"Mr. Pickering, I pride myself in knowing what's going on around me," she said, making the hair prickle on my neck with how close she had come to the thoughts in my head that very minute. "Have I missed something in your personal life, overlooked an occasion to offer my congratulations?"

"Ma'am?" I said stupidly.

"Do I understand that you've become engaged?"

"Oh, no, ma'am. Maybe you're referring to a bit of subterfuge on Billy Lamme's part. I've been copying out in a fair hand his letters to a young lady in Boston. In my spare time."

"I see. Not your own love affair at all."

"No, ma'am."

It was never surprising to me what information came her way, so I didn't comment on the matter.

"But you yourself, do you have no interest in matrimony, Mr. Pickering?"

"There hasn't been much time . . ."

"Mr. Pickering are you giving me to understand that you don't have a romantic interest because I don't allow you enough time to pursue one?"

I certainly didn't want her to think that! Even if it was true. I searched my mind to find the words to let her know how much

I valued my association with her and how reluctant I'd be to change it by one jot or tittle.

"Ma'am," I said, "you've given me something to live for. I wouldn't change nothing about my life."

"Thank you for your loyalty, Mr. Pickering. It was a happy day when you answered my advertisement. You're my rock, Mr. Pickering. I depend on you."

"And I hope to never let you down, ma'am."

"There is something you might be able to help me with, Mr. Pickering, something quite outside your usual duties. However, I hesitate to ask because you're too valuable to me to risk your esteem—"

"Mrs. Coolidge," I said forcefully, "I'd do anything for you. You've only to ask."

"Very well. I'm concerned about the passage of time, Mr. Pickering. It's something I've no control over, and requires, let us say, *strategies* to get around its limitations."

I hadn't a clue where she was leading, but I nodded and sat forward in my chair, eagerly, to let her know I was willing to take on any assignment she saw fit to give me. She paid me well, but it wasn't primarily the money that made me willing to sacrifice my bodily comfort to her service. Mine was the devotion, say, of a fine bird dog towards its master, mine the light you see shining in its eyes as it silently pleads for an opportunity to demonstrate that devotion.

"Anything I can do, Mrs. Coolidge, you've only to ask," I said again.

"You're not averse to the state of matrimony, are you? Nothing in your character that would prevent intimate association with a woman?"

"No, indeed! As a matter of fact, my thoughts lately had turned to that very subject, perhaps because of helping old Billy write his letters."

"I see. Then perhaps my query is timely. I must admit I've tried talking myself out of this, but the more I've thought on it, the better the choice becomes. You have all the qualities I'm looking for, seriousness of purpose, high moral character, stamina and physical strength, no bad habits. In short, I have only one reservation, Mr. Pickering. How do you feel about convert-

51

ing to our faith? It's imperative that the children be brought up in the Church."

"The children?"

"Oh, Mr. Pickering, there *must* be children, and plenty of them."

"Why, I've no objection at all to converting, Mrs. Coolidge. I'd welcome any spiritual challenge you were to set me as a way of demonstrating my worthiness, though I know I never can be worthy, ma'am."

"Nonsense. You'll do."

I felt an incredulous smile hovering at the edges of my mouth. "Then . . . am I to understand that you'd welcome a proposal of matrimony?"

"I suppose you're concerned about the age difference. You're—what?—thirteen years older than Edith?"

"Edith?"

"My daughter, sir. I'm suggesting that you court my daughter."

~~~~~

EDITH COOLIDGE PICKERING

In January I reciprocated some of the hospitality that had been extended me during my debutante season by giving a small dinner party. The real purpose was to introduce Charlotte to my friends, though I found it a cruel and vexing fate to be the instrument of Charlotte's diluting herself among my acquaintances. But since it was important to her to be recognized by the better families, to rise above the social station assigned to poor working girls, and since I didn't value my own social connections to any large degree, I was happy to use them in Charlotte's behalf to secure for her a place in society. I would've been glad to turn over any resource I had, but not only was that difficult to do, I was ironically conscious that the more I did for Charlotte, the more avenues I gave her to escape me.

An ancillary benefit to my party was the pleasure Mama took in my willingness, finally, to make an effort, a pleasure I didn't want to spoil by giving away that Charlotte was the only reason I was extending myself. In fact, in general, I instinctively downplayed Charlotte's importance to me, avoiding her name when I could, even to Meg. If Charlotte and I had an engagement, I pretended that others were invited too. If I talked to Charlotte on the telephone for an hour, I would hang up and remark that Jane So-and-So was such an enthusiastic conversationalist it was impossible to get off the line. In retrospect, I was right to fear Mama's reaction and should've made an even greater effort to hide my love.

However, a heart in love is full of charity and boundless optimism and I argued to myself that Mama and Meg, if they could but see beyond the barriers of their own narrow outlook, would probably be glad for me, might even come to accept the oddness of my choice one day and rejoice in my happiness. I could not afford to put that theory to the test, however, before I found out how Charlotte herself would receive such a revelation. On that score I turned out to be hopelessly naive.

Having been brought up in a Catholic girls' school, I knew that passionate friendships existed between girls, that such friendships were discouraged by the nuns, but that no one considered them really invidious. These friendships, rather, were taken to be a stage that adolescent girls passed through on their way to becoming women and to choosing a male companion with whom to spend their lives. Indeed, I myself had observed the waxing and waning of these associations. Girls would go about arm in arm with a new friend, isolate themselves to sit and whisper during lunch, write poetry and love letters vowing eternal fealty, then break apart for real or perceived injury, often propelling the injured party into the arms of a former enemy. I had played the game myself, but deep down, I knew there was a difference: for me it was no game.

In the weeks that followed that soul-shattering meeting in Mrs. Kempner's drawing room, Charlotte had become my best friend. We dined together several evenings a week, went to shows at the Grand Opera House, took long walks on the wind-scoured beach. Her unusual situation, that of having the grace, the comportment, the mien of a society girl, yet having to earn her bread and live in rented quarters, came about in this way:

Charlotte had been brought up in a well-to-do home, educated privately, prepared for a life in society, when suddenly her father was wiped out by a business miscalculation of such magnitude that he took down a number of friends with him. The shame was so great that he put a pistol to his temple and took his own life. Everything was sold to satisfy the creditors, and Charlotte and her mother were turned out in the streets. Charlotte's mother could not accept this terrible reversal of fortunes and became somewhat simple or "confused," and had she not been taken in by poor relatives somewhere out in the bayous, might have wound up in some dismal institution for psychotics. Charlotte had little choice but seek her fortune, and decided that too many people in New Orleans knew her father's sad story to remain there. She chose to move to Galveston because it was a place with which she had pleasant associations from a childhood vacation.

"Just think!" I exclaimed. "We might have met as children! But I would have remembered anyone like you."

"You're too kind. All the while I was taking my secretarial training and learning to operate a typewriter, I longed for a friend from my own social class to talk to. I've been so good, released all my pride to do this thing, but despite my most earnest intentions, I've never quite reconciled myself to a life of poverty. Perhaps with your patronage I shall meet a man who will lift me up again."

"It's not just men who have such power," I replied. "My mother is one of the wealthiest women on the island."

"But I know! I admire her enormously. I can't imagine what it must be like to be her daughter. Don't you expect that after awhile you'll put aside your art and join her in business, mother and daughter, shoulder to shoulder? I confess the thought gives me goosebumps."

"I don't even know what my mother does all day. What's more, she doesn't care for me to know. She likes it that I'm growing up a perfectly useless creature. She only wishes I'd do it more. She can hardly contain herself now that I'm old enough to get married and begin having babies."

"You sound as if you don't like babies," said Charlotte with a laugh.

"Well, I don't. They're brats. I can't stand the idea of one growing inside my body. It's monstrous!"

Charlotte's laughter grew merrier still. "You artists are so temperamental! You intrigue me."

"And I am intrigued by you. You're the first girl who's let me into her inner thoughts so that I might begin to understand the feminine mind."

"But you're a girl!"

"Yes. Physically. Mentally too, I suppose. In fact, in many ways I'm more feminine than most girls I know, but with this difference: I don't long to have a man make love to me. Do you?"

Charlotte rolled her enchanting glassy eyes and thought about it, smiling. "I won't give myself cheaply," she said after awhile. "I would have to fetch a high price for my virtue— marriage, a position in society, perhaps an income of my own. I really *ought* to try to get Mother out of the swamp."

"But what if you had all that already? Would you *crave* a man to complete you as a woman?"

"I hadn't thought about it. I confess—and only because you are my most intimate and beloved friend—" she said, laughing and throwing her arms around me with an affectionate kiss, "—that I never think of men but what I first think of their pocketbook!"

Her answer satisfied me. I knew plenty of girls who were completely man-crazy and would've gone off with any sod that would have them. If Miss Lattimore could think about romance in such cold-blooded and calculating terms, then she might give herself to a bidder who did not wear trousers.

That conversation took place on the beach, but later, in my room—in the new house, a large airy apartment overlooking Avenue P—we started work as artist and model. I no longer worried about being caught with a friend in dishabille in my room as I was too old to be treated like a child. I took my place behind my easel and Charlotte took hers on a straight- backed chair in the window, the pale winter sun feebly illuminating her, a bit of sheeting for modesty's sake, but mostly the draping was allowed to drift where it would because Charlotte had grown used to my seemingly disinterested scrutiny.

I was working on a series of charcoal drawings to determine how I would paint Charlotte. I couldn't decide between a pastoral setting, Charlotte got up as a shepherdess, thin tissue of fabric blown back by the wind to reveal the tender outline of her frail feminine frame. Or, a lady Romantic poet in yards of pale taffeta cut so deeply into the bodice that the pink aureoles of her nipples peeped out over the top of their confinement.

"I used to draw my friend Amy this way. Hundreds of sketches of her hands, her eyes, the back of her neck where it joins the shoulder, and just beyond, the curve of her jaw," I remarked.

"Did she like it?"

"I believe she was flattered."

"I am. I've never had the trained eye of an artist fastened on me before. It feels as though you see through to my bones."

"Oh, but I do. And then I imagine the bones with muscles attached and layers of epidermis on that."

"Ugh! I hate to think of my body as it will look in the grave. To feel my own eye socket and to know that someday it will be empty."

"I'm sorry, darling. Think instead of life. You've cast a pall over my drawing."

"The day is too gray," she said, stretching her limbs from their confining pose. "I'm cold now."

"I'll call down and get Meg to fix us cups of chocolate."

"When do you start the actual work? I'm eager to see what you make of all these studies." Charlotte came over to look at the work on my easel. "You're so good! I wish I really thought I looked like that."

"You can't step outside your own body to see yourself; I can. You are beautiful. You have the bones—sorry!—that artists like to draw." I kissed her lightly on the mouth and she laughed and twirled away to the pile of clothes on the bed to get dressed, oblivious to my admiring gaze, or perhaps, completely aware of it and playing up to it.

I put off working with color for several reasons. First, I intentionally tarried to prolong the hours we were shut up alone together in my room, much of it filled with giggling conversation and girlish exchange. Secondly, I hesitated to get started because I was having such a hard time maintaining a professional distance from my subject while bending a critical eye on her delicious naked person. My heart palpitated, my mouth dried out, my hands quivered for yearning of her.

But an even more serious rumination delayed my hand, a sudden overwhelming volley of doubt that began to assail me when I picked up my work again after an interlude of more than a year—the year I had wasted following Miss Winters' benighted formula for social success, which included a calculated lack of seriousness, for it was believed that young men valued those women most who were purely ornamental. But no matter how slowly I carried forward the project, I couldn't seem to evoke on my pad the images I saw in my head. The delayed frustration I used to feel upon later study of my pictures of Amy was now operating simultaneously with my hand, so that even as I lay down a line, I jeered at myself for not getting it right.

I blamed Mama for this and couldn't bear to think that she had gotten what she wanted, that by forcing me to lose a year in pointless social interaction she had made me not only *not progress* but actually *decline* in ability. What bitter irony that Mama would hire someone to teach me the proper colors and styles to wear, how to comport myself at a dinner dance, how to interview a ladies maid, but not hire me an instructor to show me how to improve my one God-given talent! I could hardly endure the knowledge that I fell into that most ignominious of categories—among artists as well as entrepreneurs—of having an ambition that exceeded my grasp. No amount of desire, I was certain, could make up for a deficiency of talent. Was that me? It was during the charcoals of Charlotte that I first began to suspect this was so.

Such a revelation would have been completely shattering had it not come to me during a period of optimism engendered by my growing intimacy with Charlotte, who seemed to hold nothing back from me, but to meet every overture with enthusiastic affection. I could bear the failure of my hopes and dreams as an artist as long as my hope of becoming Charlotte's lover prospered. There seemed even to be some cosmic significance in our meeting when we did. Perhaps God had sent her to me at that very moment to compensate for becoming conscious of my lack of talent.

And yet, it was necessary to produce actual work to justify keeping Charlotte with me, and so I dazzled her untrained eye with cheap tricks I had learnt from Mr. Chalmers—*pretty* drawings.

"Oh, darling! You're so good!"

"Oh, it's nothing. Just a few ideas as they occur to me. I still can't decide between the shepherdess and the poet."

"I can hardly wait till you get started!"

In spite of the pleasure it gave me to have Charlotte's heavenly form prettily disposed in front of me, draped in one of Mama's linen sheets, I knew that I had dawdled about as long as I could and that she would begin to wonder if I did not soon stretch canvas and begin to work in color. The dinner party gave me an excuse to put away my artist's tools for awhile and offer up distraction to Charlotte, who was giddily feminine about clothes and hair-dos.

I had offered my absurd collection of gowns that Miss Winters had outfitted me with for Charlotte to choose from, as the right clothes for the occasion could easily have set her back a month's salary. Since she couldn't decide between the peach and the white, I had them both altered to show off her narrow ribcage and ivory shoulders.

The party was to be on a Saturday, but there was much to do to get ready for it, so Charlotte left her job early that Friday, telling her employer that she had a slight sore throat. I sent Rallings for her and she arrived at our house just after dark with a good deal more luggage than was strictly required for a weekend visit. I happily installed her in the bedroom next to mine, although if my plans worked out, she wouldn't even rumple the sheets. I knew that Mama would work late, for she was on the board of a maritime insurance company that met one evening a month, happily *that* evening. I had gotten rid of Meg too by convincing her to take her friend Viola, nursemaid of the children next door, to see the new talking picture at The Rialto.

Charlotte and I ate bowls of Meg's savory lamb stew on the enamel table in the kitchen, happily chattering about our seat-ing arrangement for the following night. I had cut out a rectangle of pasteboard to represent our dining room table and small colored circles for the guests, pink for the ladies, blue for the gentlemen.

"I'm so cross with Mama for insisting I invite Mr. Pickering," I said. "He's old as the hills and the most sober-sided gentleman on the island!"

Charlotte reached out and maneuvered two colored circles to new locations. "What about putting Josephine Lark next to him?"

"As hostess, I really ought to keep him close to me. He won't know a soul—this being a young people's party."

"How old is he?"

"Thirty at least—the same age my brother Ned would be if he had lived. But I suppose Mr. Pickering seems older because of his beige personality."

Charlotte eyed the pieces dubiously and moved them back to their original places. "What a shame," she said. "If it weren't for the beige Mr. Pickering, we could've had one more single young man with expectations of inheriting his father's substantial fortune."

"Mr. Pickering may be penniless today, but he has expectations. Mama quite dotes on him. In fact—you'll laugh at this—I used to think Mama might marry him."

"Indeed?!"

"Then I went through a period of thinking how absurd and childish was my notion, because she's old enough to be his mother. But guess what? I'm back to thinking he would be perfect for her! A woman who's worth as much as Mama can afford to be eccentric. However, except for plunging into commerce, Mama continues to adhere rigidly to the code of behavior she's tried so hard to instill in me. It would scandalize her, I'm sure, to consider marrying a penniless young man who works for her."

"If you don't subscribe to her code, Edith, then whose code do you live by? You do go to church don't you?"

"Have to—it's a requirement of all who dwell in this house. But I don't go to confession any more."

"Why not?" Charlotte's glassy eyes opened wider, reflecting

more light. "Have you been naughty and done something you can't tell the priest?"

I smiled mysteriously. "No, but thoughts are sins too, you know." We both laughed. "When I was young, I thought that artists were the most devout of the religious, but that was because I saw nothing but Church art, heard nothing but Church music, read nothing but sermons and other devotional literature. Now I know that artists are the very *worst* nonconformists."

"You mean, that they don't believe?"

"I mean that they claim for themselves the right to live a bohemian life style."

Charlotte, herself a lapsed Episcopalian, had told me that after what happened to her family, she couldn't bear to piously bend a knee and thank God for her blessings.

"What does that mean, a 'bohemian life style'?"

"It means that artists cannot be expected to live within the ordinary moral framework. I myself, for example, have no wish to have a husband dictating my every move. In fact, there's a movement among artist colonies in New York and London and Paris called 'free love.'"

Charlotte laughed and reached out to slap me gently on the back of the hand. "You're *terrible!*"

I enjoyed the fleeting sensation of corrupter, although I was surely one of the most innocent girls in the world, seeing as how I had avoided going out with men, falling in love with them, sparking in parked cars on the beach as my contemporaries did.

"The women take lovers, discard them, choose another," I said, with an airy wave of my hand. "It's all very free and easy. They even, some of them, take women lovers."

If I had shocked Charlotte, she gave no sign. Her brow furrowed and she sighed loudly. "Once again, it comes down to money. If I behaved that way, people would call me a common slut."

I seized her slender almost boneless hand, lying near mine on the white enamel table. "I earnestly desire that I might free you of penury, that you would never have to go to your office again and type."

"You're so sweet to me! You do so much for me! I'll be eter-

60

nally grateful to you for all that you do!" She smiled and caught her breath, glanced down at the facsimile of our dining room table. "And if all goes well, my future husband will be one of these little blue circles! Oh, I hope he has tons of money!"

I despaired of making Charlotte understand my meaning. In truth, I wasn't sure how her objections *could* be got around, for there was no doubt that such objections were valid. No one was more sensible than I of being dependent on another's generosity. For although I had never in my life had to worry about where my next meal would come from, every penny that came my way was doled out by Mama and had to be accounted for.

We had been raised (me and my departed sisters and brothers) with a proper respect for money, the connection constantly reminded us of Mama's (and before her, Papa's) labor and the good life that we enjoyed. We did not waste our money or take it for granted. We thanked God for it. Although I had a closetful of beautiful dresses—because it was proper and expected of me—Mama spent very little on herself, being content to aim for quality and durability rather than fashion. Profits were to be plowed back into the business to make more business. Charity was given those that could not help themselves, though grudgingly, for Mama was of the opinion that if a person didn't have enough to eat it was because they weren't trying hard enough. There was opportunity enough for all, and she didn't see why she should be asked to subsidize the shiftless.

I was naive about money matters. While in theory my family was as wealthy as any of those Charlotte was angling to join, I could not envision Mama ever allowing me to independently control my own "expectations," which I vaguely understood to include money left me by my father's will, though of course Mama had it all invested for me. It would never be required that I understand or handle money. One day she would turn over my fortune to a husband who had given her reason to believe she could trust his perspicacity. I could be ignorant and blame it on my artistic mind if I liked for not being a proper vessel for thoughts of enterprise, but it wasn't even necessary that I excuse myself. Mama had never required me to be clever. It wasn't my mind she valued, it was my womb. It had never occurred to me until talking over Charlotte's finances with her that my salvation might lie in an area I had never bothered to explore. I resolved to ask Mama particulars about my money in the very near future.

Not wishing to be up when Mama came in, I suggested to Charlotte that we retire to my room and wash our hair and do it up in papers. I ran a hot bath for Charlotte and bade her let me help her wash her hair. Our sessions at the easel had made her proudly unselfconscious of her body. She sauntered past me nude and gracefully folded herself into the tub. I sat beside her on the floor and sponged hot water over her white slippery back. The water reddened the skin below the waterline and each vertebra stood out in isolation along her spine. She slipped down against the slope of the tub and regarded me dreamily.

"This puts me in mind of an oriental pasha being ministered to by concubines," she said.

"I'm your slave," I whispered, sluicing water between her breasts.

"Then I command you to think of me always as your truest friend."

"Always," I said.

"We'll live in houses side by side. Our little children will be best friends."

"I told you—I shan't have children."

"Oh, but you must! How can you bear to miss having children? And besides, darling, you're an only child. What would your mama do with all her money if she didn't leave it to you and you to your children?"

I shuddered. "I don't know! I hate having someone expect something from me. I just want to be who I am."

Charlotte reached out and stroked my cheek with her wet hand. "No one can stop you being that. You just have to compromise a little. Be who you like on the inside. On the outside, you can seem to conform to whatever they want you to be. Don't you see? The key to getting along is to be like water—appear to take the shape of the container you're in. When you are defeated, be absolutely gracious in defeat, otherwise you merely create more resistance. I tell you truly, darling, these are lessons I've learned most painfully during these past three years. A clever woman can have anything in the world she wishes."

Afterwards, in chaste white flannel, we lay cheek to cheek,

our legs braided, our arms laced about each other to warm up the cold bed.

"Oh, Charlotte," I breathed, "I love you so!"

"And I you, darling Edith! I swear we shall be eternal friends!"

~~~~~

Saturday mornings, Mama made it a practice to eat breakfast with me and give me my weekly infusion of maternal attention. I did not in the least look forward to sitting down to breakfast after my delicious night in Charlotte's arms. I knew that my coloring must be unnaturally heightened, my eyes bright, my manner brittle and nervous. I couldn't do as Charlotte suggested and dissemble with grace. Not towards a mama with such penetrating eyes. Mama had discouraged me in my youth thinking I could ever put anything over on her by catching me out in every fib. But Charlotte gave me the benefit of her radiant example, appearing positively to beam at the prospect of having breakfast with my parent.

"Good morning, Edith, Charlotte. Did you sleep well?"

I let Charlotte answer that. "Oh, very well, indeed. My, how late you must have been at your meeting, Mrs. Coolidge! I don't wonder that you're not exhausted working so hard."

"Fiddle-dee-dee," murmured Mama, turning her attention to my silence.

"Good morning, Missus," said Meg, bringing a china pot into the breakfast room and pouring out coffee for Mama without being asked. "Good morning, young ladies. Today's the big day! You were too excited about your fancy doings to sleep, weren't you? I heard noises like little mice rustling all night."

I felt the color in my cheeks deepen and reached for a piece of toast and began buttering it.

"Yes, it's terribly exciting," said Charlotte. She looked at my mother. "Thank you, Mrs. Coolidge, for having me as a guest in your home and allowing us to throw this splendid party."

"What charming manners," said my mother approvingly. "Edith, where are your manners?"

"Oh, sorry. Toast, Mama?"

63

"Thank you." She buttered her toast and took a bite before speaking again. "I understand from my daughter that you're in insurance, Miss Lattimore."

Charlotte glanced at me and giggled. "To be truthful, ma'am, I'm in 'typing.'"

"We can't get by without good typists."

"I work at it very hard, but I'm afraid my fingers are not at all nimble."

"Pity." Mama's fine gray eyes swung round to me. "Mr. Pickering tells me he is looking forward to this evening. Thank you for obliging me by inviting him. Mr. Pickering is all alone in the world, you know. I'm afraid a bachelor gentleman living alone gives too little attention to his own comfort and recreation."

"I'm afraid he's fated to be horribly bored at our party. There'll be no one his age—" Charlotte's foot bumped mine under the table and I amended my reply. "But we'll do our very best to see that he has a good time."

"Mrs. Coolidge, I've been dying to tell you how much I admire you," said Charlotte, so prettily that I longed to reach for her hand under the table. "You're an inspiration to the young women of my generation. The gentlemen in my office speak of you with awe in their voices. It quite makes me proud of my sex."

"You flatter me, Miss Lattimore. I was blessed with a head for business, though as you may know, I would never have exercised it if my dear husband had not passed on."

"So I understand from your admiring daughter."

Mama looked at me somewhat more kindly and I realized that Charlotte had just given me a graphic demonstration of how water bends to the pleasure of its container.

~~~~~

The three of us, Meg, Charlotte and I, put in a very hard day getting ready for the party. Meg had gotten in a caterer for the evening and supervised a staff of three in the kitchen. I did the flowers, and Charlotte set the table, using Mama's best dishes and crystal. At six o'clock we rushed upstairs to get ready. Charlotte wore the peach, at the last moment deciding that white should be reserved for brides. I had been waiting for the moment she got into her gown before giving her a silver bracelet that had belonged to my sister Fern and miraculously escaped the Storm by being in the vault of a jeweler having its clasp repaired.

"Oh, it's beautiful! I'll treasure it always," said Charlotte, sudden tears springing to her eyes. "You're such a darling, you know. I really love you." We hugged each other, mindful of hairdos and rouged lips. "Wish me luck," she whispered. And for a single moment I managed to be unselfish and wish for her the outcome she most wanted, contacts that would lead to a husband to rescue her from poverty.

I went down the stairs first, as we had arranged, so that Charlotte might make a better entrance after a few people had arrived. I found Meg giving the table a last-minute inspection.

"She sets a lovely table. Not a thing out of place," Meg said approvingly.

"Is anybody here yet?"

"Only Mr. Pickering, Miss. I put him in the drawing room and gave him a glass of sherry."

Why couldn't he have the decency to arrive late!? "I can't imagine why Mama insisted I invite him. He's too old for these people," I said peevishly.

"I reckon it was because he were such good friends with your brother Ned's," said Meg mildly.

"I suppose I'd better go in and say hello. Goodness! What shall we talk about? I know nothing whatever about accounts."

I fixed a smile on my face and unhurriedly approached the drawing room. Mr. Pickering was standing at the fireplace with his arms behind him, gaunt, silent, with no social graces that I could discern. He reminded me of an earlier, beardless Abe Lincoln. Or perhaps a mortician. I sighed. He was not likely to contribute to the animation of dinner conversation. But then, I didn't expect to be charmed by anyone I had invited to my dinner party, since the only person I truly wanted to be with was my house guest.

~~~~~

65

CHARLES OREN PICKERING

I would never have had the impertinence to look upon one as dainty and high-born as Miss Coolidge without her mother giving me explicit encouragement. I arrived punctually and waited nervously in the drawing room, realizing that I had made a social gaffe being on time. I had accepted a little glass of foul-tasting spirits, but only because I lacked the presence of mind to turn it down. I secretly deposited it among some other glassware on the mantel and hoped it would be collected later and not remarked on.

After awhile I heard the patter of lady's heels on the hard-wood floor and Miss Coolidge swept into the drawing room and placed a moist little hand in mine and smiled up at me. I saw right away that my years in the counting house would stand me in poor stead in this new endeavor. It was one thing to sit back two thousand miles away and polish up a compliment to a lady, making as many drafts as called for, but quite another to get off a compliment while that sparkling personage stared right into your face.

"Thank you so much for obliging me by coming to my little dinner party," she said. "Miss Lattimore hasn't come down yet. Have you met my house guest, Mr. Pickering?"

"No, ma'am, don't believe I've had the pleasure."

"I'll be sure to introduce you. Oh, good, there's someone at the door! One worries, you know, at the last minute that no one will show up."

"I can't imagine anybody with such poor manners," I said.

"I'll just be a moment. Excuse me."

I realized as she pulled her little white hand out of mine that I had failed to let go of it. I kicked myself for not somehow managing to practice a bit more making light conversation, maybe with some of the girls at the office. I would have to take steps immediately to remedy that deficiency. It made me sweat through my evening jacket to think of having to get through a whole evening of light social chitchat.

~~~~~

I got through the evening tolerably well, despite having Miss Coolidge right at my elbow during dinner. I felt a hundred years old among that glittering company and wondered if Mrs. Coolidge's wisdom in these matters could be relied upon. It seemed to me that Miss Edith could pick and choose among the young men there, that there was no earthly reason why she might want me. I knew most of those boys' fathers and could calculate to the nearest million the net worth represented at that table. Except for a little money laid by, what did I have to offer?

The guest of honor was Miss Coolidge's closest friend, a lovely young lady named Miss Charlotte Lattimore, who surely had the nicest manners I ever saw. The men were tripping over themselves to fetch things for her. After dinner she sat down at the piano and played one tune after another, without once having to resort to the music.

As I fumbled one opportunity after another to make conversation with the young ladies who came over to try to draw me out as their mamas had no doubt taught them to do, I determined that I wouldn't try to seek another engagement with Miss Coolidge face to face, but write her a nice note on the morrow thanking her for including me and asking to see her again. I couldn't bear the thought of good manners forcing her to agree to something that her mama was making her do.

~~~~~

EDITH COOLIDGE PICKERING

For weeks after our dinner party, Charlotte was drunk with success. Three men had asked if they might call on her, and she had made dates with them all. Two were millionaire's sons, and the other had a grandfather who had been Governor of the State of Texas. I was torn between envy of the men for being able to openly ask for what they wanted and pride of my darling Charlotte, who easily had been the most beautiful and accomplished girl at the party. (Of course, that was almost guaranteed by our careful selection of girls.) Charlotte had seized the opportunity given her to demonstrate that she deserved to be restored to the lofty firmament from which she had fallen. Several of the girls there that night told me later how sad it was that a girl of Miss Lattimore's accomplishments had to pound away on a typewriter every day, but they admired her so much for doing so with such good heart and hoped, as they knew I must, that my friend would soon regain her rightful place in society.

Yes, I did wish it for her, for it was clear that I wouldn't be the one to save Charlotte. When finally I got up the nerve to ask Mama about Papa's provisions for me, I did so under the guise of concern for my welfare, not that I was inquiring into the possibility that I might one day be free of her control. She replied that Papa had provided for all his children, but had wisely left the administration of those affairs in her hands. When the time came, she would discuss my financial affairs with my husband, since I had never shown the slightest interest or aptitude in handling my own affairs.

I slunk off to my room in defeat and cried because I knew it was true. I had not the spunk to defy Mama to her face nor the cleverness and heart to dissemble. There was nothing I could do but reconcile myself to Charlotte making a brilliant marriage, and hoping that she intended to keep her word and remain close to me. If she did, our greater freedom lay in marriage, for it was clear that matrimony on her side would immediately free up five and a half days a week that were presently unavailable to me.

As time went on and Charlotte continued to be her affectionate self with me, I gradually came to realize that neither of us had the stomach for defying conventional morals. She, better than I, was making the best of circumstances, winning points all around for her grace. I should have learned by her example, for I only made things harder for myself by resisting Mama's dictum that I take my rightful place in society.

On Saturday mornings Mama now devoted an hour to going over my invitations and eyeing the social column for opportunities. A brief list of eligible young men willing to escort me emerged—none who were in love with me—and although I flitted from place to place in my elegant gowns, the only events that gave me unalloyed pleasure were the ones that included Charlotte.

Outwardly, Charlotte was as affectionate and warm with me as ever, returning my embraces, allowing me to kiss her on the lips when we were alone. But my daydream of claiming her ivory body remained frustrated. Somehow, without ever directly repulsing me, Charlotte deflected my timid advances. Even the proposed portrait was indefinitely postponed as Charlotte's time was absorbed by ever-increasing social demands.

As to offers that came *my* way after the dinner party, it was not surprising that since I had not put myself out to be charming, none of the men bothered with more than perfunctory notes thanking me for being a splendid hostess and introducing them to the scintillating Miss Lattimore. Only one of them asked to see me again, Mr. Pickering. I didn't bother to reply.

Chapter Four

CHARLES OREN PICKERING

My social life took flight in the weeks following Miss Coolidge's dinner party, that spring in the year ought-nine. I knew my success was very little due to my own efforts, but that Mrs. Coolidge was unobtrusively arranging for Galveston's young hostesses to suddenly crave my company in their drawing rooms. Edith was often at these same parties, but if Mrs. Coolidge hoped to engender affection by our mere proximity, I'm afraid she must have been sorely disappointed, for Edith, no matter how many times we encountered one another, barely acknowledged me. I didn't see her warm up to any of the young fellows either, and decided that she was a good deal shyer than I had given her credit from seeing her in her own home. I began to understand why Mrs. Coolidge was taking a personal hand in the management of her daughter's social life.

Mrs. Coolidge was the most discreet of managers, never asking me directly how I got on with her daughter, and I was too mortified at my lack of progress to tell her we didn't get on at all. I was stymied how to proceed further. Maybe a fellow who had spent a good deal more time with the ladies than I could figure out how to get past Miss Coolidge's reserve. As for me, I almost wished I'd been left to suffer in my obscurity. Other ladies seemed to take to me, more than one rescuing me from social ignominy by engaging me in conversation, or perhaps asking me to take her in to supper, or inviting me to join some little party she was putting together in the future. I might've enjoyed getting to know one or two of these young ladies, but I was conscious that I was only there through the good offices of Mrs. Coolidge and it weren't for the purpose of getting up a friendship with some other young lady. So I would check with Mrs. Coolidge first to see if she thought it likely that Edith would be attending that particular function, and if she seemed discouraging, I would decline with regret. I could tell that Mrs. Coolidge was gratified by the seriousness with which I undertook the assignment she had given me.

Then something quite unexpected interrupted my campaign to win Edith Coolidge's cool little hand.

To my very great surprise and undeniable disappointment, Billy Lamme fell head over heels in love with some local girl and asked me to write a letter terminating his/my long-distance relationship with Miss Hazel Brookside. I had been aware that Billy was growing less and less interested in the letters I wrote, often casually glancing over my efforts with nothing more than, "Yeah, that'll do," before stuffing them into an envelope. But it was a blow nonetheless when he made his request, one that brought me up short and caused me to realize that I had been expressing my own, not Billy's, sentiments in those letters.

And so, very much cast down, I sat down to write my last letter to Miss Brookside, whose picture I would miss there on my writing desk—kept there for inspiration, I had explained to Billy. I decided, there being nothing left to lose, that my last act would be to tell that remarkable Boston girl the truth.

"Dear Miss Brookside," I wrote. "I must confess my part in a deceitful charade that has been carried out at your dear expense. The writer of these missives is not who you have been led to believe. Long ago Billy Lamme turned over the job to me, Mr. Charles Pickering, who very much regrets the deception this entailed and begs your most humble pardon. I will miss your sweet missives, Miss Brookside, and hope that you are not too much cast down by the fact that Mr. Lamme wishes to end the correspondence. I will completely understand your indignant response to such an insult and can only beg your eventual forgiveness for my part in it. But the truth is that I'm a solitary

71

fellow and I've taken advantage of Mr. Lamme's entree with your charming self to fill my lonely hours composing what I hoped would be phrases to delight a lady's heart. I'm sure that you shall wish to have nothing more to do with me, my lady, but please write one last time if only to reproach me. Until then, I can only pray that you will find it in your heart to someday forgive an act that is, I'm sure, unforgivable. Sincerely and with great humbleness, Your Servant, Charles O. Pickering."

I expected in reply only hurt silence, but in due time I espied a familiar feminine hand among the meager sheaf of letters slipped under the door of my room from the morning post. With quickening heart, I hurried to my writing table to snatch up the letter-opener, feeling that I clutched my very future and fortune to my bosom. All those months I had been Billy Lamme's ghostwriter, I had acutely envied him. I knew that I should be much the poorer if Miss Brookside lambasted me for fooling her. With trembling hand, I opened her reply.

"Dear Mr. Pickering," it said. "Sir, I should take more joy from having turned the tables but for your evident pain. My friends and I have been having a little fun at your expense, I'm afraid. I immediately realized that the dull young man I met last summer was not in the least capable of composing the charming letters I've received these many months. I decided to play along with the prank, in fact, to share the joke with one or two of my girlfriends, who have helped me compose my responses. But I find that the joke is, after all, on me, for I confess to a burning curiosity to meet my correspondent, whom, I am glad to learn, is not a composite as 'Miss Brookside' is. Suppose we set aside artifice and deception, Mr. Pickering, and see what might come of honesty for a change? If you are willing, I am. I've always longed to visit your beautiful Gulf Coast city and this summer would suit my schedule admirably. In truth and honesty, Miss Hazel Lorene Brookside."

I stretched out on my narrow bachelor bed stunned with incredulous joy, a thousand thoughts bottlenecked in my brain trying to get my attention all at the same time. Would Miss Brookside like me once she met me in person? What did it mean when a young lady traveled all that way to see a man? Dear God, could it mean she loved me? Where would I put her up? How would I entertain her? What would Mrs. Coolidge say when I told her that I couldn't possibly go on hoping to get somewhere with Edith? I tell you, it was almost too much for this old bachelor's brain!

It took me two nights to compose a suitable response to Miss Brookside's letter. I told her that with all my heart I wanted nothing but honesty to flow betwixt us. I sent her a photograph of me so that she might be armed with the facts. I knew mine was not the countenance to bowl over a lady, but I hoped to counter Miss Brookside's probable repugnance with some indication of my prospects, so that she might know that I was at least better fixed than Billy Lamme. More than once I had wondered how a man of his station had the audacity to approach a young lady of Miss Brookside's breeding, but I reckoned it was because he had met her while he was out of town that he had been able to pass himself off as worthy of her. The truth was that neither of us were up to a young lady of Miss Brookside's caliber, but I came a good sight nearer.

But only because of Mrs. Coolidge's sponsorship, I reminded myself, thinking of all the graceful homes in which lately I had supped. I breathed a sigh of dread as I thought about telling my patroness about this new development. Mayhap it would even affect my employment, for Mrs. Coolidge might decide she could do without me entirely if I was no longer a prospective son-in-law. Of course, I'd been with the Cotton Company long before Mrs. Coolidge broached her plan to make me her son-in-law.

After a sleepless night, I hurried in to work prepared to immediately get the matter off my chest. I knew there was no possibility of settling down to business until I did.

"I could cheerfully wring Edith's neck for letting you get away, Mr. Pickering," said Mrs. Coolidge. "Well, we've both done all that we can do. To show you how grateful I am at your many months of trying to make headway with my obstinate daughter, I hope that you will let me show Miss Brookside our true Galveston hospitality by inviting her to stay at my house while she's in town. And if, my dear Mr. Pickering, you should persuade the young woman to marry you, I will do everything in my power to see that your bride is properly introduced to Galveston society."

For a moment I was overcome with emotion as a vision of a future I had never dared dream for myself rose before my eyes. As one door closed, another had miraculously opened. And then I flung myself to my knees in front of Mrs. Coolidge, grabbed her hand and kissed it.

"Oh, do stop!" she exclaimed. "We've got a quarter of an hour to go over the Mayfield file. Fetch it and meet me in the conference room."

~~~~~

EDITH COOLIDGE PICKERING

The spring after my debutante season I seemed to go to one wedding after another, including Charlotte Lattimore's, to Mr. Walter Miller, not top drawer unfortunately, but a man with prospects on his mother's side, and who in the here and now would be able to provide for a wife adequately. I went with Charlotte to look at the little house he had bought for them.

"I didn't want to go through any more struggle," said Charlotte, sighing, "but it'll be years before Walter sees a dime of inheritance money. If he had been the first to ask, I would've turned him down, as I turned down those other two. It's extremely hard for an outsider to evaluate these things. Were it not for your invaluable help, I might have made a worse mistake."

"I'm sorry I let you down. I didn't know his money was in trust."

"No, there's no way you could've know. However, dear one, you might've known if you spent more time out in society. You simply don't pay attention to these things."

"No, I know. At any rate, he'll be rich someday."

"Yes, there is that."

"And once you have children, who knows, maybe his mother's people will think better of their plan to keep him poor."

"It's very tricky, letting it be known that you're available, but not saying no so often you earn the reputation as a flirt. I simply had to say yes to him. Janine Rodgers told her dinner guests one night, right in front of me, that she declared but what I was collecting proposals to see how many I could get."

"Yes, I heard about Janine's *bon mot*. She's simply horribly jealous of you, darling."

"And so I panicked and vowed to say yes to the very next one that asked me—*voila*!" Charlotte held up the hand that sported a tiny diamond solitaire in mock triumph.

"I positively hate it that we women can never make decisions independent of the question of money!" I replied savagely. Then I took Charlotte by the elbow and turned her to face me. "How would you live if you had an independent income, Char?"

She laughed, but I knew she was only putting a brave face on her rash act. "I suppose I'd use it to snare myself an even bigger income."

"Char, you'll never be happy here. Don't marry him."

"I have to. You know that. Don't undermine me. I need your support and love particularly at this moment. It's terribly *small*, isn't it?"

"I dare say he spent all he could on it."

"Never mind. At least I'll be able to march into Mr. Yates office and tell him I don't have to work for him any more. I've been terrified he would read the society news and discover it on his own and fire me. After next week, it won't matter."

"What about . . . are you scared? I mean, about having to go to bed with him?"

Charlotte regarded me affectionately. "You silly goose! It's not like being drawn and quartered. You just shut your eyes and it's over quickly, though I am somewhat repulsed by the untidiness of the act."

I shuddered. "It would be like torture to me! I can never endure that, no matter what Mama says."

"Then, you're very fortunate you have a mama to support you," said Charlotte lightly. "Let's go upstairs and look at the torture chamber."

We stood together just inside the doorway of the larger bedroom at the front of the house, staring in awe at the place where

Charlotte's bridal bed would very soon be delivered, our fertile imaginations conjuring up the scene that would shortly take place there. I saw Charlotte's white body, bound from each limb to the four posters of a bed, stretched naked and writhing while a demonic creature cruelly pierced her again and again. I turned away weeping and rushed from the room.

~~~~~

The love life of another of my dinner guests flourished around that time, Mr. Charles Pickering's, who had discovered a Boston girl to marry him, sight unseen. "That's the *only* way he could get someone to marry him," I told Charlotte. Mama scolded me for letting the eligible Mr. Pickering get away, and warned me that I would rue the day. Now I would have to shop in the general marketplace, competing with girls with far more proficiency than I had bothered to acquire. Most likely I would end up with the marked-down merchandise.

"Had you accepted Mr. Pickering for your lover," she said, "I would've made him my partner and you would've enjoyed the benefits of that partnership. As it is, you'll pick some young man who knows nothing about the Coolidge Cotton Company and he'll annoy me by expecting me to make him rich."

To ameliorate her fury with me, I put myself out to be useful to Mr. Pickering's Boston bride-to-be, writing to offer my services in the many preparations that must necessarily proceed before she ever arrived in Galveston. A lively correspondence developed and soon I found myself acting as Miss Brookside's agent for her own sweet sake. It was certain that her wooden fiance was incapable of making these arrangements.

I found it a sore temptation to catechize Miss Brookside on the logic of agreeing to marry a man she had never met, at the very least to pen her a frank appraisal of her bridegroom. But I reasoned that she could easily have learned that Mr. Pickering was, for me, "the one that got away" and attribute my remarks to sour grapes. Nevertheless, I felt dishonest for saying nothing, for making no move whatever to prepare her. I salved my conscience by telling myself that if she truly found that she despised the gentleman, she could get back on the train and return to Boston, her reputation intact, for all they would say in her own circle was that Mr. Pickering had proved to be an uncouth Texan and she had exercised admirable sense in backing out of her plans.

Of course, another benefit of the enormous undertaking of arranging a wedding for an out-of-town bride was to distract myself from the cruel blow to my spirits when Charlotte, showing not the slightest regret that she had not landed a bigger fish, left for a three-month's honeymoon in Europe, a present from the groom's wealthy family. I acutely envied her ability to manage her emotions and despaired that I would ever learn to disguise how I felt.

I adored Hazel Brookside at first sight. She was not beautiful, but she had such a spirited and gay personality, was so spontaneous and natural in her affections, that I, indeed, a host of instant admirers, was soon singing her praises. The bashful Mr. Pickering was one giant blush over his good fortune. Miss Brookside quite won my heart in the instant that she beheld her true love for the first time and didn't reject him, for Mr. Pickering was palpably aquiver with that expectation and made me feel quite sorry for him, as I'm sure many of the ladies in our party felt who met Miss Brookside's train. Indeed, an audible murmur of relief swept through the crowd when she stepped down to the platform, looked about her with an expectant smile, found him standing there ready to receive her, and broke into a delighted laugh.

"Oh, darling Mr. Pickering!" she exclaimed, and several of the girls who had wished good things for Mr. Pickering started a spontaneous ovation by clapping their gloved hands. The terribly romantic story of Mr. Pickering's long-distance suit was told and retold among our acquaintances, guaranteeing the happy couple a flurry of pre-nuptial parties in their honor, so that my job was made easier.

During the several weeks leading up to the last week of July date that the couple had selected in order to give us time for all needful preparations, Miss Brookside was our houseguest and stayed in the bedroom that adjoined mine and shared a bath. Once again I felt that God had sent me diversion just when I was most acutely conscious of my loss of Charlotte—now Mrs. Miller.

Although it had always been my wont to fall in love with

women I admired, my secret passion for Hazel was of a different quality than my previous loves. Perhaps I would have felt about a sister the way I did her, had my sister Fern or Mary lived. She had even whiter skin than Charlotte, the milk white of a redhead. Her hair was the thickest, loveliest stuff I ever beheld, a rich coppery brown, auburn in the sunlight. She welcomed vigorous brushing and would allow me to plait it for her each night in a long braid down her back.

Eventually I felt I knew her well enough to venture the question that was, perhaps, in all our minds. Why had a girl so brimming with zest and spirit committed the impetuous act of accepting a man she had never met, agreeing to live with him in a place that, in her part of the country, was viewed as the edge of the civilized world?

"Because I'm a girl," she said. "This 'impetuous act' of mine is the equivalent of my brethren going out West to seek their fortunes in the gold fields. Females make adventure on a smaller but no less exciting scale. Everyone I know was doing the expected thing, and I felt rebellious."

"Isn't it curious that the unexpected thing for you is the expected thing for me, that an act of true courage on my part was to say no to something that for you is an adventure." Then I grew confused, worrying that she would feel I had turned down Mr. Pickering and she had been his second choice. I decided to face this issue straight on. "I'm sure you've heard the rumors that Mama encouraged Mr. Pickering to look upon me with favor. But his heart was never in it because he was writing those letters for Mr. Lamme."

"I'm glad you told me. I sensed a certain reserve in your behavior toward Charles. I do hope the outcome in no wise hurt you, as it would give me great pain to know that I was indirectly the instrument of injuring someone who has been so kind to me."

I felt tears well into my eyes. "No," I replied. "I love another. Someone I can never marry. Please don't mention it to anyone. I cannot tell Mama, but somehow I must get around her insistence that I marry and replenish our depleted house."

"I can hardly imagine losing almost your entire family the way you did. There are bound to be repercussions for generations to come."

"If there are any generations to come. It all depends on me, you see."

Hazel gently patted a tear from my cheek with her finger. "Don't cry, dear one. It'll all work out. I'm humbled by the news of your unrequited love. You surely know that the feeling I bear for Charles is not that kind of love. I suppose that the greater part of my feeling for him is respect and admiration. As for passion, I had no expectation of enjoying that rarified emotion and am therefore not disappointed that I do not feel it."

"Oh, Hazel! I wondered, as indeed any girl must wonder, especially one who has never been made love to by a man."

"I would be frightened to be in the grip of a terrible emotion such as passion. It makes women do the most frightful things. Much nicer all around, I think, to enjoy a quieter, saner love, one that does not incapacitate the brain."

We laughed together, perhaps in mutual relief at reaching an understanding. It was the closest Hazel ever came to admitting that she was not in love with Charles Pickering.

~~~~~

MEG GALLOWAY

Sundays was my day off, the day I went to Mass and then directly afterwards went over to Dad's to do a little cleaning for him and fix him a nice dinner. He had not remarried, but a number of widow ladies in the neighborhood took an interest in his welfare, so I didn't worry about him living alone, even though he was over sixty. He had bought a small house near the Strand that he fixed up to suit himself, hardly any furniture to speak of, but nearly everywhere you looked, books, books, books, since there was no woman in his life to object to the peculiar value he placed in the airy substance of ideas over comfort. He installed a shelf or two here and there, but he weren't handy with tools, my dad, and mostly the books piled up around his ears until I come over and straightened them for him.

79

Every time I performed that chore, I was put in mind of the day I dusted Mr. Herrick Coolidge's books—that weren't shabby old used volumes like my father toted home—the day Mrs. Coolidge asked me to go with her and Edith to England. And every time, I re-thought that decision I had made to stay home and tried to figure out how things would've gone different in my life had I gone. I was a cheerful and forward-looking enough lass before tangling with that hurricane, more friendly and out-going too—had even managed to attract me a beau. But now, I wouldn't suffer no man to look at me. I couldn't bear to see them cut their eyes quickly off to something else, so I kept my head ducked down when I went out and didn't meet nobody's eye. All I had to do to put myself in a funk for days was catch sight of a looking glass and see what a sloppy piece of work I was.

The only way to become cheerful again was to count my blessings. I might never know the joy of keeping my own home, nursing my own child, but I had Miss Edith and Mrs. Coolidge. They had very little in the way of family connections either, but were happy to share their lives with me. I'd see Mrs. Coolidge's name mentioned in the newspaper and feel just as proud as I would if my own mama had made all those old graybeards that had formerly done business with her husband take her seriously. I rejoiced over Miss Edith's good tidings too, but like as not I was called upon to commiserate with the poor lamb when she ran to her room and bawled.

She seemed to do a lot of bawling that summer, what with one young lady after another getting married, and after Mrs. Coolidge had gone to all that bother and expense to properly launch her and nobody asking for her hand. I know how bitter it must have been to be asked to help with a bridal shower here, a wedding there, a reception, and to see her friends desert her for husbands.

I knowed Edith was to blame for her troubles, for finding fault with every young man that paid her any interest, but I didn't believe in adding to her troubles by telling her so, unlike Mrs. Coolidge, who hardly let a day go by without criticizing the girl and berating her for not trying harder. Edith's problem was she was too honest to pretend she liked a boy just 'cause he come from a good family and had all the traits Mrs. Coolidge wanted

80

for her. I knowed that some of those young ladies whose weddings Miss Edith went to didn't give a hoot about the man they were marrying, but were just marrying him 'cause he was a good catch. But Miss Edith would never do that. If she didn't like a body, she let the whole world know it just by the way she poked out her bottom lip. That friend of hers, Miss Charlotte, that one was a little hussy if you ask me, only using Edith to get to the better class of men, but Miss Edith couldn't see it and liked to cried her eyes out when her grand plans for her friend actually worked and she caught a husband.

No, I didn't believe in criticizing or giving advice—that was Mrs. Coolidge's department. My part was to try to console Edith after she got her poor heart broken, time and again. She was a tenderhearted little thing and took up with one girlfriend after another 'cause she never did win her mama's love and sought it in the affection of her friends. When she was little, she used to get that kind of love from me, but once she got older, I couldn't fill that need no more. It used to break my heart to try to comfort her when she took one of her spells of despondency and cried in my arms that nobody was ever going to love her. It didn't do no good to tell her she'd always have my love, 'cause she knew that. She counted on it. I was like an old comfortable bathrobe you slip into once all the people who count have gone home and you don't care how you look any more. But I valued that place above all others, 'cause Edith was the child I never got to have, the hearth and home I was never going to have. So, through all her hardships and adversities growing up, I was the one person she could count on to love her for herself and not forsake her when something else come along.

I knew Edith's pattern. She would throw herself into a friendship, or giving a party or whatnot, with all the enthusiasm in her generous nature. Then the enthusiasm would run its course and like as not, she'd end up getting her heart broke 'cause she'd expected one thing and got something else. She'd get so despondent she'd take to her bed, but it wouldn't be long before she was right back throwing herself into something else—a never-ending cycle of despondency and giddy elation. When Mr. Pickering dropped all pretense of courting her and found himself a more cooperative bride up North, Miss Edith took to

81

her bed for weeks, only to emerge to plan his wedding. It just beat all I ever see. Nobody could ever predict what that girl would take it in her head to do.

The whole household lent itself to the purpose of uniting Mr. Charles and his yankee bride, who we could hardly understand she talked so fast and said her words funny. But she was a nice enough young lady and it sure perked up everybody's spirits to have a wedding in the house. Miss Edith explained to me that the couple wasn't getting married in the Church 'cause Mr. Charles was halfway through his conversion and Miss Hazel was something else, I forget just what, some religion I'd never heard of, and so they thought it'd be better to just get married in Mrs. Coolidge's front parlor with a very small wedding party, then have a big reception at the Beach Hotel.

I was wrung out from all the comings and goings, all the special errands entailed by the wedding, not to mention having the extra work of houseguests. There was not only Miss Hazel, but a whole bevy of her friends that come down to see her married. Her family had come too, but thank the good Lord they put up at the hotel. I needed my day off in the worst way, but Miss Edith made me promise I wouldn't spend the night, but come back and make sure all those people had their supper. We'd made do without a cook for years, but that summer Mrs. Coolidge had told me to be on the lookout for someone and I'd recommended my friend Lucille Frenche for the job. She was brand-new that week and too shy to mingle with people, so I had to hurry back.

I fixed Dad sandwiches, did a little washing for him, and hurried back to Mrs. Coolidge's. As always when the trolley turned west at the beach—now a tolerable sight higher than it seemed like it ought to be—I scanned the horizon for impending weather. We were approaching the deadliest month of the year, August, when most bad storms hit—except of course for the storm from hell that had set a standard for all later storms to be compared to. The Gulf was peaceful, the jetties full of fishermen, casting into the summer-warmed waters. Dad's big old plate of broth, I thought. It'd be a pretty day for the wedding tomorrow.

Next morning I woke at my usual hour, 5:30, and spent five

minutes on my knees thanking God for my health and all the good things in life, then jumped into my clothes and hurried down to the kitchen to help Lucille with breakfast for the staff, an extra burden with three new temporary helpers.

"Mrs. Frenche," I said. "Does it seem to you the surf sounds louder than usual?"

She paused for a second to tune out the household noises and she heard it too. After awhile, Joe, the man hired to help Mr. Rallings jockey automobiles around for the wedding guests, come in and sat down just as we started eating and said that twenty-foot seas were running and that three dozen fishermen had nearly drowned last night on Bettison's Fishing Pier until a pilot boat sent a yawl in close enough to pluck them off just before the whole she-bang collapsed.

"Dear God," I whispered, losing my stomach for breakfast. "I reckon I better go wake Mrs. Coolidge and tell her."

We all looked at the clock, still an hour yet before the gentry was out of bed. "But she'd want to know," I said.

"Wait thirty minutes," said Lucille. "Thirty minutes won't make no difference."

I tried to go about my work, but I couldn't keep my mind on what I was doing. I'd pick something up and carry it around for awhile, then set it down and pick something else up. Finally I didn't say nothing to Lucille, but went up to quietly rap on Mrs. Coolidge's door. She answered right away and I found her sitting on the edge of the bed, barefooted and wearing her long gown, two thin gray braids hanging down her back almost making her look like a girl.

"Miz Coolidge, I thought I better tell you right away, they seems to be a hurricane brewing."

"I heard the surf come up towards morning." She slipped out of bed and slid her feet into her house slippers and pulled on a robe. "Let's go look," she said, and we clumb up to the third floor where she had made a half-hearted attempt to duplicate Mr. Coolidge's old library, though it was a much smaller room and didn't have no books. Miss Edith's easel and paint supplies were stored in there.

But the room boasted a little widow's walk that stuck out over the roofs of the kitchen and outhouses and I knowed she'd

83

built it to remind her of that nice broad porch Mr. Coolidge had off the back of the old house. Finally this little porch was being put to the use she had always had in mind—to look at the weather.

"I wondered how long it would take to put our new seawall to the test," she said, seeming to draw strength from the enormous energy roaring towards us. "You were afraid of storms even before the big one, weren't you, Meg?"

"Yes'm. That's why I couldn't bring myself to go across the ocean with you and Edith. I was afraid we'd run into one and there'd be no place to hide."

"It's this island that affords us no place to hide. But we keep trying our tricks on the old sea goddess. Well, let's see if this trick is enough to keep her out."

The wind was blowing straight out of the south at forty knots, ripping at our clothes and blowing Mrs. Coolidge's skinny little braids straight out behind her. I had a sudden vivid recollection of the wind tearing the clothes off my body, of my strong young muscles cramped with pain as I fought to hang on to that big carved timber that had held up Mr. Coolidge's roof, and in the end was useless except to keep alive one seventeen-year-old girl broken in body and spirit. I wanted to get off the island right that minute, get on the streetcar and head north.

Mrs. Coolidge turned to me and gripped my arm. "I'm going down there!"

"Where?"

"To the seawall to see how she's doing!"

"Oh, Miz Coolidge, don't do that!"

Heads were poking out of every door when we got back down to the second floor. "What's going on?" first one then another cried.

"Hurricane," said Mrs. Coolidge. "We're going down to the seawall. Come go with us if you want to see something magnificent."

Those yankee houseguests acted like somebody had dropped in and invited 'em to a come-as-you-are party. Such a deal of excited chattering and bustling around you never saw! The ladies grabbed up shawls for their heads and the gentlemen pulled on their trousers. "Come go with us, Meg!" urged Edith. "I won't let you stay here by yourself. You'll see there's nothing to worry about. Hurricanes are just nuisances now. Maybe you won't be so scared of them if you once see one tamed."

The only reason I went was because I knew it hadn't helped me none before to hang back and try to arrange for my own safekeeping. I grabbed up a scarf and went too, although I thought it was foolhardy to treat a hurricane like some kind of spectacle. We had enough cars to carry the lot of us, and everybody went, help too, and soon we saw that we weren't the only ones that wanted to see first-hand what a tamed hurricane looked like.

The storm flags were flying by the time we parked and piled out of the cars. Some who had come to watch the fun were brave—or crazy—enough to go right up to the edge of the seawall and stare right into the teeth of the wind, but I stayed back a respectful distance. She was a tiger on the prowl, had got up her appetite for blood, only to find herself thwarted by our puny little wall. She was pacing up and down, snarling and spitting, temporarily defeated, but she was figuring a way to get past our defenses. A wise person didn't reach through the bars to taunt an enraged beast.

The folks from Boston had seen nor'westers blow in their part of the country and weren't awfully impressed with this little blow that had come up on the Texas coast. The waves come crashing in, one after the other, but they did just what the engineers intended them to do, curved up in great foamy arcs and spouted in the air like fountains. The wind picked off the spume and drenched us sightseers. When everybody was good and wet and had seen enough, we went home and fixed a big breakfast and went about our business like we had good sense.

The power failed when the wind got up to sixty knots, and that old familiar keening began to drown out all other sounds. I was nervous as a cat in a roomful of rockers, but it never did get no worse. Mr. Pickering arrived and joined the party around the breakfast table and a lively debate ensued as to whether to go ahead with the wedding or wait. The young people were all for going ahead, but the grayer heads thought they ought to put it off a day. I noticed that Mrs. Coolidge took no part in this debate until everybody was at sixes and sevens and appealed to her to decide the matter. "Let the celebration begin," she said.

85

"You'll always be able to remember your anniversary, Mr. Pickering. It was the day twentieth century technology finally made this island safe for human habitation."

~~~~~

EDITH COOLIDGE PICKERING

I had hoped to see a good deal more of Charlotte once she was back home and settled into her little house. But she was very busy fixing things up, giving parties to repay the kindnesses done to her during her courting days, and cementing relationships with the people she wanted to cultivate. I was on her guest list often, but no more often than other girls of her acquaintance, I noticed. But it didn't matter. I preferred to see Charlotte without the crowds. I made it a practice to drop in on her at least once a week and take her some little present for the house. Since her marriage, there was a change in her that made me feel somewhat shy around her, as if she had crossed over into a bourne I would never know. We were no longer united in our ignorance, could no longer engage in silly idle conjecture about conjugal relations. She knew what it was like to have a man make love to her. She had done it. She was pregnant. She had returned from her honeymoon that way.

Mama continued to arrange my social schedule and to not let me do what I wanted, which was to stay at home, lock myself in my room and daub paint on canvas. I was too depressed to want to do anything else, but if I protested the never-ending grind of evenings out, Mama would light into me.

"Ungrateful silly baggage! You think I'm required to treat you like the Queen of Egypt? Buy you gowns and send you off to fetes night after night? There's only two of us, Edith. My job is to run Papa's empire. Your job is to get married and have children! Don't you ever forget that! If you don't do what is required of you, I'll turn you out, d'you hear me? I'll have nothing more

86

to do with a girl who refuses to pull her own weight! You'll see what happens if you don't co-operate. I'll not support a barren old spinster, do you hear me?"

Another time, when I got up the courage to plead for art school again, she coldly told me, "It's time you stopped deluding yourself, Edith. If you had any real talent, it would've come out on its own. You don't need art school to coax it out of you. Did anybody teach me how to run a business? Your Papa didn't even let me handle money! But I learned, didn't I? The only things in life worth knowing are those things you bother to find out for yourself. Stop sniveling about how you might've been a great artist! You have in your power to do one thing, and that's all that's required of you, my girl. Do it!"

You would think such brutal speeches would totally destroy me, but I had heard those and similar themes from Mama all my life. I knew she didn't believe in me. It didn't matter: I had stopped believing in myself.

Mama grew even testier about my failure to produce grandchildren for her as my friends began having children. Charlotte had a boy, Daniel Allen Miller, a perfect, fat-cheeked, blue-eyed infant that I would hold and pretend that somehow Charlotte and I had produced. It was very pleasant to visit Charlotte in her little house and pretend that the three of us were a family, to pretend that Walter would not come home and claim them. Charlotte was very kind to me and would let me lie next to her on the bed when she nursed the baby. I would look on with devotion and passion, but at the same time be overcome by the strangest sense that I would never truly belong anywhere on this earth, a creature that was neither fish nor fowl.

Hazel and Charles' first child was a little girl, whom they asked if they could name after Mama. She said yes, and told me that she had agreed because she despaired I would ever have a little girl to name after her. Mama gave Charles a nice raise and an even grander title, and the Pickerings bought a nice home just down the street from ours. I often visited in their home and watched Hazel nurse her baby, though watching Hazel with a baby at her breast did not elicit the same complicated feelings that it did to watch Charlotte.

The sad story of how I got my second chance with Charles

I shall leave for another story-teller. Meg was there and saw it all, God help us.

~~~~~

MEG GALLOWAY

We were an island, with the Gulf of Mexico and five hundred miles of open water to our south, West Bay and Galveston Bay to our north. Only a wagon bridge and the Santa Fe railroad bridge connected us to the mainland before the 1900 hurricane, both made out of wood and vulnerable to wind, water and fire. But in 1912 we finally got ourselves a weather-proof, fire-proof causeway, and Governor Colquitt and his party led a parade of fifteen hundred cars over the new causeway bridge to dedicate it.

I was now in charge of the house and the employees, even though I wasn't yet quite thirty years old. I could take off near any time I wanted, though I seldom did 'cause I took my responsibilities so hard. However, I determined that I wanted to see Houston and ride that new Galveston-Houston Electric Railway over the new causeway. I had never been any further than Texas City in my life, which there weren't a lot to see there, and I had a hankering to see the Bayou City, which was growing like a toadstool. The trip was advertised to take only an hour and nineteen minutes and I was fearful my neck would snap going that rate, but Dad was going too and I figured if a man his age could tolerate the trip, I could too.

We passed through pretty green farmland along the way, flat coastal plains, and I saw running alongside us barges and ships on the "big ditch"—the new Houston Ship Channel that took business right on past Galveston and Texas City, and which I'd often enough heard Mrs. Coolidge castigate. The business interests, though, didn't seem to be much impressed that we'd whupped nature to her knees with our fancy engineering, our seawall and grade raising to make ourselves high and dry. Our enemies had taken advantage of our misfortune to bypass us, subduing the waters of the Gulf by passing it first through Galveston Bay, then channeling it between the banks of Buffalo Bayou, to arrive in downtown Houston as tame as a sewer line and about as exciting. Nobody'd ever want to go down and stand about the wharves of the Houston Ship Channel just for the romance of the thing. It was maritime without the spirit of the sea. It was cold-eyed commerce with none of the grace and charm of our island. It was whupping Nature till she was a spiritless thing, a slow-gliding, muddy sycophant licking at the boots of industry.

So, you can see I weren't much impressed with Houston. All hustle and no go, I said to Dad, and he shook his head at the savagery of the inhabitants going about their business and said he preferred the pace we kept back home. We had ourselves a good lunch at the Rice Hotel and strolled downtown between the skyscrapers, something I didn't expect we'd ever see on Galveston, 'cause the first big blow'd knock 'em down. And then we headed back to the train station, as satisfied with ourselves as if we'd made an excursion across the ocean and seen Europe.

I had my own little car—Mrs. Coolidge had insisted I learn to drive so I wouldn't be a burden to her—and I dropped Dad off at his house and went home. It was getting on towards sunset and I noticed the lights blazing at our house as I turned the corner onto P Street. There were a lot of cars parked out front too, and I hurried and put up my car and rushed across the backyard to see what the matter was.

Edith was in the kitchen watching out the back window for me. "Oh, thank God you're here, Meg. The most terrible thing has happened. Hazel . . ." And she broke into tears and fell on my neck sobbing. It took awhile to get the story out. Mrs. Pickering, pregnant with her second child, had gone into early labor and been taken to John Sealy Hospital where the doctors said that either the baby or the mother would have to be sacrificed. Mr. Charles begged them to save his wife, and they operated, but it weren't any use. Both were pronounced dead at six o'clock that afternoon. Little Faith had been brung over to our house earlier in the day and any minute they were expecting the poor bereaved father, who had called with the news from the hospital.

"She knew she was dying, Meg. Oh, it was horrible," wailed Edith, who had been let in to see the poor young dying girl for a few minutes. "She asked me to look after them, after Charles and little Faith."

There never was a sadder man that I ever see in my life as Mr. Charles when he finally come into Mrs. Coolidge's house that evening, I suppose because he didn't know where else to go. It was the second family he'd lost and I knowed this one was by far the worst, 'cause this was the family he'd made himself. He'd a felt better maybe if he could've wept, but his long sad face just got longer and his sad eyes were dry and kind of vacant like.

Over the next few days we kept little Faith, who was two years old and big enough to keep asking for her Mommy, though she was a good brave little thing and didn't cry. Miss Edith would take her in her lap and try not to cry in front of her, but nobody could give her any answer as to why her mommy didn't come for her. Mr. Charles was no good at all with the child. His long arms would hang there useless and I'd want to say to him, oh, for pity sake, Mr. Charles, just pick her up! But he'd stand around looking awkward and uncomfortable, take food if we pressed it on him, and then he'd head back to the office, seeming to take refuge in his work. Edith and me went off to interview the Pickering housekeeper to see what needed doing to clear out poor Miss Hazel's things. A month after the poor dear thing was laid in her grave, Miss Edith said she was going to marry Charles Pickering and make a good home for little Faith.

Chapter Five

CHARLES OREN PICKERING

When Hazel was taken from me, something seemed to die inside my breast. I knew people wanted to see some feeling from me, but I couldn't oblige them. I would've liked to cry for her, for my son who also died on the operating table, but my heart felt like a desert. I didn't feel anything. My wife had felt things for me and now she was gone, taking that sense organ with her. Thank God for Mrs. Coolidge. She and Edith and Meg Galloway handled things so smoothly I hardly had to make a decision. All I had to do was get up and go to work every day. All I could do was get up and go to work every day.

One evening about a month after the funeral, Mrs. Coolidge called me into her office after the other employees had gone home and I saw that she had something on her mind.

"Mr. Pickering," she said, "nobody grieves any more than I do for your losses because I've been through it and know how it feels to lose a spouse and a child. At the same time, I know you're like me and wish people would quit bothering you with their sympathy. You'd like to just get on with your work and not mope around thinking about it."

"Yes, ma'am, that's the truth. I just don't know what'd I do if I didn't have my work."

"You know that I wanted you for Edith, Mr. Pickering, and now the opportunity has arisen again. She's learned a few lessons from her debutante days when she thought she'd always be young and sought after. If you don't help me out, she's going to wind up an old maid and I won't get my grandkids."

I spread my hands helplessly. "What can I do, Mrs. Coolidge? She doesn't seem to take to me."

"Ask her to marry you. She'll say yes. I intend to make my son-in-law a partner in this business—and I want it to be you. I can trust you. You're good with numbers and I need somebody like that. I didn't get enough training early in life to do the sums the way you do. It's too much for one person to carry all on her own."

"I'm honored you think so much of me and will strive to always be worthy of your trust, ma'am," I told her.

"You won't find me ungrateful," she said simply.

I had grave doubts that anything at all had changed in Miss Edith's feelings toward me, but I had changed. I had been a husband and was now a father. I mixed with the most important business people in town and was taken seriously by them. I had prospects that, certainly, didn't put me on a par with Miss Edith, but I had something else that put me ahead of any other man who might present himself to her: I had her mama's blessing. There was, too, the fact that I had a young child who needed a mother.

And so, not bothering to get all het up about it like I might've done in the past, I left work early and dropped in at Mrs. Coolidge's house like I usually did to hear Faith say her bedtime prayers. She was still staying with Edith and Meg 'cause their house had become more familiar to her than her own empty home. Edith went out and I helped Faith through her "Now I Lay Me." With a lump in my throat, I kissed her on the cheek and pulled the covers up tight. I turned around and saw that Edith was standing in the hall watching me. I got up and slowly walked towards her, and there on the landing, with no decoration whatsoever, asked her to marry me.

"Miss Edith, will you marry me and be my little girl's mommy?" I said.

And she, equally shunning blandishment, said without hesitation: "Yes, I will, Charles. I told Hazel I would do that. It's for her sake, not because Mama wants me to that I'm doing this. You

92

must promise me that you won't push yourself on me. If you ever do, I'll run away and you'll never see me again. Do you promise?"

It was like a curtain had parted, giving me a glimpse of a landscape I had been unable to imagine. Now I understood what Miss Edith was afraid of. "I'll be the tenderest and most considerate of lovers," I said. "You have nothing to fear in me."

"No, you don't understand. I don't want a lover at all," she said. "But maybe Mama will be happy that you've already got a little girl named Faith."

And she turned and went down the stairs. It was then I realized that neither of us had said a word about love.

~~~~~

EDITH COOLIDGE PICKERING

It was decided that my wedding would be a subdued affair, in keeping with the bereavement of the groom, who was in the curious position of being asked to both mourn and celebrate at the same time. Father Kirwin hurriedly completed Mr. Pickering's instruction to become a Catholic and married us with only a handful of friends looking on. We weren't even going on a honeymoon—my suggestion—since there was little Faith to consider.

I wanted to move down the street to Mr. Pickering's house, but that would've meant taking Meg with me and leaving Mama all by herself, so I acceded to their wishes and stayed where I was. Mr. Pickering seemed happy to rid himself of the house Hazel had spent so much energy and money fixing up to suit her. He used the money from the sale to remodel the carriage house to make it a proper garage for automobiles, with living quarters over it for employees. He seemed right happy to do that, to make an investment in Mama's house, sort of like proof he had an interest there.

As far as everyone else was concerned, Mr. Pickering would share my bedroom and bath, and use the smaller bedroom next door as his dressing room. But in reality, he spent every night in that room, keeping his word not to bother me.

Charlotte gave a tea in my honor a week or so after my wedding and invited only married ladies, all former school friends of mine. I was treated like the newest member of a club which had hitherto been closed to me, not letting on to a soul that I was a fraudulent insider. The ladies chattered on about intimate matters, childbirth, how their husbands were about their spending money, about new curtains and servant problems. And I felt as left out as I always did, only worse, because the older I got the more final was the knowledge that I would never get what I wanted, never be allowed to live the only way that seemed genuine to me, never have my passion returned. Charlotte seemed almost common to me, sharing recipes and anecdotes with the other young married ladies. Seeing my pensiveness, she threw her arms around me and kissed me on the cheek.

"Oh, my darling Edith, I'm so glad you're finally one of us! That you finally got your Charles!"

I unclasped her arms and hurried off to the bathroom to pat cold water on my face and prevent an outbreak of frustrated tears. "Isn't she a darling?" I heard Charlotte stage whisper to the others. "She was very close to Hazel." The ladies were even kinder to me upon my return.

I could hardly tolerate the assumptions that were made about me now that I presumably slept with a man, the glances at my waistline to see if I had managed to get pregnant yet, the knowing little smiles of the household staff when someone would ask me or Charles how we had slept. For his part, I'm sure my husband was being as patient and reasonable as any bridegroom can be. Yet, he didn't *really* understand, and I couldn't explain to him that I would never welcome him into my bed.

Every evening, once he thought I was in bed, Charles would tap gently on the connecting door, and whether I answered or not, would come in and kneel by my bedside, hold my hand and press kisses into my palm and wish me a good night. I knew that he was waiting for me to invite him to stay, and I appre-

94

ciated that he wasn't more forceful. However, the nightly gentle unspoken pressure of it was driving me wild. And yet there wasn't a soul I could complain to, for I didn't want anybody to find out that I had married a man I had no intention of sleeping with.

I let these things bother me to such a degree that I was slow to appreciate how I had improved my lot: Charles made a brilliant foil to fend off Mama. I had done what she asked and was now his wife, which took precedence over being her daughter. I saw no more of him than I did her, for they were *together!*—putting in long tedious hours at the office, no longer housed in left-over space above the warehouse, but in spiffy new quarters on the Strand.

For whole days together I was left to amuse myself. When the weather grew warm, I took little Faith and her nurse to the beach, and while they played in the sand or napped under the umbrella, I worked at my sketch book. I had decided to take up my brush again, and this time make no effort to produce serious art, but simply amuse myself. If I couldn't be a Mary Cassatt, I would decorate the walls with pleasing little seascapes.

The second major improvement to my life was that I no longer had to attend a dreary procession of social functions in search of a husband. I cared nothing at all for society and would gladly have let my membership in that heartless institution lapse. However, from time to time Mama would rouse herself to notice that no one ever came to our house and would urge me to extend myself. I, in turn, would drop the responsibility on Meg and she would get up a party of some sort, to which my only duty would be to provide the guest list, then attend and try to be charming. My two housemates would tear themselves away from the office to mingle with my guests, as if they were doing me a favor.

In this way we got on fairly smoothly until one morning about three months after my wedding when I woke up with Mama standing over me, livid.

"What made you think you could get away with such a cheap trick, you deceitful girl?" she shouted at me. "I have to find out from the servants that you're not sleeping with your husband! How dare you try to sneak out of your commitment this way!"

"But Mama, I did what you wanted. You've got a grandchild and a son-in-law. . . ."

The look she gave me was one of pure hatred. "You defy me? I will break you, Edith. You are not my child! I will throw you out on the street with nothing but the clothes on your back! What's wrong with you that you're such an unnatural daughter? I thought this, this *thing* with silly girls would blow over once they all got married and had families of their own. Oh, you ungrateful, you *recalcitrant* girl! I am so angry and humiliated! To think that I foisted you off on that sweet and unsuspecting, that *saintlike* Mr. Pickering!"

She stormed out of my bedroom, then just as furiously stormed right back in. "Get up and put something on. I'm throwing you out of the house."

"But Mama!" I protested. "Think how it will look!"

"*You* think how it will look. I'm through with you, do you hear me? I'll make Charles Pickering the richest man on the island and his daughter the queen of Galveston society. You'll know nothing about it, though, because you'll be waiting on tables or making beds, or if you're smart enough to learn, typing in some law office. Don't you see that this cuts both ways? You're right—I don't need you—you outsmarted yourself this time, Edith. You're nothing but a whiny, stupid, foot-dragging little milksop that I have absolutely no use for. You'll see, my girl. You'll see!"

I was hysterical by then. Meg came rushing to my rescue, but one look from Mama stopped her and she turned around and fled back to safety. Mama furiously yanked a dress from my wardrobe, tore off my nightdress and forced the dress down over my head. "You think you can fool with me, my girl!" she kept saying. "We'll see how you like the streets and the alleys. We'll see how long you can survive without the protection of a family and a home that you think you owe nothing to!"

Meg had run after Charles, who was on his way to the office and had gotten as far as pulling the car out of the garage. Suddenly he was there, pulling Mama off of me. "Mother Coolidge! Don't do that! Don't do that to my wife!" Dazed, she let him pull her away from me and the two of them stood staring down at me, naked and crying piteously on my bed, the torn dress pulled ludicrously across my bare bosom.

"I could kill her," said my mother. "I could just kill the girl. I'm so sorry, Charles, that I inflicted this on you." Shaken by her outburst, she walked unsteadily out of the room. Charles picked up my nightdress and offered it to me to cover myself.

"I didn't tell her," he said mournfully.

"She always finds out everything," I said. I ignored the proffered nightdress and struggled out of the torn street dress. I pulled the rumpled sheet over myself and huddled in my bed shaking. "I hate her. I hate her. I hate her."

Charles went over and closed the door and came back and sat on the edge of the bed. "Why did you marry me?" he said softly.

"So she wouldn't do . . . *that* to me," I said, breaking into sobs again. He didn't touch me, but continued to regard me mournfully.

"You don't love me and . . . forgive me for saying this, Edith . . . it doesn't seem to me that you care very much for little Faith. She seems always to be with her nurse and to regard Meg as her mother."

The justness of his accusation overwhelmed me with misery. It was one thing to hate Mama, who had no softness to her, whose very hardness my hatred bounced off without hurting. But it wasn't the same hating Charles, who was as soft and vulnerable as Mama was hard. I was used to Mama's betrayal, but to hear reproach from Charles was bitter indeed. I must be very bad to have warranted his criticism.

"I don't like men," I whispered. "I've always been this way. I can't understand it myself so I can't explain it to you. The very thought . . . of touching you sickens me."

He covered his face with his long narrow hands and I knew he suffered, that he was probably reviewing his unending streak of bad luck, beginning with the loss of his entire family to the hurricane, losing his beloved Hazel and unborn son, and now being saddled with a woman who didn't want him to touch her.

He took his hands away from his face and I saw that there was not the slightest trace of tears, but then, I already knew that about him, that he had no tears left. "I thought you'd come around sooner or later," he said.

"I'm sorry."

There was, of course, no adequate response and he moved

heavily out of the room and I heard him go down the stairs. Meg came to me then and I had her draw a bath for me. I felt bruised all over, though Mama had not actually struck me. My injuries were spiritual. I wanted to sink under the hot water and let it fill my lungs and drown me. There seemed to be no solution to my problems, no way to compensate those who loved me for how I had failed them. I let out my breath and slid down in the tub until the water came to my nostrils. I closed my eyes and remembered the one time I had caressed Charlotte's naked body in that very tub and how that single moment was all of heaven I was ever likely to know. I began crying again because I knew I hadn't the nerve to kill myself. I was too cowardly to defend myself against Mama, too cowardly to do the right thing with the man I had married, and too utterly cowardly to take my own life.

I lay in the hot water and wept until the water grew cold and I had to climb out and get in bed to get warm again. Nobody came near me all day, not even Meg, and I knew Mama had forbidden it. I watched the light gradually leave one side of the room and fill up the other. I listened to the busy chatter and clank of servants downstairs and the hush that came over them as they walked past my room. I decided that if I could not take an active role in killing myself I would do it passively and simply stay in bed until I died, refusing food and water, which, in any case, was not offered.

The hunger was not bothersome, but I grew so thirsty I had to go back on my plan to the extent of sneaking into the bathroom to drink water from the tap and use the commode. I heard Mama and Charles come home, heard the subdued timbre of their voices emanating from the dining room, and much later, heard Charles in the bathroom. But he didn't bother me with his gentle silent pleading, in fact, didn't even come in to say goodnight. During the wee hours I slipped downstairs and got a cold biscuit to eat.

The next day the same thing happened, everybody went about their business as if I didn't exist. Again I watched the sun come up on one side of the house and go down on the other, heard Charles and Mama come home and have supper in the dining room. Then, like they always did, they sat in the parlor reading until eleven when I heard Charles come up and go to bed. It wasn't the easiest death in the world, I reflected, lying in bed waiting for death to come to you.

Still, I persisted and lasted through another full day with the same boring things happening. By now I was attuned to the sounds of the street, the mailman setting off barking dogs as he neared our house, the clatter of trash cans as they were emptied onto the wagon, the jostle and noise of horses and cars over on the seawall swell louder as evening traffic headed home from work. Again Mama and Charles came home for dinner—they seemed to have company tonight, Mr. Galloway, I thought, and Meg had joined them—and then the sounds shifted to the front of the house where the four of them had an animated conversation, punctuated by occasional laughter. I was enraged that they were laughing while I was upstairs doing my best to die.

Finally, that night, I could stand no more and sneaked down after the house got still to Meg's room to find out what Mama had said. Meg gasped and nearly screamed when I slipped through the door. She was in bed, tucked up against the pillows, writing on a stack of little white notecards, which was how she planned meals and grocery buying.

"You nearly scared me to death!" she exclaimed. "You want me to get up and fix you an egg?"

"No. I'm starving myself. What did Mama tell you?"

"She said we was to go on about our business till you come down on your own," she said.

"Is she still mad?"

"Oh, Miss Edith, you and Miz Coolidge are like fire and ice. I don't know what to do. I'm in the middle."

"You know, don't you, why she's mad at me?"

"I do, ma'am. The whole house heard."

I could tell from the look on Meg's face that she wasn't greatly sympathetic to my side of the argument. "*You've* never slept with a man," I pointed out.

"I didn't marry one neither."

"But you were engaged. Did he touch you, your young man?"

"Touched me all over. And I liked it too. How can you be so cruel to Mr. Charles, honey? It don't hurt a woman to let a man touch her. That's what she's made for. Lots of delicate ladies lie down with their big old husbands every night and you don't see them making a fuss about it. It's what married women do, what makes them different than maidens."

"But you've never done it! You don't know how odious it might be."

"Now, listen, miss. It can't be all that bad, all right? There's certain things in life a body has to do, and this is one of them." When Meg was angry or upset, the scar on her forehead reddened. Then her expression relented. "It's my fault for spoiling you, letting you do whatever you want. Anything comes along you don't want to do, you don't have no discipline to make yourself do it. But you know how hard and firm your mother is."

"Yes," I said dully.

"She's not going to go away and she's not going to give up 'till you do your duty. It's too important to her. It's the only thing she's ever asked of you, Edith." She reached out a hand to smooth my tumbled hair. "I know, I know. Maybe if she'd been a little more loving to you, you wouldn't mind so much doing something for her. You're just holding out because you know she wants it of you. It's the only way you know how to fight back, the one thing you got to bargain with, poor little waif. There, there, honey, don't cry. Your eyes are bloodshot enough as it is."

"I *can't*, Meg. I can't! Don't you understand? Giving myself to a man seems to me horrible and unnatural!"

"Killing yourself is horrible and unnatural too, but you're willing to contemplate that," said Meg. "Even though it means perdition to your eternal soul. Now why don't you grow up, Miss Edith, and go up there and make amends to that poor man you married knowing full well you weren't going to be a wife to him? Go on, else I can't help you. Your Mama won't let me."

"Don't make me, Meg."

"I've never taken a hard line with you, Miss, and it's been your ruination. I blame myself as much as anybody. Don't you know how that poor man must be hurting 'cause you've rejected him, and him lost that sweet wife and little baby? Go on, honey, do it and get it over with. Then you'll know it ain't too bad. And if you don't, you're never gonna get back in your Mama's good graces. When she says something, she means it. She's not going to let this blow over and let you go on about your life."

Sniffing, I left Meg's room and slowly climbed the stairs.

She was right. They were all right. My problem wasn't exotic, it was just that I hated having to do something I didn't want to do. But I could do this. I could go in there and lie still with my eyes closed like Charlotte did, like Hazel did, like all the married women I knew did and let that man poke at me. If that's what they all wanted, what it took to make 'em happy, be damned to them! I could do it. I would bend so they wouldn't break me, then I'd do what I damn well pleased.

I tapped on Mr. Pickering's door and heard his bewildered response. "It's your wife," I said, "come to give you comfort."

~~~~~

MEG GALLOWAY

Seems like my part in all this is to describe the brutal weather. But you can't have lives being lived out on Galveston Island without what you take into account the periodic visits of the Storm Goddess, that raging tigress who loves to re-invent herself and visit our shores in new guises to test our defenses. Oh, mortals, your name is complacency!

That little storm we had in ought nine was just a teaser to make us smug and satisfied with ourselves, to feel that we had at last outsmarted the primitive beast with our uptown improvements. When she come prowling around again, August of 1915, she wore a new and terrifying aspect. This time we didn't jump in our automobiles and run down to the seawall to laugh at her efforts. This time the beast unleashed the ferocity of the 1900 hurricane and piled up a storm surge three inches higher.

We got warning nearly a week ahead of the storm, but not many people responded. Our household was in an uproar with the impending birth of Mrs. Coolidge's first grandchild. Edith was having a fit not wanting to go through with it and her mama seemed to take an extra glee telling her there were precious few things in life you got any choice about and this was definitely not

101

one of them, that that baby was coming whether Edith threw one of her famous hissy tantrums or not. I got impatient with Mrs. Coolidge and told her she weren't helping matters, and she saw the sense of what I was saying and left Edith's bedroom.

Dr. Brown come and looked at Edith and said it wasn't time, that the contractions weren't hard nor were they very close together, that he'd give the mother a tranquilizer if it weren't for the baby, and for us to try to calm Edith down.

Well, we done the best we could! Over the past year I thought Miss Edith had settled down and accepted her lot as a woman. I'd look in on the family having their dinner, Mr. Charles at one end of the table, Mrs. Coolidge at the other, Edith and little Faith, who was growing into such a nice little girl—had her mama's coppery-colored hair—and they'd all be talking so normal and seeming to enjoy one another's company. And I'd think, hallelujah! Praise the Lord! The lion has laid down with the lamb! Miss Edith was going out to see her friends now and then, and ever once in awhile having them over to see her. She was painting her little seashore pictures and not being bothered by Faith, who was good as gold and nobody should ever have been bothered with, but Edith just didn't take to mothering like she thought she would when she promised Miss Hazel she'd look after her baby.

Relations between the couple seemed to be more or less what you'd expect 'em to be. There weren't no more rumpled sheets on Mr. Charles's bed in the morning, and Miss Edith seemed to tolerate her mother and her husband with calmness, if not joy.

And then Miss Edith got pregnant and everything changed.

First off, she claimed she wasn't pregnant, that she was just gaining weight. I didn't see any harm in letting her deny it, knowing the facts would just naturally assert themselves eventually. But one morning before I even come out of my bedroom I heard an awful scream and ran out to the kitchen to behold Annie, the girl who helped with the heavy cleaning, seeming to be strangling Miss Edith. I knocked the girl aside and Miss Edith vomited all over both of us. "What on earth are you doing!" I shouted. "She was trying to kill herself!" shrieked Annie, which brought the whole household to the kitchen. Miss Edith vomited again and I realized from the smell that she had drunk lye water.

"Oh, good Lord!" I cried. "Run fetch the doctor somebody."

Edith pretty much had the lye out of her system before the doctor got there, but she had bad burns on her mouth and down her throat that hurt her something terrible. No harm come to the baby, which she had now admitted really existed, 'cause she had tried with that desperate measure to get rid of it. After that, Mrs. Coolidge said one of us had to be with Miss Edith all the time, to never let her out of our sight. Well, that was no easy task, what with Miss Edith's taste for solitude.

But it turned out not to be necessary, for every time Miss Edith had one of her conniption fits, she'd settle down afterwards and accept whatever it was she had been fighting. You knew that if you could just survive the storm, there'd be a period of greater peace afterwards, just like with our weather there on the coast.

And so Miss Edith plumped out and rosied up and began to embroider bibs and said she was going to name that baby Harry after her father Herrick. Her mother said she wasn't going to do no such thing 'cause it were going to be a girl and we'd call her Emily. I began to think motherhood was going to do the trick and finally make our headstrong Miss Edith grow up.

But come time for that baby to be born, Miss Edith was pacing her room, talking out of her head, saying she wasn't going to be there when it happened. Mama and Charles thought they could make her do something, but a body always has a choice, always, she says. And she just wasn't going to do it, that's all. She was going to find some way out of it.

Once again, the 24-hour watches commenced. I took most of them 'cause I was the only one that could settle Miss Edith down. I'd treat her like my big baby, pull her into my lap and rock her, sing her lullabies and rub her forehead. I could get her to sleep, make her stop pacing and swearing—where she heard such words I'll never know, but when she was in her tempers, she'd let out language I've only heard down on the docks.

Mr. Charles was keeping us posted on the weather, and by the fourteenth of August, we knew the hurricane was coming ashore at Galveston. Mr. Charles sent Faith and her nurse and all the rest of the household help north on the train, but the three of us stayed with Miss Edith. I'd watch her for two hours, then Mrs. Coolidge would take my place and let me catch a nap, that way we spelled each other round-the-clock. At one point I was so tired I couldn't go to sleep so I went up to the widow's walk on the third floor to look out at the weather.

Long heavy swells were coming in and already the seawall was sending geysers shooting skyward. The sky was streaked with long swirling arcs of clouds we call mare's tails, the outer bands of the hurricane, that in the northern hemisphere rotate in a counter-clockwise motion. All the next day we waited for something to happen, for Miss Edith to get down to business and start pushing out that baby, for the sky to let go and rain on us. All that night I took my turn sitting by the bedside, listening for the wind, listening for the crash of the surf to worsen, feeling the unbearable tension in the atmosphere as that terrible storm stalked us.

When it come my turn to sleep, I lay in my bed there behind the kitchen and listened with renewed concentration for the storm to commence, for Mrs. Coolidge to yell down the stairs to fetch the doctor. But in spite of myself, my tired eyes closed and I slept. In the early morning hours of August 15, I woke up to the smell of coffee. I got up, just as tired as when I laid down, and pulled on my clothes and went out to find Mrs. Coolidge boiling coffee in the pot. "No," she said briefly, in answer to my unspoken question.

"First babies," I said. I went to look out the back window, and again she anticipated my question. "Hasn't come ashore yet. You want to get out while the gettin's good?"

"No, ma'am. I'll stay. Miss Edith needs me."

"The last train's leaving at noon. I won't blame you a bit if you're on it."

It's funny how when you're scared you swear you'll never do something or other as long as you live, but then you have a long safe period and you sort of forget what the fear was like. It was that way with me and the storm that broke all my bones and near tore my hide off. I still had the scars and the limp to prove it had happened, and I still got uneasy when there was just a little old summer thunderstorm, and I had sworn I would never stay on the island if another big blow come up. But there I was, and it seemed more terrible to me by far to desert the family than it did to stay and face another storm.

104

"I'll stay," I said. And that was the end of it. I rustled us up some breakfast, and Mr. Charles come down and the three of us ate it at the enamel table in the kitchen, all of so worn out I probably looked as gray and out of focus to them as they looked to me. For her part, Miss Edith was sleeping to beat the band, refreshing herself for the next bout.

In 1900, the Storm to top all storms came ashore fast, afore people had a chance to escape, but the storm of 1915 took her own sweet time, seeming to take careful aim to do the most harm. All that day, all that night, we waited, both for the birth of Emily and for the monster hurricane to come. Miss Edith was completely out of the mood for histrionics by that night and was saving herself for the birth of that child. The contractions would start up good and strong, fall into a regular pattern, and Miss Edith would grunt and sweat and cry, then there'd be a lull and she'd fall asleep for a couple of hours. Then it'd all start over again.

Mrs. Coolidge, who had birthed nine babies, had seen every type of delivery, from those that just popped right out to those that took three days. But in every one of those other instances, the mother were looking forward to the birth and co-operating with all her heart. Miss Edith was resisting, like she always done, to the bitter end. Mrs. Coolidge, in a pet, slapped Edith in the face and shouted at her, "Start pushing, you monster! You're going to kill yourself and her!" I thought it was odd at the time that Mrs. Coolidge called the baby a "her" and later, when it turned out to be a girl, I thought to myself, she never considered for a moment that it wouldn't be a girl, that the baby wasn't her replacement here on God's earth. Eventually Miss Edith didn't have no choice but push. Nature just takes a hand and sees to it.

Both events began in earnest on the evening of the sixteenth. The rain began to hit the house in great furious swathes. Miss Edith began to grunt and grit her teeth, hold her breath and squeeze her eyes shut. Then she'd fall back exhausted and turn white again and we'd bathe her face and fan her. Mr. Charles went for the doctor but come back after an hour and said he'd only made it six blocks and had to leave the car and get back as best he could on foot. Power lines and trees littered the streets, the water was rising on P.

It was the only time I ever seen Mrs. Coolidge worried and scared. It wasn't for Edith's sake, nor was it because another big hurricane was breathing down our necks, catching her at home this time and not in Europe. No, it was for the sake of little Emily who was struggling to come into the world. Her mama was making a desperate effort to help her too. When it got down to the necessaries, I was proud of my girl. Of course, Miss Edith didn't have no choice by then. She'd been in labor three days, only the last three hours strong, but she was worn out, and Mrs. Coolidge was near about in tears for fear Edith wouldn't have the last bit of strength required of her. I looked at Mr. Charles, standing there helpless, excluded from this woman's work, and knowed what was going through his head, that he was fixing to be asked to make that terrible choice again between wife or baby. Maybe this time he would say, "Save my baby."

Just before midnight, with the howling fury of the hurricane threatening to take the roof off, with five feet of water downstairs, under nothing but the light of a coal oil lamp, Emily's little thatch of black hair appeared and we commenced to begging Miss Edith to work a little harder, one last time, push, baby, push! And Miss Edith sucked in her breath and gathered herself together and heaved with all her might and pushed that baby out of there. What blessed relief! How we all burst into joyful tears and rushed around wrapping that precious baby up and beating on Miss Edith in our joy and telling her she done good! Mr. Charles was so relieved he staggered to his knees and buried his face in the bedclothes at his wife's side.

It were a terrible hurricane, that one that finally come ashore on August 16, 1915, back before we gave names to the beasts, ever bit as bad as the brute force of the 1900 hurricane, and lasting twice as long. This time, though, we had our seawall, and the water only rose five or six feet inside homes along the wall and in downtown businesses. Everything was torn up from the wind, of course. But after pounding us for two days, the beast wore herself out and slunk away.

As usual, there were some mighty peculiar effects of the storm. The *Allison Doura*, a three-masted schooner, was pushed all the way from Mobile, Alabama and carried right over the seawall into Fort Crockett, where the soldiers scrambled aboard and rescued the crew. An interurban train from Houston, keeping to its regular schedule, made the mistake of heading over the causeway in spite of the raging fury of the storm. At the draw-bridge, the power went off and the passengers got out and crawled along the rails to the Causeway Inn at Virginia Point, which washed away during the night drowning sixteen people. The storm was so powerful she tossed fifteen-ton riprap granite blocks around like children's toys, and this time smashed our water main, not by destroying the concrete causeway the main ran under, but by washing away the earthen approaches to the causeway. We were left with a bridge you couldn't get to. Three hundred people—instead of the twelve to fourteen thousand in the earlier storm—died, mostly in outlying areas not protected by the seawall.

Sitting right on the beach behind the seawall was the new Galvez Hotel, just opened in 1911 by Isaac Kempner and some other old-name Galveston investors, including Mrs. Coolidge. The orchestra played all night so people could distract themselves dancing. To us three—now four—souls perched there in the house overlooking the Gulf, the storm seemed never to end and complicated the task of caring for a newborn and an exhausted young mother. The downstairs was so deep in water Mr. Charles was the only one tall enough to get through it and find us something to eat.

Baby Emily had it made in the nourishment department, her own personal source being right there. And right at first Miss Edith was too worn out to protest, but as she slowly got her strength back, she cried and carried on so when we tried to get her to let Emily nurse that we ended up feeding the poor baby cow's milk from a bottle, which didn't agree with her, until we found a girl with a babe of her own willing to let Emily suckle her.

It took ten days to get the water back on and the electricity restored. Mr. Charles, as soon as he could, went downtown to see what damage the offices and warehouses had sustained. The water had risen in the Strand five or six feet, but the Coolidge Cotton Company had its offices upstairs on the second floor and only the reception area was affected. The jetties and wharves stood.

107

It was well into September by the time ships that had been blown miles onto dry land were dug out and refloated, before trains began running again. The city hauled off more than a thousand wagon loads of debris. Salt water ruined all the pretty landscaping that had flourished on the island after the raising, including everything in our yard. But we took our losses in stride, considering it a reasonable price, I suppose, to go on living in our island paradise. If our seawall hadn't held, you wouldn't have found anybody willing to put a dime back into rebuilding Galveston.

~~~~~

EDITH COOLIDGE PICKERING

There was never any question whose child she was: She belonged to Charles and Mama, the real couple, who unfortunately had to use me, a most awkward and unmanageable tool, to achieve their ends. Oh, such a pair! They were united in their single-minded pursuit of money, neither one of them for the money itself but because business was the venue in which they applied themselves and money its natural by-product. Neither of them cared a fig for the things money would buy, although both had a taste for powerful automobiles and always went down and bought the new models as they arrived. Nor did they care for entertaining, except for the business that can be accomplished over a dinner table or standing around with a cocktail in one's hand. Neither of them played golf, nor read books, nor took vacations, nor went to plays, nor had any appreciation of music or art. They were a pair of automatons that got wound up back in 1900 and were still running. If you asked them what they cared about, they'd say, "The future."

And somehow the future was embodied in Emily, their daughter, the child they had through me but was really theirs, who came into the world in a manner befitting a woman of Mama's awesome power. What a fitting tribute for Nature to pay

108

the child of their unholy union! I was wounded and sullen after the birth. I didn't want to see that child, didn't want her gnawing at me with her little gums. My breasts gushed hot and unpleasant every time they brought her near me, but I screamed when they tried to make me nurse her. Mama couldn't throw me out now! I had bought my freedom. She could threaten all she liked, but I had finally gained the upper hand.

Nevertheless, I didn't feel like getting out of bed for a long time. Meg would coax me into the bathtub and I would look down at my poochy flaccid belly, scarred all over, the lesions running down my thighs as far as my knees, and I'd break down and sob. "Ruined," I'd say. And Meg would try to soothe me by saying those scars were precious to the sight of the man who loved me. I would get sick just thinking about him seeing my body, ever having to endure him touching me again.

Charlotte came to see me when I got better. She cooed over Emily like they all did and brought a little silver loving cup with her name and birthday engraved on it. Meg had fixed my hair and helped me into a pretty bed jacket. It didn't matter—I looked blotchy and ugly anyway, and I knew that Charlotte would never look at me like she used to. She confided that she was trying to get pregnant again, but was having trouble, and I just stared at her like she was off her head.

"Meg says your spirits are poorly, honey. I know you feel blue when it's all finally over with, but just think about little Emily. Meg says they're having to feed her with a bottle. You got all that good milk going to waste."

"It hurts."

"I know, hon, but you get toughened up after awhile. I got to where I kinda liked it. If I had any milk left, I'd nurse little Emily for you. They say she won't have any immunity if you don't."

I waved my hand as if to make the subject go away. "Emily's got more parents than any child you know. She'll be well taken care of. They don't need me any more for anything. That's why I'm free."

"Listen to you! Why do you make things so hard on yourself, darlin'?" I didn't answer, and Charlotte sighed. "I have to run now. The workers are at my house cutting up a tree that fell against that little side porch. Everything's such a mess! I hate everything getting torn up like this. Walter says we ought to move to Houston, but all those cousins of his would get everything and he'd never see a cent if we did. You have to be there, on the spot, show up every day and represent yourself, I tell him."

"Would you have married him if Mama had given me my money and let me do anything I liked with it?"

Charlotte sighed impatiently. "Of course I would! We're girls, you ninny. I couldn't stand to be talked about and pointed out like those horrid old women who live together and flaunt it, Dovie and Opal. Ugh!"

"It didn't mean anything to you?"

"I am very fond of you! Of course it meant something. It was girlish and sweet, but I don't want to think about it any more. Edith, honey, you're my friend and I care about you, so listen to me! Get out of this bed before it grows to your backside! Get out and do things, see people. People are all the time asking me if I've seen you. I know it seems like these feelings will last forever, but girls get like that after having a baby."

"Did you?"

"Well, no, not me, but some girls I've heard about do. And it takes them awhile to snap out of it, but you gotta try. Tell you what," she said in a perky voice, "you get out of this bed and I'll come back next week and take you for a ride in my new car. We'll go down on the beach just like the old times and I'll let you draw me. Okay, sweetie?"

"Char, did Mama make you come?"

Her face turned pink. "No, of course not, silly. She told me you were ailing and I thought a visit from me might cheer you up." She laughed and stood up and pulled on her little white crocheted half-handers. "Did it?"

"No."

"I didn't think so. All right, but you listen to me, Edith Pickering. I'm gonna come get you next week, so you be ready. We're going to take that spin. 'Bye now."

In spite of myself, her visit did cheer me. The prospect of being alone with Charlotte performed its old magic. The thought of getting out of the house and seeing the beach again sounded pleasant. Slowly I began to pull myself out of the black hole into which I had fallen.

Chapter Six

FAITH KOHL COOLIDGE

January 6, 1919

Teddy Roosevelt died today. We always said Papa looked like him, with his big waxed moustache and thin hair on top. Papa loved for us to say it because Mr. Roosevelt was a particular hero of his and if, Papa always said, he had been younger and not had so many children, he would've joined up to fight with him in Cuba.

It is always good to begin the new year with praise and thanksgiving for the many blessings God has bestowed upon us. I cannot think of the things I've to be grateful for without first naming my dear Charles, for how would I get on without him?—me, untutored in the things boys are taught, raised to look after a family and live out my life on a small domestic stage. Without Charles' instant grasp of numbers, without his gentle and courteous way of explaining them to me, I would never be able to make an intelligent decision about things.

Yes, we make a wonderful team, my son-in-law and I. I only regret that he must put up with my obstinate and difficult daughter. She does as she pleases these days, which is never to the benefit of anyone but herself, nor takes the slightest responsibility for the home, leaving it all for Meg to do. When Emily was a baby, she pushed her off on a wet-nurse so that Emily, like Faith, looks to Meg for permission to do something, a decision on what to wear. Faith is good with her little sister, taking responsibility for her like a little mother. Emily is bereft when Faith leaves for school.

I am too busy to remedy these matters and don't think that I could anyway, not if I had all the time in the world. Something is wrong with Edith and Lord knows I've tried: discipline and harshness, understanding and love. But the girl evades us all by seeming to go off to her own little world. No argument has the slightest effect on her, not for the children's sake, her husband's, even her own sorry self. I regret having raised such a thankless girl and sorry I got Charles to marry her. At least he's a grown man and can get away from her most of the time and make a satisfying life for himself with his work. But the girls, being just babes, don't have that luxury. They need something more than a nurse and a housekeeper. Emily is growing up with no clear understanding of who she belongs to. Poor Charles is awkward with children, stands around helpless unless there's action to be taken. I have that masculine cast of mind too, feel that I shouldn't be called upon to do it all, earn the bread, keep a roof over their heads, and wipe their noses too.

It never improves my spirits to indulge myself on the subject of Edith! I wear myself out and accomplish nothing wallowing around in this bitterness, allowing myself to imagine what life would have been like had it been Mary or dear Fern I took with me on that trip! By now Fern and young Joe O'Malley would have given me a houseful of grandchildren. Instead, Joe married Rema Prince, added four O'Malleys to the clan, and has a thriving law practice going with George Bradley. I sent the boys a little work this week to see how they handle it. I wouldn't be adverse to moving my affairs to a young energetic firm like O'Malley, Bradley. T'would be their making.

~~~~~

MEG GALLOWAY

Here I am stuck with the storm bulletins again. We were afraid that Emily's fourth birthday would be spoiled by approaching bad weather. The girl *would* be born right in the middle of hurricane season, so it shouldn't surprise us the Storm Goddess threatened to join the party.

It turned out that little Emily's party was not spoiled by the storm (only by some foolishness of her mother's.) The storm came later, and afterwards, just like we always do, we tarted things up with paint and powder, pretended that nothing had changed. People had their theories about why the storms were coming so regular. A Pentecostal preacher was quoted in the paper as saying these were the very storms mentioned in the Bible as a sign that the world was coming to an end. And the priest, not wanting to add any luster to the message of the fire-and-brimstoner, said if that was so why hadn't the world ended in the last century when Galveston had eleven hurricanes? But I guess he didn't want to miss out on the opportunity to scare folks into righteousness, for he added that it never hurt to pay attention to signs and portents.

Old-timers said it was because we'd built the seawall in the first place, that we were tempting her, like. Others said there was a scientific explanation for it, that the seawall was so big (they were talking of extending it on out to 61st Street) that it created a disturbance in the magnetic field that attracted bad weather our way. I went along with Dad's theory that storms just naturally hit ever ten years or thereabouts and our island was stretched out there in the big middle of the long curving Texas coastline and got most of it. I'm real practical in that respect. I go to church and pray every day, but I don't put no stock in mysteries and the supernatural.

But sometimes I'm tempted to feel that the house of Coolidge lived under some kind of cloud. We just couldn't seem to go along for very long without tragedy striking from out of the blue.

It was the fall after Emily turned four and we'd cleaned up after that season's hurricane. There were a number of adults in the house, a gardener, cook, housemaid, all charged with looking after the little ones, but we were in a period of welcome tranquility and not on our guard so much, what with Miss Edith behaving herself for weeks on end, at that moment happily planning some kind of get-together with her friend Charlotte Miller.

113

It was Sunday and I'd been to church and gone over to Dad's afterwards to fix him a bite to eat. We'd just got set down when the phone rang and a scared young housemaid told me I better get home quick. She didn't want to tell me over the phone what it was for fear I'd have a wreck on the way home, which was an aggravation, 'cause then I had to drive all the way across town with my heart stuck up against my throat thinking something had happened to Emily. Good Lord, if anything happened to that baby, there'd just be no reason to go on, I thought. Mrs. Coolidge would give up. And if she give up, everybody else would too.

Dr. Brown's car was sitting in front of our house, in his haste, the door left open and some papers blowing out. Neighbors had come out of their houses and were standing around in our yard looking up at the windows. As soon as I stepped out of my car, I heard a high keening wail that I knew was Edith's. Mr. Charles' car pulled up right behind mine and we both pushed through the crowd to get inside and find out what had happened. On the enamel table in the kitchen there was a little body covered by a white bedsheet, a bright red spot of blood soaked through and spreading out on the sheet. Mr. Charles and I stood there gaping at that sight in horror, then I noticed the little shoes dangling out the end—Faith's. The little figure was too long to be Emily. It was Faith, and she was dead or they wouldn't of covered her face up. I turned to Mr. Charles to offer him my arms to weep in, but he just sort of shuffled his feet and bobbed his adam's apple up and down and turned and walked out of the room, everybody falling back to let him pass.

A new kitchen girl, Ida, was standing there with her apron to her nose and I pulled her aside and asked her what happened.

"The girls were upstairs with Miss Edith," she said. "We thought she was looking out for 'em. First time I knowed they were out on that catwalk was when a dark shadow come down past the window there where I was working. She never screamed nor nothing, ma'am. I thought it was a bird, but I said something to Cook and she stepped to the door to see what it was, 'cause she seen the shadow too, said the room grew dark for just an instant like the Angel of Death had passed over the house, and sure enough it had, Miss."

I followed Mr. Charles upstairs to his wife, who was quiet now, 'cause the doctor had given her a shot to put her to sleep, but even in sleep she moaned. I looked around for Emily and when I didn't see her, I run upstairs real quick to see if she was still up there on that third floor balcony. There wasn't no one up there. I looked over the rail to see where Faith had fallen. Mrs. Coolidge had several times said we ought to bring the rail up higher so a child couldn't climb over, but I could see how in a spirit of adventure a child might clamber out on the roof tiles. Below me on the paving stones outside the kitchen areaway was a small dark circle of blood. Mrs. Coolidge wasn't home yet. I thought, she mustn't see that, and hurried back downstairs to get a bucket and wash it off.

I was stooped over my labor, vigorously scrubbing the stones when I looked up and saw Mrs. Coolidge standing at the kitchen window. I set my bucket aside and wiped my hands on the hem of my good Sunday dress and hurried in to be with her.

"Where's Emily?" she said, her voice sounding weak and low.

"She's not up there," I said. "I closed and locked that door."

"Look for her, please." She turned and went upstairs.

I knew all Emily's little hiding places. When her mother was cross with her or people had left her alone for too long, she'd take her doll and hide in the back of her mama's closet or in the big closet under the stairwell and amuse herself until we come looking for her. She was the bravest little thing about the dark, seemed to find solace in it. I found her under the stairs, clutching her doll, tears dried on her face. She had that look that said she knew she had been bad.

"Come to Nana, darlin'," I said. "We'll go to my room and read a story, all right?"

But then I remembered that we'd have to go through the kitchen to get to my room, so I took her out of the house through the front door. The neighbors had heard what had happened by then and there was a chorus of sympathy for the little girl that was left. My head felt stuffed with tears wanting to get out, but I dared not break down in front of Emily.

"Were you girls playing on the stairs?" I said.

115

"Uhhuh."

"And you went in your mama's studio like you weren't supposed to?" She nodded solemnly. "What kind of game were you and Faith playing, Emily?"

"Hide and seek. I couldn't find Faith though, Nana. She went over the rail and I couldn't find her."

"Did you . . . see her go over the rail?"

Emily shook her head no. "But I know that's where she went."

"What did you do?"

"I went to tell Mama, but she was talking on the phone and told me not to bother her, so I went and sat on the stairs to wait for Faith to come back, only she didn't come back and I got scared."

"Why did you go into Mommy's paint room, Emily? You know you're not supposed to go there."

"Faith said Mommy didn't care what we did." Emily suddenly threw her arms around my neck. "I was waiting for you, Nana."

"Poor little thing," I murmured, unable to hold back the tears. "All alone now and probably always will be."

~~~~~

EDITH COOLIDGE PICKERING

And so the darkness closed in on me again. I took to my bed and hoped that this time death would not pass me by. What was the use? Every time I fought the darkness and gained a little, the darkness caught up with me and settled the score with a vengeance. Faith had been told a dozen times not to go near my studio, but the minute I turned my back she took Emily up there. I remember how Mary and I used to play out on Papa's verandah, we called it, a big wide porch up on the third floor so he could look out at an unobstructed view of the Gulf. Papa was a businessman, but he loved the sea and often mentioned how he wished he'd gone to sea. And Mama would scold him and say that he wished no such thing, boats always made him ill. Papa had a big black moustache that he waxed to keep out of his mouth, and when he grinned, he looked like Teddy Roosevelt.

I know that Mama and Charles blame me. I blame myself. Yet how could I have kept Faith from climbing out on that roof? Children are adventurous and the places you forbid them access have the greatest attraction. I remember once my brother Ned jumping from the roof into a big pile of brush and tree trimmings the gardener had stacked right under that porch and all of us wanted to follow him and do the same thing, but Fern wouldn't let us, and we ran downstairs to see if Ned had hurt himself. He was limping a little because he'd sprained his ankle, but he pretended like it didn't hurt a bit. So how come one child got off with a swollen ankle and the other smashed her little skull in? For one thing, Mama had that big patio out there laid with stone, whereas it used to be full of coarse grass which died every time seawater came in. Mama had just replanted everything after the storm. The new trees and bushes were just switches. By the time they get big enough to afford any shade, another storm'll come along and knock 'em down again. Why does she bother? Why do any of us bother?

When the darkness closes in, my mind goes on and on like this, conjuring up images of death and destruction. After Faith's accident, I lay stunned for weeks, unable to even get out of bed to use the toilet. I had just gotten back with Charlotte, who after the birth of her second child realized a few things about her situation. One, although having another baby meant Walter had to move them into a bigger house, he was barely making ends meet— couldn't, for instance, get a housekeeper like Charlotte wanted—she had to make do with a daymaid and take care of both children day and night. All of which was beginning to sink in on her that she'd be dead and buried by the time that skinflint uncle of Walter's let go of any money. She fretted about how impatient she'd been as a girl and how she wished she'd held out longer. If she had, she might've caught herself a Moody or a Kempner or a Sealy. Instead she wound up with a Nobody. I could not entirely mourn the return of Charlotte's senses, because when she got realistic, she realized how important I was to her.

Mama has turned into some sort of living legend. Everywhere I go people tell stories about her, the sharp deals she makes, how she's a "twentieth century woman," always keeping up with the times, moving into insurance, banking, hotels at the right time, shipping sulphur now in addition to cotton and grain. But one thing she never changes, one thing she seems almost superstitious about, is the name Papa gave the company back when the only thing the Coolidge Cotton Company did was export cotton. I know why she keeps the name: Mama and the Coolidge Cotton Company are the only Coolidges left in the world.

Charlotte and I were never both down at the same time, but were like a seesaw, one up, the other down, taking turns rallying one another. When I felt down, I just gave in to it, but Charlotte didn't like to admit when she was depressed because she felt like it said something about her character (her mama was institutionalized by then.) After the birth of Aaron, it was her turn to be down and I tried to cheer her up, suggesting we throw a big party at The Galvez as soon as she got her figure back. The date we had talked about, I discovered when I got home and looked at my calendar, was Thanksgiving weekend and that's what I was doing the moment Faith fell, calling Charlotte to tell her we couldn't possibly have a dinner dance that weekend because everybody would be gone, or else they'd all be home but with a houseful of company.

I later clearly recalled seeing the girls playing right outside my bedroom door on the stairs. They had a little game they always liked to play with animal crackers. Faith would hide them randomly up and down the balusters and Emily would crawl up and down looking for them, eating them as she found them. When I didn't see them any more, I thought they'd disappeared below stairs, not up. How could I have known they would go up? They were forbidden to go up to the third floor because that's where the help had their sleeping quarters.

Nor were they allowed to go in my studio, which Mama had resisted me having for years, but I finally got. Had it fixed up just the way I liked, too, with those dark lugubrious curtains

118

pulled off the windows to let in the southern light, the wide stretch of blue waters sparkling off the ceiling, privacy and quiet up there under the eaves. What happened was a terrible, a stupid, a senseless accident. *But it wasn't my fault.*

Charles and Mama were so angry with me they wouldn't look at me. If Meg Galloway had been in charge when this happened, they would've said poor Meg, it happened while she had her back turned, kids will be kids. But it happened while I was supposed to be watching them and now they have an excuse to hate me forever.

When Dr. Brown comes and jabs that needle in me, I can turn off my brain and float on the blackness and it is my friend.

~~~~~

EMILY PICKERING DOUGLAS

I don't really remember the day my sister fell. I think that I remember Faith, though. A child playing on the stairs with me. A game we used to play with animal crackers. Or maybe Meg told me those things to keep Faith's memory alive for me. I do recall that always, way back to my earliest memory, my mama lay in her room with a black scarf over her eyes and I had to be quiet on the landing or she would holler out at me to hush up, her head was splitting. I remember that sometimes she screamed and I thought Daddy was hurting her and I would run into her bedroom and try to defend her. And Nana would take me down to her room and let me spend the night with her instead of in my nursery, which was lonely and I was afraid of.

Nana was my own name for Meg Galloway, who was like a mother to me. I liked it downstairs with Nana next to the kitchen. Nana would let me cuddle up to her and would sing me Scottish songs her mama used to sing to her, and sometimes she cried for her mama and I would pat her cheeks and tell her she could be my little girl for awhile, and I would sing the same

119

songs to her. And when Mrs. Frenche made pies, Nana would let me sit on a tall stool and cut out the pie crust that was left over and make cinnamon men with raisin eyes that got puffy in the oven.

Grandmama and Papa were gone all the time because they had to run the Coolidge Cotton Company. There was a hole in my quilt and I pulled cotton out of it and my nurse got on to me about it. When I was little I thought Grandmama and Papa had something to do with quilts.

I wanted a little sister or a brother more than anything in the world. I learned in catechism that you always got what you prayed for, so every night when I said my prayers, I asked for a brother or sister. Nana told me it was best if I quit praying for that 'cause there were some things God needed help with from down below. I didn't understand, because Nana said that babies came from God and that they were found under the covers of the Mommy's bed. Mrs. Frenche said babies came in a basket with a pink or blue blanket, depending on if it was a girl or boy. Mr. Gomez said babies come out of their mommy's tummy and I ran into the house to enlighten Nana and she frowned and said she'd have a talk with Mr. Gomez.

When I was eight, Mama took me to be enrolled at the Ursuline Academy, a Catholic girls' school. My great grand-father's name was on a carved stone, but my friends didn't know he was kin to me because his name was Kohl. Mama says that since we're all girls, Grandmama, her, and me, we always have to give up our identity when we get married, that someday I won't be a Pickering. Her friend Mrs. Miller got a divorce (she's not Catholic) but she was still a Miller afterwards. She and my momma were very good friends and always wanted to do every-thing together. Mama had lots of secrets and said I had to help her keep them, that if I didn't, she might get sick and die.

I would never tell on Mama, not in a hundred million years. I would stand watch at the front window of her bedroom when she was talking on the phone, keeping a lookout for Papa's car or Grandmama's. If I saw them—which I never did—I was to tell Mama so she could get off the phone. Mama was sad sometimes and cried and wouldn't come out of her room. I would fetch a wet rag for her face and rub her feet. Sometimes she hurt so bad the doctor had to come and give her a shot. Grandmama said there was nothing wrong with her, but Mama said Grandmama was just mean and never loved her like she did my Aunt Fern, who died in the 1900 hurricane. She said that Grandmama and Papa never got over the hurricane and that's why they hate her. But I didn't hate her. I loved Mama. She was so pretty when she got all fixed up to go to a party. I liked her best when she was getting ready to go see Mrs. Miller, because she was always at her most festive.

~~~~~

When I was eleven, my best friends were Ruth Myers and India Kenneally. The three of us formed the Mata Hari Girls Spy Club to find out what the nuns and our parents didn't want us to know, for it was clear there was a conspiracy afoot to keep us ignorant. Sister Rosario, in charge of hygiene and sports, set an inspiring example of how a young lady might live in the physical world but avoid all reference to her physical self. In fact, the word "body" was slightly shameful and not to be used except in private. Our bodies didn't belong to us, but were merely temporary receptacles for our souls. But that didn't mean we were allowed to abuse our bodies, which was somehow different than the saints mortifying their flesh to attain purity. Ruth brought many a hygiene class to an abrupt end by trying to get Sister Rosario to elaborate on this abuse issue so we could be sure to avoid abusing our bodies by accident, but Sister Rosario would never bite.

The Mata Haris were supposed to find out one Fact of Life to share at each meeting, but I hardly ever made my quota since I lived in a house full of elderly celibates and could not be expected to have access to much information. Mine were the only parents I knew who slept in separate bedrooms. Nevertheless, I spied on them when I could.

When Mama realized that I had begun to pay attention to her side of telephone conversations, she banished me from her room. But I found a way around this. Sometimes she would yell down the stairs that she was expecting a call and for nobody to

121

answer the phone when it rang. I would pick it up at the exact moment she did and sometimes be rewarded by getting to hear both sides of the conversation. I never learned anything, though, because her caller was nearly always Mrs. Miller and the only things they talked about was getting out of their houses to meet each other, what they were going to wear, where they would go and who they might see there.

Ruth Meyers, a year older than India and me, was full of worldly information. She was the only girl I knew who had actually seen her parents doing it, although they were under the cover at the time and all Ruth could tell us about it was that her father had been on top and that he had sounded like a pig, while her mother had lain silent. I was certain my mother would never let my father lie on top of her and sound like a pig, but the fact that I was born, Ruth said, proved they did this. Ruth conjectured that my father sneaked in to see Mama late at night after I was asleep, and I tried to prove this by checking the extra pillow every morning in Mama's bed to see if it had been slept on. The pillow was always smooth.

Mama didn't even like Papa to touch her. Once he came into the dining room and brushed against her shoulder accidentally while taking his place at the table. She recoiled as if something loathsome had touched her, and Grandmama flung her water glass against the wall and told her to go to her room if she couldn't act like a human being. Papa said after she burst into tears and left the room, "That's all right, Faith. I'm used to that."

We sat for a picture once when I was a baby. I'm sitting on Mama's lap and Faith is standing in front of Papa, who has his arm around Mama's waist. I'm sure we never sat like that in real life.

Once, over at India Kenneally's house, we shared a cigarette that Ruth had snitched from her mama's purse and drank sherry from a cut-glass decanter. It was vile stuff, tasted like the worst medicine in the world, and made my head swim. India made us swear our super-secret vow of silence and then she fetched from its hiding place her mother's pessary, which we passed around to look at. We didn't know how the thing worked or what it did, but we knew it had something to do with sex.

At the same time that the nuns collaborated with our parents to keep us ignorant, they were under the imperative to socialize us so that we could converse with boys without stammering and dance with them without killing them. Therefore, our school had dances with the boys from Kirwin to give us practice at these skills. Everybody hated those dances, especially the boys, who would have to be bodily shoved at us, giggling and waiting for them across the room. I was always one of the last ones asked because I was small for my age and not very pretty. Spencer O'Malley, who had wonderful manners, always danced with me and any other girls who were left stranded. He was going to be a priest and was already practicing how to be nice to everyone, even the social lepers.

I loved Spencer but didn't tell anyone, not even my fellow girl spies. It was too painful and wonderful a secret. Spencer had lovely brown skin and whitey blond hair and eyelashes. I knew that he only asked me to dance because he was nice, but that didn't stop me making up stories about him in my head. The stories were always the same, with slight variations. Spencer would decide he couldn't become a priest because he was in love with me. We would get married and sleep in the same bed. I never imagined us doing it, which I secretly thought was horrible, but we would hold hands and kiss, stare into each other's eyes like Mary Pickford and Douglas Fairbanks did. And I would be beautiful.

When I was twelve, Mama wanted to take me to Europe, which was a tradition that Grandmama had started, but didn't want Mama to continue. They had a terrible fight about it. This time, instead of Grandmama winning like she always did, and Mama locking herself in her room for days on end, Mama appealed to Papa and he said he didn't see why Mama couldn't go to Europe if she wanted. And why not take me? I was old enough now to look after myself. I saw the look they exchanged. Papa rarely opposed Grandmama. "All right," she said quietly, "but only if Meg goes too." Mama and I both begged Meg to say yes, but she got so upset she came down with one of *her* headaches and had to stay in her room all day. That night everybody was silent and angry around the dinner table.

"Well, it's clear you must have your way," said Grandmama.

"I won't require Meg to do this if she doesn't want to. You can go, but not in August or September. Wait until spring, June, I think." I knew that Grandmama was thinking about the weather. So we had to wait six whole months to take our trip. Mama arranged for me to miss the last few weeks of school since the trip was supposed to be educational. We planned to visit picture galleries, hear fine symphonies, and see cities and buildings that were in my history book.

That whole time waiting for our trip, Mama was in a fine mood, excited and happy as she made plans, wrote off for tickets, booked excursions and sight-seeing trips, bought me new clothes and a new trunk to pack them in. One day we were downtown shopping when she spotted a darling little blue hat decorated with peafowl feathers and she rushed into the store to buy it.

"Don't tell anyone," she said. "This hat is a present for a friend." I knew which friend.

Papa and Meg came to the wharf to see us off. Grandmama claimed she was too busy and had said goodbye to me the night before and prayed over me. I could tell that Mama was glad Grandmama had not come and that she was impatient with Papa for being there. She said she hated long goodbyes and didn't want them coming on board, so Papa and Meg stayed on the wharf while we stood at the rail waiting for the ship to get underway. Mama fidgeted and fussed, asked several passing crewmen how long it would be, but finally they pulled in the gangway and the *Emma Lewis* slowly moved away from the wharf. Meg cried and waved her handkerchief, mouthed the words "I'm sorry!"— she meant for not going with me, and Papa looked more solemn than usual.

But Mama was ecstatic! She had finally won some kind of victory over Grandmama. Straight away I found out what it was. As soon as the faces on shore were too small to recognize, Charlotte Miller silently came up and joined us at the rail. I immediately noticed that she was wearing the little hat with peafowl feathers. Mother turned to her and yelped, then the two women hugged each other and thumped each other on the back as if they had pulled off a coup. Listening to them, I began to understand that they had planned all along to take this trip

124

together. I wondered what Mama would've done had Meg agreed to go with us. Probably told her she couldn't and to not tell Grandmama.

In many ways, that week at sea was the best time I ever had with Mama. She laughed a lot and hugged and kissed Mrs. Miller and me in her happiness. I had never seen anyone sleep with Mama before, but Mrs. Miller slept with her, Mama said because it was so lonesome for Charlotte all by herself. I was tempted to be jealous of Mrs. Miller because Mama was so affectionate with her. (She found my own touch vaguely irritating. "Don't touch, darling," she would say. "It's too warm.") But on that trip she was generous with her caresses.

Mrs. Miller had two sons, one older, one younger than me, but they lived with their father. I was very curious about her, about her being divorced, about her boys living with their father, but I was not allowed to ask questions. As a girl spy, however, I had my ways. One of which was to read Mama's journal, which is how I learned that she and Mrs. Miller had been planning that trip for nearly a year and that Mama was paying for it.

Reading Mama's journal every night was like having listened to a foreign language all day and only having access to a phrase book afterwards to see what people had been saying to you. Each night when I slipped into the bathroom to read Mama's journal (whose clasp any girl spy could easily defeat with a hairpin), hers and Mrs. Miller's behavior would become clear to me. For the most part.

What I didn't understand was why Grandmama detested Mrs. Miller so much that she wasn't allowed in our home. Meg said it was because Mrs. Miller had divorced her husband and was a shameless little social climber. But we knew other people who weren't Catholic and got divorced. Mama claimed that Grandmama hated her friends because she wanted to make her life a misery. Naturally I was taken into their confidence and promised I would die before I told on them.

In London we met some people that Mama knew, and she and Charlotte seemed very glad to run across them in the lobby of our hotel, but I later read in Mama's journal that she wasn't happy at all about crossing the ocean and running into someone she knew from back home. Mr. Kelly was quite gallant and

125

wanted to include us in their party, which caused ill feelings because Mama didn't want to and Mrs. Miller did. Mama had been so sunny and cheerful while we were at sea, but all that changed very suddenly in London. She and Mrs. Miller quarreled about it and slept in different beds that night.

The next day Mama sent me off to the Albert and Victoria Museum on my own. I was quite proud of myself for finding my way across the city, spending the morning at the museum, having lunch on my own, then finding my way back to the hotel. I had never done anything half so adventurous before. Meg would never have stood for me riding in cabs by myself! But instead of congratulating me for my independence, Mama handed me more English money and told me to go downstairs and have my dinner. I saw that she and Mrs. Miller were locked in a tense discussion.

It was too early for dinner, so I dawdled in the lobby, looked in shop windows, talked to an English girl whose father worked at the hotel, and in that way passed the time until the dinner hour. It felt very strange to sit all alone at a starchy white tablecloth with grownup diners all around me looking at me curiously, wondering how I happened to be on my own. I tried to make the meal last a long time. Eventually I was stuffed and all the dishes had been taken away. I counted out the correct money for my meal and went out to the lobby, where, to my surprise, I saw Mrs. Miller with all her luggage gathered around her feet, waiting for the doorman to get her a cab. She saw me, but turned the other way like she didn't want to speak to me. I was afraid to go up to our room because I knew that Mama would be in a bad mood over Mrs. Miller leaving. At home during Mama's long bouts of illness, I had Meg to keep me from being lonesome, but I had no one here in England and I was afraid of having to look after Mama without a grownup around.

I found Mama weeping hysterically. I could hear her before I even got the door open. I didn't know what to do. Meg always called the doctor, but I wasn't sure I should do that in a foreign city. I crept to her side and whispered "Mama?" and she stopped crying for a minute and stared at me with tragic red wet eyes. "She's gone!" she cried, and opened her mouth and began wailing again. "Please don't, Mama," I begged. But she didn't seem to hear me. I got a wet rag and brought it to her, got in bed with her and patted her while she cried and cried. Gradually she cried herself out and got calm enough to fall asleep. I was afraid to move for fear she would wake up and start crying again. Finally I fell asleep too, my arm in a cramped position that woke me later with pins and needles.

We were in the hotel for six days. I was afraid to tell anyone that Mama was sick, so I would bring her food, which she generally wouldn't eat, and I kept asking the maid not to clean our room. On the third day the concierge came to the room and said our reservation was up, did we wish to extend? I said yes, of course, like I knew what I was talking about. After he was gone, Mama roused herself and got up and bathed her face, which was swollen and shiny. Then she went back to bed for another three days.

When she finally got up, Mama acted as if she had been gone. She asked me questions about which day it was and what I had been doing. I pretended that I hadn't been the least bit afraid, but the truth was that I was extremely relieved when Mama decided to come back to me, relieved that an adult was in charge again.

We had missed a whole week of our itinerary, but we made up for it by skipping Paris. Her old self again, Mama pressed ahead to cross the Alps and get to Italy. I knew that she hoped to catch up with Mrs. Miller in Venice, assuming that Mrs. Miller had kept to the schedule.

When we checked into our hotel in Venice, Mama asked the desk clerk if Mrs. Charlotte Miller had checked in ahead of her, that they had come in separate conveyances. He looked in his book but said there didn't appear to be a Mrs. Miller staying at the hotel. Mama was very irritated and made him check again. He did so and said in English, "Sorry, Madame. Another time, then?" Mama thought for a moment and said. "Is there a Mr. Roy Kelly staying here?" "Oh, yes," was the immediate reply. "Mr. and Mrs. Kelly stay in the bridal suite. May I send up your compliments, Madame?"

I waited for the outburst, but Mama somehow kept her calm all the way to our room. "It's someone else," she said. "She wouldn't do this to me. She wouldn't. She wouldn't." Suddenly she reached over and grabbed me by the shoulders. "Go find out which room he's in, Mr. Roy Kelly. Go there and knock on the door. See if Charlotte answers. Don't say anything, but come back to me and tell me at once."

"All right, Mama," I said. I went back down in the cage-like lift and approached the desk. The honeymoon suite was on the second floor. I took the stairs, practicing what I would say when I got there. I knocked politely and waited. Mr. Kelly answered the door wearing a maroon silk dressing gown.

"Well, hello, little girl," he said to me in a jovial voice. "Where's your mama?"

"Emily!" said Mrs. Miller, suddenly appearing beside him. "Excuse us, Roy, I'll only be a minute." Mrs. Miller hurried me along the corridor until we came to a corner and were out of sight of Mr. Kelly. "Where is she? Is she terribly upset?"

"She sent me to see if you were with Mr. Kelly."

Mrs. Miller had on a robe too, pink quilted satin that I had seen her wear a lot in our stateroom on the boat. She had her arms crossed and a thoughtful frown on her face. "Tell you what, Emily, it'll go a lot better for you if you tell her you didn't see me. Tell her Mr. Kelly got married and his wife's name is Elizabeth, okay? It's not really lying, sweetie, it's saving your own skin." She sighed impatiently. "Look, I can't be responsible for her. She's too much for anyone! I'm not going to let guilt or gratitude dictate my behavior. Go, Emily! Go back to her. Tell her you didn't see me."

She turned and left. I peeped around the corner and saw that Mr. Kelly was still standing in front of their room waiting for her. As she approached him, he chuckled and held out his arms to her. They embraced and went into the room and shut the door.

I didn't dare take so much time that Mama grew impatient with me and came to find out where I was. Would she believe me if I told her Charlotte Miller's lie? Would we run into the happy couple in the lobby or dining room? How could I get Mama safely back home where Grandmama and Meg could look after us?

~~~~~

EDITH COOLIDGE PICKERING

It was just as well that Emily came down sick our first day in Venice. I had lost all taste for travel after Charlotte's desertion and only wanted to get back home to Galveston, back to my room where I could fall apart and nobody would care. Emily seemed much improved a mere twenty-four hours later, and I was quite relieved, for ever since losing Faith, I've been terrified some tragedy might befall Emily while she's in my care. I knew that was why Mama didn't want to let her go with me, that the tension I felt between Mama and Charles was her desire to continue punishing me for what happened to Faith and his willingness to give me the benefit of the doubt, which Mama is never willing to do.

Some will surely say that I got what was coming to me, that I let Charlotte take advantage of me. But the poor girl lost everything in her divorce and had forgotten how cruel and unforgiving people can be. Only I understood. Walter had lied to her about his prospects. He was never going to have money and she saw herself turning into a domestic drudge. I would give anything if I had the nerve to get a divorce like she did. But Charlotte can take a chance like that, she is capable of earning a living. Mama kept me from learning anything that would allow me the slightest independence.

Charlotte is different from me in another way too. She tolerates my love for her, it amuses her, she uses it when she wants something, but it means nothing to her. I know that now. I saw how she flirted with Roy Kelly in London. I suspected that she quarreled with me on purpose so that she could join him, but it appears now that she was deluded by yet another man—when will she ever learn?

After traveling night and day to get to Venice, I found that after all Mr. Kelly had a wife in tow, apparently had had a bride stashed away in London and didn't tell Charlotte. When I heard this, I realized that I was wrong to think Charlotte would continue on with our itinerary and knew she had gone home instead in a fit of pique. I longed to see her and make up for my own

129

bad temper. I simply can't help myself! I feel so wretched and impotent when she won't see things my way!

Emily's indisposition gave me an excuse to cut our trip short. There's some consolation knowing that I shall be given credit for having taken the sensible and virtuous course of hurrying home with an ailing child.

~~~~~

To my amazement, Charlotte was not home after all. Her landlady blithely reported that Mrs. Miller had gone overseas on a fancy vacation with her friend. "But I'm her friend," I wanted to say, then I realized how I had been hoodwinked. I had to wait all day for Emily to get home from school before I got any satisfaction.

"Did you lie to me!?" I demanded of her. Instantly the guilt on her face gave me my answer. "Did Charlotte put you up to it? Tell me what happened! Tell me, Emily!"

"I didn't want you to be sick again, Mama," she quavered, her lower lip trembling. Meg Galloway has a sixth sense about turmoil in the house, or maybe she heard me raise my voice, for almost at once she came into my room to see why I was shouting at Emily.

"Now, now, Miss Edith. Don't take on so with the child," she said.

"You stay out of this, Meg! This is my child—or has Mama convinced you otherwise? Look at me, Emily! What happened when I sent you to Mr. Kelly's room? Speak up!"

"Mrs. Miller told me to tell you that he was married to someone named Elizabeth."

Despair washed over me so heavily that I knew I couldn't stand the horror of my life another instant. I ran out of the room and down the hall to the stairs, which I took up to my little studio on the third floor. It had not been opened in a long time. The air was stale and still. I rushed across the room and yanked open the balcony doors and without hesitation climbed up on the rail, closed my eyes, and leaped.

~~~~~

MEG GALLOWAY

Poor lamb. She never got over little Faith's death, which we all blamed her for, whether we meant to or not. That's why she chose the exact same death that ended Faith's life. Only, in the intervening years, the trees Mrs. Coolidge planted after the house was raised had grown twenty feet tall, with brushy limbs that reached out like protecting arms to break Miss Edith's fall. By the time I got to the rail and looked down, she was already sitting up screaming with pain. I hollered for Mrs. Frenche to call the doctor and he sent the ambulance. I didn't call Mrs. Coolidge to tell her what happened until after the ambulance was already on its way with Miss Edith sedated in the back.

She and Mr. Charles went to the hospital and after awhile they called me to find out what had happened just before she jumped. I told her I didn't know, but it were my opinion Edith had intended to kill herself.

~~~~~

EMILY PICKERING DOUGLAS

When I was thirteen, my mother leaped from the same balcony from which my sister Faith fell, attempting to take her own life. But she was not a lucky woman, she only broke her leg.

However, as Mercutio says when Romeo asks him how bad is his injury, the wound may not have been as wide as a church nor as deep as a grave, but it would do. Mama's injuries were enough to get her started on the long journey toward the death she longed for. She refused to recover, to mend, to get out of bed. She refused to take an interest in life again, no matter how often Meg chided her, Grandmama upbraided her, Papa solemnly attempted to humor her.

When I think back to those years that Mama lay in her bed trying to die, I think of a quiet house, empty except for me, the sick woman, and the household staff, all going about our busi-

131

ness conscious of the slow tragedy going on upstairs, our only concession to it to tiptoe past Mama's room and lower our voices in the stairwell and entry hall. It took her two years to die, which she passed in a dull stupor of morphine for the pain she claimed she felt in her leg and spine. My grandmother tried more than once to shame Mama out of bed, but Mama had learned the trick of shutting out whatever she didn't want to hear. Each time, Grandmama left the sick room in defeat.

Once, I telephoned Mrs. Miller and begged her to come see Mama. She didn't want to, I could tell, but she did anyway. It seems that she had not married Mr. Kelly after all. She said that she was sick of Galveston, that it was a cheat and a fraud, that it would never let in an outsider like her, she was moving to Houston where she would've gone years ago if hadn't been for Walter. He had remarried and was being nasty about her seeing the boys. Mama was barely aware she had company and said to me that evening when I washed her face, "I dreamed Charlotte came to see me."

When I was fifteen and Mama was forty, I finally lost her. The doctor wrote on the death certificate, "Cause of death, blocked bowels." It was an ignominious end for a woman who had been exalted by her passion and hindered by her lack of courage. For me there was not a great deal of difference in having a sickly mother who never came downstairs and not having one at all, for through it all, I had Grandmama and Meg.

BOOK II

Galveston, 1928–1968

Chapter Seven

I dream of Atlantis. The old dream where the world has turned to water, where substance has turned to insubstance. The very air is gray and wet. I gasp for air. I try to run, but the surf catches at my legs and makes them heavy. Everywhere are struggling figures in the watery air. The elements are confused. Air has turned to water and water to air. Fire is quenched and earth submerged. My clothes cling to me and the wind plucks them from my body till I run naked through this watery place, adding my tears to the deluge. Is there nowhere a dry substantial piece of land? Dark figures struggle beside me, but we are lost, we are damned souls awaiting a watery hell.

But I must fight! Must draw air into my bursting lungs! Air, that precious commodity we take for granted! But I find only water. I gasp. I fight. I pull at the curtains until my husband reaches up and gently shakes me awake. What a fool I am! Here I stand, in our bed, tugging at the curtains above us like a crazed thing. At once I feel relieved to find that I am only dreaming. I'm also terribly afraid.

"Was it the drowning dream?" he says, and he, born on the island, understands like no other. "I'm here, Emily, I'm here," he croons, and the terror recedes.

I can't lie back down just yet. We must get up and pull on our warm robes and slippers, pad out to the kitchen and make cups of tea. We must sit across from each other and I must let him stroke my hand and speak of everyday things, how the roof will need inspecting after the thunderstorm we had tonight, the sound of which must have loosed my old nemesis to enter the sanctity of my dreams to whisper in my ear: "Fear death by water." With a shudder, I push the monster out of my head and breathe in the good dry air, bathe my face in the cold fluorescent light above the kitchen sink, let the good solid objects of my kitchen restore my confidence in air, in dry things, in the reality of wakefulness.

~~~~~

Several years ago Spencer gave me an odd gift, an electric typewriter from his law office. They were switching over to computers and he thought I might find a use for the machine. I dare say he had noticed the litter of notecards that fluttered in my wake. I hadn't the courage at that point to face an entire sheet of paper.

The words began as a trickle—epigrams I wrote under photographs to explain what my camera never seemed to capture. There they are, my first words, in an old album. As the years roll by, the explanations grow lengthier. There's a point, oh, sometime in the sixties, where the words gradually edge out the photos in the albums. You can guess the rest: I threw away my camera and started writing. Interesting that Spencer gave me that old typewriter: Lawrence had given me *his* old camera.

My mother was a painter, not very good, I've heard, so perhaps this artistic bent comes from her. I had an itch one day and couldn't think of anything to scratch it with but art. I recall painting a few awful pictures before Lawrence came to us in Mexico and wisely advised me to stop at once, offering me his camera instead, since he was dying and would soon not need it. Lawrence was a poet. I wonder that he didn't get me started writing. But since I was barely literate when I met him, how could he have known?

The sisters at Ursuline Academy used to mark up my papers in despair and accuse me of being purposely thick-headed. The wellspring of words lay dormant, and to tell the truth, Lawrence's helpfulness may have postponed my writing by several years, for after his death I felt bound to learn to operate the camera to prove his assertion that I had a "beautiful soul."

I was never good at landscapes, but generally found things around the house to point my camera at. I have dozens of pictures of sloe-eyed Aurora, our beautiful young housekeeper, and Gilberto, her dimple-kneed baby. And of course those early albums are full of photographs of the dispossessed souls who trekked down from the North. Our house became a way station for misfits like Harding and me: Chiefly was Franklin Poe, an old army buddy of Harding's who had lived in Monterrey for years, and his wife Zaida. Frank and Harding had both been career Army (grunts, not officers) and seemed to know hundreds of men. Harding was only truly comfortable with men, and only men like himself—he could never think of anything to say to Lawrence.

Some of my old crowd came too. India Kenneally married a geologist who followed the scent of oil around the world; Mimi Sinclair came several times, never with the same husband; Jack Tarnow, whom I had dated briefly in high school before throwing him over for his twin Tommie. And Peter Bright, my favorite of the old Galveston crowd, brought his bride Alma to Monterrey for a honeymoon, then came on down to Tres Hermanas to spend a few days with us. Alma reminded me of cotton candy on a stick—and was about as nutritious for Peter. Later, they had two boys, whom she half-raised before running off with another man and leaving them to Peter. She was the one who told me that Harding had given Ruth "a dose of clap" on their honeymoon. Their grandson Dan is the one who built the deck on my beach house, and then later . . . well, we'll get to all that, won't we?

Peter Bright had been as wild as me before he got married. We were together that night the police rounded up the patrons of the Sui Jen the night I turned twenty-one. Some three hundred revelers all went to jail together. Just before Peter left Tres Hermanas to go home, he took me aside and told me he was shocked at the depravity that passed for ordinary living at my house, the all-night drinking parties, the remorseless hangovers, the failure of morals and slackness of ambition. No, that's not what he said. He only said that he thought it was pretty rotten the way we carried on. I was too proud to let him know that my household was not in my control, so I laughed and accused him of letting Alma turn him into a fuddy- duddy. I didn't think I would ever see Peter again.

I was wrong. Eventually we did come back to Galveston and I saw quite a lot of Peter Bright. In fact, when he retired from shrimping, he bought one of the houses in Fair Isle Estates that had been damaged by Hurricane Alicia, lived there while he rebuilt, then he sold it and bought another house that had been trashed by renters. (Oh, dear, I see it's going to take some discipline to keep from jumping ahead.)

One person who did not pass through my *salon*, for reasons that will become clear, was Ruth Meyers, my best friend in high school. For many years I didn't even know where Ruth was living. I wanted to ask her mother so I could write, but I didn't get the courage to write that letter until after Harding died. The letter came back unopened and I was ashamed to mention it to Mrs. Meyers. I don't know to this day if Ruth or the post office sent it back. She died only two years after Harding did, she of liver cancer, he of cirrhosis of the liver.

I had something to say about all these people and the countless others I persuaded to pose for me over the years, but the camera was not my mouthpiece. As has been true of so many things in my life, I came to writing with no forethought or planning, something that seemed to just "happen" to me. I wish I had been a different sort of woman, the kind who causes things to happen, but that was my grandmother, you see, not me.

The trickle of words took forty years to swell into a torrent, an unstoppable deluge, like the storm surge that accompanies our West Indian hurricanes. It was with intense relief that I seized on Spencer's old typewriter and a Gregg typing manual, turned on the spigot of words, which my awkward fingers could barely keep up with. I had so much to say!

I began with the journals of my grandmother and mother, which Meg Galloway had saved for me. I plumped up the words from what I knew myself and what Meg had told me. It was

138

important to understand those women, I believed, so that I might begin to understand myself.

You'll find it surprising perhaps, that I felt Mama's absence so keenly when she had never really been my companion. But I did miss her, though not because of an empty house. In fact, Grandmama's house was home to more servants than to those being served. Mr. Gomez, our gardener, lived over the garage and was in his eighties. He had been with Grandmama since she built the new house and wasn't likely to be sent packing just because he could no longer carry out his duties. A younger man was employed to do the actual work, while Mr. Gomez, the "head gardener," looked on. I recall a rapid turnover in the position below him.

Mrs. Frenche, the cook, suffered rheumatoid arthritis and had to be carried up and down the stairs by Lewis, the younger man (only in his sixties) who looked after things in general. We did not call him a butler for fear of seeming undemocratic. Then there was the housemaid's position that was filled for short periods of time by able-bodied young women just before they got married. And there was Meg Galloway.

After my mother died, Meg sat me down and told me I was in charge of things, the lady of the house, that they were all to do my bidding now and I must learn to be a proper young lady and always be a credit to my grandmother.

Ever since I could remember, my grandmother had been someone who was written about in the newspapers, always with some reference to her father being one of the founders, not only of a large fortune, but of the city itself. Our family's money endowed a hospital wing for the state's chief medical college, the University of Texas Medical Branch, which grew to employ over 7,000 people. A street was named for my grandmother, a bust unveiled in the Rosenberg Library. I was often asked to represent her at ceremonial functions, but I was not comfortable in that role and when asked to speak, would nearly die of fright.

My grandmother, naturally, didn't want me to turn out as poorly as my mother had, and for a long time after my mother's death, made an effort to spend more time with me, several nights a week coming home to dinner, both she and my father, so we could be a "family." Otherwise, I took my meals in the

139

kitchen with Meg. But I turned out to have little in common with my mother, gave Grandmama no cause for alarm, and so she eventually relaxed her vigilance and let me sink back into obscurity.

Still my best friends were Ruth Meyers and India Kenneally, with whom I had trudged through seven years of parochial school, fellow members of the by then-defunct Mata Hari Girl Spies. Meg asked me to look over the odd collection of novels in Mama's room and see which I wanted to keep and which give to the library. I was not bookish and the task held no appeal. I almost told Meg to give them all to the library. Luckily for me, I made a haphazard inspection of the pile and recognized one that Charlotte Miller had bought in London and that she and Mama had sat up in bed breathlessly reading one night. Idly I flipped through the pages and my eyes lit upon this passage:

> *And it seemed she was like the sea, nothing but dark waves rising and heaving, heaving with a great swell, so that slowly her whole darkness was in motion, and she was ocean rolling its dark, dumb mass. Oh, and far down inside her the deeps parted and rolled asunder, in long, far-travelling billows, and ever, at the quick of her, the depths parted and rolled asunder, from the centre of soft plunging, as the plunger went deeper and deeper and deeper disclosed, and heavier the billows of her rolled away to some shore, uncovering her, and closer and closer plunged the palpable unknown, and further and further rolled the waves of herself away from herself, leaving her, till suddenly, in a soft, shuddering convulsion, the quick of all her plasm was touched, she knew herself touched, the consummation was upon her, and she was gone. She was gone, she was not, and she was born: a woman.*
> —(1959, NAL edition of *Lady Chatterley's Lover*, p. 163)

It was D.H. Lawrence's *Lady Chatterley's Lover*, published the year we went to England and banned in this country for years. Immediately I had the good sense to realize what I had and to know that my lackluster reputation as a girl spy was about to be burnished.

"Where did you get that!?" exclaimed Ruth. "Don't you know the whole world is talking about that book?"

"It has a lot of dirty words in it," I said happily. India Kenneally grabbed the book and started reading out loud in an awestruck voice:

"Tha'art real, tha art! Tha'rt real, even a bit of a bitch. Here tha shits an' here tha pisses: an' I lay my hand on 'em both an' like thee for it. I like thee for it. Tha's got a proper, woman's arse, proud of itself. It's none ashamed of itself, this isna."

—(p. 208)

"Oh, my God," whispered Ruth, falling back in a near perfect imitation of a faint. "It's all there, everything they don't want us to know!"

And soon the secrets lay open to us too, putting our sophistication and dearly acquired wisdom to shame. Such silence! Such large incredulous eyes! Our mouths held in awestruck little O's while India read aloud Lawrence's perfervid prose!

We couldn't read the whole thing in one sitting, of course, but we vowed to do what our teachers had always recommended, savor the entire literary classic. This good intention went by the wayside as we encountered long tedious passages about politics and coal, which we would skip to get to the scenes in the hut when Mellors mutters his crude Anglo-Saxon love epithets in Constance Chatterley's ear. When we left off our study, we would walk home in a daze of unfocused passion. Ruth was charged with keeping the volatile volume, since her mother had a job and never paid any attention to what Ruth read, which I sometimes later blamed for how far ahead of us Ruth got. We were all in love with Mellors and had to develop a code for speaking of our obsession in front of others. Ruth swore she would never marry a man who didn't adore her arsehole. I said I would never marry a man like Clifford, who reminded me too much of my mother.

At fifteen, we were experienced, decadent, world-wise and weary. We were addicted to nicotine, adept at maintaining the level of the sherry bottles, and so loyal to each other that we never got caught. But that was no particular feat at my house. The adults were all preoccupied with their own matters, too busy to spend the time to find out what lay beyond the innocent-looking facade I presented to the world. Papa and Grandmama had their work, Meg had the smooth-running of Grandmama's household, a task she often said she wasn't worthy of and which she took extremely seriously. Meg saw more of me than the others, but she had a glaring deficiency in the sniffing out of wrongdoing—she was incapable of thinking ill of someone she loved.

141

I had long since outgrown my crush on Spencer O'Malley, who had given up the idea of becoming a priest and declared his intention of going into law like his uncle George. Spencer, of course, like India and myself (not so much Ruth, for reasons I shall go into later) belonged to a small select group of Catholics with money who were encouraged to unite with others of our "set" for friendship, and, it went without saying, matrimony.

But Ruth and I had discovered that the real fun was outside our "set"—trysts with island boys who were not from such good homes. India did not go along on these outings, having met the limits of her adventurousness in the reading of D. H. Lawrence. But she didn't tell on us when we did and allowed us to use her for an alibi.

The Tarnow twins, proud owners of a disreputable old jalopy, would pick us up on the corner behind India's house. We would ride around with them after school for as long as we could, ducking when we saw familiar vehicles. Once we drove right past Papa, who blinked at me in surprise, but at the dinner table that night, I swore it wasn't me and he believed me because of my reputation for veracity.

The Tarnow boys were decent young chaps who could be forgiven for being somewhat dazzled by the grand houses we lived in and were eager to oblige our desire to misbehave. The extent of our perversions, however, was a little harmless necking among the sand dunes and a lot of smoking and swearing. Occasionally, the boys would lay their hands on a little moonshine whiskey or we would steal some of our parents' bootleg hooch. But, of course, I didn't dare go home drunk, when it was already something of a trial to explain the smell of tobacco from which I constantly reeked. (Ruth's father was a chain-smoker, I explained.)

Neither of us were in love with the Tarnows. For one thing, we couldn't tell them apart to keep them from switching on us, which I knew they did so they could both kiss Ruth, who was by far the prettier. We met some of their friends occasionally, although Ruth and I discouraged their bringing along other girls to add to the competition. Peter Bright, already out of school and working on his father's shrimper, was not impressed with our claims to degeneracy.

142

"You'll get tired of slumming, Miss Emily," he told me, "then you'll run right back to your society swells to choose a husband."

"I will not!" I protested hotly. If only my grandmother could've heard!

Spencer O'Malley asked me to be his date for our first big society party, the winter cotillion at The Galvez Hotel. As I got dressed, I remembered watching Mama get dressed for parties and how I had sighed and longed for the day that I would be allowed to wear long dresses and put up my hair. Mama had hated her society duties, unless Charlotte Miller was involved, of course, and now I, before even being properly launched in society, shared her boredom, which I knew better than to admit out loud.

Grandmama came into my room while Meg hurriedly took up a place where my hem dragged the floor. "Very pretty," she said.

"I'm not pretty," I said, reaching up to pinch my cheeks because my reflection did not please me.

"Hold still," said Meg. "Pretty is as pretty does, Miss."

My grandmother joined me in the frame of the mirror, looking at me approvingly. "Prettiness should not be a woman's number one attraction," she said. "Virtue should. So you've caught you a beau, Emily?"

For a moment I thought she meant Tommie Tarnow and I gave her a startled look in the long mirror. Then I realized she meant Spencer O'Malley. "Just for the dance, Grandmama. I think he likes a girl named Rose who lives in Houston."

"Nonsense! He would never have a girl who wasn't BOI."

"I don't think that means as much as it used to, Grandmama," I told her gently. "I mean, you know, that old toughness and immunity and stuff."

"There's more to it than that, my girl. It takes a special kind of spirit to live here."

"A special kind of crazy," I retorted. "I heard (I couldn't say I heard it from a shrimper's son) that we're overdue for another big hurricane, since we haven't had one in thirteen years."

"And when it comes," said Grandmama serenely, "we'll take it in stride like we always do. A Houston girl would pick up her skirts and run."

When she left the room, I said to Meg, "Why does she want me to like Spencer O'Malley?"

Crawling around on the floor at my feet with her mouth full of straight pins, Meg's reply was somewhat mumbled. "I suppose 'cause he's got the same virtues as has Mr. Charles."

"Spencer is like Papa?" I wrinkled my nose in disbelief. What could these grown women see that I couldn't?

Meg sat back on her haunches and took the pins out of her mouth. "They both be serious and respectable gentlemen, dutiful in their love of the Lord, eager to do what's expected of them."

Needless to say, this resounding endorsement further depressed the value of Spencer's stock.

In fact, I was feeling quite resentful by the time he picked me up that evening in his father's Oldsmobile, looking very serious indeed, with the consciousness of weighty responsibility on his slim shoulders. To my embarrassment, Meg had alerted Mrs. Frenche and Florence to come to the door of the kitchen to see me off. You'd have thought I was leaving for my honeymoon.

Spencer appeared completely abashed by my long dress and formal coiffure, and after a glancing smile, ignored me and concentrated on his driving. I suppose he had gone to a lot of trouble to polish up his father's car, but with the egoism of youth, my focus was intensely on myself. I felt extremely grownup and experienced, felt that I was being forced to go out with someone quite beneath me in experience. Brazenly, I snapped open my purse and fetched out a Chesterfield.

"Want one?" I said.

"Well, um, my father might smell it."

"I'll roll down the window."

The wind was coming strong out of the southeast, knocking the waves into the big square granite boulders with such violence the water atomized and misted our windows. For warmth, I was wearing my grandmother's mink stole. I pushed it back off my shoulders to expose my insignificant decollete. The cold was damp and unpleasant, but I pretended to enjoy it as I puffed away on my cigarette. I pretended to enjoy my smoke too, but actually I was acutely conscious of Spencer's disapproval. I felt shamed and therefore obliged to further misbehave.

144

I got my opportunity when three uninvited boys from Texas City crashed the dance. We knew they didn't belong because of their clothes, ordinary suits, not very nice ones at that. To get even with Spencer for going around trying to get up enough support to eject the gate crashers, I danced with one named Roger Hollis whose brown wooly blazer I can still recall against my fingertips. I made Roger feel so welcome that he invited me to step behind a large potted plant and take a snort of bootleg whiskey from a dented silver hip flask.

The stuff took my breath away. Instantly my head felt woozy the way it did when we drank sherry at India Kenneally's house. I decided I would only dance with Roger and his friends, since mine were being such pills. I felt everyone's eyes on me. Spencer's cheeks developed two dark red stains under his tan. The chaperones gathered and put their heads together, darting disapproving looks at me over their shoulders. Roger was getting nervous at all the attention and suddenly yanked me out the door leading to the south lawn where his friends had already regrouped.

"Hey, Rog, we're leaving. We didn't expect to stand out like this."

"Yeah, well, we're just as good as they are," said Roger defiantly. "We gotta right. Whaddya say, sweetheart?" he said, appealing to me.

I looked back toward the windows and saw faces looking out at us. If they left, I would be on my own to face their censure.

"Take me with you," I said.

Roger shook his head in disbelief. "You kiddin'? That swell you're with would sic the law on me."

"It's a free country," said one of the other boys. "She can leave a party if she wants to."

"Yeah," said the other. "You got any money on you? We could get another bottle."

I had brought only a token handbag, but I pretended there was a possibility of finding cash in the bottom of it. Already the boys were beginning to edge toward the parking lot. Grandmama's stole was inside and I was freezing in the chilly damp air. All of a sudden Roger took off his tacky brown coat and placed it around my shoulders.

"Here, you'll freeze to death. So what are you gonna do?"

The coat smelled as if it had hung in a diner absorbing grease-laden molecules and the smell of passing lower-class patrons. I saw Roger clearly for a moment, as Grandmama would, as Clifford Chatterley would, as a boy whose father worked in our equivalent of a coal pit, a Texas City chemical plant, a boy who would himself work there someday, a boy who thought he could pass himself off as one of the "swells" by wearing his one good suit. A sudden sadness washed over me to realize that Grandmama had trained me to see Roger and his friends that way, see him with the same veiled contempt Clifford Chatterley had seen his gamekeeper. And, like Lady Chatterley, I would not find love in my precious set but would have to go looking for it among the proletariat.

"I'm going with you," I said, hurrying across the grass to catch up with Roger's friends.

Or perhaps I thought of all that later. Maybe all I wanted at the time was to not let Roger know that his dirty coat repelled me. Suddenly it was a race to get out of the parking lot before we were stopped. I was hot property, stolen from my rightful owner. In a flash, I had achieved worth.

Naturally I look back on that rash act with astonishment, climbing into the car with three strange youths full of illegal booze. No telling what might have happened to me! But it was soon apparent that these were innocents who had no idea what to do with their stolen society girl. Roger and I, in the backseat, kept an eye out for the police and thought we saw them everywhere. To foil our presumed pursuers, the driver headed to the causeway and back to the boys' home turf where they felt more confident.

I didn't learn Roger's full name that night—I think he kept it from me on purpose—but I did learn that a boy's kisses could make up for my pathetic lack of affection at home. Roger's friend parked the car in a cow pasture, and he and the other boy took a walk in the cold to give us privacy. It was my good fortune that Roger was neither as sexually experienced nor as aggressive as Lady Chatterley's working man, that he committed no more savagery on my person than to kiss my lips till they bled. The next day I would wake up and cherish their dryness as proof that the whole thing had not been a dream.

146

Too soon it was over. The friends, wet and cold, crept apologetically back into the car and offered to go to sleep. I wished like anything I had brought money with me so I could buy them liquor. As we drove back across the causeway, the sky was beginning to lighten, but Roger and I were still counting the ways two pairs of human lips can combine.

In the many years I've known Spencer, I've deplored many things about him, but never his loyalty. I spotted his father's car parked a block from my house and knew that he was waiting for me so I wouldn't get in trouble. Well, if he thought I was going to be grateful! But the sight of him asleep in the front seat filled me with guilt and contrition. Giving my illicit companion one last embrace, I jumped out of the car and waved goodbye as Roger and his pals sped off. Then I walked down the street and woke up Spencer.

Had there been more light, he would have seen me as I later saw myself, hair disheveled, white dress rumpled and soiled, blotches of color on my neck, lips bruised and puffy, but above all, a look of triumph in my black eyes.

"I'm sorry, Spence," I told him, "but it was just that you were so stuffy about everything. Are you going to tell Grandmama?"

"Of course not. Are you all right?"

"Sure. We just drove around."

Even though he had fallen from a great height in my estimation, I suddenly felt very fond of Spencer for proving that he was more loyal to me than he was to my grandmother, a bit of knowledge I would shamelessly exploit in the months to come.

"Thanks, Spencer," I said, and heartlessly left him there, unkissed.

I dreamed about Roger for weeks, hoped he would call and ask me out, planned the scene I would make if Grandmama said I couldn't go. But Roger, apparently, had had his fling with society and I learned that he got married and became a fireman. Fourteen years later I read in a month-old Galveston newspaper mailed to me in Mexico by Meg, that Roger Hollis was listed among the dead in that other great catastrophe that defines our part of the world to outsiders, the Texas City explosion.

~~~~~

147

Ruth Meyers had always been one of the "older" girls at school, actually only a year older than I, but years older in genuine worldliness. We didn't become close until I was a senior and she was out of school working. By then she and her mother had been dropped from polite society because of the Meyers' divorce. Ruth was the youngest of seven children and her father was a drunk. When Ruth graduated, Mrs. Meyers decided enough was enough and got a divorce in spite of the Church's dictum against legal remedies for an unhappy marriage.

They lost their home and had to move to a tiny apartment over a grocery store, an apartment so small that mother and daughter shared a single bed. Later, after my own graduation, I would spend a lot of time there and Mrs. Meyers would sleep on the couch so we girls could be together. Mrs. Meyers would've been only forty at the time, but she was so exhausted-looking that she seemed much older to me. However, she ended up outliving Ruth, as I've mentioned.

When Ruth's parents divorced, my grandmother forbade me to see her any more, but for once I stood up to Grandmama and said I didn't care what a person's parents had done, I was going to stick by my friend. I was getting too old to be treated like a child, and she seemed to recognize that. Shortly afterwards I overheard her tell my father that it was time I went away to school. She had wanted to send me when I was fifteen, but Mama's illness prevented it. My father, never one to disagree with his mother-in-law, merely observed that conditions in Europe worried him. Nonsense, said my grandmother, the convent she supported in Nantes, France was the perfect containment for a girl until she reached a marriageable age—at which age Grandmama expected to turn me over to the care of a husband of her choosing.

I was terrified that she would really do it, but Ruth and my other friends gave me the courage to simply say no. "Grandmama, I will not be sent away from my friends," I told her. Seeing that she was unmoved by loyalty to friends, I invoked Spencer, who had said no such thing. "Besides, Spencer said that he would marry somebody else if I went away."

"The boy adores you," she said firmly, but I could see her conviction waver. "If you don't get an education, Emily, you'll always have to trust others to take care of your money. And girl, after your father and I are gone, you'll see just how big a job that is."

"Then I ought to go to work in Papa's office so I can start learning." This had been Ruth's contribution when we brainstormed over my dilemma, and I immediately saw its beauty when Grandmama smiled. She liked the idea enormously. She thought it was spunky. It was what she would have done under the circumstances.

And, there was the fact that I was only a middling scholar at the Academy. (Since I'm in an academic vein, let me quench your undoubted curiosity about whether or not I ever finished reading *Lady Chatterley's Lover*. I didn't, not for some fifteen years, when I met the poet Lawrence Edgar Payne, whose name recalled for me the forbidden pleasures of the Lawrence who had been introduced to me as a pornographer. When I again took up Lady C., I read her as literature.)

Today it is inconceivable that my folks planned to turn over a complex business empire to an uneducated person. But of course, they planned no such thing. They expected my husband to look after both me and the business matters they would leave me, which gave them the right to voice a strong opinion in who I married. I knew the requirements of this perfect mate well: BOI, Catholic, "our set."

My grandmother never suggested to me that I ought to go to college. For one thing, I was not considered particularly bright, and for another, educated women were like men who had to use their hands to make a living, not quite the *thing*, my dear. The proper education for a girl like me prepared her to rule society and the home.

In any case, I had another year with the Ursuline sisters. It was decided that I would go to work for Papa the following summer and begin to learn the business, that is, if I didn't get married right away. Perhaps I could take a secretarial training course. Everyone believed I would be married long before any such shocking thing came to pass.

Spencer left for the University of Texas to pursue the goal he and his family had chosen for him of becoming a lawyer, without the slightest resentment that his life was being molded

149

into a shape chosen by others. He would not begin to experience doubt that the system might be flawed until a mad assassin robbed our nation of its first Catholic president, until he himself was robbed of his youngest son in a conflict that was still three wars away.

When he was nineteen, however, and leaving home for the first time, Spencer was supremely satisfied with his life, happy to oblige his family by studying law, glad to court the girl everybody had decided he should marry, although that was something we never directly discussed.

It's difficult for me to recall just what I believed about myself at the time, but I think that in the back of my mind I thought Spencer, older and smarter, was right, that I would one day feel differently and want to "settle down" and marry him and have many children. It was all terribly far off in the future though.

In the meantime I told him about the boys I dated when he was away at school; I smoked in front of him; and, since Prohibition had failed to sober the nation and the Eighteenth Amendment was repealed the year I graduated, I ordered legal cocktails when we went out. Spencer was unimpressed with my attempts to shock him. I was a fish, he said, fighting the line, one of the reds he loved to tire out until it became docile and willing to swim into his net.

And so I might, had Ruth not met her handsome soldier.

Chapter Eight

Harding Douglas was an orphan who had been raised by an aunt and uncle. He suffered a terrible childhood, grew up feeling that he owed these relatives for every bite he ate, indeed, the air he breathed. His unmarried mother, only fourteen when he was born, got in the car with a stranger only weeks after his birth and was never heard from again. They didn't know if she got up a romance with the stranger whose car she entered or if the stranger had murdered her. No one in the small Kansas town where Harding grew up ever claimed to be his father.

Perhaps the only ennobling story from Harding's younger years was that one of his teachers realized he was being ill-treated and attempted to adopt him. My heart has always been gladdened at the thought that someone was willing to interfere, to actually take a family to court to right an injustice—this in a time when child beating was considered a family's private business. However, I can't help wondering if Harding's losing that earlier case didn't account for the perseverance he showed in prosecuting my case many years later, attempting to wrest from my family what he felt they owed me.

At any rate, the Douglases testified in court that they loved Harding exactly as they loved their other children and couldn't give him up. Harding was worth something to them, I might add, a stipend they received from the county for his keep.

Probably too, they were concerned that he would tell people how ill they had used him if they let him go.

In these matters, I think I am reporting fact, but it is entirely possible that I am only reporting my unthinking loyalty to Harding. I met the Douglases once, early in our marriage when we traveled up through the Midwest. I expected some sort of monsters, at the very least to see their sins in their hardened eyes. Instead, I found an old farm couple, neither prosperous nor poor, nor particularly large people, as Harding had described them. They were, however, noticeably discomfitted about our being there, possibly because the last time they had seen their nephew was the day he knocked his uncle down and ran off to join the Army.

I believe that for many years the Army was the family that Harding had always wanted, his Army buddies closer to him than any brothers. Ruth and I met him in 1936, the year I turned twenty-one and inherited my mother's money, which had been left her by her father, Herrick Coolidge, drowned in the great storm. The money had been held in trust for me all my life, but more about that trust later.

I was absolutely forbidden to socialize with soldiers, which made them enormously attractive to me, of course. Harding was posted to the Army's Third Attack Group at Fort Crockett, his job to maintain aircraft. It so happened that during Harding's years in the military, the United States was between wars, so the only action he saw was in barroom brawls, the only foreign soil, that of Galveston Island.

Weekends when Harding was on duty and couldn't take Ruth out, I would spend the night with her, also forbidden to me, but by then I routinely defied my grandmother. Mrs. Meyers, Ruth's divorced mother, would sleep on the couch so that Ruth and I could be together. Ruth seemed so grown up to me, blowing her cigarette smoke out the window, whispering details of her stirring love affair with Harding in my ear, recalling for me the days she had read aloud panty-dampening scenes from D.H. Lawrence to her convent- educated and protected friends. Now she was Constance Chatterley and had found her Mellors. I envied her acutely and despaired that I would ever meet my game-keeper!

152

Ruth lost her virginity on her very first date with Harding, she said—somewhat proudly—because he simply wouldn't take no for an answer. I was thrilled to know someone intimately who had gone through that rite of passage leading to fully-fledged womanhood. I felt hopelessly left behind. Harding was such a grownup man, a different species from those we palled around with and teased in backseats. I was terribly in love with him, but Ruth didn't mind. Perhaps she believed, as I did, that experiencing love second-hand was as close as I would ever get.

I was small for my age and, despite strenuous efforts to learn about "real" life, extremely ill-prepared for life beyond Grandmama's care. Girls from whom information about their bodies is willfully withheld invent fantastic beliefs. I'm not sure we fully realized how girls got pregnant. We believed that the rending of the hymen was a painful and bloody procedure, that we would be fundamentally changed by this act and that people would be able to tell. Ruth said that was nonsense, just one of the myths they told us to keep us virgins. There really wasn't much to it, she reported, D.H. Lawrence notwithstanding. The actual event took far less time that it did to read about it.

I was almost a full year younger than Ruth. My own attempts to become a fully- fledged woman were still inconclusive. Once I came in late from a date with Tommie Tarnow—though I claimed to have been with Spencer—and happened to meet my father in the foyer. He never had the least idea how to make conversation with young people, nor when was an appropriate time to make his errant stabs. We were joined by my grandmother, whose sharp little eyes inspected me minutely and found a blot on my skirt. I looked down and there was some of Tommie Tarnow's bodily fluids wetting my hem. I went scarlet with embarrassment, claimed I had dumped ice cream on myself, and raced upstairs to scrub the telltale spot before anyone could see it up close.

Ruth's blasé crossing of that line made me wonder if I weren't kidding myself, if, in spite of my long-running flirt with danger, I wasn't saving myself for Spencer. And if I fooled myself in that matter, maybe I did so in others? Perhaps in the end I would tamely submit to my grandmother's plan for my life. It was then that I realized what an enormous amount of courage it would take to break away.

In my small, piecemeal fashion, however, I did break away. Ruth, more and more with her lover, left me to the younger crowd. There were Mimi Sinclair, the Tarnow twins—Jack and Tommie—Peter Bright, and at different times, other BOI kids whose folks did not appear at my grandmother's dining table. I was with my friends almost every night, but I told them at home that I was with Ruth, or with Spencer when he wasn't away at school.

My friendship with Spencer is one of the few things from those years that I recall without pain, though he assures me the same is not true for him. When he was home from Austin, I was always the first person he called. Our dates were not real dates, not romantic dates, for I used him as a sounding board, would tell him who I was in love with and seek his advice on getting this other one to like me. He was like a big brother, only I knew that he was waiting for me to grow up and take him seriously. Thank goodness he didn't patronize me, nor try to reform me.

I've tried to imagine what I must have seemed like to Spencer in those days. Perhaps I was *his* little bit of rebellion. But of course I wasn't content until I had carried rebellion too far, even for my tolerant friend Spencer.

Quite often I merely used Spencer to get out of the house, didn't remain with him when we ran across some of my "real" friends. Spencer pretended he didn't care. He too had a "serious" girl, Rose Mataglia, a banker's daughter, whom he eventually married. He confessed that Rose was not very exciting, but that she was the perfect girl to marry and have children with. I confided my heartbreaking crush in an older man, a soldier, though I kept to myself the rest of the secret, that he was Ruth's beau.

"He treats me like I'm thirteen years old," I complained.

"Good," said Spencer, "because you are."

In fact, Harding teased me mercilessly, knew that I was in love with him, and taunted me by forcing me to chauffeur him and Ruth around while they made love in the backseat.

But sometimes I didn't give Spencer the slip. Sometimes I stayed with him and let him remind me of all the reasons I liked him. Today I understand my behavior differently than I did then. Now I'm inclined to believe that I mistreated Spencer because I secretly feared I would disappoint him if I played it straight, if I ever seriously tried to be the "perfect wife and mother of his children." Since I didn't believe I could live up to the expectations of a nice boy like Spencer, I wouldn't try. I would be a madcap instead.

Spencer was following his father and his uncle into the family law business, taking his rightful place in our small, elite set, not in the least interested in changing the status quo. One part of me hated him for being so correct and conservative, another part of me admired him for being able to conform. I'm sorry to say that I didn't get to see the moon from Spencer's backseat.

As I awkwardly came of age, so did the city of Galveston. Citizens were seriously debating at the time, just as I did, whose values they would follow, the old power elite—the Sealys, the Kempners, the Moodys, my grandmother and the church groups; or gangsters—the brothers Sam and Rose Maceo, Dutch Voight, Ollie J. Quinn, all of whom made tremendous fortunes during Prohibition running rum, and after Prohibition, dealing vice.

The success of one of the boys who had been with Roger the night they "kidnapped" me from my first cotillion perhaps illustrates the allure of the mob life. The driver of the car that night had been a Texas City boy named Deke Butts, who later got a job running errands for Sam Maceo. In no time Deke was able to afford his own automobile, fancy clothes, and was making the circuit of nightclubs with a bleach blonde on his arm, an example to make us all think twice about sticking to the straight and narrow—the same moral dilemma faced by youngsters growing up in America's drug-torn ghettos today.

But for the Galveston of the thirties, there was a big difference. It wasn't just individuals who profited from the activity of mobsters, our whole city was vitalized by their clandestine commerce. The mob boys were BOI. Rather than run off to foreign climes to spend their money, they invested at home. While the old money built hospitals and libraries, mob money built glittering nightclubs that featured casino style gambling, big bands, Hollywood entertainers, and hardwood dance floors big enough

155

for five hundred dancers. Galveston had been a party town since the middle of the nineteenth century when it staged its first Mardi Gras festival, since Prohibition when its deserted beaches offered perfect cover for the unloading of illegal liquor, since the turn of the century when 900 prostitutes worked notorious Fat Alley in the block off Market, Postoffice, 28th and 29th streets. Now "entertainment" went mainstream.

The tension between these two elements defined the politics and the culture of Galveston for decades, first one side then the other gaining preeminence in the hearts of its citizens.

From time to time, the do-gooders would agitate to get rid of prostitution, drugs, illegal alcohol and gambling. When enough pressure was brought to bear, the state would send in the Texas Rangers, but there was profound ambivalence on all sides about how far to go. In fact, Galveston didn't make up its mind to make sin illegal until the 1950's after nearly all the old elite heads of family were dead, as were their counterparts in the mob.

I celebrated my birthday, August 16, with a quiet dinner at home with Grandmama and Papa, then later at the Sui Jen (pronounced "Swee Rin," and later revamped to become the infamous Balinese Room) which was at the end of a two-hundred-foot pier jutting out into the Gulf. Peter Bright was the only one of our old crowd still around to celebrate with me. Everybody else seemed to have gotten married, gone on to higher education, or moved to the mainland where there were jobs. I was working for my father at the Coolidge Cotton Company "learning the business," and Peter's family owned a shrimp boat and he was the only son. Harding and Ruth had gotten married that summer and were preparing to move to the West Coast. Even Spencer had forgotten this was my all-important day of freedom and was taking Rose Mataglia to hear a famous opera singer.

I felt desperate that life was passing me by, that I didn't know how to catch up. So what if I was twenty-one? Nothing at all had changed. I was still treated like a child at home and hadn't the least idea how to become my own person.

I must have communicated some of these feelings to Peter, for he gallantly proposed to me. We told the people at the next table that we were going to get married and they sent us cham-

156

pagne. I tried to drink enough to get drunk, but I nearly always got sick long before that happened. I simply didn't have the capacity to lose myself.

All of a sudden absolute pandemonium broke out as blue-suited officers poured onto the dance floor. Peter and I were rudely herded, along with everybody else, toward the exit and taken in paddy wagons to the police station. I wept with disappointment. It was so typical of my life to have my private independence day interrupted by the sin patrol. I just knew my grandmother was behind it.

Eventually Police Chief Tony Messina spotted me among the bedraggled detainees and immediately escorted me into his office and called my grandmother. Rather than fetch me herself, which would have been humiliation enough, she sent someone from O'Malley, Bradley and Tate, which alerted reporters covering the story that someone with a reputation worth ruining had been netted in the raid. Strangely, I thought of Spencer as the flashbulbs popped in my face, worried that he would no longer be able to justify his friendship with me to family and friends.

My picture was on the front page of *The Galveston Daily News* the next morning with the headline "Coolidge Granddaughter Arrested." I envied Peter Bright, left in jail to go before the magistrate and pay his twenty-five-dollar fine and be home in time for breakfast. I forgot all about our "engagement."

I had been working in my father's office ever since I graduated, but had shown no aptitude for business and had not been promoted beyond menial tasks. Everyone knew that the only reason I was tolerated was that I was kinfolk. Dancing most nights till the wee hours did nothing for my punctuality. Nor did increased proximity to my father endear me to him. In fact, I seemed to embarrass him even when I wasn't getting my picture in the newspaper. The day after the storm of unwanted publicity, I resolved to go to the office as usual to show them I was unbowed and unbroken. I could tell by the way my co-workers' eyes veered away from me that they pitied my poor father having me for an only child.

I sat at my poky little desk in the corner, trying to focus on my make-work tasks—all so hideously boring, my cheeks burning, equally torn between quitting that instant and turning over

157

a new leaf, begging Grandmama's forgiveness and starting right in being good. If getting arrested for dancing at the Sui Jen capped my career of crime, would Grandmama love humanity less and begin to love her only living descendant more? I didn't think so. I had been good for eighteen years and it hadn't made any difference. The obverse had been true, though; when I became "bad," they managed to dislike me more.

Among Papa's office staff, Mr. Galloway, the old man who had been in charge of bookkeeping for Coolidge Cotton Company since before I was born, was my one ally, united with me in our common desire to thwart Grandmama's ban on smoking, which she enforced not only because of the fire hazard, but because she despised the use of nicotine almost as much as she did alcohol. Meg's father was a tall skinny old man with enormous white eyebrows that cast a shadow over his blue eyes, one of which he would wink slightly to invite me out for a smoke. I left my desk and joined him on the fire escape which had a view of the wharves.

"Did Meg ever do anything that you didn't want her to do?" I asked him.

"Meg doesn't have your temperament," said Mr. Galloway mildly.

"But what if she did something really bad? Would you still love her?" I persisted.

I can see now that I had begun to suspect the existence of unconditional love, to realize that even those children who brought shame and disgrace on their families did not lose their families' love. Peter Bright, a child of fisher folk, the humblest strata of island society, had lost none of the value his family placed on him for our little escapade. He had told them everything and they had laughed with him and told him to be more careful next time. Neither had Ruth Meyers ever had to hide things from her mother, although Ruth did everything I did and worse. Yet Mrs. Meyers continued to dote on Ruth, her last chick in the nest.

I had always believed that my family was peculiar because Grandmama and Papa had lost all their kin in the great storm, but here was a man, Mr. Galloway, with an identical history. He had lost his wife in the storm and only had Meg left. The survival of the Galloways depended on Meg as much as the survival of the Coolidge-Pickerings depended on me, yet I had never heard the old man express the slightest regret that Meg had not married and given him grandchildren.

Mr. Galloway had no answer for me, could not imagine Meg getting in trouble—nor could I.

"If I had a daughter, I wouldn't care what she did, I'd love her anyway," I said.

I went back to my desk and took a telephone message for my father, but my mind wasn't on my work and I promptly forgot the message. Later in the day, when I came back from lunch, I had managed to gain enough perspective on the events of the night before to realize that my real hurt was that more had not been made of my birthday. I had unconsciously looked forward to this event as somehow being the turning point of my life, the time from which everything would begin to get better, when my folks would begin to treat me as a significant and honored member of the family, an adult, someone whose wishes would be consulted, whose ideas, few though they may be, would not be dismissed out of hand, someone who had a chance of one day being treated as an equal, God forbid. But the morning after that totally random event of being among the mass arrest showed me the folly of expecting different treatment merely for having become a year older. It would take a lot more birthdays for Grandmama to regard me differently.

When I came back to the office, my father was purple in the face and sputtering with indignation about having missed an important luncheon, thanks to my carelessness. My father rarely had anything at all to say to me and left important matters, such as my religious training and the acquisition of social skills, to Grandmama. But the public exposure of my face and morals in the newspaper had apparently brought all his other grievances against me to an intolerable pitch of irritation, and this, causing him to lose face among his business peers, pushed him over the line.

"You imbecile!" he shouted at me.

I felt my face turn scarlet. He had never spoken harshly to me before and now he had done so in front of others, people who didn't even like me because I was imagined to have a spe-

159

cial "in" with the boss. Before anyone could have the satisfaction of seeing me in tears, I ran out of the office and down to the ladies room, where I defiantly lit a cigarette and planned my revenge. I would move out today, get my own apartment, learn how to live my own life. I would show them the significance of my turning twenty-one. They couldn't treat me like a child a minute longer!

Before I could put this bold plan into action, Grandmama swept through the door and caught me smoking. Mouth pinched into a grim line, pendulous little cheeks aquiver, she drew herself up to her full four feet eleven inches, unclinched her jaw and said: "Emily, you're fired. Leave at once."

I had imagined that if ever I pushed Grandmama far enough to fire me, I would feel nothing but triumph. But as I let myself into our house in the middle of the day, I was so discouraged and depressed that I went up to Mama's old third floor painting studio, opened the French doors, and went out on the widow's walk. I stood at the railing and looked out at the sparkling blue Gulf and realized that I had come there to contemplate taking my own life. The scene below me, the lush green tree tops, taller and more cushiony now than when Mama had jumped, seemed to beckon me, seemed to say, you will never find happiness in this life.

I leaned over the railing to see if the flagstones below were visible, testing my balance, my nerve. A leap from a particular spot on the walkway would just clear the trees. But even as I calculated what it would take to end my own life, I knew it was no use. I would endure a great deal more suffering before I put to the test that my pitiful life was worse than purgatory. After all, I had very little in common with Mama; I was really far more like my grandmother, which is perhaps why she felt she had to break me. Mama didn't lift a finger to save herself, never rebelled, never tried to get out. She could have taken the money left her by her father and gone to New York to study painting. Instead, her only act of defiance was to curl up and die.

I heard the telephone ring somewhere far below me, heard someone call my name. Instantly I felt more hopeful—one of my friends was calling to see if I wanted to go out tonight. "Who is it?" I called down the stairwell.

160

"Mrs. Douglas, Miss. Are you home?"

Mrs. Douglas? Ruth! I sprang to the telephone, forgetting that I had been reflecting on suicide only a moment before and remembering only that on top of everything else, I was about to lose my best friend.

"I called to say goodbye," said Ruth. "We leave tomorrow."

"Oh, but you can't, Ruth! Not without a proper goodbye. We'll go to dinner, the three of us."

"Money's a little tight, Em."

"It'll be my treat, silly! I've finally got my own money. And guess what? Grandmama fired me today for smoking!" I forced a less than hearty laugh. "Isn't that too much?"

"Harding's friends are giving him a party. Maybe I could go out for a little bit. Just for old time's sake," Ruth said wistfully.

"I'll meet you at the Dinner Club at eight!"

"All right," she agreed.

As a testament to the resilience of youth, I recall that I promptly went out and got my hair done.

~~~~~

I hadn't seen Ruth in weeks and was somewhat startled at her appearance. Being a redhead, she was naturally pale, with milk-white skin which didn't tolerate the sun as mine did. But now Ruth's pallor gleamed in the near dark of a rear table at the Hollywood Dinner Club.

Ruth tossed off my concern by claiming she was recovering from a flu bug. I let the subject lapse for two quite opposite reasons, the first, my natural self-centeredness: The young don't really believe that others have feelings. The second, at odds with the first, was youthful diffidence. I wasn't confident of my right to know things about people, even my oldest friend. With more experience I would realize that I was supposed to ask, supposed to pry a little, show a little concern. But I took Ruth at her word and let it go, therefore not learning until Peter Bright's silly young bride told me many months later that Ruth had undergone treatment for a venereal disease, a wedding present from her new husband. I don't know whether Ruth was feeling rotten physically, mentally, or both.

161

I didn't know what to do about the undercurrents except chatter inanely. "Don't you miss the old days?" I said. "Everybody's gotten married except me and Peter." I laughed suddenly, having forgotten in all the excitement of getting arrested and getting fired that I had also gotten engaged. "Peter asked me to marry him last night! Can you imagine if I had taken him seriously!"

"We were such idiots," commented Ruth.

I felt put in my place. Marriage had matured Ruth. Now she was not merely a year older, but a generation older, more like my mother. I longed to ask if she was happy. Was it still exciting to make love to a man after you had married him? But I said nothing of the sort, sensing that her replies would be negative. I didn't really want to know that being married to big handsome Harding Douglas hadn't made Ruth happy—tell me no truths.

To keep disillusionment at bay, we ordered drinks which neither of us cared for, and I kept introducing topics that revealed the total failure of our sympathy for one another.

"Oh, I didn't tell you! I'm moving out—getting my own apartment," I said.

"I thought you said you got fired today."

"Oh, I'm through working for my family!"

"Oh, yes, you don't have to do anything you don't want to do—you've got your own money now."

She sounded bitter, which I found extremely unfair. My whole adolescence I had had to borrow from friends because Grandmama thought that being broke would keep me out of trouble. (It didn't work in my teens, nor did it work in my twenties or thirties.)

Ruth's strange mood I interpreted as narrowly and selfishly as you'd expect: it was simply one more thing in a disastrous twenty-four hours that wasn't going my way. Rather disingenuously, I attempted to get back in my friend's good graces. Ruth had always liked being the grownup one in our relationship, the one whose advice was sought, the one who knew the answers. I appealed to this aspect of our friendship by again making myself childish and dependent.

"When did you start feeling like an adult, Ruth? I keep wait-

162

ing for it to happen to me, but what if it never does? Was it getting married that made you feel like a grownup?"

Ruth exhaled a great cloud of smoke over her head and thought about my question for such a long time I thought she had forgotten about it. "No, it was before that, back when Mommy and Daddy got divorced. We lost all our society friends, you know, not because of the Church, but because she had to go to work in that grocery store. I guess that's when I quit believing in childhood."

"Do you think I ought to marry Peter?"

"What about Spencer?"

I shrugged off Spencer. "He hasn't asked. And he won't, either, not until everything's just so. He'll probably already own a house and have china in the cupboard by the time he carries a bride over the threshold. Oh, look, isn't that—!" I blushed. It was Harding, one of a noisy contingent of servicemen and their dates, whom the waiters were trying to accommodate by scurrying around dislodging people and pushing tables together. But Ruth, I saw, had noticed him before I had, was staring at him narrowly, smoke curling around her face, almost coming out her ears. I braced for an explosion, but there was none.

Only the most outrageous behavior could have saved the moment, and Harding Douglas was perfectly up to it. He swooped down on Ruth and kissed her as if nothing could have pleased him more than finding his bride there. His loyalties obviously divided, he tried to get the two groups to conjoin, but Ruth wouldn't budge, merely sat stonily smoking her cigarette and let him extricate himself from this difficulty. The woman Harding seemed to have been paired with a moment before stood icily watching us, then had a powwow with her friends and stormed off to the powder room. Harding sat down with us and began teasing me. I didn't mind being used to ease the hostilities between husband and wife.

"Does Grandma know you're out so late?" he said, ostentatiously peering at his wristwatch.

"Cut it out!" said Ruth irritably.

"For your information," I replied, "I was twenty-one yesterday."

Apparently neither of them read *The Galveston Daily News*

163

and knew of my fame. I told them how Peter Bright and I had been carted off to jail with several hundred others, omitting the conclusion, my special treatment. Harding was as eager as I to take Ruth's mind off the woman who had bustled off to the powder room, and my piece of news was as good as any to get us out of there.

"Twenty-one!" he exclaimed. "And I thought you were just a baby. Well, this calls for a celebration. Come on, let's get out of here. I was the odd man," he added carelessly, "so it's just as well I ran into you two."

He said something to one of his buddies at the other table and a moment later we were out in the parking lot.

"You drive, babe," he said, tossing me his car keys. "I've had too much to drink."

I expected him to get in back with Ruth as he always used to do, but instead, he climbed in front with me. I realized he had let me drive so he wouldn't have to face Ruth, though he didn't seem particularly uneasy by his wife's silence in the backseat.

"Where shall we go?" I said. How did I end up in the middle of this? At least I now understood the reason for Ruth's mood—she had known Harding was out tomcatting around. "Ruth?" How often I've wondered why Ruth simply didn't say she wanted to go home. I would've driven myself home first and turned the car over to Harding and that would have been that. I never would have seen either of them again.

But going home would've meant they had to be alone, so Ruth said: "Surprise me."

Harding seemed completely at his ease, threw his big arm expansively across the back of the seat, caressed my neck with his fingers. Warmth crept up my neck and spread across my face in a blush: I liked it too much. I started the car and got us turned around. The car was new, purchased just before they got married—a Buick, if I remember. Harding claimed I was a natural behind the wheel, but Ruth wasn't allowed to touch the machine because she didn't have the coordination for driving.

"The Turf Club?" I suggested. "I haven't been there for awhile."

Harding laughed and made some comment about my "blue blood." I wouldn't have suggested the place had I known that

164

Harding was going to pay for everything and further distress Ruth with money troubles.

As soon as we were seated and had drinks in front of us, Harding slipped away on a mysterious errand. I was afraid it had something to do with that woman he had left at the Hollywood, so I tried to distract Ruth, make her laugh. I realize now that I was equally motivated by a desire for her not to destroy my idealism about true love, and to stop being part of the general conspiracy to spoil my birthday and cheat me of the attention I deserved for turning twenty-one. Today, of course, I'm ashamed of asking Ruth to pretend for my sake that she had not just caught her husband of barely three months out with another woman, for heartlessly discounting her feelings and thinking only of myself. I blame the sins of selfishness and a willingness to self-deceive for my taking part in the events of that night, which was the last time I ever saw Ruth and which determined the course of my own life.

Harding returned with a little troupe from the kitchen and a hastily decorated cake sporting a single sparkler. The band struck up "Happy Birthday" and several hundred people burst into song, not even knowing whose birthday it was. Harding led me out on the dance floor, where, flushed with happiness, I waved at Ruth every time we whirled past. What must the poor girl have felt as she watched her husband take up with me where he had left off with that anonymous girl at the Hollywood?

I felt that life owed me some fun after the indignities I had suffered, and I calmed my guilty feelings about having my good time at Ruth's expense by noting that Harding, not Ruth, was the one who was behaving with perfect manners. Repeatedly he asked Ruth to dance, but she turned him down. She sat at the table, nursing her drink, smoking, watching while Harding whirled me around on the dance floor till we were dizzy and breathless.

I had forgotten how handsome Harding was. As we danced, I fell in love with him all over again. I have many photos of Harding in uniform—none that I took—he was out of the Army by the time Lawrence gave me his camera. In all these pictures, he sits amid a litter of bottles and glasses with other men in uniform. Sometimes there's a wife or girlfriend present, their hair worn in those dreadful pre-war piles, dark lipstick, everyone smoking and apparently having a wonderful time.

Today I am inclined to be more critical of Harding's looks in these pictures, to notice the incipient ravages of alcoholism and unhealthy living. He seems not really handsome to me, certainly not in a noble or gentlemanly way, but twenty-one found me in full rebellion against anything that might be construed as good for me. What he lacked in sophistication, Harding made up for in virility and sheer size. Yes, he was impressiveness in mufti—which has won many a girl's heart before mine. At the worst of Harding's illness he was so emaciated that I could roll him over in bed all by myself, but back then he weighed close to two hundred and fifty pounds and didn't have a bit of fat on him. Obviously we were a gross example of opposites attracting, he so massive, so fair-haired, me so small and dark. I was fascinated with his size, marveled at the volume of liquor he could put away and still function, qualities that would soon not thrill me at all.

Many of the same patrons who had been carted off to jail the night before had arranged for their freedom as easily as I had, and we laughed and joked with one another about our celebrity. When one place became tiresome, we moved on to another, the Del Mar, the Sui Jen, which was already open for business again. It seemed to me that life had been concentrated into this pure essence: club-hopping with a blond giant in uniform who paid me extravagant attention. It was a mad, delightful life, and the best part was that Grandmama would've been furious!

Ruth neither endorsed nor condemned our erratic itinerary, but went along with us as if indulging two willful and not very funny children. At some point she went to sleep in the backseat and I was afraid we would have to call it a night, but Harding had a solution. He stopped and got a bottle and we headed out to West Beach. Nothing mattered except that the night not end.

With Ruth asleep, Harding grew bolder about touching me, and I stopped pretending I wanted him to quit. He offered me swigs of whiskey and I took them, but in spite of all I had drunk, I had never felt more alert. I drove in a huge circle, Seawall

Boulevard to 61st Street, down Broadway and back to the sea-wall. I kept remembering the night I had run off with Roger from the cotillion and how I had infuriated and at the same time enlightened Spencer when he realized what a pathetic little mutt I was, trailing after people, hoping someone would take me home. My awful neediness was the reason Spencer kept just out of arm's reach. I scared him, as I would anyone with any sense. Tears of pure self pity rolled down my cheeks.

But there was no one to notice my tears. I had outlasted my companions. Harding was slumped in the seat beside me, his heavy head pressed against my upper arm and breast. I felt protective toward my friends and vowed to look after them and see they came to no harm.

I had no clear cut plan, thought I would merely drive until the others woke up, I think, but Ruth abruptly sat up and demanded that I stop. Responding to the panic in her voice, I veered sharply left and bounced to a stop among the sand dunes. Ruth tumbled out the door on the far side from me and began vomiting. Harding sat up and peered out at the Gulf of Mexico, visible straight ahead in the pale beam of our head-lights.

"Where are we?"

"Um, on the beach."

"Don't get us stuck." Then he sank back down to his cozy place against my breasts. "Stop!" I hissed at him when his little bites became more insistent. I was less concerned about propriety than I was about Ruth finding out. But Ruth was in no condition to find out anything. We heartlessly ignored her pathetic retching, and it didn't occur to me to get out and help her. Harding pulled my blouse out of my waistband and put a hand inside. We tussled and giggled to see whether his hand would stay where it was or advance further.

After an interminable delay, Ruth crawled back in the car and lay in the back moaning.

"Just lie down and be still, Ruth," I told her, trying to sound sober and responsible. "I'll take you home now."

Harding pretended to give up the struggle and took his hand out of my blouse, but all of a sudden he turned his head in my lap and closed his jaws around a big bite of mons Venus,

167

destroying my pose of concern for Ruth. I screamed and giggled, jerked my knees up, crashing his head into the steering wheel, and we were swept away on gales of hysterical laughter, from which I recovered only with great difficulty.

"Stop now, behave yourself!" I said, trying to sound stern. "I have to take Ruth home."

I managed to get the car in reverse, but nothing happened when I stepped on the accelerator. I didn't know what was wrong, thought the problem lay in my fuddled perception. I floorboarded the accelerator. The engine roared and behind us twin plumes of sand redly ignited in the taillights.

"Aw, shit," said Harding, collapsing in defeat against my thigh. "You've got us stuck." He groped under the seat for something and a moment later came up with a flashlight and got out, lurching and swearing in the deep sand. I rolled down my window and listened while he inspected each wheel and cursed it. Finally he came to my window and stuck his head in.

"Forget it, goddamn thing's buried to the axles," he informed me. "We'll be here all night."

I should have felt some remorse, but the fact is, I wasn't the least bit sorry we couldn't leave. I noticed Harding eyeing Ruth in the backseat, at the same time, softly massaging my nearer shoulder.

"Come on, let's take a walk," he said. "I gotta clear my head before I dig us out."

I didn't wait to be asked twice, but with obscene haste abandoned my sick friend. The breeze was blowing a steady thirty knots out of the southeast, pushing the tide high up the beach. Clouds raced overhead, switching the moon on and off. On the day before this, twenty-one years earlier, my mother had struggled to give me birth while a hurricane raged. Mama would have left with thousands of other islanders if she had not been in labor. I came very close to *not* being born on the island.

As we went away and left Ruth, I felt compelled to mention her. "What's wrong with Ruth?"

Harding shrugged. "She gets these headaches."

He took my hand and shoved it into his pants pocket where coins hot from his thigh pressed against my skin. Ahead of us, off Bolivar Point, the new day sent out pale pink exploratory fingers. I felt completely alive and awake. I felt beautiful and sought after. The clouds raced across the face of the moon, giving me the sensation of actually being able to feel the earth hurtle through space. I turned to look at Harding, my beautiful companion, facing into the wind, his straight dark blond hair blown back from his face, his khaki shirt open at the throat. He freed my hand and fumbled for a cigarette, offered me a drag. The wind quickly burned the cigarette to ash. Harding's pace was leisurely, but I had to trot to keep up, a Pekingese on an outing with a Great Dane.

My flimsy high-heeled sandals kept filling with sand and tripping me, so Harding bent down and took them off and put them in his jacket pocket. Then he hefted me into his arms and turned and walked into the dunes. He folded up suddenly and we were lying against the coarse vegetation and sand, kissing each other passionately. He pulled himself away long enough to shrug out of his coat and spread it for us to sit on. We were somewhat protected from the wind by the sand dune, and Harding further shielded me with his big body. I neatly fit the hollow under his arm against his ribs, like Eve returning to her mythic origins. I was entirely willing to fall into a dreamy swoon and do anything Harding liked, but he wanted to talk.

"Ruth says you're a goddamn millionaire, Little Emily."

I struggled to sit up. "I've got two whole dollars left," I joked. "Need a loan?"

"But don't you get some money or something now that you're twenty-one?"

"I'm supposed to get my mother's money."

"How much?"

"I don't know. My grandmother has it all invested. My mother was sick for a long time before she died, so she turned it all over to Grandmama. Probably she'll dole it out to me a few dollars a week for the rest of my life."

Possibly my father had explained that to me. Or Spencer. And maybe I've confused the chronology and it wasn't that night that we had this conversation. But I'm sure of what Harding said when I told him that Grandmama could either give me the money, or not, as she chose.

"But it's your money. The law's on your side."

169

In spite of my brave words to Ruth about moving out and living on my own, I had not imagined myself living opulently, only getting by, living in a small apartment and working for my living like everybody else. I wasn't like Mama, who had associated exclusively with the island's privileged class; I drew my ideas and aspirations from the island's working children.

Nor had I been taught the dangers of discussing my fortune with a strange man. Instead, I was flattered that Harding was interested in me, that he had thought of me in any terms, other than that I was too short, dark, plain, and young to fool with. If he chose to be impressed with my theoretical wealth, so be it. For myself, insofar as I had considered the money at all, I figured it would only serve as another prong to my grandmother's toasting fork, on which I perpetually seemed to turn. I tried to be honest, to explain something of this to Harding, but he had his own ideas about wealth and assumed that everything I told him would change now that I had achieved my majority.

"What's it like living in a big house with servants to wait on you hand and foot?"

"Are you kidding? They're all allowed to boss me around."

"You don't look twenty-one. In fact, I thought you were a little kid."

"I'm only a year younger than Ruth."

"What did you get for your birthday?"

"Nothing much. My father gave me this ring that was my mother's. That was nice, but then today he called me an imbecile in front of the other employees and my grandmother fired me. What are you looking for?"

"Something to give you for your birthday." Harding searched his pockets, considered for a moment the hand that wore a thin gold wedding band as if he might give that to me. He pulled a chain from his shirt and peered at his dog tags, fingered the insignia on his shirt collar. "What can I give Little Emily for her birthday that will be real special, something she'll always remember ol' Harding by?" he said.

"How about a kiss?" I suggested, trying to sound arch.

"Just a kiss? Well then, it'll have to be a good one."

He pulled me into his lap so that I straddled him, and he wrapped his great arms around me, two or three times it seemed, before kissing me. Everything, I suddenly realized, had been a prologue to this. From the moment we first saw each other in the Hollywood Dinner Club, we had been maneuvering toward this end, watching for our opportunity. We would've had to invent something if Ruth had not gotten ill, if we had not gotten stuck in the sand.

I can't even excuse myself by claiming that I thought Harding was in love with me or would ever want to see me again. I was simply a little opportunist, taking love where I found it, unhampered by inconvenient morals. That afternoon I had casually considered suicide; that night I casually committed adultery with my best friend's husband.

Not that I didn't try to excuse myself. I told myself that Ruth didn't really love Harding any more—anybody could see that. I told myself that probably she didn't care what he did. And since they were leaving on the morrow, she wouldn't have to be hurt by the fact that it was me and not the girl he had been with.

I knew that Harding wouldn't stop with just a kiss, that I was playing with fire, that he wasn't like the young men whom I egged on, then pushed away when things went too far. I was determined to go through with it this time and not back out. I twisted aside my underclothes so he could get closer to me, finally implored him to take me. And Harding was wise enough to hold back until I demanded satisfaction. Once I gave him the word, everything changed.

Suddenly he was terrifyingly businesslike. He stripped off my underpants and unbuttoned himself, lay back against the dunes and arranged me on top of him. I was shaking with the cold and with suppressed excitement when he gripped my bare buttocks in his hands and tried to ease me down on him, but I gasped and writhed away from what seemed an impossible fit. He merely gripped me tighter and pulled me down with more authority so that I had no option but meet him straight on. A spasm of white hot cramp wrenched my tender female organs, shocking all desire out of me.

I grunted and opened my mouth to protest, but he didn't wait to hear what I thought about it, but thrust into me again and again. The scream congealed on my lips. I felt boneless and malleable. I tried vainly to hold myself away from the driving

171

pain, but his big hands held me like a vise. I writhed in pain no less agonizing than the mental pain of once having envied Constance Chatterley when Mellors obsessively searched out her hidden places, seeking to possess her as no man ever had, exciting her astonishment at what she was able to bear. What foolish prepubescent virgins we had been, reading those humid passages to each other, moaning with suppressed ecstasy and longing for the lover who would use us that way! And now I was finally getting exactly what I had wished for and could only hold on for dear life, hoping the great shaft didn't divide me into my two deceitful selves. A woman didn't write that book! This was what I deserved for betraying Ruth, this cruel scouring that seemed to go on forever, a pain I could never become inured to.

But finally it concluded in a series of violent spasms. Harding fell back against the sand, spent and out of breath, gasping, "Baby, baby, baby."

I crawled off into the dunes, weeping and disbelieving. I held my poor maimed self and rocked with the pain, worse than any cramp I'd ever had. Peeing, I sensed, would be pure torture, and if I stood up, blood would surely pour into my shoes. Harding hardly seemed human to me at that moment. He reached a dazed hand out toward me, but I was too far away.

"Honey, why didn't you tell me you were new at this?" he said, getting his breath back. "Goddamn, if I'd known—how'd you expect me to know?—you're out with a different guy every goddamn night of the week."

"They always stop when I tell them to," I said accusingly, hating him.

He rolled over and grabbed me by the wrist, pulled me forcibly back into his lap. "Hey, babe, don't you know I just made you a woman? My woman?"

I wanted to be comforted, wanted to be assured that the sordid and painful experience I had just undergone wasn't all there was to grownup love. I was so disappointed I wanted to cry if this was what all the excitement was about, the act that had launched a million impassioned phrases. Or maybe I was like Mama, who had written into her journal how she hated for Papa to touch her. The thought that I might have inherited some strange unwomanly tendency from her was so threatening that I curled up tight against Harding and willed myself to fall back under his spell.

"That teasing shit is one of them society girl games that don't work with real men," he explained. "You said you wanted it—begged me for it—how was I to know you didn't really mean it?"

"What am I going to do? I can't walk back to the car like this!" Indeed, it seemed unlikely to me that I would ever walk again. "I think I'm . . . *injured!*"

"Let's . . . think," said Harding, sounding a bit nervous. "You got a hanky or something?"

I didn't, but there was a scrap of white embroidered fabric pinned in my breast pocket. He took it, and to my embarrassment, reached between my legs with the rag and wiped me, then held the cloth up to the moon to see if there was any blood. Even I was forced to concede only the barest trace of some dark substance.

"There, see, you're not ruined." He sounded relieved. "Next time you'll be a champ. You'll see, babe, I can make it beautiful for you."

It was a bit late for moral outrage, but perhaps because he dismissed my pain so easily, I demurred. "Next time! There can never be a next time! You're Ruth's husband! This is terrible what we've done! She must never know about it!"

Inexplicably, Harding grinned and shook his head slightly. "Can't you tell it's all over between Ruth and me? Listen, let's talk about me and you—"

"Over! Really?"

"Why do you think I was with someone else tonight? Not that she means anything, understand—one of my buddies fixed me up with her—I don't even know her. But, you and me, kid— I got a crazy idea that we could be something really special."

Reality was changing so fast I could hardly keep up. "You . . .? Harding, are you serious? You aren't just saying that because you're drunk?"

"Honey, I know exactly what I'm saying. Maybe you'll be surprised about this, but all those times I was teasing you? I was really wondering what it'd be like with you. God, you're so sweet and tight! I know I ain't no society swell—but, hell, if them jerks knew anything about women you'd've lost that sweet little cherry of yours before now." The wind whipped his hair in both our faces. His hands were doing things to me that felt good. I could scarcely believe my body was capable of feeling passion again after the indignity it had just suffered. Maybe I wasn't like Mama after all.

"You know what I'd do if you were mine?" Harding said. "I'd carry you around in my arms from morning till night and make sweet love to you till the roosters crowed. We'd still be on our honeymoon when we were eighty."

I wasn't ready just then to contemplate a vigorous love life. "I don't know . . ." I said doubtfully.

"Hell, don't worry about the first time, honey! Think about someday when you're rarin' to go and I'm an old man and can't get it up. That's the way it is, you know. Women last a whole lot longer than men. What'd'you say, Emily?"

"About what?"

"Could you love a guy like me? Look here when I'm talking to you, honey!" He turned my face up to his. "Could you love a big palooka like me?"

"Yes," I whispered. "I've always loved you."

"You're not worried about me being divorced?"

"Are you?"

"Not yet, but I'm gonna be. If you'll have me. Would you marry me if I was free?" He kissed my fingers, one at a time. "I'll be more careful next time. You just got me excited and I went a little crazy. Next time it'll be in a bed, real nice and slow."

"You're not going to leave tomorrow?"

I wanted more than anything to grab on to this bright hope Harding held out to me, but there was so much to fear: He was asking me to be a woman for him, face the certain perils of defying the Church and my folks, not to mention a lifetime of adult physical love with him, which I was not at all certain I was up to.

All previous defiance melted into childish pranks compared to this. What would Grandmama do? And what about Ruth!? There could be no shabbier treatment of a best friend than to lie down on the ground with her new husband. Suddenly I quailed at the thought of having to go back to the car to face her. And we would surely have to in a few minutes, for even then the air was growing palpably grayer. If we could just stay on the beach forever and never face any of them—all those people who had claims on us!

"I'll just let her go on to California," Harding was saying. "It was her idea. She wanted to get me away from my buddies."

"I thought you loved Ruth. I used to envy her when you were in the backseat and I drove you around."

Harding wrote off his entire relationship with Ruth in a few words. "Aw, it was okay for awhile. She was one thing back when we were dating, but something else after we got married—nag, nag, nag, never happy with anything I did for her."

"She seems sort of unhappy . . ." How willing I was to make Ruth the villain! "What's wrong with her—why is she sick?"

"Oh, that—nothing. All taken care of now. Nothing you have to worry about, hear? Here's what we'll do—I'll put her on the bus and you and I'll head on down to Monterrey where I got this buddy named Frank Poe. We'll lay low until things cool off. What'd'ya say, babe? How does that sound to you?"

I wasn't capable at that moment of sorting out complex moral issues. All I really heard was that someone finally wanted me, which made up for everything, the pain I had just gone through, my dread of having to go through it again if we got married and slept together every night, even the terrible fact that we now had to break the news to everyone we knew.

For all Harding's faults, he showed great sensitivity in playing to my needs. I would never be alone again. He wanted to marry me, not just have an affair. In time, he said, my family would accept him, even if the Church didn't. I didn't argue, but I knew better. Grandmama would disown me, but I didn't need her money. Harding was right, Mama's money would be enough for us. And anyway, had my family's money ever brought me the slightest happiness?

It was ironic and appropriate that all I had ever asked of my folks was a little attention. Now they would have to give it to me, but it would come too late. I was legally free of them and would meet my needs in my own way. There was nothing they could do to stop me. Nor could the Church stop me. Hadn't Ruth and I always said we wouldn't be happy till we got ourselves excommunicated?

"I'll take care of everything," Harding was saying. "All you have to do is wait for my call, okay?"

I clung to him in sudden panic. "No! I can't let you go. I'll never see you again!"

"My little baby," he cooed, rocking me. To be held in a pair of strong arms, to be assured that everything was going to be all right, that my own salvation was being taken out of my inept hands—what blessed relief. With what willingness I turned myself over to him!

"How long do you think it will be?" I said, steeling myself, trying to be brave.

"Shouldn't be more than a couple of days, honey."

"What do you have to do?"

"Don't ask, don't ask me any questions about that stuff. I'll take care of it and all you have to do is be ready to go when you get the word. That is, if you're serious and not playing one of your schoolgirl games with me."

It seemed quite incredible that he could doubt *my* seriousness. "I want to be your wife, Harding. I just don't see. . . ."

"I'll take care of it," he repeated. "Now, you're not to say a word to anybody. If your grandmother can stop you, she will. She'll use the law, the Army, God-knows what all. But I guaran-damn-tee you the old bitch won't stand by and let some guy like me steal her little darling, so you're gonna have to play it real cool."

I knew he was right, but he had the reasons wrong. Grandmama would hold on to me not because she loved me, but because I was *hers*. Neither of us mentioned my papa. He was a cipher as far as my raising was concerned, and even people who barely knew me seemed to sense that Grandmama held all the power.

Harding began tucking his khaki shirt into his pants. "When everything's ready, I'll call and tell you I'm on my way. Don't take anything with you, understand? That'll tip 'em off. Just your purse, or whatever you take when you go out."

Breathlessly I agreed, but none of it seemed real. God wouldn't let me get away with such a thing. He would be on Grandmama's side and intervene in some terrible way. Harding smoothed my hair. "Fix yourself up some, hon. Get your clothes

176

back on. We gotta git, gotta dig the goddamned car out of the sand or we won't have no wheels to take us to Mexico."

At the thought of facing Ruth, my mind snapped back to reality. My God, I had just conspired with my best friend's husband to elope to Mexico! Sensing that second thoughts had me paralyzed, Harding pulled me back into his arms and came up with the one saving thought:

"Emily, don't worry about her—she'll be glad to see the last of me. You'll be doing her a favor."

The car wasn't nearly as far away as I had imagined. Ruth could have stumbled on us at any time. Nor was I as injured as I had expected to be. In fact, as I walked along beside Harding, I felt quite proud of myself. I was a real woman now, carried a little bit of my lover inside me. We stopped to kiss again and again to assure each other we really would go through with our plan.

"You'll really call, won't you?" I pleaded, just before giving him up, possibly forever.

"The only thing that can stop me is a knife between the ribs," he declared. "Now listen—I'm counting on you to use a little sense—don't go packing a lot of goddamned stuff—we can buy what you need later. And don't trust *any*body!"

I felt like a beautiful heroine in the movies, bravely seeing my man off to war. When we were in sight of the car, Harding reached over and touched my mouth with the tip of one finger, marking his place. He laughed suddenly.

"I got myself a million-dollar baby!"

For Ruth's benefit I fixed an innocent look on my face, but it was wasted, she hardly stirred when I got in the car. Harding went out on the highway and about ten minutes later came back with a man in a pickup to pull us out. In no time, we were heading into the rising sun. Ruth sat up and yawned, said she felt better. I couldn't look at her.

I had dozens of questions, but could ask none of them. I bit my lip and contented myself with the pressure of Harding's fingers underneath a fold of my skirt, letting me know we were still connected in spirit. I felt suddenly shy, seeing him in the light, his seeing me. He would see that I wasn't beautiful and would perhaps regret what had happened. Our pact was made by two strangers in the dark, not Ruth's husband and best friend, not this exhausted, emotionally wrung out, strangely silent pair. Ruth didn't seem to notice our monosyllables, but talked about what all there was to do before they left. Our plan to go to Mexico seemed like a fantasy I had dreamed up in the night. But here was the reality of Harding's fingers touching my leg, his repeated looks in my direction. What color were his eyes? I had never noticed before. Dark, though, not blue as I would've guessed. We looked at the same time and our eyes caught. Brown, he had brown eyes.

I performed my part perfectly. Harding let me out on the side street so I could go through the backyard. I had done that hundreds of times, my grandmother knew my trick, but had given up trying to stop me. I turned around and gave Ruth a quick hug, probably she thought I was too distraught about losing her to say anything. I didn't look at Harding for fear I would give myself away. I ran for the safety of the yard, stood at the corner of the garage and watched their car disappear, Ruth still in the backseat. Would they go home and make up? Would Harding come to his senses? Why would a man want me when he could have my beautiful friend Ruth?

I went upstairs and lay on my bed for hours, neither asleep nor fully awake, but in a kind of trance in which I relived over and over every word spoken, every embrace and caress we had shared on that dark beach. I was alternately elated and cast into the deepest despair, certain he would come for me, equally certain he wouldn't.

Meanwhile the hot August sun drove away the moon and dispelled the chill of the dawn, making our frantic capers of the night before seem slightly mad, unreal. Yet on the coverlet under me was the gritty reality of sand sifting out of my clothes. I really had lain on the beach in Harding's arms and done the unthinkable!

I postponed bathing, washing away the sweet substance of Harding himself. Would he really leave Ruth and take me to Mexico? Or would he, in the light of day, soberly reassess the facts: that Ruth was ten times prettier than me, years more mature. Would he shamefacedly confess what he had done and ask her forgiveness, blame it all on liquor? Maybe they had just used me to get even with each other, and now they would make up, pack the car, and put me and Galveston far behind them, start a new life in California.

But I kept remembering all the sweet things Harding had said. I had to believe he meant them, that he would come back for me. If I didn't believe, I would have to kill myself in despair. Who was I fooling with my brave talk of moving out on my own? Anyone could see that I didn't have the least idea how to go about it. And yet, I couldn't endure any more of this terrible loneliness. If Harding didn't rescue me, I might do what Mama had done, lie in my bed and wait to die.

I crept to my bureau to look at my purses and choose the right one for Mexico.

Chapter Nine

My grandmother rarely gave any indication that she noticed me, but later I realized she must have been paying close attention to me virtually from the moment I came back from that night on the beach with Harding. I thought I was going about my business normally, but I now see that as I waited for the call that was to save my life, I gave my housemates all the clues they needed to deduce that I was going through a very disturbing time. I quit eating; I was easily startled; I turned down all invitations; I obsessively watched the front of our house from Mama's old front bedroom window. If I did go out, on my return, I questioned Meg and Mrs. Frenche so closely about my telephone messages that they became quite touchy on the subject.

One of my errands was to go to the bank to withdraw the money I had saved from my earnings—not much—I was a spendthrift at heart and once I had money, generously treated the friends who had supported me throughout my poverty. I was worried about Harding and me having enough money to make our escape, since Ruth had said money was tight.

And during it all, I worried—not about what Ruth might be going through, nor about the certain perdition of my soul—that I wouldn't get to put my family and friends through this trauma, worried that I was being a fool, that Harding didn't really intend to run away with me, that what he had said was just something handsome men promised virgins they had ravished.

The call did not come the next day, nor the day after, nor the day after that. A week went by and all I knew was that Harding and Ruth were no longer at their old address. I didn't dare call Mrs. Meyers and ask her where Ruth was. Maybe Ruth knew by now what I had done. Maybe she had already spread the word to her mother, and thence out into the community.

I teetered on the verge of despair. When, in later years, I grieved over Harding's weaknesses and failures, I forced myself to recount the awful minutes of that week as they crept by and how I willed him to call, could not endure the thought that he might stand me up. I wanted him more than I wanted life. If I didn't get him, if he didn't call, I was prepared to commit some desperate, though unspecified, act. I could never afterward tell myself that I had not cooperated fully with my undoing.

I was too distracted with my thoughts to notice how eerily peaceful things were at home.

Eight days after my second twenty-first birthday celebration, I was so depressed I could hardly speak. There was no longer any reason to hope that Harding's call would come. Both my folks came home for dinner that night, which in itself was somewhat unusual. I stared at my plate and let their humdrum conversation flow past me. At the earliest opportunity I excused myself and crept up to my room. It was time to consider desperate remedies.

I lay on my bed with the little purse I had packed for flight pressed to my heart. What would it be? A sharp blade? A long walk into the Gulf? A leap from the widow's walk?

Suddenly Lewis tapped on my door and said that I had a visitor. I nearly knocked him over getting out the door. How like Harding to brazenly walk into Grandmama's house and carry me off! I had to get down there before Grandmama could interrogate him and scare him away! Clutching the little bag that contained a change of underwear, a toothbrush, and all the cash I could lay my hands on, about four hundred dollars, I arrived in the drawing room breathless, to meet—Spencer. I expect my eyes bugged from my head.

My grandmother said, "Look who's here, Emily, come to

181

take you for a drive. I told him you've looked quite peaked lately."

Suddenly I realized that it was all planned, that she had got Spencer there on purpose. Wordlessly I turned and walked out of the house, too stunned to think how to protect myself from the blow that had fallen, for I had no doubt that if Grandmama knew there was reason to enlist Spencer's aid, she had already taken steps to prevent the disaster.

Spencer, blushing to the roots of his cropped whitey-blond hair, hurried after me, but I got to the car first, yanked open my own door and threw myself in, suddenly conscious that my purse had underwear in it. We rode in silence for several minutes while I chose among the various attitudes available to me. Finally outrage won out.

"What are you doing here, Spencer!?"

He tried to sound casual. "I've been home all summer—not that you noticed. I go back next week."

"My grandmother put you up to this."

"Put me up to what?"

"Don't you turn on me too, Spence! What does she know? What has she done? Tell me!"

"Nothing that I know of."

"Liar! Well it won't do her any good. She can't stop me. I'm twenty-one now and I can do what I damn well please!"

Spencer paid attention to his driving and kept a determinedly neutral expression on his face. It was not quite dark out. Finally he jerked the wheel over to the curb and impatiently turned off the engine, apparently unable to argue cogently and drive at the same time. We were on the seawall at the very spot where the city of Galveston would one day build a Pleasure Pier, which would operate at a loss for a number of years and be sold to a developer who would tear it down and build The Flagship Hotel, which stands there today.

Spencer, too, had decided on an attitude. "Look," he said, "none of that has anything to do with me. The only reason I'm here is to argue my own case. Quit looking at me like I'm the enemy."

I knew then that Grandmama had found out about and crushed my plans. Maybe Mr. Wilbur at the bank had told her about the money. Maybe she had had me followed. However it came about, I now had my answer: Harding wasn't going to call. I collapsed in grief.

"Emily, stop! I can't stand to see you cry. What do you want me to do—I'll do it!"

"You! You're just her stooge!" Spencer seemed like a little boy to me after being with Harding. I could hardly look at him.

"Come on, Emily, be fair. I've never ratted on you in your life."

"If you're my friend, tell me what she did. Help me undo it! What does she know?"

Spencer sighed deeply, obviously resenting his role in this matter. "She knows you're gonna run off with this character—"

"How does she know that?!"

"What does it matter, Emily? You're right about them not being able to stop you. Oh, God! Emily, please don't do this!"

He looked like he might burst into tears himself. Two spots of vivid color stained the sharp points of his cheekbones, like they had that night when he watched me dance with Roger. He had been shaving for years, but there was still a suggestion of peach fuzz around his eyes, which, with his little boy hair-cut made him seem foolish saying these things. But he pleaded grownup feelings. He clasped the hand nearest him and kissed it.

"Emily, why do you have to be so dense? Don't you know I love you?"

I had always known, but it didn't matter. He was just Spencer, the boy I had grown up with, not the grown man I could have if Grandmama would stop interfering with my life.

"Spencer, I don't have time for this! You've got to tell me what you know. Where is he?"

"Who?"

"You know who—Harding! I told you a long time ago I was in love with him. I told you he was older and that Grandmama wouldn't like him. But you don't begrudge me my happiness, do you? You don't want to see me miserable, do you? Help me!"

Spencer took a swipe at his eyes and cleared his throat. His voice sounded deeper with the effort to hold back tears. "I have to argue these cases all the time, see, in mock court. But this is

183

one case I can't win just by having the best argument. All I can do is beg you, Emily, *please* don't run off with this guy. Marry me. I always thought we would someday, when we grew up. I thought you meant to."

"Everybody thought it but me," I answered bitterly.

"You were supposed to get all this out of your system," he said.

"Get what out of my system?" I cried. "Get it out of my system that I need love and affection, tenderness and touching once in awhile?"

"You never wanted those things from me."

"No, I didn't. We were friends, pals. It wouldn't have felt right."

"Every time I came home from Austin people would be dying to tell me what you had been up to—drunk, dancing till dawn, out with three guys at one time—" (The Tarnow twins and Peter, we were celebrating Tommie's buying a second-hand fishing boat.) "And I always want to say to those people—Emily's not really like that. She just does those things because . . . I don't know why, Emily. I respect your grandmother a lot, but I realize she's probably not the easiest person in the world to live with. I mean, I mean. . . ."

Spencer could never in his life tell a falsehood, not even to gain the girl he loved. He was bound at that moment to express his own frustration with my absurd behavior.

"I mean, but Emily, does that give you the right to act like an idiot? The guy's AWOL from the Army! They say he's a drunk—damn it, Emily—he's married, for Chrissake—Ruth Meyer's husband. What are you thinking of?!"

Seeing my stony face, he realized he had let passion cause him to lose track of his argument. "Em, I've tried to be a friend to you every way I know how. I just wish it had been enough. Inside, I believe you're a decent person, that you wouldn't do things like this if. . . . And I'd still—if you said the word, Emily—I'd still—" He hesitated and gulped. "I'd marry you right this minute! Run away with me, Emily. I'm the one you're supposed to be with, not some . . . alcoholic, married soldier."

"Where is he?" I said calmly, ignoring his proposal, which didn't mean anything, was just their last-ditch effort to keep me in the fold. "Where is he? If you know and don't tell me, Spencer, I'll never speak to you again, not if I live to be a hundred."

Spencer knew it was hopeless. "You just won't listen," he said sadly. "God, we're both gonna regret this night."

He started the car and drove slowly away from the curb. A mile or so further down the coastline, he parked again, across from the entrance to Ft. Crockett. He held up his wristwatch and checked the time. I felt my pulse pick up speed.

"What are we doing here?"

"Shut up, Emily!" he said savagely.

I sat very still and tried to figure out what was going on, what was about to happen, and what did Spencer have to do with it?

"Spencer . . ."

"Not another word, Emily! Or so help me, I'll take you back to your grandmother and wash my hands of this whole stupid mess!"

Across the street, a man came out the Seawall entrance of the military base, a tall man in civilian clothes whom I didn't immediately recognize. He looked up and down the street, across at us sitting in the dark car, then reached into his pocket for a cigarette. When he cupped his hands over the flaring match, I finally realized it was Harding.

"Oh, Spence, you darling!" I flung myself across the car seat and kissed him, but he pushed me away.

"Get out of here! And don't you ever accuse me of not loving you, Emily."

I didn't hang around to argue about it, but jumped out of the car and ran after the figure, now walking east along Seawall Boulevard. "Harding! Harding!"

Harding stopped, incredulous, and waited for me.

"Goddamn, baby, what's going on?"

"I don't know, but if you still want me, we've got to get out of here fast."

"I don't know where the bastards have my car. You got any money?"

"Four hundred dollars."

"We'll get a cab." Suddenly he stopped. "How did you know they were going to let me out?"

185

"I didn't. I didn't know anything. A friend came and got me and brought me here. I waited all week for you to call."

Harding frowned and flung aside his just lit cigarette. "Something's screwy. It's a trap, I feel it. Who was this friend?"

"I think . . . I think he told Grandmama he would keep me away from you and instead . . . he brought me to you." I was only just beginning to appreciate Spencer's sacrifice. "Let you out of where? You mean, you couldn't come for me, couldn't call me?"

"Hell, no. I've been in the slammer since Tuesday. I put Ruth on the bus—"

"Did you tell her?"

"Are you kidding? I was down on the wharf selling a couple of guys my stuff to raise money, and all of a sudden the shore patrol's picking me up throwing me in the stockade without so much as a by your leave. I figured your old lady was behind it."

"Maybe Mr. Wilbur at the bank told her I took out all my money."

"You don't think this guy's gonna tell her what he did?"

"I think he's covering for me. But let's not wait around to find out. Oh, Harding, is it true, you really want me? This was the worst week of my life."

"You and me both, honey." He grinned suddenly. Even with several days' stubble on his chin he looked good enough to break my heart. "Just proves to me they know someone's trying to make off with their treasure. Come on, babe, let's go see if we can find my car. If we can't, we'll get there by bus, or by God use our thumbs. But we're gonna get there one way or the other. Baby, you're gonna love Frank and Zaida. You know any Spanish?"

~~~~~

I learned my new husband's less admirable qualities gradually, like most wives do. There wasn't a single moment in time when I woke up and realized what I had done. Relationships are too complex for that. Before the first anniversary, I had learned to cry over his drinking, just as Ruth had done, but knowing her fate, I didn't nag him.

I found out that Harding could not make me pregnant only

after a number of years thinking I had been lucky. I believe that repeated exposure to venereal disease, or perhaps the side effects of treatment, made him sterile. (Ruth remarried and had three children.) But the subject was closed as far as Harding was concerned. Any mention of it was a question of his manhood. Eventually I went in secret to a doctor in Mexico whose opinion was that I wasn't at fault for our not having children. The news came at a particularly low point for me, a time when I was inclined to believe that God knew what he was doing in depriving me and Harding of young lives to influence.

It took Harding several weeks to get his affairs in order, to get the divorce from Ruth, and to square things with the Army, which chose to discharge him dishonorably rather than prosecute him for desertion. If Harding had not believed he was marrying a rich girl, he might have been less willing to walk away and leave the Army's piddling compensation for his ten years' service. However, in accepting his ignominious fate, he missed World War II.

We stayed, during those first few crazy weeks, with Frank and Zaida in a cramped and unattractive house in Monterrey, Mexico. (Compared to the places Harding and I would live over the next eight years, the Poe home was roomy and well-furnished.) Franklin had spent twenty years in the Army and retired at the age of forty with a pension handsome enough to live in Mexico without expending any further effort in life.

It would be easy to belittle my naive younger self for supposing, as I did, that Harding would have little incentive to marry me since I had let him "have his way" with me. But I did worry about it, right up to the moment we stood before a small rotund Mexican official and exchanged vows, coached by Frank and Zaida, who spoke the language fluently.

I wrote a long anguished letter to Ruth, trying to explain myself, but even I realized that my motives would be apparent to anyone: I had a total disregard for anyone's feelings but my own. I tore up the letter and didn't write again until after Harding died in 1958.

With almost embarrassing alacrity, we returned to Galveston to look for a lawyer who could tell us what I could expect from my family. I was terrified that Grandmama would have Harding arrested again, or somehow have me bodily carried back to her house. I dreaded an accidental meeting with her or Papa, but I needn't have worried; Galveston society flowed in well-insulated layers from one another. (There was only one accidental meeting, but I'll relate the scene in its time.)

Harding's lawyer learned what I already knew, that O'Malley, Bradley and Tate guarded the Coolidge-Pickering interests, that Grandmama was executrix of my mother's estate and could keep me from seeing any substantial sums until I was thirty years old, and even after that, I would require my father's approval for withdrawals over a certain amount.

It was obvious the will had been structured to protect a frivolous, if not dangerously willful person. I recognized my grandmother's hand in this and realized that my mother probably had had little to do with the document other than signing it. Obviously, my grandmother had tried to protect future generations should I happen to turn out like my mother.

Harding refused to accept that his bride was worth so much but that he could access so little. Over the next eight years he went through a number of lawyers seeking the answer he wanted to hear. There had to be a way around the clause that put his wife perpetually under the thumb of her family.

Our money didn't last. We were amazingly profligate, spent money on foolish things and didn't have enough for essentials. I parted with my rings and trinkets, including the little coral ring that had belonged to my mother—without a sigh, feeling myself fully compensated by Harding's love.

Harding was more careful the next time he made love to me than he had been on that beautiful and terrible night of my deflowering, but I discovered that we were essentially at odds in the matter of sex. It seemed to me that I might get used to it, come to even like it, if Harding didn't want it so often and if he weren't so *vigorous* in taking his pleasure. His appetite was unquenchable. I longed for a mature married lady friend I could ask questions, but mine didn't seem the sort of problem one could discuss with anyone. (Even if I'd had a mother, in 1936, I might not have felt free to broach the subject of sex with her.) I might have unburdened myself to Zaida, had we remained in Mexico that first trip. Did her husband want sex several times a day? How did one *physically* manage? As a new bride, I crept about, raw and miserable, trying to do nothing that might arouse my virile mate's hair-trigger libido.

Harding, who had none of my lifelong associations with the island, often said that he hated Galveston and that he would rather live anywhere in the world. However, it was not convenient to live elsewhere and pursue his legal claim against my family. I heartily wished Harding didn't care about it so much, but I went along with whatever he wanted in that and most matters. Every month I had to go in person to the Kempner Street law offices of Grandmama's attorneys to get my money, my "allowance," as I thought of it. The amount was generous enough for us to live on, had we managed properly, but frugality was in neither of our characters.

Harding loved to party and went out most nights whether I went with him or not (a circumstance I didn't like at first, but which I eventually found preferable to staying home accidentally arousing and having to satisfy my husband's insatiable desires.) Our money was always used up before the month was out. Harding, big, blonde and likeable, never seemed to run short of people to borrow from, including his lawyers, whom he not only didn't pay, but borrowed from against our expectations. Evidently they believed, as Harding did, that it would all be worth it someday.

We had obtained furnished rooms over a house on Post-office Street, where nights were punctuated with the revelry of sailors on shore leave. Prostitutes lived on either side of us. Nights when Harding was out drinking with his friends, I was terrified a drunken sailor would get into the wrong house and find me.

Having been reared in a gracious home with full domestic help, I had never learned to cook, clean or mend. I was the classic well-meaning bride who nearly poisons her husband and burns down the house. At first Harding was charmed by this proof of my gentle upbringing, but like any husband he soon tired of unappetizing meals and a filthy home.

One day he came home with a cookbook, not new, I realized, turning its pages. Some woman had consulted this cookbook, spattered its pages, written notes to herself in its margins, noted, for example, that the custard on page 234 needed to cook five minutes longer than the time suggested. From whose kitchen had Harding acquired this cookbook? Why did she give it up? But Harding didn't like to be asked about his comings and goings, always had many mysterious plans afoot, and I soon learned they included other women.

Naturally I was hurt. I thought that Harding would leave me as he had left Ruth, and I waited for the ax to fall. It never did, and I slowly came to realize why: I had something Ruth didn't have, a fortune. I was so diffident about my looks and whatever other charms I had that it was easy for me to believe Harding had married me for my money. I remember thinking that it was not all bad that Harding let off some of his sexual energy elsewhere.

A few years ago, I went through that universal civic experience called "jury duty," and following a friend's advice, took along a novel to read. Not knowing how long I might spend in the court house, I selected *Bleak House*, whose intimidating size had kept it on my shelf for a number of years. On the flyleaf I was startled to see Lawrence's name in fading black ink, Lawrence Edgar Payne, one of his personal volumes, and I recalled that he had given me that book. It was a posthumous joke. He had known full well how Dickens' bleak generational saga applied to my life.

That day, I was not selected to judge my peer, but I did get interested in the Victorian legal system and learned that long before a pair of impecunious Galveston petitioners forfeited any chance they might have had for happiness by pinning all their hopes on the probate court, their fate had been foreshadowed by the Jarndyces in the High Court of Chancery.

When we took on the defenders of my mother's will, Harding confidently predicted it might take a year or so to make my family "cough up the cash." At worst, he darkly predicted, we might have to hang on till "the old bitch" "kicked the bucket." I hated for Harding to talk about Grandmama that way. I had absorbed enough moral training to believe that God wouldn't allow us to profit from her death, but I didn't tell Harding this. I was afraid that if he believed, as I did, that we would never get the money, he would consider me a poor bargain and give up on me as well.

Having never had money, Harding didn't know that money seldom makes up for emotional deprivation, that in matters of affection and family give and take, I was as deprived as he. Even in our tawdry circumstances, I was far happier than I had been at home. Harding was a jolly companion who seldom allowed himself to get down about anything. And his tastes were simple. He had a lot of energy, though, and couldn't bear staying cooped up in our tiny apartment (nor later in our roomy villa). Our home, wherever we lived, seemed filled to capacity when Harding was in it. Even the bed was too small—he had to sleep with his feet dangling off the end. I was glad for him to get out, but I cried when he didn't come home when I thought he should.

It never occurred to me that Harding ought to work, that his getting a job might solve many of our problems, that he might have had a focus for his fierce energy, that we would've been able to pay our bills. But in those days he filled my world so completely that I simply accepted whatever he did without question. His seven years' seniority made me feel so young and foolish that I deferred all questions to him. If he made money, he made it gambling or in some mysterious "deal," and lost it the same way. He knew scores of men from his military days and never lacked for companions or opportunities for adventure.

I recall those two years on Postoffice Street as the most magical and, at the same time, the most miserable of my life. I didn't in the least miss the comfort and security of Grandmama's house, yet I knew I didn't fit into my new life any better. I counted on our circumstances changing, of course, when we got my money.

In the meantime, Spencer O'Malley graduated from the University of Texas and joined his uncle's law firm. On my monthly errand to collect my check, we took pains not to run into one another. I had read about his engagement party in the newspaper, a rather breathless account of what the society debs wore, complete with a softly glowing portrait of Rose Mataglia, who looked every bit as pretty and accomplished as Spence deserved. I wouldn't allow myself to think about his heroic attempt to save me from the fate of being married to Harding. I wondered how much he knew about my married life, if he felt that his fears for me had been justified, and if he was tremendously relieved that I had turned him down.

I rarely saw my old friends, not only because of the layering effect, but because I didn't go out much. Once, I could not have imagined living anywhere else, but now I longed for the day we could leave the island. The Galveston I had known was no longer my home; I had traded it for a dingy apartment on Post-office Street and a pair of strong arms.

Today, I regret that Grandmama died without getting to know me as an adult. The last time I saw her she was still very angry with me, and I with her. Not enough time had passed for us to see each other in any but the old familiar way.

I remember that it was September, the month the wind dies on the island and the air becomes so thick and hot you can hardly breathe. Mosquitoes, unhampered by the wind, swarmed, and people with money went somewhere else for a month. Our apartment was hot and airless, the pavement below blazing. Harding had gone to New Orleans with some old boot camp buddies who had turned up in Galveston to defend the coast against German invasion. I hadn't wanted him to go, of course, but he never let a wife's wishes unduly influence him, especially if it meant losing face with his "buddies."

I had learned to dread old buddies showing up, because it invariably meant they would take Harding away from me and return him the worse for drink. How would I survive the desolate days until he returned? I had no life of my own, no friends, amusements, nothing but books and the radio. I rarely went out on the streets by myself. My nights were full of vague terrors.

But somehow I summoned the courage to take a long walk to the seawall to try to catch a breeze off the water. I stood looking out at the Gulf, which I recalled Meg Galloway calling "a big bowl of lukewarm broth." Even Meg had turned out to be more loyal to Grandmama than she was to me. But then, I hadn't bothered to tell her where I was, had I? The prevailing breeze, out of the southwest, drove the current along the great curve of the Texas coast, arriving on our shores with a freight of effluvial mud. Galveston waters are only blue when the wind shifts and comes at us from the southeast.

My thoughts turned to Spencer and how many of our scenes

192

had been played out here on the seawall. I missed him and wished we could have one of our intimate chatty conversations. A horn hooted behind me and I turned, half expecting it to be Spencer, but it was Grandmama—eighty-one and still driving herself. For a moment I stood my ground, contemplating flight. Under the influence of Harding's single-minded fanaticism, she had achieved an almost monstrous stature in my mind. It seemed that even meeting her gaze might cause me some injury.

But she was so tiny and erect, so fierce-looking, sitting there behind the wheel, that my heart melted, and I longed for her love as fervently as I had as a child. She, much more than my mother, had raised me, put the stamp of her taste and opinions on me, whether I liked them or not. And no matter how she thwarted my desires, I knew that she did so because she believed it was for my own good. I composed the flutter in my heart and walked over to the car and leaned down to look in the window.

"Hello, Grandmama."

"Emily."

"It's . . . nice to see you."

"Wouldn't hurt you to call once in awhile."

"I didn't think you'd want me to." I was ashamed suddenly of having feared and hated her, especially seeing she was so frail. Had she been ill? Why hadn't I been told? But then I realized I had given up my right to hear family news. Suddenly I was conscious of my shabby clothing and cheap haircut. I should have dressed up more if I was going to leave my own part of town.

"Where's your young man?" she said, looking not at me as she asked this question, but out at the Gulf.

"Away at the moment."

"I suppose you think I'm merely being mean not to let you have your mother's money."

I certainly would have said so five minutes earlier, but seeing her in the flesh after such a long time worked its old magic on me and destroyed my confidence in my rightness.

"I'm sure you think you're doing what's good for me," I said quietly. "You always did."

"What do you suppose Harding Douglas would do with twenty million dollars, Emily?"

She waited, but I had no answer. Or rather, I had too decided

193

an answer. I blushed deeply, wondering how much she actually knew about Harding, about our life together. Did she have us spied on?

"That's what my accountant tells me I'm worth," she said. "Would he do something useful with the money, do you suppose?"

"Don't say ugly things about Harding—"

"*I've* said nothing. Your silence says it for me."

"He wasn't born with money."

"That's right. And neither of you have demonstrated the least bit of sense in handling what little money you do have. A lot of good can be done with twenty million dollars. I won't have it frittered away by fools. You're my flesh and blood, Emily, but I'll disown you before I let you tear down what I've built."

"Keep your money, Grandmama!" I exclaimed, stung into bitterness. "It's all you ever cared about. You never cared about me. Harding has his faults, but at least he touches me, at least he tells me he loves me!"

Grandmama's eyes filmed over and she looked out at the water again, her eyes mirroring crescents of blue.

"I forgot how to be tender, Emily. It was all taken out of me by the storm. I had to harden myself to survive. I'm sorry I didn't love you the way you wanted. I thought your mother would—"

"Don't you talk to me about my mother! She threw herself from the housetop because she didn't feel loved in your house!"

"You don't know what you're talking about! Your mother was a whining, self-indulgent, spoiled creature. She never thought of anybody but herself. She wanted to run off and do something shameful and I wouldn't let her. That's why she jumped off the house. She didn't even have sense enough to do that right."

Tears had blinded my vision. I wanted to run away, but at the same time I was morbidly fascinated to hear these great secrets openly talked about. Later, of course, I realized that my grandmother probably knew she would never have another chance to speak of these things. Unknown to me, she had already suffered her first mild heart attack and had begun to seriously curtail her business and social activities.

194

"I won't let you starve," she said, matter-of-factly, as if reporting that she would renew a magazine subscription for me. "I've left instructions with young Spencer O'Malley—"

"Spencer!?"

"George is retiring. Spencer now handles probate matters for the firm. There's no reason to take my business elsewhere. Spencer has always had a level head on his shoulders, demonstrated maturity and common sense beyond his years. By the way, I plan to dance at his wedding next month. He's marrying Rose Mataglia."

Mention of Spencer, of his approaching nuptials, was perhaps unwise. She had unnerved herself. For a long moment she gripped the steering wheel and said nothing, apparently getting her emotions under control before trusting her voice again. Tears flowed freely down my cheeks. If she had said nothing else, perhaps I would have jumped in the car with her, hugged her, forgiven her everything. But Grandmama wasn't like that. She had hardened herself years before I was born and probably couldn't remember how to access the softer, more feminine emotions.

"Emily, do you repent this terrible thing you've done? Do you wish to come home?"

How would I have answered if she had been around to ask me later, say, after two more years of marriage to Harding? Even then the question conjured up a sudden yearning for my old room, the well-planned meals, the orderliness and grace of Grandmama's house, even to sit in the drawing room with Papa, whom I thought of so seldom that it was a shock to think of him now.

I shook my head, recalling too vividly the loneliness of those elegant rooms, remembering that the drawing room and gracious dining room often had contained only myself until I was old enough to seek entertainment outside our home as my elders did.

"No, Grandmama. You taught me—the Church taught me—that a woman's place is with her husband—until death."

I wouldn't stoop to asking her if this was the dictum she had cited to keep my mother from running off with Charlotte Miller. I felt a momentary satisfaction seeing Grandmama boxed in by her own rules, but she accepted my answer with the dignity strong people seem to muster to accept things they don't like.

"Very well," she said. "I'll not give you enough money to mount an effective campaign against my own interests, Emily, but if you're ever truly in need, apply to Spencer O'Malley. Goodbye. And you can tell Harding Douglas for me that he did *not* marry an heiress."

It was years before Spencer explained to me the meaning of that remark. Shortly before he took me to meet Harding, Grandmama had already been to see Harding and ask him what he would take to give me up. Spencer, not present at that meeting, was of course understandably short on details. But Grandmama's parting shot led me to deduce what Harding's answer had been: "I don't need your money—I'm about to marry an heiress."

They were both dead before I knew anything about this unseemly confrontation, but I was humiliated and outraged in retrospect to think of them sitting down to bargain for me as if I were chattel.

Why, you might ask, didn't Harding tell me about turning her down? I can only suppose he didn't brag about thwarting her, as he could have been expected to do, because he wasn't proud of something in his own behavior. For example, perhaps he had agreed in principle to being bought off by engaging in haggling in the first place, but being greedy, pushed her to her limit and she broke off negotiations.

Oh, what exquisite irony it was for Grandmama to put Spencer in charge of her fortune! True to her word, she left me a moderate income for life, pegged, via a cryptic formula, to the cost of living. As soon as Harding learned that supplication to my old boyfriend could cut through the formula, he urged me to go see Spencer and find out how much slack there was in the system.

It was the one thing I refused Harding. Surely he wouldn't have asked had he known about Spencer's chivalrous last minute proposal. Spencer became, in Harding's lexicon "your society swell boyfriend"—as in, "Go see your society swell boyfriend and pick up your check." I followed Spencer's brilliant career, his and Rose's social life, the births of their children and other mile-

196

stones, in the newspaper. Without the slightest fuss, my old friend fit into his appointed place among Galveston's elite. Further, he accepted his role as defender of Grandmama's will against the predations of his rival for his first love.

The battle went on for years. Harding collected cartons and cartons of papers, fired one lawyer and hired another. There was a predictable cycle to his relationship with a new attorney. At first there would be a great deal of enthusiasm, new motions filed, more paper generated. There would be depositions and hearings and stays and continuances, setbacks. And as it gradually became apparent that O'Malley, Bradley and Tate were equal to Grandmama's faith in them, the latest attorney would become harder and harder to get hold of, finally would stop taking Harding's calls altogether.

Strangers on the street familiar with the particulars of my case would wish me luck. Reporters, finding the whole affair unspeakably romantic, would write stories about me—the last person left alive on earth with Coolidge blood flowing in her veins, deprived of the Coolidge millions. I was portrayed as an innocent, trapped by love between awesome forces.

After Grandmama died and a fresh flurry of briefs were filed in the case, Harding decided that I should butter up my old man—I was also Charles Pickering's only heir, and he was not slated to die poor either. Harding didn't know Papa as I did and feared that now my grandmother was out of the way, my father would take it in his head to marry a young thing and start producing children who would challenge my claim.

I was not averse to getting closer to my father, though not for the reason Harding wanted me to. During the war, my father moved out of Grandmama's fin de siecle house and into a suite at The Galvez Hotel, not because he feared Germans might land in the backyard, but, I think, because living alone in the house became unbearable. When Mr. Galloway retired, Meg moved back home to care for him, and Papa converted the huge old house into five apartments for married GI's and their families.

I would love to report that in his last days my father and I managed to bridge the chasm that had always existed between us, and to a certain extent, we did. In the spring of 1944, he suffered a series of strokes and spent several weeks in John Sealy

Hospital. I would go and sit with him and try to make out what he was trying to tell me. He hardly ever talked about my mother, but he recounted for me the details of his courtship of Hazel Brookside, which I've laid out for you here. And then he was gone.

Eight years after I married Harding, he and I sat down in the conference room of the law offices of O'Malley, Bradley and Tate in the Stewart Title Building on Kempner Street to listen to Spencer O'Malley read the terms of my father's will. Harding was terribly keyed up, had bought a new navy hopsack blazer in the certainty that we were about to become wealthy beyond his wildest dreams. It was painful having to sit at that great expanse of polished walnut and listen to Spencer drily recite facts that intimately affected me. There followed a long litany of bequests to various charities and organizations. As these amounts added up, I could feel Harding's forearm in its navy blue hopsack tense beneath my fingers. Would there be anything left when all these bequests were honored? Finally Spencer got to me, reading in a flat, unemotional, legal voice. To his beloved daughter Emily, my father left my grandmother's house and a piece of property I had never heard about out on West Beach. Further, he left me the family pictures. The residue of the estate was to be put in trust and paid to me upon the death of my husband Harding Douglas.

I felt the muscle in Harding's arm jerk inside his new coat. The blood rushed to his face and he leaped from his chair and ran out of the room. Spencer looked at me for the first time, a look of pity and pain. "Thank you, Spencer," I murmured and got up to go look for Harding.

I couldn't find Harding anywhere and deduced that he had gone off to get drunk. I started walking toward Seawall Boulevard, but turned onto Avenue P and walked down to Grandmama's house—all the reward I got for being the last surviving member of a wealthy nineteenth-century family.

It never occurred to us to drive out and inspect that other piece of property my father had left me. West Beach back then was deemed practically worthless because it had no hurricane protection. Therefore I never saw the modest little house my father maintained as a weekend getaway, in the general area of which I eventually built Fair Isle Estates. Papa's little cabin was completely obliterated by Carla in 1961, and when I finally went out to look at the place, I couldn't be sure where it had stood—though I was fairly confident that I myself stood practically on top of the very dune where I had lain with Harding and lost my virginity.

~~~~~

Four generations of my family had tried to take root in that poor soil, but like Galveston, we were barely holding our own. Harding decided there was no reason to tolerate Galveston another minute, and within days of that terrible confrontation in the offices of O'Malley, Bradley and Tate, we packed up and left for the mountains south of Monterrey.

Harding abandoned the lawsuit and decided to take Frank Poe's advice and settle in a place where our income would allow us to live in the manner Harding craved. In Galveston we had been failures, inconsequential, hopelessly eclipsed by our social betters; in Monterrey we were persons of means, at the top of the heap. We bought a shabby old villa in the mountains above the picturesque village of Tres Hermanas. Opposite and above us stood the blazing white walls of a beautiful old convent that housed a TB sanitarium and hospice, run by an order of nuns. Those white walls towering above us reminded me daily of my distance from the Church and eventually led to my finding my way back to it. Harding went in quite another direction. His hospitality became legendary, soon attracting a stream of visitors from the North.

Among them was Lawrence.

~~~~~

It's been half a century since I set up housekeeping in the villa overlooking the tiny backward village of Tres Hermanas, difficult now for me to recall exactly how I felt about myself. Certainly I had begun to grow up a little, to read books, to wonder about things, even before Lawrence came into my life and added new urgency to my mission to find out who I was in my own right, not as a reflection of Harding or Grandmama.

I've spent many idle moments since Lawrence's death won-

199

dering what shape my life might have taken had I never met him, or conversely, had he lived. Would I have left Harding to be with him? Yes, I think so. But, I realize, there's no guarantee we would have been happy, no more so than there was for me and Harding. But Lawrence died young, quickly becoming a saint in my private pantheon. And saints get to go on being saints, don't they, since they aren't around to disappoint us?

Of one thing I am certain: I had at least figured out that Harding was not to be my rescuer, indeed, that he would be lucky to rescue himself. I knew by then that Harding was not merely a heavy drinker; he had a drink in his hand from the earliest I saw him in the morning until he finally slept—or passed out—at night, though I was seldom around to witness that latter stage of his day. And yet, he was rarely falling-down drunk. But why do I go on? The litany of complaints a wife has about a drinking husband are too well known to litter my page. I will speak of his health, though, since that became important.

I was worried about Harding's health long before a friend of ours, a medical doctor and, I might add, himself a heavy drinker (as most of our friends were), told me that Harding's liver was enlarged. (Zaida later wrote me that Dr. Peña outlived his patient by only a year.) Harding's complexion, always on the ruddy side, in his forties, turned several shades darker from constant exposure to the sun and from high blood pressure. The magnificent towering physique that had once frightened and excited me, seemed to shrink every year. The face that I had fallen in love with, that I thought handsome beyond my poor ability to attract, coarsened and seemed to want to avoid my sober-eyed scrutiny.

Harding was afraid that I would leave him—not that having that fear altered his behavior. I didn't threaten, cajole or reason, though I might have done all those things if not for Zaida's constant example before me; it was plain to see that such strategies had not worked with Frank. Their marriage was a series of bust-ups and reunions, varying only in degree. Sometimes Zaida would make a grand exit, pack her bags and go home to her mother in Texas, but most of the time, she ran no farther than our house, where she would stay until Frank wooed her back with promises of reform. Frank's reforms lasted only until

Harding and their other drinking buddies shamed and bullied him back into the world of men, and Zaida would return to her impotent threats.

My response was to cease to care what Harding did. By the time I met Lawrence, I had been married twelve years. I still shared a roof with Harding, but we had become husband and wife in name only, stuck with each other because of our stubbornness. I felt that I deserved to have to face this man every day whom I had used to hurt everyone who had meant anything to me. And Harding stayed because I had money. If he left me, he could not take my money with him.

I remember vividly the occasion when I first got up enough self respect to refuse Harding sex, the end of our marital intimacy. There were always houseguests, but I had given up feeling I owed these people any special attention; the only reason they were there was to drink Harding's liquor. One night, with the typical complement of unwanted guests under my roof, I went off to bed at my usual hour only to be awakened by someone stealthily climbing into bed with me. Something warned me it wasn't Harding.

"Who is it?" I said sharply. The man was naked and tried to hush my questions by kissing me, pulling my gown up and initiating sex, but I would have none of it. I tried to roll away from him and reach the light, but he struggled to keep me in the bed, all without saying a word. By then I knew good and well it wasn't Harding, whose body was as familiar to me as my own. This person was much smaller than Harding, though almost anyone could have subdued me if sufficiently motivated. This person was not that motivated and besides, was hampered by the knowledge that he was in the wrong. Finally he gave up the struggle and swore.

"Damn it! Why can't you just hold still, lady? I could get you a baby. Joyce and I had three kids in four years."

In a final indignant burst I flung out of bed and reached the light. Sitting sheepishly in my bed was Sidney Poe, Franklin's brother, one of his and Harding's good buddies, naked, drunk, but completely cognizant that I had him to dead to rights.

"Did Harding put you up to this?"

He was fumbling with his clothes and too ashamed to answer. I flounced out of the room to look for Harding. I found

201

him passed out under the dining room table, his cheek resting uncomfortably against the cool saltillo tiles. He didn't respond when I prodded him with my foot and called his name. I knew it was no use talking to him in that condition; I would have to wait till morning to vent my moral outrage. I went back to my room and, since there was not a lock on the door, shoved the bed against it, though I doubted anyone would try to bother me again that night.

Harding claimed total ignorance of the matter, but I didn't believe him. He really wasn't a very good liar, could never meet my eyes when he had done something he was ashamed of. I knew that he had sent Sidney to my bed in a misguided attempt to make up for what was missing in my life, indirectly acknowledging that he had let me down, cheated me of motherhood. Perhaps it was unfair of me to use that incident to have a lock installed on my bedroom door and to lock it against Harding, or perhaps you think I should have taken this step years before when I first suspected my husband was unfaithful to me. But in my long association with culpability, where did I draw the line? I had cooperated fully with my corrupter. Harding wasn't to blame for expecting me to continue to do so.

It was during this period that Harding began to call me, with ironic deference, Miss Emily, having once heard Meg Galloway call me that. It was also the beginning of his finding travel more congenial than staying home inflicting his buddies on me. Harding had easily acquired Spanish, while I could do little but hold simple conversations with Aurora about household matters. Harding loved Mexico as he had never loved any of the dozens of places in the U.S. he had lived as a soldier, especially Galveston. Within the limits of our income, he traveled widely, from La Paz to Merida, Nogales to Acapulco, down into Central and South America. He sailed, fished, hunted, always with a cohort of males, and, I'm sure, here and there the fugitive female or two. All activities, though, served only as a venue for their drinking.

I met Lawrence in the winter of 1945. I was thirty years old, had had plenty of leisure to repent, as my grandmother would have put it. One day I opened my door and found him there, holding out a twig of bougainvillea he had broken off one of my bushes.

"Madam," he said with a courtly bow. "Could this lowly token persuade you to offer your hearth to an oppressed and weary stranger?"

I laughed. "An American!" I had spoken nothing but Spanish for weeks. Harding and crew were sailing down to Tampico. I matched the stranger's courtliness. "The promise, sir, of a conversation in a civil tongue is enough to win you entrance to my hearth, even dinner if you like. My husband is away at the moment." Then I became flustered because I had not meant to sound flirtatious. I looked more closely at the young man before me and noticed his pallor and terrible emaciation.

"You're ill."

"No, madam, I am dying," said Lawrence. "A resident on yon mountaintop." He nodded toward the hospice across the valley, run by the Sisters of the Immaculate Conception. "Lawrence Edgar Payne at your service. Poet, soldier of fortune, consumptive. I've been told to warn people of that fact before I seek their hospitality."

"Oh, well, I'm sure . . ." Sympathy at a first meeting did not seem in order, so I merely said: "I'm Emily Douglas. Please come in and let me offer you refreshment. And do let's have a long chat. What can I get you? Is it too early in the day for a drink?"

"The sisters don't let me drink," he said, with a grin. "So, of course, I always drink when I get out."

I led him in to a pretty little patio in the center of the house and rang for Aurora.

"You're free, then, to come and go?" I said, then blushed with embarrassment. "Anyway, don't worry on my account. I was born on the island—Galveston—they say we have an inherited immunity to everything. I'm sure that any day now they'll find a cure—"

"A lovely thought, but I've been warned against hope. I've decided to view my disease as an advantage—the ultimate freedom. Why, I could rob a bank and they could do nothing worse to me than Fate has already done."

"Mr. Payne, you're making me quite uncomfortable."

"I apologize," he said gracefully. He had pale eyes with dark centers, a thin face that knew suffering. He was younger than I, by five or six years at least. "My freedom doesn't give me the right to rob others of their peace of mind. Please call me Lawrence. I tried to meet you in church Sunday morning."

"I . . . I was lost in my thoughts and didn't notice. You're Catholic?"

"I was once, a long time ago. I went to church hoping to train my thoughts on more lofty themes than the ones that lately have occupied me. I was advised to get my spiritual house in order."

"Did you . . . succeed?"

"Now that's an interesting question," he said, sitting eagerly forward in his seat. "I was making progress. Had my bag packed, so to speak, whispered all my filthy secrets into the hoary ear of Father Scanlon, paid the cock I owed to Asclepius, then suddenly—you might find this very odd—but suddenly it occurred to me that I was rushing into things, that I had fallen in love with the idea of suffering the same tragic death as John Keats, Frederic Chopin, even my namesake D. H. Lawrence—"

I caught my breath, as if feeling the prod of destiny at mention of that magical name. The young man before me noted my reaction, but continued on.

"I mean, why should I fall in so readily with the suggestion of doctors who had lied to me about everything else? Well, I tell you, I lost all heart for the journey after that. Don't give a damn now whether I go or not. What do you make of this, Mrs. Douglas?"

"I don't wonder at all," I said feelingly. "I myself haven't the slightest desire to make the . . . the trip you're talking about. And you shouldn't either, Mr. Payne. Why, you're far too young to be . . . well, looking forward to . . ."

"It wasn't so much looking forward to the trip, dear lady, as accepting the inevitable graciously, or so I believed. And please, call me Lawrence. Or Larry. Anything but mister. I don't have time for ritual."

"All right. Lawrence." I tried out his name on my tongue and wondered if I should tell him about the Mata Hari Girl Spies, about our schoolgirl giggles and trustful acceptance that a forbidden novel portrayed life as it really was. "I was once a great fan of D. H. Lawrence. Well, more of a voyeur than fan. Do

204

you mind if I ask . . . what made you change your mind, lose interest in the, er, trip?"

Lawrence gave me a seraphic smile. "I was sent a vision. Perhaps you saw it too, in that very church where you went about your prayers so earnestly, dear pilgrim. I went there seeking a miracle, and by heavens, the old magician pulled one off. Sunday morning, the creak of knees, the mumble of the humble, the smell of burning wax—and there she was—the angel I had hoped to find. When one asks for a sign and receives same, one would have to be an ingrate or a fool not to accept the dispensation. I was given, at the outside, three months by the boys in white. But my holy visitant planted the thought that I might tarry on terra firma longer if I had anything to live for."

Aurora had appeared to serve us. I looked up at her, shocked to find I was sitting in my own home, speaking in my normal voice, serving a guest in the ordinary way.

"We have Mexican beer, wine and other spirits, not to mention a number of delectable teas," I said.

He looked at me cannily. "You're the tea drinker."

"There is much solace in a cup of tea."

"And much need for solace?"

He knows Harding, I thought. "Aurora, a pot of Earl Grey please."

"Yes, Mees Emily."

When we were alone again, I pondered the morality of quizzing a dying man about his motives. Why had he, knowing my husband was away, come to my house? How came he to our part of the world in the first place? Was he really a poet? Perhaps the freedom he mentioned gave him the right to tell me anything he liked. My experience with men had taught me a healthy suspicion; however, something in Lawrence Payne's manner convinced me that he was not a dissembler. I decided to let his statements about himself stand unchallenged. If that was humoring, so be it. I tacitly agreed to play his game—if he was to be believed, his last.

"I've only just found my way back to the Church," I said.

"I myself am quite devout," he replied, placing a thin white hand over his heart. "Devoutly agnostic, that is. But there's something to that old saying about a dearth of unbelievers in the foxhole. The prospect of my imminent departure to the great beyond made the urge irresistible to go back one more time to hear the old arguments." He smiled. "My supplication rewarded me with a peep behind the curtain, but instead of the old magician, I found a raven-haired beauty made of corporeal flesh, a beauty, moreover, in obvious metaphysical pain. Suffering marred the purity of that dear angel's marble brow. I forgot my own silly errand in rapt admiration of her beauty. My dear, I solemnly swear to you that nothing made of silver, nothing paved with gold, not the gaudiest goddamn plumage imaginable can compensate me for the loss of beauty."

"Please, Lawrence, you shouldn't feed my vanity. I'm a very ordinary person. You happened to witness my return to the Church after the absence of a dozen years. I'm still overcome with emotion when I hear the liturgy."

His slightly sardonic expression softened. "Too bad it doesn't affect me that way. All I hear is the rote-quoted Latin, the old lies, the old cant. If there is a great spirit, he's not an old man, he's a beautiful woman. I swear I never felt more spiritual than in the presence of feminine beauty. So, go ahead and worship your god, transcendent beauty, and I'll bask in your reflected glory. Second-hand salvation is better than none, I say."

"Oh, dear, Lawrence, what blasphemy you speak!" I said with an embarrassed laugh.

His jaunty grin returned. "Then teach me, Beauty, teach me to worship, teach me to die with dignity. You must know that your prayers drew me to you."

I shook my head slowly. "Lawrence, I'm disturbed. I don't know what to say. I admit there's more than a slight coincidence to our both being at early Mass in this remote village—"

"Ah, yes, that old trick of seeing the hand of God in every pattern, every whorl on the tortilla. It's the human mind that imposes pattern, Beauty. See here—your goodness is already having an affect on me. I'll confess my first sin: I knew you would be there."

I laughed. "If you set out to deceive me, you'll find it no Herculean task. I believe anything people tell me about themselves, for I can never believe they'd bother to lie."

"I'll accept that as absolution. Harry Brink is my uncle.

My poor mother couldn't stand watching me die so she sent me here where the sisters of mercy can tend me when I grow too weak to gad about the countryside speaking riddles to beautiful women."

I shook my head in mock dismay over his flattery. "I was too distracted by this . . . religious fervor I'm experiencing to come to dinner when Agnes invited me the other night."

"I had specially asked her to get you there."

"Really? Surely we haven't met?"

"No, I've seen you, though, in the village, going about your errands. You've disturbed more than my slumber."

"Are you really a poet?"

"All dying men are poets. Haven't you noticed how they gather 'round the bedside to record last words?"

"And you . . . you're really . . . It distresses me very much to think . . . I don't want to get to know someone who is . . ." I couldn't finish my sentence.

"It is asking a lot, isn't it?" he admitted.

"No, no. I would gladly . . . do anything . . . to make it easier. Don't think I'm so selfish I can't lay aside my brooding over the eternal mysteries, my impatience with my tedious life, my banal daily routine—"

He had noticed one of my canvases on a nearby easel, a child's head inspired by Aurora's son Gilberto. "You paint, dear angel?"

"Not well, I'm afraid."

"It's not your medium. I should advise you to find another. Do you own a camera?"

"Why, no."

"I have a nice one I don't need any more. I'll bring it when I come tomorrow."

"Are you . . . coming tomorrow?"

He stared at me with his intense pale eyes. "I'll be with you every day and we'll have our little talks . . . until the end. But promise me that when I stop coming down, you won't come to me. I have my vanity too. Anyway, you belong here, below. The world needs your beauty. And there are other men over whose death you must preside. And now, my dear, I must go while I still have strength to get back up the mountain."

207

I suddenly realized he had learned about me from Dr. Peña. I didn't know whether to be grateful or cry.

"I can drive you in the car."

He smiled, seraphic again. "Then we can talk awhile longer."

~~~~~

Lawrence's generation was the last to know the devastation of tuberculosis, the AIDS of its time, a virus that killed perhaps a billion people during the nineteenth and early twentieth century, peasants and poets, rich and poor. Only a few months after Lawrence's tragic early death, streptomycin, the first exotic antibiotic would begin clinical trials and be hailed as a miracle drug.

It may seem foolhardy for Lawrence to have abandoned hope in medicine, but to him it was profligate to spend his last precious days in a sterile white American hospital. And so he left his loving family and set off to see what he could of the world until he grew too weak and sought refuge on our mountain. He had hoped in his travels to find God, peace, anything to help him accept death. He was also retracing the footsteps of a hero, Hart Crane. Perhaps he found what he was looking for in me. I found what I was looking for in him: joy.

Every morning we tumbled from our beds—me in the bedroom I no longer shared with my sometime companion, he in his clean white cell on the mountaintop—each of us delirious with happiness that we would soon be together. Lawrence's death sentence lent our love urgency, poignancy, and yes, freedom from convention, attributes of any love, I think.

Lawrence took care not to infect me or my household with his disease. I tend to forget when I am thinking about my love affair with him, that it was not physical, unless you count the way my eyes were devoted to his eyes, how my heart sang at first catching a glimpse of his uncle's car or the old village taxi making its way up my side of the mountain, unless you count the lightness and quickness that came into my body when I thought of him.

Yet, in the ordinary sense, I never made love to Lawrence, never placed my lips on his, didn't even hold his dear hand, though I would've taken all those risks had he let me. My love for Harding had been a showy blossom crowning the summit of youth and beauty, but like all carnal things, had withered and died, leaving hardly a memory of itself. But this love, having little to do with flesh, has lived on in my mind as a thing of beauty, and kept the memory of Lawrence immediate despite the span of years.

Harding and I, careless and brash in youth, had flaunted our love, made a great spectacle of ourselves by flying in the face of accepted morality. But there was no need for posturing in this love. I neither denied my relationship with Lawrence nor advertised it. His illness moved him beyond ordinary custom and he took me with him.

If he had been confined to his bed all morning, he came to me in the evening, and we sat up, late into the night, on the little patio and talked until he was tired, sometimes till morning. I gave up smoking for fear the smoke would irritate his fragile lungs. Harding came and went, mildly puzzled at my friendship with a young dying poet.

Lawrence was young, but it seemed to me he had read everything. In the company of Harding and his friends, I passed for an intellectual; but in the presence of genuine learning, my ignorance was soon exposed. Nearly every week I sent off to New York for books whose titles Lawrence casually mentioned. While he rested to be with me, I read, vainly trying to become his intellectual equal.

Before his illness reached an acute stage, he had taught poetry at City University of New York, published two volumes of his own verse, and written a foreword for a new edition of Hart Crane's poetry. He jested that if he had made Carl Sandburg his muse, he might have lived longer. Hart Crane, too, had fled to Mexico, and when he was thirty-three, leaped from a ship in the Gulf of Mexico, from whence his body was never recovered. Lawrence could only envy the thirty-three years. To match Crane's longevity he would need prove his doctors wrong by six years.

I didn't realize, until I was happy with Lawrence, how terribly unhappy I had been before. And though it saddened me almost beyond enduring to watch Lawrence grow feeble, my sadness was ameliorated by the certain knowledge of what life

209

would have been like without him. I might eventually have joined Crane's missing corpse in the Gulf of Mexico, a more romantic leap than my mother had made.

I had promised not to see Lawrence once he was unable to leave the hospice, but fortunately he was no more willing to make me keep my promise than I was able to fulfill it. We found that we could not afford to disdain time in the interest of our vanity. When finally he couldn't leave his room, I made daily pilgrimages to his side of the mountain, taking him tempting foods, books. I read to him when he felt up to it, sat quietly at his side when he didn't. The view of the surrounding mountains, the valley below, the messy sprawl of the village—a dark patch of lichens on the mountain's flank—are part of my mental landscape. Any time I like, I can sit again in that small hard wooden chair and hear the rale in Lawrence's chest, see his pale, pain-filled eyes seek out mine for assurance that he was not alone. Father Scanlon visited daily too, hoping for a deathbed conversion, but Lawrence told him that Jesus and Mary had nothing to offer that Emily had not already given him.

I had been so close to turning my ill-spent life over to the Church, as I had once intended in youth, but life—in the form of death—intruded. The seductive power of vanity, having been chosen among women to sit at the dying man's side, was enough to turn me from a life of seclusion, contemplation and prayer.

But don't think it was all one-sided. Lawrence gave me so many spiritual gifts I hardly know how to enumerate them. Loving him taught me truly to disengage from the vulgar life around me, to live in its midst, but not be part of it. They were emotional children who mistook feverish activity for living, who in their search for abandonment wasted the precious stuff of life. Theirs was unreflective life, hardly distinguishable from the mental life of brutes. And yet, Lawrence also taught me to be compassionate, to realize that we each strive for what we can reach.

One afternoon I left him sleeping and went home, exhausted with pity and sorrow. I lay down in our little patio, where we had spent so many pleasant hours, and slipped into a troubled dream. Someone had given me something to hold, a heavy burden. I wanted to let it go because my arms were breaking, but I was loathe to disappoint the person who had entrusted the burden to me. As it slipped away and was lost, I cried as if my heart would break. I awoke with tears on my face.

I hurried to find Aurora to see if there had been any calls, but there were none. I didn't want to disturb Lawrence by calling to see about him, so I went ahead with my plans for that evening. A few weeks before, on one of our last outings together, I had taken Lawrence to the south rim of the valley, which offered a breathtaking view of the village below, the white stones of the convent and hospice above, and towering over all, the sawtooth Sierra Madre Mountains.

"Set your camera up here," said Lawrence. "And do it right at the moment the balance of light shifts to nighttime."

I could see what he was suggesting, the dramatic lights and darks, high places and low, sublime and mundane—all captured in a single frame. Even as I pictured the scene as my camera would see it, I composed the words that I would write under the picture when I pasted it into my album, already fat with pictures of Aurora and baby Gilberto.

And so I came back now to get the picture while there was still time for Lawrence to see it. I set up my camera and watched for that unholy moment when overweening light loses the battle with the dark prince, when attenuated shadow lay stretched on the ground before separating to join the night. I opened the shutter. In that instant, the setting sun caromed off the windows of the convent, setting the mountaintop on fire and blinding my camera's eye. I turned up my face in wonder to gaze at the gaudy spectacle of Nature herself teaching the artist humility. That which I attempted to capture on black and white film blinded my lens with bloodstained red, incandescent gold and vivid peach, lime-green, and lemon, delicate pinks, mauves and lavenders, purple, and finally, low on the eastern horizon, indigo.

As everything below me was overtaken by the night, I stood on the only point of light left in the world, suddenly overcome with grief. Tears that had hovered near the surface of my eyes for weeks burst forth and washed and purified my spirit.

I packed my camera and tripod, my heavy camera bag, into the car, and followed my headlights down the mountain. When I got home, Father Scanlon was waiting to tell me that Lawrence was gone.

211

Chapter Ten

I think of Harding and Lawrence as having defined polar aspects of my personality: the carnal and the ethereal; the physical and the spiritual; body and intellect. In Harding, I got far more than I bargained for, a physical relationship more vigorous than any I supposed existed; in Lawrence, my intellectual love, I was banned from physical contact of any sort and learned to love in my head.

I seemed destined to tread the perimeter of life, never stride boldly up the middle. I wondered if other women allowed themselves to be so defined by what or whom they love? Yes, there was Mama and her frustrating, one-sided love for Charlotte Miller; Grandmama, who translated a desire to found a dynasty into a passion for business; and Meg Galloway, whose devotion to a family that no longer existed was evident in the way she still lived in Grandmama's old house and mailed me rent checks every month—despite the fact that the family she once served had dwindled to a single member and that one fled to a remote valley in Mexico.

When I locked my bedroom door against Harding, I found that I was able to focus on my neglected intellectual development, spurred on, of course, by my desire to be worthy of Lawrence, who claimed to find me "a brilliant naif." (He also claimed to find me beautiful, so we know something was wrong with his perception, right?) At any rate, for several years after Lawrence entered and left my life so dramatically, I worked hard with my camera, certain that I was meant to do something important, something in the arts. I never painted again after the portrait of Aurora's little Gilberto (whom I suspect was fathered by one of Harding's blue-eyed gringo buddies, possibly the virile Poe brother.)

But somehow, art eluded me. Often I would leave my camera untouched for days and simply write in my journal, which should have clued me in. But, you see, I had no education beyond what the Ursuline sisters had given me, no confidence in my native intelligence or the value of my life experiences. Moreover, Lawrence had engendered in me such reverence for words—his medium—that I dared not think I might claim that avenue for myself. So, while Lawrence awakened my intellect, alas, he also unintentionally stifled it—ironically, in much the same way that Harding stifled me sexually. Both men, by being such adepts in their own "area," made me feel like a pale shadow behind their colossal selves. Sometimes I wrote things that made me quite happy, but I couldn't foresee that I would ever want to share these words with anyone. I'm sorry to be the sort of woman who requires a man to unlock her secrets, but perhaps the reverse is also true, that I've helped unlock a few men.

It was Spencer O'Malley who taught me to explore the middle ground.

~~~~~

Lawrence lived another eight months after coming to Tres Hermanas to die. They were months, I like to think, that he would not have had if he had stayed at home and followed doctor's orders. Certainly, I believe, those months meant more to him for having known me, which is not as egotistical as it may seem, since I am only claiming that my company was better than a protracted stay in the hospital.

But my purpose here is not to gloat over whatever small role I played in my dear Lawrence's tragically brief life, but to relate my own story. (Oh, dear, how did that change? I set out to tell Mama's and Grandmama's stories!) But to continue:

213

Lawrence was right that there were more deaths for me to preside over. Perhaps being so close to death himself gave him this insight, or, more plausibly, the doctor he shared with my husband, Dr. Peña, indiscreetly let it be known that Harding Douglas himself was none too healthy.

It was Harding's idea to come home to Galveston once his health became too bad to permit him to stay gone as much as he liked. I suspect, also, that he thought I might find more to amuse myself in my home town and secretly feared I would leave him if forced to spend too much time in his company. At any rate, his friends had proven fickle and had no use for him when he was no longer able to entertain them.

Perhaps it seems strange that Harding chose to return to Galveston after maligning the place so, but there were few other places he could claim as home. He had left Kansas when he went into boot camp, and had belonged to the Army until he married me.

And so, in 1958, we came back to the island to find it much changed since we left in '44. Price Daniel had made things hot for the Maceos and other mobsters and put a thousand people out of work in the first big purge of gambling. The blow to the economy was so devastating that even the old elite wondered if closing down gaming was really necessary. It was certain that the great commercial era of my grandfather's day could not be rebuilt—by then it was clear to any would-be investor that Galveston was piteously at the mercy of Mother Nature—or the Sea Goddess, as Meg Galloway calls her, the evil twin, perhaps, of the Mother of Mercy.

And so, over the decade of the fifties, the status quo gradually reasserted itself. Galveston backslid and returned to the way of life it knew best, like an alcoholic returning to the bottle, a comparison I'm all too qualified to make. Gambling and prostitution thrived.

But finally a new attorney general was elected, Will Wilson, who brought fresh ambition and renewed energy to the task of forcing Galveston into the fold of civilized municipalities. Wilson launched a major campaign to clean up vice on the island once and for all, force businessmen to obey the law, coerce civic leaders into developing fresh sources of revenue. In an epic raid, the Texas Rangers sledge hammered thousands of slot machines. In all, forty-seven clubs, bingo establishments and houses of prostitution were closed down.

Had Harding been well enough to seek adventure away from home those last years of his life, he might have had a hard time finding adventure to suit his taste. But those were quiet years for us, spent in a rented house. My own house, the one Grandmama had built at the turn of the century, which had sustained damage from repeated batterings by the sea, was subdivided and lived in by renters who had no knowledge of the grand old building's history. Meg Galloway, now in her seventies, had moved into the large ground floor apartment after her father died, still loyal to her post, and not only mailing me rent checks and newspapers, but writing newsy letters to keep me informed of local events. Meg was glad I came back, but Harding and I were virtually ignored by everybody else, especially my old society friends. Since Harding was not out making new buddies, we seldom saw people.

Each trip to the hospital I supposed would be Harding's last. And in the wake of each crisis, he would swear new oaths of fealty to sobriety. But he simply couldn't follow through with them and was forced to absurd leaps in logic to explain his continued dependence: that he could handle it this time, that booze had nothing to do with his health anyway, that, yes, drink had destroyed him, but it was too late to do anything about it now and he might as well die a happy man. To save my own sanity, I ignored as much as possible both his repeated failures to stay on the wagon and his deteriorating condition.

The only pictures I have from that dark time are the ones taken by a photographer for *The Galveston Daily News*. One day a reporter called and said he was writing a story about me. I told him to go right ahead, but to expect no cooperation from me. He countered with the irrefutable argument that he would do the story whether I had any "input" or not, so that if I wanted to avoid inaccuracies, I would answer his questions.

I greatly disliked and resented the intrusion, but I wasn't eager to see lies printed about me in the newspaper, so I reluctantly agreed to answer only those questions I thought were anybody's business. The young man, who was familiar with the

215

names Coolidge and Pickering only because they were on buildings and plaques around the city, did the sort of story that I had become quite familiar with in the years before we left Galveston. It's amazing how much sympathy a small female figure elicits when she is perceived as the enemy of the powerful, the monied, the aristocratic, especially if she has aligned herself with the common people, and even more especially in that era when the young were burning their draft cards. In that and other fatuous articles that found their way into print during the sixties, I am portrayed as a heroine in a class struggle, as an aging hippie, as a woman who married for love. Somehow the press and public have always had need to see my long- running struggle with Grandmama as somehow noble, classic, mythic. Never mind that I didn't see it in those terms myself, or even that I disavowed my own reasons at that writing. Later, when I made a remark critical of American policy in Vietnam, (that's making me seem very high-brow indeed; all I said was that I didn't think our boys should be sent there) it was construed as further evidence of my anarchic tendencies and I became even more popular in certain circles: Rebellion had become fashionable.

But back to the pictures. As a gesture of his gratitude, the young reporter sent me the extra prints of the pictures that accompanied that article—ugly things, black and white glossies, showing all our defects. Yes, I do look like a woman who cares nothing for fashion, who might be an anarchist. And Harding looks like an old ill man. But they're the only pictures I have of him in what was for him old age. He wasn't even sixty when he died. I had no idea what effect his aging was having on me.

~~~~~

Today, from the grand vantage of seventy-five years (at this writing—I do write terribly slow) I can laugh when I recount my words to Spencer when he took me out to see the property on West Beach my father had left me.

"I want to build a house out here, Spence, a place to end my days."

Harding was in the hospital again, more to give me a break from nursing than anything else. I hadn't told him that when he

216

was "away" Spencer and I saw each other. We pretended we had business to discuss, but really, each occasion was a celebration of the endurance of our miraculous friendship. Today we were together because it was my birthday and Spencer thought it a shame for me to spend it in the hospital. He was the one who had suggested we come look at the land.

"Let's see," he said, "if you're as long-lived as your grandmother, you've got another thirty or forty years before your days end."

"There's more to living than longevity," I replied. "Is this the place?"

"I should've brought along the plat to be sure. There used to be a road out here, before Carla."

I was amazed that large residential neighborhoods were being built on West Beach, especially after Carla just two years earlier. (Harding and I rode out the storm in a Houston hotel and returned to find Grandmama's house had endured yet another storm, though as usual the yard had to be replanted.) Carla was no bigger than the great storms early in the century, but each hurricane that made a direct hit on America's coastal cities was more costly than the one before for the simple reason that there was more to blow away, not to mention that property values along the finite coastline continued to go up.

Spencer and I got out and waded through the sand to see if we could find any traces of my father's house. It had been only a slight thing to begin with and weakened by years of neglect. Carla had taken away every trace of it.

Being again in Spencer's company gave me a more honest barometer of my age. He was eighteen months older than I, yet as fit, as trim, as unlined and jaunty as ever. His face was brown from fishing, his hair, white as in his youth, he still wore in a crewcut.

"What's Grandmama got saved up for me, Spence? Am I dipping into principle yet?"

Usually I avoided the possibility of controversy by not mentioning the subject that had brought us such disharmony. However, Harding's medical treatment had exhausted our ordinary income, and I had been forced to exercise the option that allowed me to tap into the principle of my delayed inheritance by mere application to Spencer. It was that first terribly awkward visit—in which Spencer humanely spared me as much embarrassment as he could by swiftly writing out a personal check in the amount I named—that had led to this, our cautious attempts to reestablish friendship.

I had made it clear that I was not interested in being included in his wife's social plans, nor was it fitting that we have dinner out or that I entertain him at my house; so, from time to time Spence would call and suggest a car trip of some sort: out West Beach to see my land, into Houston on some legal errand, a ride on the Bolivar ferry to watch the dolphins cavort alongside the ship. I did not mention these outings to Harding, and though I had no way of knowing for sure, I suspected Spencer did not mention them to Rose.

Now Spencer's clear untroubled blue eyes sought mine and he answered as briefly and succinctly as possible: "You're going to be very rich, Emily."

~~~~~

Upon our return to Galveston, Harding had reopened "my" case. The lawyer he found, a Mr. Brandon, a newcomer to Galveston who knew nothing of the long history of the case, accepted with alacrity the assignment of finding out why justice had ground so exceedingly slow in this matter. I thought it would give Harding's restless mind something to do, fiddling with the cartons of folders again, talking on the telephone to his lawyer, drawing up suggested plans of attack on a yellow legal pad, delving into his surprisingly well-stocked law library. I was confident that Spencer would not have the least trouble parrying these inept thrusts, though it wouldn't have hurt my feelings in the least had we won. Spencer had profited richly over the years taking care of my money. I didn't want to get into the frame of mind, however, in which I began to think all my troubles could be solved by winning the case, or that not winning would somehow ruin my life.

That day, when I returned from my outing with Spencer, Harding looked up eagerly from his yellow pad. Papers were spread across his bed, shuffled into untidy piles. Harding was making himself a "To Do" list for when he got out of the hospital.

"Ah, Emily, you're here!" (The Miss Emily era ended when he was reduced to summoning me to his bedside dozens of times a day.) "Did you pick up the papers I asked for?"

I had told Mr. Brandon not to embarrass me by filing any more actions in my behalf, but to please let my husband believe that he was still diligently pursuing the case. For a consideration, he was agreeable. His secretary ran off extra copies of whatever else she was working on, with Harding's name typed in. He complained about Brandon's "inefficiency."

"Yes, darling, here they are. Is this your dinner?"

"Wasn't too hungry."

"You don't like it when they pour the stuff down a tube, Harding."

"I ate the potatoes."

"I saw. . . ."

His eyes had a spectral brilliance and seemed to miss nothing these days. "Who?"

"Oh, not who, what. I saw our land out on West Beach this afternoon."

"I've been meaning to get out there and take a look at that. What do you think? Is it worth anything?"

"Darling, you'll never believe it! It may be the very stretch of beach where you made me yours."

Harding looked pleased with himself. "No kidding! Maybe we'll run out there when I get out." He began to shuffle his papers again. "Would you put these away, darling? I'm a little tired. Careful! They're in order. I want Brandon to follow up on this motion today. It's imperative that he get it filed before the courthouse closes this afternoon."

"Yes, all right. I'll take them with me when I go."

"I thought he might be in after while and take them himself."

"He's very busy, you know. You keep him very busy."

I watched him doze for a bit. How I loathed hospitals. I was familiar with this one from when Papa died, though we were in a new wing. I was not good at this sort of work, watching men die. Harding made the third.

I stepped over to the window. We were on the fourth floor and had a view of the north side of the island, the Port of Galveston, the cranes that handled containerized goods, the superstructure of ships lined up to receive cargo, and beyond that, the vast skyline of cracking towers that made up the Texas City petro-chemical industry. I thought of my anonymous young lover, Roger, who had slipped over to our side of the bay to steal a waltz and a few kisses from a rebellious debutante. In the Texas City explosion of 1947, Roger and more than two thousand plant workers and residents had been injured or killed.

The fire had started with an explosion in the hold of a French cargo ship loaded with ammonium nitrate—fertilizer—and spread when burning shrapnel pierced natural gas storage tanks on shore. Houses for a mile around collapsed, and a barge was blown out of the water and dropped on dry ground. There was no one to put out the ensuing fire—the entire fire department, including my abductor Roger, died in the initial explosion. The city burned to the ground, which is why the disaster is also referred to as the Texas City fire. Many of the injured had been brought there to John Sealy Hospital.

Perhaps my mind dwelled on disaster because I felt so vulnerable. I turned back to Harding and watched a nurse check the IV flow, take his emaciated arm and feel for a pulse. She had brought with her several ounces of vodka to feed him, which the doctor had explained was necessary, for if Harding's system did not receive the poison it was used to, he could go into shock and die. I left the room so I wouldn't have to watch him drink it.

Could I have done more? Should I have left him? I had always believed that by not campaigning vigorously for temperance, I was giving Harding nothing to rebel against and thereby saving us from the Punch and Judy show of Frank and Zaida's marriage. I had believed that leaving it entirely up to him whether he drank or not was being smart, using reverse psychology on him—all right, if you want to kill yourself, go ahead, I'll not stop you.

But now, belatedly, I was realizing that whether I meant to endorse his drinking or not, I had done so by the mere fact of supporting him. If he had had to work, he might have been forced years ago to answer to an employer and gotten help for his problem. But I, in requiring nothing of him, had inadvertently enabled him to an early grave.

In my own defense, however, I must plead that I had often considered using the power of the purse to control my husband, but all it took to deter me was to remember what my response had always been when Grandmama threatened to withhold her money from me. I could grant Harding no less spirit and resolve than it had taken for me to walk away from a fortune. But money was more important to Harding, perhaps it would have made a good weapon. (It seems that half my life I'm faced with a decision between two distasteful choices and that I spend the other half second-guessing myself.)

I wandered the hospital, driven by a vague desire for something, but what? Something to eat? A cup of tea? I knew what it was. In times of stress, I invariably craved a cigarette, but I wouldn't let myself have one. I couldn't forget how poor Lawrence had struggled to get air into his ravaged lungs. Here I was, back in the hospital only half an hour and crazy to get out, go anywhere. It was so sweet of Spencer to remember my birthday and to wish for me to spend it elsewhere, if only for an hour, but it made coming back worse. Harding hadn't remembered yet that it was my birthday and I disliked having to remind him. What a true friend Spence had been to me! In spite of Harding's harassing lawsuits, he steadfastly refused to regard me as his enemy. It was good that we had been able to stay friends, that we could still laugh together. How I wished . . .

I stopped before I could say it, shocked with myself. I didn't wish any such thing! It would've spoiled everything if Spencer and I had gotten married. We would have been so ill-suited. I would have embarrassed him. Anyway, we weren't in love, except maybe when we were thirteen, fourteen. By the time I started dating I already knew that Spencer wasn't the one. And it was certainly ridiculous to think of having a romance now at our age. He was happily married to Rose, had grandchildren, enjoyed a comfortable life, an important role in society.

I found myself sobbing, there in the drab anonymous waiting room on the fourth floor of John Sealy Hospital. What a terrible mess I had made of my life! So stubborn! No one had ever been able to tell me anything. No, I had to find out for myself what the consequences were of defying every convention, going against all I had been taught by the Church, the nuns, Grandmama, and to a lesser extent by my other two family members, Mama and Papa. Spencer and Rose had four lovely children, were greatly admired by numbers of people, had made a valuable contribution to community life. What did I have for all my vaunted freedom to do exactly as I wished? Here's what I had: the right to be utterly alone in the world.

I helped myself to a handful of tissues the hospital thoughtfully provided for people who had to use this overbright public place to shed their tears. I reached also for the only weapon I had ever had, defiance. I vowed to go find a cigarette machine and buy myself a pack of smokes, or at the very least, bum one from somebody.

Out in the hall, I wandered drearily in search of a smoker with a friendly face. I found such a person standing outside the snack bar, a fat young man, smoking nervously, jerkily, his eyes darting fearfully about.

"Excuse me, could I beg or buy a cigarette from you?" I said. "I quit years ago, but. . . ."

"This is no time to quit," he muttered, digging a crumpled pack out of his jeans pocket. I straightened the unfamiliar object between my fingertips and he snapped open a Zippo lighter and lit me. I inhaled and felt an instantaneous quickening of my pulse. My head felt light. The taste in my mouth was monstrous.

"They don't taste like I remember," I said.

"No, they taste like shit," he agreed. "It's the drug we're after, just the drug."

"Thanks," I said, and turned to go back to "my" end of the corridor. When I was out of sight of the donor, I stubbed out the cigarette. It wasn't what I wanted after all. Ahead of me there was a commotion in the hall, a cluster of blue-clad hospital employees in front of Harding's door, I realized. I hurried forward, but Harding's doctor, a young man who seemed hardly old enough to be out of college, met me and turned me into another corridor.

"I'd rather you didn't go in just now," he said.

"What's happening?"

"Um. It's the end, Mrs. Douglas." I knew it was, of course. I

222

stared at him and knew that my eyes were red, that I looked terrible. "I'm sorry," he said. "They go like that. Their heart just . . . stops. We tried to revive him, but it was no good."

"Yes."

"Is there someone . . ."

"No."

The young man glanced about him hopelessly, looking for someone to attach me to. "Can I call someone?"

I looked at him and said the cruellest thing. "I'm the last of my kind, Dr. Stevenson. There is no one else."

And then I went to the phone to call Spencer because he was the only one I could think of who might care that I had just lost my husband.

~~~~~

For the last time in the role of hopeful, one on the outside looking in, I sat at the polished mahogany table in the conference room of O'Malley, Bradley and Tate. The only person in the firm now who owned any of those names was Spencer. The old conservative family law firm had a different look. A young woman lawyer, severe and competent, had joined the firm, and an equally young Hispanic male. At the front desk was now a beautiful young black woman who did interesting things to her hair. (If I seem to describe everyone as young, I'm afraid it's one of the idiosyncrasies of old age.)

Spencer, once a junior member of the staff, was now the senior partner. I listened while he outlined the assets that now to be turned over to me without further interference from the law, assets that had been carefully tended by Spencer's uncle, then by Spencer himself, now worth many times over their original value. I had had to see the deaths of Mama, Grandmama, Papa and Harding to get this money, and had long intended to refuse it, force on O'Malley, Bradley and Tate the awkward problem of figuring out what to do with an unclaimed fortune. In imagining such a scenario, however, I had forgotten one thing: there was absolutely no one left to be hurt by such a gesture but myself. Without a backboard, a basketball describes a harmless arc and crashes to the floor.

The young woman attorney, Brenda Lynch, her name was, tapped a Bic thoughtfully against her legal pad. "Gosh, Mrs. Douglas, what will you do with all that?"

That was the question, wasn't it? Her livelihood and others depended on my answer. The Coolidge-Pickering estate was the bread and butter account for O'Malley, Bradley & Tate. Miss Lynch herself probably spent half her time seeing to the various investments and charitable trusts Grandmama had set up.

"My plans are quite modest," I replied. "Like most people, I've long wished to own my own home." Spencer visibly relaxed. I think he had been holding his breath, waiting to see what I might do to myself in the name of rebellion.

"Mr. O'Malley," I said—the formality for the benefit of his colleagues, "you've done such a good job looking after the Coolidge-Pickering estate that I shall rely on your advice. I plan to live quite simply, and as you know, I have no heirs. I'm in agreement with Grandmama's philosophy that the money should do some good, but you see, we may differ on our definition of good. I'll draw up a list of my own worthy causes. However, I would prefer not to find myself in the role of personally interviewing petitioners."

Spencer nodded gravely. Perhaps Miss Lynch was astonished that a person who had spent her life trying to wrest control of this monstrous pile of money away from them, when it was given her, mildly agreed that they had been the best ones after all to be in charge. I smiled at them and that was that. I could now turn my attention to more cheerful matters.

~~~~~

A few weeks later, my new house rose in the air twenty feet and had a roof on it. I liked to drive out every afternoon to see how the work progressed, enjoying the smell of new- cut lumber and the busy noise of hammers and electric saws. The young men building my house were wonderfully polite and deferential to me.

Sometimes I stopped by Spencer's office to see if he wanted to go with me, though I was sensible of offending Rose by reclaiming my friendship with her husband too warmly. He was probably terribly busy, but he never acted like it. He would grab his jacket and bounce out the door with a word over his shoulder at LaKeesha, the receptionist.

I saw no reason why Spencer and I shouldn't resume our friendship. We had been friends for a number of years without romantic involvement. We were safely middle-aged, beyond the terrifying passion of youth when nothing else in the world matters but answering that passion. And yet, on my own side of the equation was a guilty pleasure in seeing him, being made to feel young. There was also the pleasure of provoking that prudish pucker to his lips. He couldn't help it, he'd been part of the establishment his entire life, and though he prided himself in changing with the times, I was still able to shock him and I still enjoyed doing so.

I was not invited to anything when Harding and I first returned to the island in '58, but after his death in the summer of '63, first one, then another of the women with whom I had gone to school tentatively included me on her guest list. I was vexed how to respond. In theory, I had no objection to seeing my oldest acquaintances, perhaps becoming friends—it wasn't out of the question. But how would I answer their polite questions? Was I to say nothing of the past thirty years? Wouldn't it be a lie to dress up in pumps and stockings, sedate afternoon wear, have my hair done, to attend their luncheons and teas? (After years of ignoring fashion, wearing comfortable shoes, dressing as I liked?) See, they were saying, your old place with us is still here. Now that your dreadful husband is dead, now that you've gotten all that money, we can ask you to our teas.

And so I decided to decline any invitations that came on an engraved card and accept only those accompanied by a hug, a kiss on the cheek, a genuine gladness to see me. Meg Galloway's were acceptable, so were Peter Bright's. Peter had never remarried after his young wife took flight and left him with two boys to raise. He was retired from skippering a shrimp boat and now did carpentry. (At that point he had not yet bought one of my houses and become my neighbor—my house was the only one for miles in either direction.)

After I moved into my house that fall, Spencer would often appear on my doorstep, unannounced, at odd times of the day, bringing with him some crazy present. Chicken necks so we could go crabbing, an old electric office typewriter, once a baggie of marijuana that a client had slipped to him just before he was arrested.

"What do you expect me to do with that?" I protested.

"Have you ever smoked it?"

"Heavens no. Harding and his friends did in Mexico. It always seemed to have the effect of making them dare each other to eat the worm in the bottom of the tequila bottle."

Young people were smoking the drug openly, defiantly, for America to see on its evening news.

"You surprise me," I told Spencer. "You've always been such a straight arrow." With his crewcut and button-down shirt, he looked ridiculous rolling a joint. "Here, let me do it. You've never even smoked a regular cigarette."

And so we sat on my porch and got silly on hemp. With the setting of the sun, it grew chilly and I suggested we move inside. Spencer reluctantly admitted it was time for him to leave. His youngest son Kirwin had beat the draft by dropping out of graduate school and volunteering for the Navy. Rose was throwing a goodbye party at the country club that evening.

"I should have been there hours ago," Spencer said, but he didn't sound particularly regretful.

I walked him to the door and he turned suddenly and hugged me. Usually we didn't touch, except upon greeting, when he invariably kissed me on the cheek. Once, when we met outside the Galveston County Courthouse, he had greeted me with his usual kiss, that intimate yet strangely formal gesture, then we had gone inside and assumed our roles as adversaries.

"What would your children say if you told them you'd spent your evening smoking pot with an old girlfriend?" I teased.

"They'd say, Dad, you old fogey, doesn't it feel good?" Spence rolled his eyes. "God, does it ever! I'm on cloud nine. Give us a kiss, Emily."

"Don't, Spence," I said uneasily. I wasn't sure I could be trusted not to fall into his arms like a silly, vapid girl. He looked somewhat shaken as he went down the stairs.

I went back inside and changed into my walking shoes, put on a sweater to ward against the November chill, prepared to

226

take my usual brisk walk along the beach. But instead I found that the marijuana had made me so sleepy I could hardly hold my eyes open. I thought if I lay down on the couch and took a ten minute refresher nap, I would feel more like going.

I lay down, in shoes and sweater, and seemed instantly to dream. Often I don't realize it's the drowning dream—it starts out innocuously, then turns malevolent. This time, I seemed to be at a party, cutting a big cake, a white wedding cake I think, surrounded by guests outside on a very green lawn. I had forgotten something and went toward the house in search of this object. Without my realizing, it had begun to rain, in fact, a hurricane was blowing, and I was torn between seeing to my guests and getting myself to high ground. In no time, I was struggling through knee-high water, desperately trying to reach the roof and safety, but the house wasn't where I thought it was. It seems that I was heading out to sea and the water was getting deeper.

I awoke in my usual panic, further confused by the fact that I was on the couch wearing shoes and a sweater. Then I remembered that I had been going to take a walk. I wondered if the weather had turned bad and caused me to have the dream, which sometimes happens. Hurricane season was long past. I opened the door and looked out. It was black as pitch out, not even a glimmer on the waves, a strong north wind driving the roar of the surf far from shore. It wasn't cold—hardly ever is in November—but the beach, nevertheless, had never seemed less attractive. I couldn't shake the idea that death and anarchy stalked the land. I felt so alone, so vulnerable out there miles from town. Anything could happen to me and no one would know about it for days. Had I ended up so alone and friendless as punishment for the sin of misusing friends like Ruth and Spencer?

Resolutely, I got a grip on myself, closed the door and turned on all the lights in the house. I put on the tea kettle and with a shock noticed that it was after midnight. I wondered if Spencer was back home from his party. I wanted so badly to pick up the telephone and hear his voice, tell him about the nightmare so he could talk it away. I picked up the receiver and listened to the dial tone. Only seven digits away, yet I had no right

227

to call him, my oldest and dearest friend. What would I say if Rose answered?

I dialed the number, prepared at any second to change my mind and slam down the receiver. Why was the impulse to call Spencer so fraught with guilt? I let the signal go out, but even as it did so, I put down the receiver, unable to complete the connection. I sat there in a cold shaking panic, thinking that I would have to get in my car and drive into town, find an all-night restaurant, just to be around other human beings. Suddenly the telephone rang practically in my hand, shattering my fragile composure and startling an involuntary scream out of me.

"Hello," I whispered when I had stilled the pounding of my heart enough to hear who was calling me so late.

"Was that you that called?"

"Spencer? How did you know?"

"What's wrong?"

"Oh, I have this silly nightmare from time to time. It's like . . . the hurricane finally gets me. I dream I'm drowning. It's probably when the wind rises like this. It's nothing, dear. Thank you for calling, thank you for picking up on my disturbed vibrations or whatever. I'm sure I'll be just fine now that I've talked to someone. I'll just . . . go back to bed now. Thanks, Spence."

"I'll be there in fifteen minutes," he said, and hung up.

He didn't give me a chance to say no. I couldn't call him back, risk getting Rose on the phone, asking her to relay the message to her husband that I wished he wouldn't come out to see me this late, that I didn't feel strong enough to do the right thing, follow the course I had decided upon.

I ran around frantically for a few minutes trying to figure out what to do before he got there, whether to jump in the shower, fix sandwiches, put on some lipstick. Finally I went out on the porch and wrapped up in an old quilt and watched for the lights of his car out on the highway.

~~~~~

That night we were the Spencer and Emily we had always wanted to be for each other. I didn't ask what he had told Rose nor what it meant that he had come to me. Nothing mattered

228

but the fact that we had finally escaped all the snares that had kept us apart, the pride, the expectations of others, the conventions we had agreed to uphold so that we might consider ourselves civilized.

"You were right to turn me away, Emily," he said, sometime late in the night. "What might I have done to a fey, spirited woman like you! I told myself that I was the only man who could love you, appreciate your wonderfulness, make you happy, but probably I would've made you miserable and destroyed in you the very thing I love."

"Tonight I'm inclined to believe that you were the one who was right, Spence, that it was I who spoiled things. If I had listened to you, it would be me weeping with you about Kirwin going to Vietnam, you'd rejoice with over Roslynn's baby. I wouldn't be an old woman living out on the edge of nowhere, I'd be a grandmother surrounded by a large loving family."

"Emily, I don't want you to ever be alone again!" said Spencer fervently. It wasn't a promise exactly, but did I deserve promises? I snuggled up to him and slept soundly.

We woke up late—excited, frightened and joyful about being together. Nothing was settled, of course, and our task now was to figure out what we had done. Was it irrevocable?

"You should have nightmares more often," Spencer said.

"I do."

"Oh, sweet Emily! I want to be with you the next time it happens. I was lying there last night thinking about you and wishing I hadn't left you, when the phone rang, just once, like a question hanging in the air. I got up and went downstairs to call you, as certain that it was you as if I'd heard you call my name."

"What on earth did you tell Rose?"

"I told her a client. . . ."

I interrupted, not wanting to know after all. "Here I've known you over forty years and I don't even know what you like for breakfast! Or perhaps you need to get back right away?"

I was prepared to return him to his rightful owner without a whimper of self-pity, to consider this an aberration never to be repeated. At that moment, strengthened by his love, I felt equipped to face the solitude again, to be outside the circle of family and society, forever looking on, disdaining and envying.

229

"We'll at least have breakfast," he said quietly, acknowledging his own jarring return to reality.

And so, we cooked together, dawdled over eating, took a bathtub bath together and climbed back between the sheets. He called his office around nine and said something about being called out of town during the night, a not unheard-of event.

Suddenly someone was knocking on the door. Even though I hadn't heard a car, I was sure it was Rose and that there was about to be a horrendous scene. But Spencer didn't seem in the least alarmed and sensibly suggested I go see who was at the door. I slipped on a robe and put the chain on the door and peeped out. It was Peter Bright. A small sailboat lay on the beach just beyond the dunes.

He had come to be with me, he said, because the president had been assassinated. He was fighting back tears. I have no recollection of what I said to Peter, only that when I came back from talking to him, Spencer was half dressed and had the radio on in the bedroom. Rose had worked on Kennedy's campaign. As Catholics, we had rejoiced less than three years earlier to see the first Catholic elected to the White House. It was impossible that our young, beloved, handsome president had been shot, and in Texas! Oh, the hatred that would be heaped on us by the rest of the nation!

"Will you be all right?" said Spencer. "I hate to leave you at a time like this."

"No, you go ahead, Spence. I'll be fine. You came when I needed you, but the night is over now." I wanted to sound strong. "Go be with Rose. I'm sure she's devastated."

Later, I drove into town to Peter's house, apologized for offering so little comfort when he had come to me, and the two of us spent the next three days watching television coverage of the funeral.

~~~~~

I wish I could report that that was all there was to Spencer's and my love affair, that the news Peter Bright brought that day shocked us into saner paths of thinking, that we were able to end what we had started before anybody got hurt. But I've told you

230

enough about myself for you to have realized by now what kind of woman I am, one who had been taught well, one who wanted to be better than she was, one who continually failed to meet her own standards. I can offer no excuse for myself other than that I was starved for a lover's touch. It seems, even though my husband had been dead only three months, that I had not had anyone to love me since Lawrence died, and as I've explained, there was no flesh involved in that love.

I had the builder come back and close in the downstairs for a garage so that Spencer's car could not be seen from the highway. I welcomed him whenever he could come, for however long he could stay. I was unforgivably happy, though when alone, I chastised myself for not remaining celibate, as I had intended, for the rest of my life.

My love for Lawrence had been such a pure and uplifting love that I did not regret not getting to know him in bed. And, of course, the inequality between Harding and me had spoiled sex between us. Now all the joys of an equal physical relationship were mine: lying in the bathtub between Spencer's legs while the water cascaded over the rim; falling asleep as if drugged after making love, only to waken in his arms and want him again; slipping off in his sailboat to Cat Island and building a fire on the beach and making love beside it, cuddled in quilts against the chill.

But as I write these words, I suddenly remember something that happened between me and Harding that I seem to have willfully forgotten, something that must be considered in any meaningful exploration of the importance I gave my sexual feelings. We had been back in Galveston only a short time. The change of scenery was good for us and allowed us to change the way we behaved toward one another. Initially, there was the question of bedrooms, who would sleep where. Harding, I recall, playfully suggested that now we were alone (for the first time in years without household help or guests) maybe we could share a room. I squashed that idea rather peremptorily with some excuse about how often he got up during the night, but I could see that he had got the idea in his head we might repair our old intimacy.

Early one morning—Harding's favorite time for sex—I

231

woke up to find him in bed with me attempting to be ardent. He had been so near death that I didn't feel like being mean to him, so I lay passively and told myself that it wouldn't hurt me to give him what he wanted this once. So what if I didn't love him any more, in fact, despised him for his repeated betrayals? I had loved him once and now he was old and dying. It was the least I could do for him. But I could see that he was not succeeding and suddenly it was very important to me that he should. It broke my heart to think of his losing something that, in his mind at least, made him who he was. And so I worked as hard as he did to help him regain his flagging manhood, but in the end we were defeated: all the medication he took had put an end to his sex life.

But now I enjoyed an unexpected mid-life flowering of my own sex life. And with Spencer, of all people! It seemed to me that all my disparate selves came together in loving Spencer, the physical, the emotional, friendship and passion, our shared past. We were equals in appetite, in taste, in adventure; equals in that he could speak of family members, old acquaintances and not have to explain who these people were. Either of us could start a sentence, apropos to nothing, and the other wouldn't be at sea.

We delighted in discovering similarities of taste and out-look. We teased ourselves into believing that we would have been ideal mates, indeed, one of those couples of whom it was said grew to look like one another. When we weren't together, we talked on the phone, and when Spencer could manage it, I went with him to Houston or Dallas on business and we did things we couldn't do at home, movies, dinner.

It was an idyllic time, that winter when love was new, pas-sion only barely explored, and the question of where it was all leading resolutely not asked. Neither did we ask ourselves if we were really justified, no matter how far apart he and Rose had drifted, in viewing what we were doing as anything but adultery.

It was only gradually that I realized that I had lost the peace of mind I had assiduously cultivated while Harding was off play-ing with the boys. It was hard to recognize in me now the self-reliant woman who had gone about her business for weeks at a time while her errant husband was away, this clinging vine who needed to hear Spencer's voice several times a day. (I might add that far from being annoyed, Spencer was delighted with this change in me.)

I found it increasingly difficult to find meaning in my petty introverted activities. I had once spent the day happily amusing myself drinking tea and reading the large numbers of newspapers and magazines I relied on while living in Mexico to keep me informed; clipping articles for my "idea" scrapbook and scribbling comments alongside; after lunch, heading out for a vigorous walk on the beach, binoculars strung about my neck; upon my return, recording my observations about sea birds, dolphins and other marine life in yet another journal I kept, my nature journal. In the evenings, I pursued an ambitious reading program of great works that Lawrence had devised for me. (Organized around the development of the English novel, beginning with the adventures of Pamela, Clarissa, Joseph Andrews, Tom Jones and Humphrey Clinker. I was, I believe, well into the nineteenth century by then, reading the dolorous novels of Hardy.)

But it was no longer enough. I wanted a companion. My day, which formerly never had enough hours to squeeze into it everything I wanted to do, now seemed endless when I was expecting a call from Spencer and it didn't come. (Married men, I learned, are not in charge of their own time.) I would finally give up and go to bed, but sit up late into the night reading, listening for his car, unable to concentrate. Finally I would turn out the light and lie there in the dark, resenting him, resenting Rose, for having to sleep by myself.

I became irritating company to myself, planning meals that he would not be there to eat with me, postponing my walk in case he got out of court early, turning down the rare invitation that came my way from the few people I wanted to see. Even worse were the times when I did accept and found that Rose O'Malley had been invited also. I wanted to dislike her, to find some flaw in her that would justify Spencer's leaving her and coming to live with me, but she was unfailingly kind to me, urged me to let her throw a party and reintroduce me to my old friends. It was painfully obvious that Spencer had been fortunate in a mate, had chosen well (while I had not and had suf-

233

fered the consequences). Many's the time such thoughts drove me home in a fit of tears, convinced of my worthlessness.

There would be days when I saw clearly that the only thing to do was to give him up. If we kept on, I would end up making him hate me. He would see that I wasn't the strong independent woman he thought me. On certain mornings I would wake up calm and resolved to do the deed, but by nightfall have made myself ill and gone to bed with headache. I came up with all the excuses I needed to put off doing anything: I had only just found him again. I had been through so much. I deserved a little happiness before I died. There was no reason to spoil everything just when we were becoming so good together.

In the end, it wasn't I who made the decision, nor was it Spencer. Call it circumstance. Spencer and Rose lost Kirwin, twenty-three years old and electrocuted on board his ship in the Sea of Japan. He never made it to Vietnam, yet he was a casualty as surely as was mine and Spencer's love. Spencer and Rose, the sorrowing parents, closed ranks to grieve for their boy. My heart broke for Spencer, but the best thing I could do for him was to send him away without guilt when finally he got the strength to come see me again.

The summer of '64 (the summer I first became aware of something called the Beatles), I finally threw off lethargy and grief, accumulated from Harding's death and having to give up Spencer, and found the strength to follow my true lights. What was needed, I decided, was an occupation. And neighbors. I formed a small development company and built half-a-dozen "spec" houses a stone's throw from my own. I called it Fair Isle.

Chapter Eleven

Fair Isle (which eventually grew to twenty-four houses) was one of several votes of confidence Galveston received during the late sixties. There were also Sea Isle and Jamaica Beach on the west end, Tiki Island on the bay near the causeway. The old Pleasure Pier, which over the years had bankrupted several developers, in 1965 became the Flagship Hotel, owned by the city of Galveston. Sea-Arama opened that year. The toll bridge across San Luis Pass opened the following year. R. E. "Bob" Smith built a yacht basin and shopping mall just beyond the medical center.

The medical center, now the University of Texas Medical Branch (UTMB), became the largest employer on the island, with the American National Insurance Company and the school district a distant second and third. Fortunes made in the nineteenth century bankrolled the expansion, building new hospitals and adding wings to old ones.

Still, Galveston's permanent population declined. The downtown district, so prosperous and bustling in Grandmama's day, deteriorated so I could hardly bear to see it on the occasions when I had business with my attorneys. Business after business forsook the island and headed north. There had been three Catholic schools in my day, now there was only one. The movie houses closed, passenger train service to Houston stopped. Scholes Field ceased to serve major airlines.

To think that a mere seventy years earlier Galveston had been a serious rival to Houston! Galveston's population has hovered around 60,000 since the '40s, while Houston went on to become the fourth-largest city in the country. On the occasions when I had to drive in Houston, I felt like a little old lady hunched over my steering wheel, terrified of the freeways and "spaghetti bowl" exchanges. Houston was all youth and muscle; we were in our dotage, Galveston and I. But both I and Galveston continued to express spasms of optimism. For my part, 1968 was the year I put my relationship with Peter Bright on a new footing.

It all started when I woke up one night with a burning pain in my abdomen. I know exactly when it was, because earlier that evening I had been watching the Democratic National Convention in Chicago on TV, at the same time holding an animated telephone conversation with Peter Bright, who was as incensed as I was at what the Chicago police were doing to the young people outside the convention hall demonstrating against the war.

As people who live alone must do, I cast my mind over my acquaintances and wondered which of them to call. My thoughts went first to Spencer, but I was so angry at him for his hawkishness about the war that I decided to punish him by not calling him. These days we could hardly conduct necessary business without quarreling about the war. It seemed extraordinary to me that he could support an illegal and immoral "police action" that had cost him his son's life. Yet at the same time, I realized that if he didn't support the war, he would have to feel that Kirwin's life had been entirely wasted. The whole divisive issue had done to us what it was doing to the country, forced us into two angry camps, with no middle ground.

And so I called Peter, though it was nearly three o'clock in the morning. He promptly drove out West Beach to fetch me into town to the emergency room. I had an inflamed appendix which had to come out. It was while filling out the admission forms that it came home to me how alone I was. I had lived with the fact that I was the last member of my family for the last quarter century, since Papa's death in 1944, yet somehow this truth had never registered as powerfully for me as it did that night I signed myself into the hospital and had no one to put down as next-of-kin, no one to give permission should some extraordinary procedure be required while I lay anesthetized. Usually I put down Spencer's name as my attorney, but that evening I couldn't bear to think of Spencer being called upon to make decisions about my body. There was no immediate remedy, of course, so I left those blanks unfilled and was wheeled into the operating room and put to sleep.

But as I lay in the hospital recovering from surgery—which passed uneventfully, requiring no one to make decisions in my behalf—I felt that I must end my solitude or die, must somehow find purpose and meaning, or die. Death had seemed the next inevitable step for me for so long, and yet I kept on living.

It would be both self-serving and untruthful if I said this dreary train of thought came to me because there was no one around to take note of my stay in the hospital. In fact, the opposite was true: An outpouring of affection was heaped on my ungrateful head. I wanted only to sleep, but people I hadn't seen in years crowded into my hospital room to see me. Well-wishers from as far away as Washington sent me flowers, telegrams and cards. I wanted to beg Peter to spirit me off to an empty room somewhere so I could get some rest.

Yet, at the same time, my vanity was tickled. They *did* care. They were afraid I would die without their having told me they cared.

Nevertheless, in the weeks of my convalescence, as I walked the beach, going a little further each day to gain back my strength and stamina, I resolved to ask Peter Bright to come live with me. It would be a liaison of convenience, for there was no passion between us. We were old friends (almost as old as Spencer and I), comrades-in-arms, fellow solitaries.

Or was it a little too cold-blooded and practical to ask a man to live with you because you despised being alone? Was it the sort of pact my grandmother had encouraged both Mama and me to enter? Never mind that you don't love him *that way*, think of what is to be gained. Unnerving thought. But one needn't be sneaky or manipulative like Grandmama had been. One could lay one's cards on the table. I determined to be absolutely honest.

~~~~~

Peter Bright, having spent most of his adult life on a shrimp boat, was aged and wrinkled by the sun and hard work. Over the bones of his face, the skin was thin and shiny, the cheeks red as apples. His eyes were an astonishing electric blue, which had earned him the sobriquet "Bright Eyes" when we were young. His long gray hair, thin and unkempt, was habitually ponytailed and jammed into a Houston Astros baseball cap. Virtually year-round, he wore denim cut-offs and rubber thongs. His feet, legs and arms were marvelously sinewy and brown. Shirtless, his body was as hard and lean as a teenaged boy's, without the slightest unnecessary flesh. I smiled to see him bound up my stairs that evening.

"Peter," I said over dinner—I confess I had put myself out more than usual to produce something palatable, "what if I were to return the compliment of the proposal you made me some—what—thirty-two years ago?—the night we were hustled off to jail for drinking bootleg whiskey at the Sui Jen—and asked you to come live with me?"

"I'd accept," he said promptly.

"Would you really, Peter? Knowing that we're not wildly infatuated with one another?"

"Why, what do you mean? I've always had a soft spot for you, old girl."

"Always?"

"Made me so cotton-pickin' mad when I saw how you were living down there in Mexico."

"I was terribly upset after you left, pulling me aside and lec-turing me about how bad we were! It would've been disloyal to Harding to tell you that it was all his doing."

"The surgery scared you, didn't it, old girl?"

"What scared me was having no one to write down as next-of-kin, the thought of dying all alone."

Peter could always be relied on to introduce practicality. "What? Dying! I'm three years older than you! That'd make you—"

"Fifty-three."

238

He cocked a bright blue eye at me like a robin eyeing a wormhole. "Want to do it up brown and get hitched?"

"No," I said quickly. "What I mean is, it'd only be, well, like an experiment, Peter. The kids are doing it, you know, living together. Free love and all that. It might not work at all— we've both lived alone so long."

"The kids do it because they want to sleep together."

There, he had me. I had no desire to sleep with Peter Bright. Defeated, I sat back and considered what to say next. Such a setback would not have deterred Grandmama, I thought.

"Tell you what, Miss Emily," said Peter, pointing the tines of his fork at me. "I'm sod poor—never have two coins to clink together—and you've got more money than you'll ever be able to spend. Sell me one of your houses under terms I can manage, and I'll move here right under your nose. You want company for dinner, I'll wash my face and hands and be right over. You want somebody to sashay down the beach with you, I'm your man. You want somebody who's handy with a wrench, I'll grab my toolbox. And if you want somebody to hold your little hand through the night, love—get my drift?"

"Perhaps we could gradually get used to togetherness," I said, hope springing to life again.

He eyed me shrewdly. "I won't hold my breath."

And so, instead of having an affair with Peter Bright, he became my neighbor. I kept an open mind about the hand-holding, but somehow I knew it wouldn't work and might even destroy our friendship. Pondering this whole question of exactly what I wanted Peter Bright to be to me, made me rethink the relationship between my grandmother and my father, Faith and Charles. Mama, on occasion—usually just before Meg summoned Dr. Brown to come poke her with his hypodermic and silence her, when she was raging at the slights the world had heaped on her head—used to accuse her mother and husband of being in league against her, used to hint at the unnaturalness of their perfect synchronization of thought and movement. And later, after Harding had blasted my innocence by bringing every sort of corruption into our villa in Tres Hermanas, I would ponder Mama's veiled accusations, think back over my own memories and wonder: Was there something *more* between them? I

239

recalled many times hearing Grandmama apologize to Papa for having "saddled" him with her wrong-headed daughter, frankly owning her part in bringing them together. Since I had grown up in Grandmama's house, it never seemed odd to me that Grandmama arranged people's lives for them. Now, of course, I saw her meddling as mere biological self-interest.

I was thirty years old before it occurred to me to ask myself why Grandmama found it necessary to arrange a marriage for Mama. When I was little, I was Mama's champion against a world that didn't understand her. But later I adopted Grandmama's view of my mother, that she was a bitter woman, a failed artist, an alternately whining and hysterical creature who lived in an upstairs bedroom and blighted my teens with her perpetual illnesses. It was only after I put away Lawrence's old Hasselblad, and the notecards began to flutter in my wake, that a different view emerged, the truth of why Grandmama and Mama had hated one another so.

It was in '68, right after Peter and I began our experiment in cohabiting—nearby houses, as we both guarded our independence so carefully that we hadn't yet decided to live under one roof—that I realized I needn't rely merely on my own faulty memory. There was a living resource I had never tapped, a storehouse of memories, a houseful of artifacts, another pair of eyes and living human memory: Meg Galloway.

Although my old nurse was eighty-five years old by the time I seriously began asking questions about my family, Meg was able-bodied and still lived in the ground-floor apartment of our old house. A handyman came around every few days to do her bidding, and a young woman came in every morning to do her shopping, cleaning, and prepare her a hot meal. Grandmama had provided for Meg so that she could lead an independent life for as long as she chose. She didn't want to go to a home, she repeatedly told me, but wanted to stay where she was. Arthritis had settled into her lame leg, making it difficult for her to get around.

In spite of the cleaning woman, the mementos of a lifetime filled the apartment so there was hardly room to take a seat. It is surprising, perhaps, that I had not achieved the same closeness to Meg that my mother had, since Meg, from the time my sister Faith fell from the roof, was the adult I looked to as a parent. But it was Mama she felt loyal to, and I was the one who went away. We wrote to each other, all those years I was in Mexico, but nevertheless, I returned a stranger to the island, seeing things with a stranger's eyes.

And so I began to interview Meg Galloway, and that's when I discovered the rich lode of family information she had, not only in her head, but piled high in the spare bedroom, the hall cupboards, filling up kitchen drawers and the piano bench, overflowing onto dresser tops and tables—old crumbling packets of letters in brown ink, tied up with string and faded ribbon, disintegrating bound volumes filled with my grandmother's handwriting, moldering photo albums displaying my grave-faced ancestors. Certainly, many of these exhibits I remembered from my youth, for example, the small locked journal my mother kept on that disastrous cruise to Europe. How brave and sneaky it was of me to wait for Mama and Charlotte to get quiet, then slip out of my bed and take that little book to the bathroom with me! Only the endorsement of the Mata Hari girl spies could've given me the courage to do such a thing. Of course, at thirteen, my reading of those anguished lines of my mother's was a far different reading than the one I gave it as an adult! Meg generously allowed me to plunder her treasures, insisting that she had saved them for me all along. The truth was, Meg, like me, was a sole survivor and had no one to leave her things to. Who would I leave mine to?

After Grandmama's death in 1938, my father moved into a suite at the Tremont Hotel so that the house might be converted into apartments for married soldiers—stationed there to guard the coast against German U-boats. Papa did very little cleaning and consolidating. In fact, knowing his distaste for dealing with emotional matters, I'd wager he moved out with his clothes and personal papers and left the rest for Meg to dispose of as she would.

"He was twenty years younger than Grandmama," I remarked to Meg, while turning the pages of the little velvet album Grandmama had taken to Europe in 1900, "and yet he only outlived her by six years."

"He were a lost soul without her, poor man," said Meg.

"Meg, there were . . . let's see . . . two or three years they lived here in the old house without me or Mama." I thought for a moment. "Without you, too, isn't that right? You were taking care of your dad?"

"Your Grandmama was up in her eighties."

"Late seventies, Meg. And she was spry. I saw her once during that time. She was still driving her own car."

"She were the sort that marched around like Caesar and then one day dropped dead. No lying abed taking her time dying, that one!"

"Well, then, if she was spry and marching around and all that, did you notice her relationship with my father change any during that time?"

Meg wrinkled her brow, the better to sharpen her memory perhaps. "I'm sure I couldn't say, Miss Emily."

"Who was here? Household staff, I mean?"

"Well, let's see now. Mrs. Frenche had gone to the home on account of her rheumatism. Mr. Gomez—goodness—he died in what?"

"Never mind him—he was an old man when I was a child. Grandmama surely had household help?"

"I recall a black girl coming over to clean for her, but she didn't live here."

"No one lived here while I was growing up," I retorted, "—except a pack of servants employed to look after me. So, it appears that at the end, it was just Grandmama and Charles? They were devoted to one another, weren't they, Meg?"

"No doubt about that, Miss Emily. Everybody knew that. Never a difference of opinion between those two."

Children take what they are given at face value because they've nothing to measure it against. Growing up, I was innocently willing to believe there was nothing more than friendship between my mother and Charlotte Miller, nee Lattimore, but among my mother's papers I found ample evidence to suggest that Mama was a frustrated lesbian, that Grandmama knew this and tried her very best to "cure" my mother by forcing her to get married.

But Grandmama had not made it so easy to penetrate her secrets. Her journals, ample, and dealing with public events and

242

business decisions—which for the most part I do not include here—seemed almost to have been written to deflect curiosity. There was not a scrap of evidence to suggest that she and my father had a love affair. If they felt passion for one another, if that passion led them to conduct a clandestine sexual affair, they did so without making a fuss about it. Among Meg Galloway's heaps of papers, I uncovered no secret cache of love letters, no keepsakes pressed into books. And obviously there could have been no issue from their union—since Grandmama was nearly forty when they met—save the very large fortune they amassed, which they were amicably agreed should not be squandered on me, even if I was the last Coolidge-Pickering.

I found myself obsessed with and thoroughly baffled by this pair as I searched my memory for clues. I recalled evenings in my youth when Faith and Charles sat in the drawing room after dinner (with Mama likely as not sulking in her room or off somewhere with Charlotte) and how they would share the evening paper and express the same reaction to things: "Did you see . . .?" "Yes, I saw." "Isn't it awful?" "They ought to be horsewhipped . . . " More than once Grandmama alludes in her journal to her "masculine cast of mind." What sort of mind did she see my father as having? He had spent his life working behind a desk, taking orders from a woman, and it appears that he was celibate for most of his life, all but the four years he was married to Hazel Brookside. I could come to no conclusions, but the facts as I knew them caused me to shake my head in wonder. Were people then really so different than they were today? Had I been hoodwinked by an elaborate charade? Did Grandmama leave behind only her "public" journals, imagining the day a biographer would delve into her long and self-abnegating public life and hoping to take the secret to her grave that she had actually had a very different private life than anyone knew?

When I became overwhelmed at the task I had set for myself, I would seek out others who had known those involved. What did Spencer make of Grandmama and Papa's relationship? Spencer was only twenty-five when Grandmama died, but he had known her all his life, had sat in on his uncle George's interviews with her as she decided the disposition of her affairs.

And he had handled hundreds of documents pertaining to those affairs.

I should take the time here to say that after the dissolution of our love affair, Spencer and I had gone right on seeing one another, for it was impossible not to—we had almost as much business between us as Faith and Charles had. I had briefly considered moving my business elsewhere, but I didn't want to seem vindictive or to add to Spencer's pain. Besides, there was the simple fact that no one else knew as much about Grandmama's business. (I still couldn't think of it as *my* business.)

I remember the first time we allowed ourselves to go to dinner after we had agreed not to see each other as lovers. In spite of our long friendship, it felt awkward to sit across the table from Spencer, painful not to reach across the table to touch his hand. Kirwin's death had been the first real tragedy of his life. I don't mean to belittle other deaths Spencer had weathered—his parents and grandparents, an older brother, but the deaths of people old enough to die is never as tragic and painful as the death of a youngster who had yet to live up to his promise. Compared to my losses, I considered Spencer and Rose extraordinarily lucky and blessed.

Spencer's response was: "Grandmama and old Charles? You must be kidding!" His mild gray-blue eyes widened at the idea. "Correct to the nth, darling! What made you think of such a thing?" I recall that we were having lunch at our favorite seafood restaurant, Gaido's, on the seawall.

"What made you *not* think of it?" I countered.

He thought for a moment, choosing his words with care. "It's revisionist history to look at the past with our knowing and jaded eyes. Here we are in the late sixties, seeing all barriers between the sexes fall away and we look back and amend the way we see our past. Suddenly it's impossible to believe that there could've been a relationship between a man and a woman that lasted over forty years and was apparently satisfying and close, without imagining them in bed together. No, Emily, I do not think Faith and Charles secretly conducted a clandestine sexual affair."

Old stuffed shirt, I thought, always sticking rigidly to the establishment view! Secretly smoldering, I picked up my salad fork and considered how best to deflate his pompousness.

244

"If I'm guilty of revisionism, you're guilty of a failed imagination. My grandmother was a dynamic and aggressive woman. Why shouldn't she be as capable as the next of gratifying her sexual urges? I grant you that my father was not a young Galahad, but he did manage to make his way in the world with little more than his charm and a good head for figures."

"Why can't the facts as we know them be enough for you? Why do you have to cheapen what they had?"

"I don't think that sex *cheapens* a relationship between a man and a woman."

"That's not what I mean," he said helplessly. "I just mean . . . why can't you leave it at that? I can't think of anyone else who would pursue such an angle about her own grandmother and father—who was married to your mother."

"He may not have been married to her when he and Grandmama had their affair."

"Affair! You've come to a conclusion with no other evidence than your suspicions, your dirty mind."

I leaned toward him across the table top and said sweetly, "Spencer, sex is not dirty."

He colored and sat back in his chair. Mustering his dignity he said: "Nevertheless, I refuse to think of a great woman like your grandmother being drawn into something sordid. I hope you won't spread groundless rumors about one of our BOI heroines."

"Stuff and nonsense!" I snapped at him. We continued our meal in silence, me on my side marshaling my thoughts for the next attack. "The Victorians, as we now know, were notoriously duplicitous about sexual matters, maintaining strait-laced decorum in public, but in private indulging the most scabrous tastes."

"I'm not sure it's fair to call them Victorians. . . ."

"Grandmama was born in 1857 and Papa in 1877. From what era do you suppose they got their ideas about sex?"

"All right, you win that one." Spencer chewed on a shrimp-tail, getting every last bit of good out of it. The empty tails were laid around the edge of his plate in a little pink fan. "It doesn't really matter, does it? It can't be proved one way or the other. So why not give them the benefit of the doubt? If it meant so much to your grandmother to hide the fact, why not let her get away with it? How does it benefit you to prove such a thing?"

245

"It isn't a theory I dreamed up and then set out to prove, Spence! It's there in every old letter I read, every old photograph, every high-flown phrase written about her in the newspapers! She is portrayed as fulfilled and complete. Why should she have felt fulfilled and complete when her dreams of founding a line of Coolidges had come to naught? It's not that I decided there must have been sex from the perspective of my dirty twentieth century mind, it's that I'm asking why we assume two such dynamic people, who apparently never had a cross word, who lived under the same roof for many years, who were united in despising my poor sick mother—why *shouldn't* they have had a sex life?"

"I find the question unseemly," he said with finality.

"Why do you assume they were any different than us?" I said, firing the coup de grace. "Were we dirty-minded for what we did? Is that why you're in such pain, my friend? That you were sinning while Kirwin went off to war?"

~~~~~

Over the years Spencer and I would find ourselves on opposite sides of the fence again and again: American policy in Vietnam, desegregation of the schools, women's rights, ecology. Each time there was an issue, we took our sides, faithful to our roles, me the rebel, he the staunch defender of the establishment. It wasn't that Spencer was an evil man intent on depriving the less fortunate of enfranchisement, merely that he was a privileged white male whose own intentions were benign, making it seem unnecessary and dangerous to change the rules. He dismissed the ERA as "unnecessary, since we're *all* covered by the Bill of Rights." Furthermore, he despised any philosophy that set "man against man." Oho! Did I make something of that all-inclusive statement! "I can understand why you would defend the status quo when you're on the side with all the power!" I shouted at him. To which he calmly replied: "I refuse to let you cast me in the role of enemy, Mrs. Douglas. Go march in the streets and burn your bra if you like. You cannot argue with my love for you."

246

With each new political awareness, I re-examined my conclusions about Faith and Edith, my foremothers. Faith rose up as a magnificent matriarch. Why, indeed, did she need a man to sleep with? She had all that *power*. And Edith? Born before her time, poor woman. Added to that, she was probably mentally ill, major depression, and was unable to do what she longed to do, seize the moment she came into her inheritance to go to New York, where she undoubtedly would have met up with some of those "bohemians" she admired, might even have met a woman like herself and settled into a lasting and satisfying relationship, instead of having to make do with Charlotte Miller, whose only interest seems to have been finding a rich husband. And if, indeed, Grandmama *was* carrying on a secret affair with my father, then I gave her even more credit for sheer audacity!

But perhaps there was a clue in the phrase she dropped more than once, her "masculine cast of mind." What did Grandmama mean by that? Did she herself feel homo-erotic stirrings and is that why she understood them in Edith and so vigorously attempted to stamp them out? We despise most in others those traits we hate in ourselves. I thought of the unsentimental way my grandmother conducted herself, dressed, wore her hair. I thought of the aggressive way she ran my grandfather's business, how she took the Coolidge Cotton Company far beyond what he had ever imagined for it and made more money than either her husband or her father before her. I thought of how she had interviewed my father, being careful not to choose a man who would challenge or eclipse her, and how, despite his lackluster performance, had made him her partner. Did Grandmama, with her masculine cast of mind, envy her daughter, born of a generation that could contemplate "bohemianism" without immediately rushing off to hang herself? Was the lack of proof of a physical relationship between Charles and Faith simply due to the fact that Faith had no desire to sleep with Charles?

And my own generation—not *mine*, but the one I was currently picked up and carried along with—was Spencer right—were we obsessed to find sex everywhere we looked?

~~~~~

247

Perhaps it goes without saying that Peter Bright was one of the earliest men I knew to march under the feminist banner. I conceived many of my ideas about the likely workings of Grandmama and Papa's relationship from how ours worked, though on such a different stage. Ours domestic, theirs public.

Peter was quite a good cook, while I never progressed beyond plain and serviceable. He had raised his two boys with very little help from their mother or any other female, and apparently did so without inflicting lasting harm on them. Often Peter would come over to my kitchen to fix our evening meal, cleaning up after himself so efficiently I didn't even have to do the pots and pans afterwards. While he diced and tossed and stirred, I rat-a-tat-tatted on the old typewriter Spencer had given me on the dining room table, which could never be used for eating. I had graduated from index cards to typing paper and was even confident enough to buy a ream at a time!

"It spoils Grandmama as a feminist hero that she apparently didn't feel the slightest sense of solidarity with her sisters," I said. "She never did anything for the women of Coolidge Cotton Company."

"Did she do anything for the men?"

"Well, no. A social conscience is pretty much a product of the late twentieth century."

"There you go."

"And do you know, Peter, I can't recall a single woman friend she had? Apparently all her relationships were connected with business."

"How many do you have, love?"

"I know hundreds of women!"

Peter rolled his bright blues and let my remark speak for itself.

"I wish there was some way to find out! The whole household knew when Charles *wasn't* sleeping with my mother. Why couldn't they have noticed the dented extra pillow in my grandmother's room? Why couldn't I have spied on them? I spied on everybody else. It never occurred to me, of course, because they were so *dull*, Grandmama a paragon of rectitude and Papa a boring old duffer."

"Your opinion about him hasn't changed," observed Peter.

"One time we were sitting around the dining room table— it wasn't often that Grandmama and Papa came home to dinner, but when they did, we made a regular production of it. At any rate, Mama was late to the table and I recall that Papa put his hand on her forearm, in greeting, I suppose, and she brushed it off with such loathing that my grandmother responded by smashing a cut-glass water tumbler against the wall and sending Mama to her room."

"What did it mean?"

"I don't know. It left a vivid impression on my memory, as you can see. I suppose it means merely that she had arranged for these two to marry and she felt it very keenly that the marriage didn't thrive. Do you know that she *forced* my mother to sleep with her husband? Apparently Mama had no intention of letting him into her bed. But when Grandmama found out, she gave Mama the choice of either submitting or getting out of the house."

"Well it's a cinch there would've been no Emily if she hadn't insisted."

"Right." I sighed. "Think I'll talk to Meg Galloway again. She's bound to have known what was going on upstairs."

I decided to pretend that I knew the truth and was only seeking confirmation from her. "What can it possibly hurt, Meg, now that they're all these many years dead, for the truth to come out? Did my grandmother sleep with Charles?"

"Lands, child! What a shocking thing to say."

"Not in this day and time, Meg. Look at what goes on on TV. Did you ever see Papa in her bedroom? Did you ever suspect they were together behind closed doors? I'm intensely interested in arriving at the truth and you may be my last hope."

"I know you're writing a book about your grandmother, but I'll not contribute to no dirt being said about her. She was a great lady and a credit to her sex. She did a lot for this city too, miss, and you could do worse than copy her example."

Meg thought me lazy and self-indulgent, and perhaps I was.

"But wouldn't it be wonderful to know what made her tick? What did she do that gave her true enjoyment? Make money?"

"Give it away, more likely. She wanted to leave her property to her children but she was thwarted in that, so she took the city

249

of Galveston to be her child. She loved this island more than anything. That were her true lover, Emily, this island. She was BOI to the core. Look among your papers for that, sweetheart. No use looking for ugly things."

My old nurse could say things to me that I wouldn't let Spencer get away with. Chastised, I relented. "I know you're right. Yes, later in life, when she knew she wouldn't have heirs, she did become a great benefactor. I suppose it's all to the good that I didn't have children, that O'Malley, Bradley and Tate were so damn-awful good at protecting Grandmama's interests against poor inept Harding's depredations. If he'd been sober, he might have been dangerous."

Still, I carried away with me another armload of papers and diligently searched for clues that would bring a twentieth century understanding to my grandmother's nineteenth century mind.

One evening in January, when I was alone, reading in bed, the phone rang and it was Spencer to tell me that Meg Galloway had been found dead by Edna, her cleaning woman. She had apparently died in her sleep, a peaceful death, a quiet ending for our faithful servant. I didn't cry at the time, though Spencer was afraid I would and offered to come out. No, I said, we mustn't console each other. No, he agreed. Meg Galloway had been one of my last links to the past. In spite of the index cards, the hopeless scrabbling through old papers, the oft-abandoned resolve to write a book—something irreplaceable slipped out of my life with Meg's death. Now I was the only one who still remembered life in that big old house on Avenue P. In a mere three generations we would all be gone.

And then I began to cry for myself and for Meg Galloway.

BOOK III

Galveston, 1980–1990

Chapter Twelve

In 1980, Spencer and I found ourselves confronting each other over yet another fence. He and a group of investors had bought a huge tract of land near San Luis Pass at the western end of the island and announced ambitious plans to build a "Galveston-West End." There were to be a second causeway to the mainland, a business and industrial park, shopping mall, exclusive residential neighborhood, condominiums, hotel, golf course—all with utter disregard to the environment and the island's history. The seawall is a good fifteen miles away.

The confrontation took place on the beach, where Spencer and a group of young men in suits had arranged for television cameras to record their scooping up of ceremonial shovelsful of sand in front of a large billboard proclaiming their monstrous hubris. Laid out impressively among the dunes were little fluttering day-glo orange flags. Our small but vocal band of environmentalists stole the spotlight, however, sparking a public debate about west end development that eventually caused repeated postponement of Spencer's plans. It was one the earliest instances on the island when concern for the environment gained precedence over the long-accepted profit motive.

I was singled out for an interview, not because I was an authority on the environment of West Beach, nor because I had the grayest head in the bunch and might possibly be the possessor of a little wisdom, but because my grandmother had been Faith Kohl Coolidge, still a name that carried moral authority, no matter what the issue. (For her part, Grandmama would not have been in the least bit sympathetic to a bunch of hooligans waving signs at her while she was busy conducting business.) I still have the tape, provided me by KHOU-TV in Houston, with my long skirt flapping in the wind, my earth shoes filling with sand, hair blowing in my eyes, indignantly questioning Spencer's sanity.

"What in God's name do they think will keep this place from blowing away in the next big storm?!" I demand. (Speaking extempore I'm all heart and no logic.) "What planet are these people from?" The camera shifts to Spencer and the young men in suits, who are muttering to themselves. "Where have they been that they're so ignorant of this island's history?!"

I was at home an hour later when Spencer stopped by on his way back to town. He was livid. "You never bother to find out the facts, do you?!" he stormed at me.

"Enlighten me," I said. "Just who is going to pay for your little mini-city when the storm surge carries it away?"

"Your grandmother would've been one of my investors!"

"My grandmother wasn't stupid enough to build on sand!" I fired back.

"Here are the facts: we have in place one of the strictest building codes in the entire world. Every structure must be designed to withstand winds of a hundred twenty-five miles an hour and a storm surge of eighteen feet. Face it, Emily, human beings have lived on this island for over a hundred and fifty years: We're not going away."

"But why, Spence? At what cost? Why not spend your zillion dollars over on the mainland where you don't have to build eighteen feet in the air, where the eco-system can tolerate having thousands more cars and people? I've never seen this side of you before, this—this *money-grubbing* side! But then, look at your past—you're the one that kept me all those years from having the money Mama intended me to have—"

"Oh, let's not drag up that one!"

"You enriched yourself at my expense!"

"You're being unfair. You're the one that ran off with that

cheap bounder Harding Douglas. He only married you for the money he thought you were worth. When you're in a more sensible frame of mind, you always thank me for sticking to business, for not letting my love for you color my business decisions."

"And now, for you to use that money to do something so crass, so big-city, so unthinking and heedless—"

"Oh, fine, you build your twenty-four houses on West Beach, but after that, it's bar the door, don't let anyone else in!"

"If any of us had had a *speck* of environmental awareness back then, I wouldn't have built these houses! I would tear them all down tomorrow, but I don't own them any more. I don't have a choice about it, but you do. You can't claim ignorance of what you're doing. That causeway you're talking about will cut right through the wetlands, disturb the nesting grounds for thousands of shore birds. Don't do it, Spencer! Get out of this silly thing while you can."

The second causeway to serve the western end of the island never found funding. Spencer's billboard grew shabby in the marine atmosphere, just like our houses and cars do, like all man-made things do on the island. I didn't change Spencer's mind; the ardent young environmentalists didn't change the developer's minds; it was the Storm Goddess that turned the trick.

It had been twenty-two years since she visited our shores. A whole generation had grown up on the island without first-hand knowledge of the awesome power of hurricanes. I boarded up my windows and headed north. Let her rip, I thought. Let her sweep it all out to sea! It's a struggle neither of us can win. She can't make us go away, we can't keep her from coming.

Alicia, which hit on August 18, 1983, was one of Galveston's worst storms, not in deaths, but in dollar losses. In twenty-two years, we had overbuilt the island, far beyond the protection of the seawall. We had put up our hundred-thousand-dollar beach houses and condominium developments just as if 1900, 1915, 1919, 1932, 1941, 1943, 1949, 1957, 1961 hadn't brought us an angry Storm Goddess pounding at our door. Out on West Beach we couldn't get back to our homes for weeks. When at last I was allowed in, I found the beach littered with collapsed beach houses, the highway an obstacle course of rusted washing machines, forlorn porcelain johns, and other wildly out-of-place domestica.

255

In spite of the damage Galveston suffered, Alicia will be remembered as the storm that rained glass down on Houston, proving that sixty miles is not far enough inland to escape the fury of a full-blown hurricane. Nestled amongst Houston's downtown skyscrapers is a graceful pink column of granite and glass which abuts a building of shorter stature topped with an old, low-tech tar and gravel roof. Alicia (call her what they would, Carla in 1961, Gilbert in 1981, we BOI's knew her true identity)—Alicia's one-hundred-mile-an-hour winds knocked out over three hundred pink glass windows with gravel bullets.

My own home had sustained serious damage—there was no longer a garage and laundry room downstairs—but I could see that my home was repairable. Many of my neighbors were not so lucky. Tornadoes had cut a zigzag path through Fair Isle, taking a roof here, clearing a foundation there, leaving nothing but a ragged set of black pilings elsewhere. At least half a dozen houses would have to be pulled down, including Peter's.

I wondered where Peter was. We had kept in touch by phone—he had insisted on riding out the storm in Galveston. As I watched the tide merrily advance to the very underpinnings of my house, I should have felt loss and confusion, a sense of looming depression at the destruction of my own hubris. Instead, I felt a fierce admiration for the Storm Goddess, as if I were standing on ground newly hallowed by her fierce handiwork. Soon the bulldozers would come and rake everything away, the re-building would begin. But just at that moment, you could almost hear the rustle of her departing skirts.

A car returning from the west end turned into the entrance of Fair Isle, going slowly to avoid the debris and enormous chugholes scoured out by the storm. It was Spencer coming back, I thought, from looking over his property. No great loss, all he had was a billboard. Nevertheless, I would be nice—Alicia had made my point for me. Spencer got out of his car and joined me on what had been a nice green lawn a few weeks before, now drowned in sand, with weird pieces of debris sticking up.

"I'm sorry, Em," he said.

I made a gesture that implied that it didn't matter. "I'm luckier than most."

"I wish you lived in town. I worry about you out here all alone."

"I've got Peter."

"Where is he?"

"Probably helping dig someone out."

"I came looking for you to tell you you were right."

"Of course I'm right. What about this time?"

"Building on this end of the island," he said ruefully. "I don't know what I was thinking of—let all those young fellows convince me somehow."

"Not BOI," I said.

Spencer laughed. "No, I expect not."

"I wonder, what do we really mean by that term, anyway? Grandmama used it a lot. It doesn't mean just the physical act of being born at John Sealy Hospital."

"Hmmm, no. I suppose it's the whole ball of wax, our shared experience and history, the thing that binds us to each other and to this gorgeous, hostile spit of sand."

"So, you've decided you're not a developer after all?"

"I believe this storm taught us something."

"Each generation has to learn it the hard way, it seems."

"Let the birds and the snakes and the sea turtles have it." He made a gesture of finality toward the western end of the island, where he had just searched in vain for scraps of his billboard and little orange flags.

"I believe I could like a man like you," I said.

Spencer put his arm around me. "Give us a kiss, Em."

And I did. It was a glorious day and we had come through another hurricane.

~~~~~

Peter Bright suffered a mild heart attack while helping one of his friends dismantle a wrecked ground-floor apartment after the storm. Perhaps that is why I insisted he move in with me. He had family, of course, which could have looked after him, two grown sons, grandchildren, in-laws. But he lived alone, and Alicia had destroyed his house. I found him at a friend's and took him home with me.

257

The heart attack was a warning, the doctor said, which made me angry because Peter Bright had lived an extremely active life, and for years had eaten right. A warning of what? That it didn't matter how well we took care of ourselves? That it didn't matter what we did in any circumstance because Fate stood ready to correct any silly notion we might have that our choices mattered? Is that what we learn from living on the island? Is that what makes us BOI? That unlike the rest of humanity, who build their houses and live on solid ground, we are never allowed to hold the illusion that we're in control?

I was tired of being the lone hold-out, the last one outside the fold, the lonely heretic, the extra single female for whom hostesses must provide. I had run out my string, gotten all the good that could be had from living on the edge. It was time to Join The Establishment. I would marry Peter as soon as I made him well. He had two sons. Each of them had married and had children, attractive, well-behaved children that I wished were mine. And if I married Peter, they would be. I would leave them my money and Grandmama would finally, in some measure, achieve her goal.

Such were my thoughts looking at Peter Bright, lying there looking surprised, the pins knocked from under him, a man used to being in control of his own body, now reduced to asking others to fetch for him. And yes, you needn't remind me that I was again setting myself up to fulfill a role that had become accustomed and familiar to me. I've spent far more time in the presence of dying men than I have with men in their virility and prime. Are dying men less frightening to me somehow?

But Peter Bright did not die, I'm happy to say. He recovered nicely and was able after a few months to move back to his own house and help put Fair Isle back together. I said nothing more about getting married—he knew it had only been said out of concern and worry for him. But we did go into partnership, he selecting damaged houses and me buying them, he and his grandson putting them back together and sharing the profits with me. After a storm there are always lots of houses for sale. These Houston people who come down here and build their pretty houses, who see the Gulf as merely a backdrop for a second home, are disillusioned when the Storm Goddess wreaks havoc and they sell cheap to us canny BOI's, who make our living selling the same pieces of real estate over and over.

Peter's grandson Dan was fifteen that summer he came down to work with his grandfather, not so much because Peter needed the help, but because the boy wanted to earn a tan and a set of hard young muscles, make some money to buy a car and meet girls.

I was not in the least surprised that Galveston wasted little time feeling sorry for herself, that she didn't lie where the storm had slammed her in stunned disbelief, but like Grandmama when she came back from Europe and saw what had happened, rolled up her sleeves and set to work. Cash flowed like water after Alicia. Everybody had a story about the insurance adjustor finding them and writing out a check on the spot, subsidized, of course, by the citizens of the Great State of Texas, whose monies were pooled to compensate those of us who choose to live in that area of greater risk. Hammers banged, saws buzzed, trucks loaded with lumber roared up and down the island, fueling a building frenzy that would revitalize the island. That's what hurricanes do. Like a prairie fire, they destroy everything in their path, leaving a clean slate for nature and humans to do their work.

~~~~~

Even before Alicia, Galveston had begun to realize that she was the caretaker of an enormous amount of nineteenth century history. The Galveston Historical Foundation lobbied tirelessly to stop the demolition of historic homes and buildings. Saved from destruction were the Williams-Tucker House, Ashton Villa, the Tremont House. I had even been enjoined from tearing down Grandmama's house, though I had expressed no plans to do so. Buildings in the Strand were being restored. There was suddenly interest in the old means of transportation, the wharves, the train depot, the trolley lines. The city acquired a tall sailing ship, the *Elissa*, which may or may not have made port in Galveston twice during the nineteenth century.

George P. Mitchell, BOI, made a fortune in oil and gas and came back to invest quite a lot of it in his old hometown, not

259

only restoring historical structures—the Balinese Room in the sixties, the old Galvez Hotel in the nineties—but also building new ones, The San Luis on Galveston Isle, a luxury hotel that opened in 1972 on the site of old Fort Crockett where Harding was a young soldier and where Grandmama had him incarcerated to keep him from running away with me. (Oh, Spencer has paid for his part in that one!) In 1985 the Mitchells revived Galveston's old Mardi Gras festival, which, along with Dickens on The Strand, brings visitors to the island in the winter.

And the renaissance continues: Pier 21—a hotel, restaurant and marina; Rainforest Pyramid—an acre of tropical forest inside a ten-story glass tower; Moody Gardens—a large recreation complex with 3-D IMAX theater.

The nineteenth century coruscations and embellishments on the old red brick warehouses that had once housed the Coolidge Cotton Company (which passed into other hands after my father's death) looked perfectly appropriate on a newly restored office complex. I attended the ceremony marking the opening and felt as tongue-tied as ever when asked to say a few words. However, I was inspired to try to tell them how Grandmama had returned to the island that terrible September, 1900, how she made her way through the ravaged streets, amid burning pyres of dead bodies and heaps of rubble, to get to the warehouse to see how quickly she could get people back to work. For she knew that was what Galveston's survival depended upon, showing the outside world that Galveston still worked.

As I left the microphone, I was applauded and patted on the back as if I had given a fine speech, but as always, standing in the shadow of that five foot giant of a woman, I felt ill-at-ease representing her. But who else did she have? Her legacy in jobs and institutions wasn't enough. The people needed a piece of Grandmama. What could I give them?

~~~~~

The old house on Avenue P, cut up into five apartments, was screaming for attention: plumbing problems, a roof leak, termites in the foundation joists. Hardly a month went by that I didn't hear from a tenant about something else that was broken or worn out. A general refurbishment was long overdue, but I dragged my heels, reluctant to perpetuate the graceless, random, hodge-podge, hither and yon pile that the house had become. Over the last fifty years half a dozen major storms and countless tenant demands had dictated the gracious rooms and halls be chopped up into poky little cubicles. Twelve foot ceilings—once necessary for cool rooms—had been lowered to a standard height so that window air conditioners operated more efficiently. And the tall narrow windows had been plugged with plywood to accommodate the deafening monstrosities. Cheap carpeting was nailed to the hardwood floors. The lovely fluted tops of the carved balusters where Faith and I had played our animal cracker games was coarsened and begrimed under dozens of layers of chalky white paint.

"I just can't deal with it," I told Peter. "I believe I shall ask Spencer to just sell the old place. Someone will want to restore it and they'll give tours through our old bedrooms." I shuddered. "If I can just hold out long enough, I'll be dead and gone and won't have to see that."

"You've been threatening to die for thirty years," said Peter. "You've got the constitution of a Franklin stove."

Maybe I am more conscious than most people of the inevitability of death because of my family's history. It is true that my body still feels the same to me as it always did. I dislike winter, but then, it always made my bones ache. My only serious illness has been a case of appendicitis. My face is wrinkled and my hair a fright, but my body is small and quick, still does what I want it to do, which, in part, I attribute to never having had children. Yes, it is silly of me to live with the constant consciousness of my own mortality, which alternately animates me with frantic energy—get it done, get it done, get it done—and lays me on my can with the most profound indolence—never mind, never mind, there's no time, there's no time.

~~~~~

In the summer of '90, instead of spending money to upgrade my rental property in town, I hired young Dan Bright to come remodel my beach house. The boy was twenty-two and had the gumption to start his own little construction business. He had worked with his grandfather every summer during high school and was a competent carpenter, had a good business head on his shoulders. Originally my idea was merely to convert an old-fashioned screened-in porch to a new-fangled "deck" like many of my neighbors now had on their houses. I considered these structures far less useful than a screened porch—no protection from the sun or mosquitoes—but they were all the rage and looked very pretty, and I didn't want to depress property values by being the lone unfashionable hold-out.

Fair Isle had become almost too upscale and yuppie for my blood, the houses owned by young two-income couples from Houston who lavished money and care on their properties, but had little time to enjoy them. Next-door was Bob Langley, gone a lot, but his girlfriend was there that whole summer because she had lost her job under rather unpleasant circumstances and was feeling too defeated to look for another. Her name was Lisa Gaines, grew up in Houston, but her people were from Trinity. She was twenty-one. Bob Langley was at least twice her age and doted on the girl, but I think she hadn't yet decided whether she loved him or merely felt grateful to him for providing her with a place to stay. I liked Lisa very much, an uncomplicated graceful creature with long dark hair and sparkling dark eyes. I wish I could say that something about her reminded me of myself, but what a fancy that would require! Lisa was tall, nearly a foot taller than me, had long, long slim brown legs, and she was quite astonishingly lovely, though she had no confidence in her looks, and even less in her intelligence.

I was back at work on Grandmama's book, having decided to let her and Mama and Charles and Meg Galloway speak for themselves. I was still totally at sea about the relationships between all of them, but not so pigheaded as I was before when I was set on overlaying some sort of modern interpretation on their behavior. If there was no proof—not even from the memory of one who was there—what could I do? All I had, as Spencer had once accused me, was intuition and suspicion.

Spencer lost his wife Rose in '89 after a prolonged battle with breast cancer. Spencer was beginning to lose a certain gaunt lost look and get back to his previous occupations, still practicing law, still wade fishing, his single mild sporting obsession. Neither of us had very much work to do any more on Grandmama's estate. Her foundations were grown children now and mostly consulted us out of deference. Much of my attention had drawn in from the outer to my inner world. I kept a pair of binoculars near my typewriter and watched the comings and goings of my neighbors. I hadn't marched against anything in years.

Bob Langley traveled in his job to far-flung parts of the world selling oilfield equipment, and his girlfriend Lisa was frequently alone. I would invite her to lunch and try not to bore her, as old people will do, about my vainglorious past. Lisa was ignorant of history, both Galveston's and the world's, had never heard of the Coolidges, and I liked this just fine. She accepted me as she found me, an old woman who lived next door, who had once lived in Mexico, which for some reason fascinated her. She loved to browse through my old albums and was much impressed by the fact that I had once been able to operate a camera, more so than she was that I now claimed to be writing a book.

"I wish I could take pictures like that," she told me. "Mine are always kind of blurry, because even on Bob's automatic camera, you have to turn this little ring thing to make it clear." Then she squinched her alarming black eyes. "I'm supposed to wear glasses, but they make me look so *icky*."

When Dan Bright came to start my building project, I saw at once that he was taken with Lisa. I warned myself not to interfere, yet I found myself putting these two young people in each other's way and warming myself with the energy that flowed between them as their awareness of one another grew. All the while I worried about poor Bob Langley—would he be awfully cut up if Lisa left him? For a younger man?

I'm afraid my over-stimulated imagination got away from me. After Lisa and Dan married, I decided, I would give them my worn-out old beach house and go live in town like Spencer wanted me to. I would make Lisa my heir and she would never have to worry again about being fired for not being quite bright enough. (It turned out that Lisa was not mentally deficient after all, though she was a slow and reluctant reader, but instead had a hearing problem that was able to be corrected after seeing my doctor.)

263

Oh, yes, I was certainly conscious, throughout my scheming and dreaming, that I was behaving like Grandmama, arranging people's lives, thinking that I knew what was best for them! But I couldn't help myself! Bob wanted Lisa to marry him and she felt she had no choice. I wanted her to have choices. She didn't have to marry an old man.

Each time I advised Dan to go take a swim and cool off (having spotted Lisa making her way down to the beach with all her tanning accouterments) I would get angry with myself and vow to stop meddling. It was immoral of me to accept Bob Langley's payments every month as his mortgagor, while secretly throwing his girlfriend in the way of Peter Bright's grandson. Then I would watch the lovely young pair romp on the beach, and I would say, it doesn't matter what I do, nature will take its course.

In August I prepared to celebrate my seventy-fifth birthday. How had I survived to such antiquity—three quarters of a century! One of the ladies on the historical committee wanted to make something of the occasion, but I pooh-poohed the idea. What would they do to top themselves if I survived to see seventy-six? I did agree to let Spencer buy me lunch. As is so very usual at that time of year, there was a hurricane in the Gulf, still undecided whether she (finally—an Emily!) would visit our shores or call upon the Yucatan Peninsula. Fair Isle slumbered under the summer sun, the sunbathers oblivious to the menace out in the Gulf. My turn had come at last in Danny's busy schedule and he was doing some measuring and making little drawings in a spiral notebook. He had convinced me to remodel the kitchen and bath as well.

Keep an eye on the weather, I told him, as I went down the stairs to my car. I smiled to myself. I saw what he had *his* eye on, a tanned slender beauty sprawled with coltish grace in a sand chair on the beach. "Oh, right," he belatedly replied, shifting his eyes to me. Please love her, I thought. Don't let her marry Bob. And then I tried to put the young people's exciting affairs out of my mind and focus on my own.

I met Spencer at Gaido's so we would have the view, not to mention the heaping platters of fresh seafood. Spencer, I could see, was secretly full of himself about something.

"Don't, for heaven's sake, spring any surprises on me,

264

Spence," I begged. "I dislike all this fuss and bother about birthdays. What is it but just another day in the life of a septuagenarian?"

Spencer was not put off by my ill temper. All I really wanted to do was get back home so I could watch what happened between Lisa and Dan! But we ordered our food and I made an effort to be good company, even though Spencer was into "remember when."

"You remember that dance I took you to, in—what—'31? You wore a lovely long dress— don't remember what color—but you had your hair up and wore your grandmother's fur wrap?"

I laughed. "You can't have remembered that night as somehow idyllic?"

"Well, of course it was! The first night I ever kissed you."

"Why, Spence! Don't you remember—that's the night I ran off with those awful boys from Texas City."

"What boys? I don't remember anything like that. It was a dance at the Galvez and we stole away from the chaperones and went out on the south lawn and you let me kiss you."

"Oh, you're hopeless!" I cried. "That was Rose, you ninny. You've got me confused with Rose."

"I do not! You're the one that's got it wrong. When I drove you home, we stopped, just about there, I think, on the sea wall and you let me kiss you again. It was the night of our first kiss, Emily, and you were sweet sixteen."

"If you say so," I said, resigned. I slathered butter on a roll and bit into it. "Wouldn't it be funny if all our versions of the past differed that much? I mean, can you imagine if Mama were alive today and *she* were writing about Grandmama?"

"How's the book coming?" Spencer got that tolerant look in his eyes. One day I was really going to surprise him!

"How can I write anything definitive when I don't *know*?"

"Are you still hung up on that, Em? For heaven's sakes, what does it matter?"

"*You* try writing a biography without knowing whether your subject had a sex life or not!"

"Do you have one?" said Spencer with seeming casualness.

"It's none of your business."

"Peter . . . ?"

265

"Not since he moved back home."

"There's been no one for me since Rose."

"Don't sound like such a martyr, it's only been a year. I used to wonder if my papa visited the ladies on Postoffice Street. You realize that if he didn't, he jolly well went without for most of his life?"

"I've never had your consuming interest in other people's sex lives."

"I see. Only in your own. Well, I must confess, Spence, I've spent far less time speculating about yours than some others I can think of."

"Oh, give it a rest, Emily. What if you could be sixteen again? Just for a day?"

I made a face. "No, sixteen wasn't very much fun. Anyway, I didn't lose my virginity until I was twenty-one—quite old by today's standards."

"Indulge me, Emily!"

"It's my birthday."

"And I want to make it wonderful for you, if you'll let me," he said irritably. "Oh, why do I bother!"

"All right, if you're going to pull a sulk." I closed my eyes and tried to think myself back half a century. The noise of the restaurant filled with tourists, was too distracting. "No, no, I can't do that. Let's be us, today, with all our wisdom and the grace of our years. Won't that do?"

"I have a surprise and you're going to spoil it."

"All right, I'm sixteen. And you're eighteen, just barely. What's the surprise?"

"I've got a room for us at the Flagship."

~~~~~

Spencer came around the car to open my door for me in the parking garage of the four-block-long pier that juts out into the Gulf. The pier was built in the thirties and had once accommodated a ballroom and an outdoor theater. I suppose it was entirely fitting that we should come here as septuagenarians pretending to be teenagers.

266

"This is so silly!" I said querulously, still wishing I'd gone home after lunch instead of indulging this foolishness.

"Now, now, you promised," said Spencer. "Where's that highly vaunted spirit of adventure?"

"I've not claimed a spirit of adventure for half a century! I just want to be left alone to be an old woman, Spence."

"Emily, *pretend*," he commanded.

"Oh, all right. We'll go in and have one drink. But I'm not going upstairs with you. I wouldn't when I was sixteen and I won't now that I'm seventy-five—and for not very different reasons, I might add."

"Sixteen," he said, hushing me.

When he opened the car door for me, I did feel just a teeny thrill of magic. There in the dimly lit garage, I could almost believe that Spencer, with his BOI tan and white crewcut, was my eighteen-year-old beau. He handled me as tenderly as if I were a long-stemmed rose. A man looking for his car hailed us and spoiled the moment, one of Spencer's clients, but Spencer gripped my elbow more firmly and rushed me into the hotel bar. A foursome of young people in blinding white tennis shorts and athletic shoes chattered near our table, looking out the large tinted window at the Gulf, speculating about the storm brewing out there.

"We'll be in Minneapolis by the time it hits," said one girl.

"They probably won't even mention it on the news back home," said another. "We'll have to get Gran to send us a postcard."

"Yes, let's," said the first woman, laughing. "Tell her to be sure to let us know if Galveston blows away."

Spencer and I gave each other a look—not BOI!—and laughed. Seas of five to six feet were already running and the sky had grown milky.

"I wonder what the latest news is?" I said. "We should have turned on the car radio. I should be home right this minute closing things up."

"There's plenty of time for that."

"There's also a hundred thousand summer people clogging up the streets," I retorted, still feeling irritable about being here instead of at home with my typewriter and my large window overlooking the beach.

"Emily, when I said there'd been no one for me since Rose, I meant, not for many years. She had gotten very frail and after that last surgery asked me to move to the other bedroom. I've almost forgotten how to be with a woman."

"I'm through with all that too. It is my goal, for whatever time I've got left, to live it without passion."

"That's not the Emily I know."

"It's time to muster a little dignity, a little self-restraint. I've developed a certain reputation—belatedly, I admit. In fact, I feel I've at last become someone my grandmother would've approved of."

"Oh, nonsense!" said Spencer impatiently. "You've just forgotten, that's all."

"What made you start remembering all of a sudden?" I asked cannily.

"Your birthday," he said shortly. "Here, I've got something for you."

He took a small cardboard box from his breast pocket and handed it to me. I opened it and found, lying on a bed of cotton wool, a brooch I had not seen in sixty odd years, but which I instantly recognized. It was a silhouette of Charlotte Lattimore. My mother had painted her own and Charlotte's profiles, then had them made up into pins so they could wear each other's likeness. I recall that Mama wore hers often until that ghastly trip to Europe.

"Where on earth did you find this?"

"Someone cleaned out a storeroom at the office and found a box of odds and ends from Meg Galloway's safe deposit. This pin was in an envelope that said 'Save for Emily.'"

"Oh, Spencer! Was there anything else?"

"Some papers that had belonged to Meg's father. No, darling, nothing about Grandmama and Charles."

"I'm so disappointed I could cry!"

"I take it you don't like my present?" he said drily. "Who is it?"

"There were a pair of them, Mama and a friend of hers."

"I wonder what went with the other one?"

"The other was Mama's profile. She gave it to her friend

268

Charlotte Lattimore. They quarreled and Mama quit wearing the pin."

"That name sounds familiar. A friend of your mother's? Is she still alive?"

"I don't know. I've always assumed not. How silly of me. I wonder if she would know anything about Faith and Charles?"

"Good heavens, Emily! Why not advertise in the paper?"

"Might not be a bad idea. Biographers do that, you know." He sighed, disgruntled, sorry, no doubt, that he had ever given me that old typewriter.

"Who was she? Or is she?"

"You'll read about her in my memoirs."

"You are keeping in mind, well, living people aren't you? Their memories might not match yours, you see. As your attorney. . . ."

I made an impatient gesture with my hand. They were *my* memories and I wasn't about to let him usurp them. "Do you remember how Grandmama's house used to smell? Sometimes you catch a whiff of it in the foyer if the tenants aren't cooking."

"What smell is that?"

"A musty smell, an attic smell, something old and fine. Wood, linen, ladies' sachet powder. It was especially strong in Meg Galloway's apartment when I used to rummage among her things looking for old letters and pictures."

"What about the room, Em? Won't you go up with me?"

"Oh, for heaven's sake, Spencer!"

"I thought you might think it was something Harding Douglas would do, something spontaneous."

"What's spontaneous about it? You planned it for days. I'm the one being asked to be spontaneous. Well, you can just go tell them you're giving it back."

I toyed with the brooch, decided not to put it on—I was wearing a cotton skirt and knit top, a new pair of Kinney sneakers. I returned the delicate little object to its bed of cotton wool. What would a girl like Lisa think of it? Would she wear it? Regard it as *icky*?

"Spencer," I said, "it's too late for us. I'm not driven by passion like I used to be. When you lost your son, I turned off all those feelings with an act of will so I wouldn't miss you so much."

"Darling."

"I've always been a woman who easily loses herself in a man. First there was Harding, then Lawrence, then you. You don't know what you're asking—that I give up myself, my hard-won solitude."

"No, only that you let me hold you for awhile. We made our choices a long time ago, Emily. I spent all these years doing what I had pledged to do and only straying once. Now I want to do what you did in your twenties—what I like. Even if it shocks the grandkids."

"I've waited a long time to hear you say that," I said, smiling in spite of myself. "I suppose it would be rather fun to go upstairs and watch the weather. Did you get a room high up so we can see something?"

"Of course I did."

"Let's at least take a look."

"Are you at all concerned about your reputation? If so, we could go up separately," he offered.

I laughed. "I've never given my reputation a thought, though I once built a garage to protect yours."

And with that, we left the bar and caught the elevator, rode up holding hands and walked out on our floor, through the carpeted and hushed corridors looking for the right number. The key had been in Spencer's pocket all along.

"Oh, you are naughty!" I said, finally feeling a slight trepidation over this enterprise of ours, a small stirring of, perhaps not desire, but adventure.

The room offered a commanding view of the Gulf. A line of ships, moving so slowly they appeared to be painted on the horizon, were heading into the channel. Spencer drew the drapes aside and pulled up chairs for us.

"I should like to be brave enough to sit here and watch a storm roll in," I said. "But I'm not. As soon as I find out the storm is heading this way, I'll skedaddle."

"Do you still have that dream?"

"Haven't for a long time."

Spencer reached across from his chair and took my hand. "I suppose I could turn on the television and catch the weather," he said, reluctantly. "Not what I had in mind, coming here."

"At least long enough to get the coordinates," I replied.

Spencer depressed the on/off button of the television set behind him. The room was instantly filled with a broadcaster's voice, which I now realized I had been hearing, muted, from the next room on the neighbor's set. Hurricane Emily continued to gather strength. Top winds were 75 miles per hour, barometer still falling. Landfall was now projected for somewhere between Corpus Christi and Grand Isle, Louisiana in the next thirty-six hours. The mayor had called for an all-out evacuation of the island beginning tomorrow morning, as it would take at least twenty-four hours to move the thousands of cars over the causeway.

Spencer groaned. "What do you think of my timing, Emily? Sixty years too late and now this."

But the news unexpectedly vitalized me. She was coming again, the Storm Goddess, and this time she was wearing my name. "We'll leave together, Spence. Tonight we'll go to my house and close the shutters and pack a few things. Then we'll go to Houston and get a room, wait out the storm."

"It was such a nice room," said Spencer, looking about him hopelessly.

"We'll come again."

The decision to leave the stifling hotel somehow liberated me. I felt suddenly affectionate towards Spencer and I took his hand as we walked down the long carpeted corridor toward the elevator. Spence pushed the button and I leaned over and kissed him on the cheek.

"You did it, Spence, you managed to surprise me."

"It's taken me seventy-five years to catch up with you, you little minx."

"I'm flattered you still want me. Maybe . . . maybe tonight I can find a way out of this barrier I've erected between us. No promises."

"Will Peter Bright mind if I love you?"

"He never has."

We drove back to Gaido's to fetch my car, then took it over to Spencer's house where he locked it in his garage for safe-keeping. He and Rose had built a lovely home on the golf course. Then we headed out the island, home. How could I ever leave my beloved beach?

271

"Spencer, what does a person have to do to adopt someone?"

"What do you mean 'someone?' A child?"

"No, an adult. I mean, is that possible, to adopt an adult?"

"Why would you want to do that?"

"Oh, to make them an heir, to give them expectations."

Spencer glanced at me with a twinkle in his eye. "Frankly, I'm surprised to hear you of all people bring up such a topic."

"Yes, rather. Well, it's an unusual situation. I hadn't expected to make any money of my own, but I have made some, and it's that money that I'd like to dispose of a little unconventionally."

"It's yours to dispose of any way you like."

"You've heard me speak of my friend Lisa?"

"Your neighbor, the one who lives with Bob what's-his-name."

"Exactly."

"Her? You want to make her your heir?"

"My own property, which you just said is mine to do with as I like."

"Yes, certainly."

"She's not to know about it. I don't want the poor girl to suddenly feel this awful burden of obligation. Although I would like for her to know how much I care for her. I'll have to think of something. . . ."

"Does she remind you of someone you know?"

"Myself in some ways, though she's quite lovely and I never was." Spencer said "Tuh!" "She grew up without much love from her family. Like mine, they meant well, but they were so busy. She's a late-bloomer like me."

Spencer chuckled. "It's one of your many charms that you've got this peculiar blindness to yourself. In this book you're writing, let somebody else write part of it. You'll never do yourself justice. Your modesty has always been one of the things I love about you."

I brushed off the compliment. Compliments make me tired. "Lisa loves the beach the same way I do. I want her to have my house, though I know it's not much in another person's eyes, but what a location! That is, if it's still standing after this week." I cast a worried glance out at the cloudy sky. A few spatters of rain had messed up the windshield.

"So, you've finally found yourself a daughter?" said Spencer quietly.

Without warning I sagged against the seat and began sobbing. "A daughter, a daughter. . . ." Spencer pulled off the road and clasped me in his arms while the paroxysm of tears shook me. "I'm fine, I'm fine," I protested, sitting up and drying my eyes with my fingertips. "How silly of me. You don't know what I've gone through lately, writing all this stuff down."

Spencer refused to release me. "And you don't know what it's done for me thinking about being with you again. I've never felt like such an old man as since Rose died. I couldn't see any reason for going on. She had been sick so long. You turn in on yourself and forget how to reach out to people."

"And then one day you take an old girlfriend to lunch and don't tell her you've got a hotel key in your pocket," I said, wiping away tears on my skirt hem. I've never been the sort of woman that came prepared for tears with a white hanky. "Come on, let's go see if Fair Isle is taking Hurricane Emily seriously."

When we turned in at the entrance, I exclaimed with satisfaction: "Ah, look at that, will you—Dan Bright's pickup in Bob Langley's carport."

Spencer O'Malley was mystified why this seemed to delight me. Several sheets of fresh yellow plywood hung off the end of the pickup's tailgate, but none of the occupants of the house were in evidence.

All over the neighborhood the clatter and echo of hammers resounded. Around the cul-de-sac, my neighbors had sprung into action to get their homes protected before the evacuation order went into effect. It took both Nancy Springer and Kai LaVelle, two young legal secretaries from Houston whom I suspected were lesbians, to wrestle a sheet of plywood to the top of the scaffold and nail it over their large south-facing window. Kai strained against the material, holding it in place, while Nancy hammered furiously. Next door, John Kimball was engaged in much the same work, only he had but to stand on his deck to do the job. His fat wife Frederica lay listlessly in one of the lounge chairs on the mid-deck where I had sat with Lisa only the night before at a barbecue. The Kimball's redheaded six-year-old Jennifer sat on the steps with her sunburned face pressed between the balusters looking like a small zoo animal longing for freedom.

I hurried up the stairs ahead of Spencer to see if I could spot Lisa. I found her just beyond the dunes, lying on a towel next to Dan Bright. Dan was propped on one elbow gazing into her eyes. Neither of them were conscious of anything else.

I clasped my hands together in joy and turned to look at Spence who was following at a more leisurely pace. "Oh, isn't it a glorious day! What a birthday you've given me!"

Suddenly it began to rain quite hard.

Chapter Thirteen

"No, I never heard Grandma mention your mother," said Mrs. Grimes, speaking of her grandmother, the former Charlotte Miller, nee Lattimore. "She died when I was in the fifth grade. I didn't even know she had been married before Grandpa, but Mama says she had two sons, uncles I've never met. They lived in Galveston, I believe. Didn't you say that was where you're from?"

"Yes, orphans of the storm, I'm afraid. What do you remember about your grandmother?" I said.

Mrs. Grimes shrugged. "The usual things. She made apple pies and used to give a dollar for every A on my report card." Mrs. Grimes's eyes dropped to the brooch fastened at the neck of my blouse—I admit that I wore it on purpose. "Funny that you should have one of those old-fashioned pins," she said. "My grandmother had one very similar to it."

"Yes, I know. I'll give you this if you like—it's your grandmother." Spencer harrumped at my side—I was giving away "his" present to me. I handed over the pin, and Mrs. Grimes—her name was Melanie though she didn't look like a Melanie—fingered it thoughtfully.

"She was classy-looking in her youth, wasn't she? I wouldn't have known it was her—she got heavy later. There was a story in the family . . . oh, well, I don't suppose I should tell tales about Grandma."

"Oh, do!" I exclaimed, not adding that collecting tales was the only reason I was there.

"Well, I don't suppose it could do any harm now. She put on airs, my grandmother, used to claim she almost married into one of those wealthy old Galveston families. If she looked like this, maybe it was true. Just imagine," she said, heaving a sigh and looking around her rather shabby suburban living room, "we might've been living like kings."

"I don't suppose you have any of your grandmother's old papers, letters, diaries, pictures perhaps, from her life in Galveston?"

"Oh, no, would've thrown it out years ago. I'm not a packrat," said Mrs. Grimes virtuously.

I set my jaw and stifled my irritation. When Spencer and I were back in the car and driving away, I exclaimed, "How provoking! Not a packrat!"

"I daresay that's how some people view your penchant for hanging on to canceled checks from 1958, m'dear," rumbled Spencer. "I'm glad you didn't ask that woman if her grandmother was a lesbian."

"You're speeding," I said irritably. "Houston has never been interested in history," I added with a sniff. "Pulling down any building with the least pretension to character and putting up these tacky glass boxes."

We were waiting out Hurricane Emily, who dithered off the coast for days and finally slipped ashore somewhere on the vast King Ranch in south Texas where she did no harm. It was Spencer who suggested we spend our time profitably while we were there and try to locate Charlotte Lattimore's family. Utilizing certain legal resources of his, we found this granddaughter, the only kin Charlotte Lattimore still had living in this part of the world, it turned out, a woman a dozen or so years younger than I.

In spite of the hastiness of this trip and its air of emergency, Spencer and I were managing to amuse ourselves quite grandly. We had spent a day or two in a hotel before removing to a luxurious high-rise apartment owned by absent friends, where every morning we lolled by the pool and read the newspapers till late in the day. We took our meals at one of the many sidewalk cafes just down the street in the museum area, napped in the afternoon when it was hot, then went out for dinner and shopping, or a movie that evening. Almost, I could have imagined going on living that way enjoying Houston's gaudy diversions.

You'll be wondering if the woman with the unseemly interest in her mother's and her grandmother's sex lives had resumed having one of her own, but I'll choose the material, thank you very much. Let some future biographer tease it out of the artifacts I leave behind.

But I haven't described our last day in Galveston, the day after my birthday! Spencer and I had awoken early, delighted to find ourselves in bed together, since natural reticence had made us unable to start out that way. He had given me plaintive and aggrieved looks aplenty, but forbore to argue his case with his lawyer's cunning and probably win, and had started out the night in the spare bedroom where I peremptorily ordered him. Afterward I lay alone in my own bed trying to convince myself that I had made the right decision. Our ages! It was well past time for us to demonstrate a little self-restraint, a little dignity. I confess to an utter failure of the imagination, an inability to picture a pair as doddering as we causing the flesh to sing.

However, my hateful old recurring nightmare rescued me from my hidebound prison. Spencer heard my muffled cries as the nightmare waters rolled over me, and hurried in to render aid and comfort. I came to my senses clasped to his bosom where I stayed for the remainder of the night. And sometime during those dark intimate hours, he asked again the question I had always before answered no.

As we prepared the next morning to evacuate, I had quite forgotten about Lisa, who had also entertained an overnight visitor. But suddenly Nancy Springer was at my door to warn us that all hell was about to bust loose if I didn't take Bob Langley in and occupy him for awhile. The poor man had gotten a stand-by flight (no two weeks at sea these days!) to get home and make sure Lisa got out of the way of the hurricane, only to find Dan Bright's pickup in his carport.

"Bring him up at once," I said to Nancy.

Spencer was amazed at the volumes of intelligence that somehow passed in that brief communication. "I'm not sure I want to see you get involved in this, Emily," he said uneasily.

"Hush, Spence. Hurry," I told Nancy, who was already halfway down the stairs. Below stood Bob Langley, hands shoved in his pockets, moodily staring out at the gray water.

"What on earth do you intend to do with him?" said Spencer. "I hope the fellow doesn't start shooting."

"Not to worry, Bob Langley is the gentlest of creatures. It breaks my heart to think how unhappy he must be!"

"I thought you were scheming how to get his girlfriend away from him."

"Which isn't to say I have no sympathy for his suffering! Hush, here he is."

It is a delicate matter to buck up a person whose world is crashing down around him, especially when you yourself think that everyone will be the better for the crash. Thanks entirely to Bob Langley's own excellent manners, he allowed us to detain him for some twenty minutes, the three of us gallantly pretending we had come together on purpose to drink coffee. The pretense came to an abrupt halt when we heard Lisa's car start up next door. Bob leaped to his feet and went out to the screened porch to watch Lisa's little red car zoom down the road behind Dan's pickup. Both vehicles stopped at Peter Bright's house, where I reckoned Dan wanted to make sure his cantankerous old grandpa planned to evacuate as the mayor had ordered. Bob set down his coffee mug and headed for the stairs.

"Don't go," I called after him, but he didn't acknowledge he heard me. I too headed for the stairs and heard Spencer bark, "Stay, Emily!" which I also ignored. Suddenly, it was as important to me that Lisa make good her escape as it had been that I make my own the night I ran off with Harding. I prayed that Lisa's impulse would not prove as destructive as mine, but no matter how it turned out, I knew she would never regret her choice—no more than I had. The lonely heart has no choice but choose love.

I ran down the road to Peter's house, glad of my strong heart and lungs, my supple legs, in trying to keep up with these young things. Lisa was sitting in her car with the engine idling, listening to Bob speak to her through the half-opened glass. I was right—Bob Langley is not the sort of man to use bullets to get his way, nor even tears. Nevertheless, I saw that Lisa was moved and upset by his argument.

Then Dan came out of his grandfather's house and stood on the deck above us. The two men locked gazes and took each other's measure. Lisa looked anxiously from one to the other, then at me, silently imploring me to do something. I put my hand on Bob Langley's elbow and he slowly relaxed and backed away from Lisa's car. Dan Bright unhurriedly descended the stairs, the very stance of his virile young body a warning. He got in his pickup and drove off without a word or glance at Lisa. She seemed uncertain for a moment, torn, between the two men. I said only, "Call me after the storm."

At once she put her car in gear and raced off after Dan.

"She's so young," Bob said. "She doesn't know what she wants."

"Neither do we," I said.

~~~~~

And so Lisa married Peter Bright's grandson, joining our two families, Peter's and mine, though not in the way we had envisioned that night five decades ago when he proposed to me in the Sui Jen. In making Lisa my legal heir, I finally have a family, though I've not made them wait for my death to do nice things for them. To start, I gave the young couple my seedy old beach house and the money to remodel it to suit them.

Having no desire to upstage Lisa and Dan's nuptials, Spencer and I were married in a quiet ceremony in the rectory, attended by only a few old friends we have known since high school. We felt we had already had our honeymoon, so we turned our attention to the project we had agreed upon, to restore Grandmama's old house.

Spencer introduced me to a young architect who has restored several other historical homes in Galveston. I was interested in restoring the house not only to its period in history, but to its place in my memory. I wanted the balusters painted the same light cream that I remembered, the red tiles returned to the roof, the oleanders planted by the back door just as they were in my grandmother's day. I wanted the old kitchen arranged just as it was back then, with the white enamel table in the middle where I used to eat my meals with Meg when Grandmama and Papa worked late at the office.

The renovation took nearly two years, during which time we lived in Spencer's house on the golf course. Lisa and Dan finished their remodeling in only a few weeks and moved right into my beloved old beach house, where I am always warmly welcomed. I am glad they are close enough to look in often on Peter. Lisa is a devoted granddaughter-in-law and often has Peter over for dinner. Bob Langley recovered from the awful blow of losing Lisa and was married the following year.

Having always loved construction, I came nearly every day to see how the work progressed on the Coolidge Mansion, as it is now called in the tourist brochures. It is very satisfying to have the partitions gone and the original gracious dimensions of the rooms restored. Cupboards and crawlspaces that hadn't seen the light of day for fifty years were suddenly revealed when the false ceilings came down. And that is where I finally found what I was looking for, my father's personal papers from the time between when I left home and he moved to the Tremont Hotel. Another delayed inheritance, a belated legacy of understanding to reward me for dropping my pigheadedness, for finally assuming my rightful place there on P Street.

My father, as had my grandmother, felt it was his moral obligation to record his private thoughts in letters and journals. Very few letters found their way back to their author, though the ones to Hazel Brookside survived since she herself returned his missives to Galveston and preserved them, tied up in a red felt candy box that I imagined still smelled faintly of chocolate. I had assumed that Papa simply ended his dialogue with himself after he married my mother, for I had found very little of a personal nature among his papers after 1913, the year they were married. Why, you ask yourselves, should I have allowed myself to be persuaded, simply on the lack of evidence, that a man who had once written so eloquently as to capture a bride sight unseen would cease his continuous writing and be content from thence on to the grave with silence? Possibly I accepted such a thesis because I had never understood my father in the first place. And that can be blamed on the success of the charade he and my grandmother played out daily for my benefit as well as for Mama and Meg and the other household staff, for the whole world. For theirs, I discovered, was an uncelebrated love.

Like my grandmother, Papa was fond of recording the minutiae of his business day, second-guessing himself, speculating, planning—but my eye skipped unerringly to the entries that chronicled his private life, compressed here as my final comments on the astonishing life of my grandmother:

~~~~~

CHARLES OREN PICKERING

I told Mrs. Coolidge not to trouble herself that Edith used me ill, told her that venomous darts fail to find their target in a heart that has become impervious to such barbs. I speak, of course, of how Mrs. Coolidge leaped to my rescue when my wife brushed aside my thoughtless gesture of fondness with utter loathing and contempt. I am moved beyond the ability of my pitiful words to express how my heart expanded when the dear lady flung her water glass at the wall and rebuked her daughter for her coldness! I knew then that my dear Faith does care, know that I mean more to her than merely the necessary male contribution to the continuance of her line. She feels something for *me*. For *me myself*, Charles O. Pickering, orphan of the storm the same as she. Our kinship is too extraordinary for the world ever to understand, and therefore no word shall ever be spoken of it. Nor would public mention serve but to corrupt the purest and finest of feelings: admiration, gratitude, respect, and yes, love. Let it remain so.

But later he writes:

This evening we sat in our accustomed places in the drawing room while Edith kept to her room above our heads. Mrs.

281

Coolidge had been out of the office all day in meetings at various locations, while I tended the regular flow of business. We therefore had had no chance for our usual intercourse and I found that I missed her as if I had not laid eyes on her for days. We chatted most amiably for about an hour, discussed various business questions that had come up in her absence, then fell silent, sitting idiotically and self-pleasedly smiling at one another.

"And how are *you*, Mr. Pickering?" she finally murmured.

"Ma'am, I was never happier in my life," I replied.

"Nor I," she said.

We shook out our newspapers and read for another three quarters of an hour. I felt my smile still hovering about my mouth and thought how foolish I would look if Meg Galloway were to come in and see me so, when Dr. Brown had been shown out a mere three hours earlier after giving my wife a powerful sedative. The thought sobered me and I felt my face relax into its usual melancholic lines. No one need know that beneath this banal exterior beats the heart of a contented man, that the poor orphan who buried his mother and father, sisters and brothers, wife and children, who has linked his life to a woman who despises him, has yet claimed a modicum of happiness by being allowed to share the life of a woman who in all the world represents the fairest of her sex, whom I find on a daily basis to be the most admirable, intelligent, virtuous and strong. A woman, furthermore, who chose me at that time of my life when I was most callow, unproven, beaten and bewildered—to share a life and a love!

~~~~~

"So you see," I told Spencer, showing him these passages, "they loved one another."

"Everyone knew that," he objected. "I thought you were looking for proof of *sex*."

Well, yes, that was the direction my quest had taken me, but after such high-minded praise as this, how could I be so worldly as to continue the search when it is clear that they themselves were satisfied with their unworldly love?—or else were far too canny to commit damning facts to paper. In a letter she writes to

Charles, which he evidently cherished for its much-handled appearance:

I don't know what I would've done had not the good Lord sent you to me. You have been my rod and my staff through the depths of adversity as well as the mountain peaks of extraordinary good fortune. My own flesh and blood disappointed me, but you, a diffident stranger, appeared and salvaged my personal fortunes and made me feel blessed in spite of reversals that might otherwise have capsized me. I am grateful, my dear Charles, for your wisdom, your loyalty, your courage, but most especially for your friendship. I shall think of you throughout Eternity, my dear Friend and hope to be reunited with you one sweet day. Yours as ever, Faith.

~~~~~

I sit on Grandmama's balcony and listen to the restless rush of the waves as the tide comes in, almost drowned out by the continual swish of traffic on Seawall Boulevard. I miss the quietness of West Beach. The air is heavy and sultry, smells faintly of dead fish. Barely a breath stirs the oleanders below. Lights twinkle on oil rigs just beyond the break of the waves. I think of Grandmama and Charles together "in Eternity" and giggle irreverently at the thought of them having to share it with Edith. Edith and Charlotte. Perhaps they can all drop their nineteenth century hypocrisy and admit what and whom they really want. But, of course, there is neither sects nor sex in heaven! I hear a brisk step behind me and Spencer appears in the doorway looking for me.

"So there you are. I thought you were still on the phone. Why are you sitting alone in the dark?"

"I believe I've finished Grandmama's story."

"What shall you do with it?"

"Stick it in the attic, I think."

Spencer laughs. "Well, I must say, as your grandmother's attorney, I almost wish you would, darling. But, of course," he hastens to add, "you must satisfy yourself as an artist."

"Oh, bother!" I answer cheerfully. "You don't mean that at

283

all. Anyway, I am satisfied. All I ever wanted was to understand them better. But perhaps. . . ."

"Perhaps?"

"When we're both dead and gone. . . ."

"At least let me clear out. Then you can say anything you like about your grandmother."

"It used to bother me a lot that you cared so much about what people think."

"It doesn't bother you any more?"

"Nothing I can do about it, is there? No, really, Spence, if there's just one thing I've proven, it's that I forgive them and hope they've forgiven me. That's all. That I love them in spite of how we all hurt each other."

"I'm sure Grandmama Faith knows that, and old Charles."

"Edith was strange, wasn't she?"

"Edith was strange."

"A little mad I think. Probably addicted to sedatives, too."

"To think she leaped from this very balcony!"

"When I started this project I thought of the House of Coolidge as, well, tragic and flawed. But do you know, after all this poking about, I believe we all got exactly what we wanted."

"I know I did," says my husband, loyally squeezing my hand.

"And Grandmama and Charles did too—they spent their whole lives together, working and playing. My mother got to play the mad tragic noncomformist. I was granted an interesting life and colorful relatives—which every writer needs—and I enjoyed a lifetime of alternately sparring with and making love to you."

"And I finally got my Emily."

"Saved the best till last, didn't we, darling? I'm terribly glad you had a full and interesting life before me, that you had your family, earned the respect of the community, discharged the great trust my grandmother left you."

"I've always loved you, Emily, always thought you were the most interesting woman I knew, the strongest—"

"Strongest! How so?"

"Strong enough to do what you wanted. Very few people do that."

284

"I don't feel I've been particularly strong, nor that I've done what I wanted. Things happened, choices arose, and I chose the path of least pain. But that's what a life looks like from the inside. As my grandmother's biographer, I had the chance to look at her life more closely. She was the strong one, not me. I'm too soft-headed and romantic. Oh, but I haven't told you the news! That was Lisa on the phone, called to say the doctor confirmed she's pregnant. The baby is due in the spring. Bob could never have given her children, you know. She says that if it's a girl she wants to name it after me."

"A Coolidge great grandchild."

"Exactly what I was thinking."

For more information about Galveston, see *GALVESTON, A HISTORY* by David G. McComb, University of Texas Press, Austin, 1986. And for a non-fiction account of the Great Storm, read *ISAAC'S STORM*, by Erik Larson, Crown, 1999. You may also view historical pictures of the devastation by visiting **www.1900Storm.com**